*O*ur Valentine To You!

Valentine's Day is a time for romance—a
celebration of love.

We hope that our valentine to you—a
collection of stories written by four of your
favorite Romance authors—will bring you the
true warmth and happiness of this special day
and prove that the spirit of St. Valentine can
live on throughout the year.

We wish you, our reader, a Valentine's Day
filled with champagne and chocolate and roses,
yes, but we wish you much more than that. We
wish you a day—and a life—filled with love.

The Editors

Valentine *my*
1991

Katherine Arthur
Debbie Macomber
Leigh Michaels
Peggy Nicholson

◆ *Harlequin*®

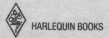 HARLEQUIN BOOKS

MY VALENTINE 1991
Copyright © 1991 by Harlequin Enterprises Ltd.
ISBN 0-373-83226-5

MY VALENTINE 1991 first printing February 1991

The publisher acknowledges the copyright holders
of the individual works as follows:

LISTEN TO YOUR HEART
Copyright © 1991 by Katherine Arthur

MY FUNNY VALENTINE
Copyright © 1991 by Debbie Macomber

SOME KIND OF HERO
Copyright © 1991 by Leigh Michaels

HARTZ AND FLOWERS
Copyright © 1991 by Peggy Nicholson

Contents

LISTEN
TO YOUR HEART

Katherine Arthur

A word from Katherine Arthur

I sometimes wonder if people think a romance writer's life has been filled with romance. After all, the experts tell you to write about what you know. If so, I should have glorious memories of Valentine's Days gone by, of lacy cards, flowers and whispered declarations of love. Instead, I remember bandaged knees that stole the glamour from a beautiful red velvet dress my mother made for me. A huge card concealing a mouse-trap device that nearly mashed my thumb. And my first date for a Valentine's dance with a boy almost a head shorter than I, who breathed heavily on my gardenia corsage and turned it brown.

But wait. Maybe it's not what really happens but what you make of it that turns imperfect reality into rapturous romance.

I remember taking some scraps of the velvet from that dress to make a gown for a tiny doll. She became a princess, with long golden hair. A Cinderella, who took me with her to endless balls and always found her nice, tall Prince Charming. Finally, I found my Prince Charming too. I threw the mousetrap away, but there were better Valentines, carefully cut from red construction paper and thick with paste where the paper lace was attached. My children brought those to me, and somewhere I've kept them all.

There have been no more brown gardenias, but there have been plenty of other catastrophes. Strangely enough, it is those and not a life of romance that started me writing. It happened this way.

My husband, a professor, decided to try his hand at farming some land that we bought, never mind that they'd used horses when he spent childhood summers on his uncle's farm. Disaster followed disaster. While towing some equipment, our pickup truck collapsed and died with a gasp and a cloud of smoke, leaving us stranded fifty miles from home on our anniversary. We tried disking a too-wet field and turned it into something resembling rock-hard bowling balls that wouldn't break up until the next year. We spent weeks trying to make hay bales come out rectangular instead of trapezoidal. And so on, and so on. It was pretty funny, the professor and his wife blundering along at tasks any real farmer knows how to do. Worth writing about, I thought. And although nothing came of those first efforts, I was hooked on writing. Soon I wrote a children's story, "The Practical Princess," and it sold. Then I tried romance and something really clicked. Now, my Cinderella could once again always find her Prince Charming, at least whenever I wasn't helping to cultivate the soybeans or grease the combine.

Sound short on romance? It isn't. I have a warm, loving, funny, fascinating husband. Life with him is a wonderful adventure. It's the sometimes disastrous but always interesting things that happen that inspire me to write. So, if your Valentine's Day sometimes falls short of your dreams, don't worry. To paraphrase the poet, "Come dream along with me, the best is yet to be."

Chapter One

BERTRAM BELLAMY shook his head and sighed heavily for emphasis. "Jamie'd better slow down and make room in her life for a good man, and stop acting as if she's married to that blasted flower shop," he said to his wife. "I'm almost sorry I ever let her get into the business."

Jamie Exeter gave her uncle a sideways glance and paused with her coffee cup halfway to her mouth. "Aunt Martha, if this is going to be Uncle Bert's annual 'We'd better get Jamie married off before another year is out' lecture, I'm going home right now," she said, wondering why she hadn't had the sense not to mention that she didn't have a date for New Year's Eve. After working in her shop from five in the morning until six at night, she'd be in no mood to go out.

"Calm down, dear, your uncle means well," her Aunt Martha said soothingly. "He does worry about you."

"Well he doesn't need to. I'm perfectly happy," Jamie said, continuing their time-honored tradition of routing difficult conversations through her aunt. "The manager told me last week that Isaiah Dunham plans to let the present store owners stay when he takes over the hotel—unless they're really incompetent. So I don't have to worry about my lease anymore. *I'm* certainly not incompetent." She smiled, in hopes of erasing the frown lines from between her uncle's bushy white eyebrows. "I'm just a little tired. I guess that's the price of success, though, and I owe it all to Uncle Bert.''

"Hmph," her uncle said, trying not to look pleased, "I'm not so sure about that. Maybe I steered you in the wrong direction."

"Aunt Martha," Jamie said plaintively, "could you remind Uncle Bert that once upon a time he was glad I worked hard and didn't waste my time chasing boys?"

"Now, Bertie," Martha Bellamy said gently, "I'm sure Jamie will get married in due time." She smiled at her niece. "Won't you, dear? When you find someone who's really right for you?"

"Of course," Jamie agreed, taking her cue from her aunt. "I'm just particular. Someday the right man will show up." She smiled at her uncle again. "Who knows, he might come walking into my shop tomorrow."

"Are you sure you'd recognize him if he did?" her uncle asked, cocking a skeptical eyebrow in Jamie's direction. "Do you know what you're looking for?"

Jamie shrugged. "I suppose I have a general idea. You know, the usual things. Intelligent and interesting, a good sense of humor. Reasonably nice-looking, gainfully employed. After that, I don't know. I guess I expect bells to ring, but that's probably silly."

"Don't be too sure about that," her uncle said. "Bells rang when I saw *my* dream girl." He reached over and squeezed his wife's hand.

"The first time I heard Bertie laugh and saw that twinkle in his big brown eyes, I knew he was the man I'd been waiting for," said her aunt.

Jamie shook her head and sighed as her aunt and uncle gazed at each other adoringly. They had been married for almost fifty years and were still in love. She occasionally brooded about the fact that she apparently wasn't destined to have such a beautiful relationship, but she always felt vaguely guilty when she did. She'd been blessed with inordinate good luck in her beloved flower shop. She had no right to expect Providence to send the perfect man her way, as well. "If I'm half as lucky as you two, I'll think I've done well," she said.

"You should give more thought to just what you want," her uncle said seriously. "The man's background, his interests, even what he looks like. Knowing what you want is half the battle of getting it."

Jamie went over to give her uncle a hug and plant a kiss on the top of his bald head. "I'll try to take your recommendation to heart," she said, then turned and kissed her aunt. "I just hope Fate dreams up as perfect a man for me as it did for you. Now, I'd better go. Tomorrow's going to be a long day. Call me if you need me to bring anything besides the wine for New Year's dinner."

"I will, dear. Drive carefully. It's drizzly out."

"Yes, Aunt Martha, I will," Jamie said.

She drove carefully along the rain-shiny St. Louis streets in the chill December wind that lashed the fine mist against her windows and shrouded the street lamps with iridescent halos. As she drove she speculated about why her aunt and uncle were so determined that she should get married now, when only a few years ago they'd seemed happy enough that she was doing well as a florist. The answer, she decided, was that they'd always assumed she'd *be* married by now, and since they were so happy together, they couldn't imagine anyone being perfectly content to be alone. Well, they didn't need to worry. She'd get along just fine, whether or not any dream man ever appeared on the scene. Not that she'd mind if one did, but dreaming didn't seem a very practical approach to finding one. Still, if she could have just what she wanted, what would he be like? Not one of the slick salesmen she met at the hotel, that was for sure. He'd be a real, rugged outdoor sort of man, not some health-club body builder. She'd prefer tall and dark-haired. Handsome wasn't necessary, but he'd have to have a strong jaw, and a sturdy, masculine-looking nose. For some reason, dinky noses on men definitely turned her off. The eyes would be most important, though. Green was her favorite color. Green, with crinkly laugh lines around them, and nicely arched brows above them. The green would be a clear, emerald green, full of deep, prismatic lights that shone when his mouth curved into a nice, wide, warm smile....

The man's image became so vivid that Jamie almost missed the turn into the driveway next to her apartment building. "Darn!" she exclaimed as she slithered around the corner. Dreaming was not only unproductive, it was dangerous. Still shaken, she came to a stop in her parking space behind the small tan-brick apartment building. In the wind-driven mist, the dimly lighted yard with its one bare tree whipping to and fro had a vaguely menacing appearance, which made Jamie shudder involuntarily.

She hurried into the building and up the back stairs to her second-floor apartment, noticing as she did that the ugly, yellowish-tan paint on the walls was peeling in several places and dirty in others, giving the place a depressing institutional appearance. She thought of complaining to the superintendent, then shook her head. If he did anything at all, he'd just come and put on another layer of the same ugly color. She paused with her key in her lock, looking at the drab hallway in sudden distaste. Maybe she should move, or even buy a house. She'd always planned that a house would come after she was married, but there was no reason anymore that it should. She could afford it now; why not do it?

"You'd like that, wouldn't you?" she said to Cyrano, the large white cat who came to rub against her legs as soon as she opened the door to her kitchen. "A house with your own yard?"

"Yow," Cyrano replied, and trotted hopefully to his food bowl, staring back at her with wide, green eyes.

"But not as much as you'd like your dinner. All right, first things first." She tossed her coat and purse onto a chair and poured dry cat food into Cyrano's bowl. "There you go," she said, then sat down at the table to watch him eat while she meditated on her new idea. Looking around her little kitchen only reinforced her sudden discontent. It was no wonder she usually didn't bother to cook. It was almost impossible to keep things organized in such a tiny space.

"Shall I see if I can find something we'd like at a reasonable price?" she asked Cyrano, who had jumped onto her lap as soon as he finished his food. He purred loudly. "I guess that's a yes," Jamie said. "Well, I won't be able to do anything about it for a while, and I expect I'd better think seriously about what my dream house should be like." She smiled to herself and rubbed Cyrano's chin. "First my dream man, now my dream house. At least I can do something about the house. I'm afraid that even if I worked at it twenty-four hours a day I couldn't dream up a real man."

Cyrano gave her a cool, green-eyed stare. "Mer-oww."

Jamie made a face at him. "Oh, really? Does that mean you think I could? You know, I said he should have green eyes, like you do." She put a finger on the large black patch on Cyrano's nose. "Maybe you're him, bewitched centuries ago by an evil spell. Shall we find out?" She framed Cyrano's furry face between her hands, then gave him a resounding kiss on the forehead. "Darn, I was afraid of that," she said, laughing as Cyrano wriggled free and stalked away, obviously disgusted. "Oh, well, it's bedtime, anyway. I've got to be at the shop by five in the morning, and that means getting up at four. Will I ever be glad when New Year's Eve is over!"

In the morning, Jamie drove through the dark, almost deserted streets to her shop, arriving just as the ornate grandfather clock in the hotel lobby struck five. Her shop, Flowers from the Heart, was in the Chateau St. Louis, an old but elegant downtown hotel. Originally it had been her Uncle Bert's. Jamie had worked there part-time when she was in high school, and when her father died and her mother elected to move to Arizona, she'd chosen to stay on with her favorite aunt and uncle. The Bellamys encouraged her to enroll in a business course so that she'd be able to take over the running of the store and eventually buy it. Now, thanks to Jamie's hard work and excellent management, she owned the business and could reasonably expect to buy her own home, too.

When her accountant stopped by in the early afternoon to pick up a corsage for his wife, she told him she wanted to check her year-end figures as soon as possible. "I'm thinking of buying a house next year, Ralph," she told him.

"Not a bad idea," Ralph agreed. "What kind of house?"

"Mmm, I'm not sure yet," Jamie replied. She handed him the lovely orchid corsage in its clear plastic box. "You must be going partying tonight."

"Yeah, we're coming to the ballroom here," Ralph said with a resigned sigh. "My wife heard that both old Isaiah Dunham and his son, Zack, will be there. She read somewhere that Zack and Cissie Bergstrom, the singer who's headlining the show, might announce their engagement tonight, and the old man's having a fit about it. She thinks things might get exciting. I couldn't care less about those celebrity romances, but my wife reads every bit of gossip she can get her hands on, so if it'll keep her happy..." He smiled and shrugged.

Jamie nodded understandingly. "I expect it's best to start the New Year off on the right foot."

"Exactly," Ralph said. "Well, see you later. Don't work too hard."

"I won't. 'Bye, Ralph," Jamie said, turning her attention to her next customer, a nervous-looking man who bought a half dozen long-stemmed red roses.

"Want to bet those aren't for his wife?" asked her assistant, Barney Wakefield, when the man had gone.

"Don't be such a cynic," Jamie said with a frown. "He's probably like Ralph, and wants to make a good beginning on the New Year. I wonder why Isaiah Dunham is here. He doesn't take over the hotel until the fifteenth of January, and I doubt he'd come just to keep track of his son. Zack Dunham must be a grown man.''

"If I had billions and one of my heirs was about to make a damned fool of himself with some gold digger, I'd sure hang around," Barney said with a grin.

"Maybe," Jamie said doubtfully. "On the other hand, he may be checking up on how well the people here run a really big event." She looked at her watch. "I think I'll make sure everything's lined up just right for the party in the Grand Ballroom. It's time for the final push to begin. Don't forget the orchid corsage for the Cavalier suite promptly at two o'clock."

"You've already reminded me three times," Barney said, giving her a resentful look.

"I know." Jamie sighed. "I'm sorry. I'm just nervous. I want everything to be perfect, you know."

She hurried to the back room of the shop where, in a climate-controlled environment, three more assistants' fingers were flying, turning masses of pink and yellow chrysanthemums, white daisies, and sprigs of fern and baby's breath into table arrangements. A fourth labored over several larger arrangements to bank the stage. Jamie carefully checked off her lists, counted canisters of still-unused flowers, and generally made sure that everything they would need was in place. Satisfied, she paused at the door and looked around. The moist, cool air was pungent with the spicy smell of the chrysanthemums. She loved that smell, just as she loved all the other flowers' wonderful scents, their varied colors and contrasting textures. How lucky she was, she thought, to be able to work at something she loved so much. She didn't need any magical dream man to make her life complete. Only an ungrateful fool would ask for anything more.

By early evening the pace had slowed and at five-thirty Jamie let Barney go home. She tidied the shelves, discarded faded flowers and arranged the few remaining bouquets in the mirrored case behind the counter. On the center shelf she placed a small bouquet of pink rosebuds and baby's breath. She always kept one on display so that she could enjoy its delicate beauty. It was, she decided, the perfect bouquet to express romantic feelings, exactly what she would want her dream man to—

"Oh, don't be silly," she muttered, bending to pick up a few scraps of greenery from the floor and toss them into the waste can. She straightened again, facing the counter, and looked out at the lights of the traffic hurrying by. Dinnertime, she thought. Everyone was going home. She might as well go, too.

She started across the room to lock the outside door when suddenly a dark male shape appeared and the door began to open. Jamie stopped. Then, as the man entered, her heart lurched and seemed to stop beating completely for so long that she thought perhaps it would never start again. When it did, it was racing frantically. For, as the man came closer, she saw that he had green eyes, sparkling with beautiful laughing lights, and his smile was the warmest she'd ever seen.

Jamie began to back up, one hand at her throat, which seemed so tight it barely permitted her to breathe. "M-may I help you?" she stammered, wondering if the apparition would vanish when she spoke.

"I certainly hope so," the man said in a deep, resonant voice, entrancing flashes of silver dancing behind the thick fringe of his dark lashes.

Jamie bolted for the relative safety of the sales counter. "Wh-what do you want?" she asked, then flushed scarlet as the man smiled and let his glance travel slowly across Jamie's lips and down the front of her pink angora sweater. His eyes moved slowly back to hers, then he looked past her, over her shoulder.

"I'd like those pink roses with the tiny white flowers mixed in," he said.

"Baby's breath," Jamie said, still staring at the man.

"What?" His brows raised questioningly.

"Th-the tiny white flowers," Jamie said. "They're called baby's breath. Because they're so sweet and delicate."

"I like that. That's nice," he said, still smiling that incredibly warm and beautiful smile.

With difficulty, Jamie drew her gaze away and turned around, fumbling for the catch on the glass door. She could see his reflection in the mirror, see his eyes watching her every move. Her hand trembled as she reached for the bouquet. *For heaven's sake, get hold of yourself, Jamie,* she scolded as she took a firm grip on the vase. *It isn't what you think. He's just another customer.*

"There you are," she said as she turned back and set the arrangement on the counter. "I'll let you have it for ten dollars. It wouldn't keep until Wednesday, anyway. Unless you want it delivered somewhere. That would be extra."

"That won't be necessary," the man said, peeling a ten from a large roll of bills he'd pulled from the pocket of his leather jacket just as a brassy-looking redhead came through the door. "Will these do, Cissie?" he asked, swiveling to look at her.

Jamie's whirling world stopped spinning with a sickening jolt. So much for dream men, she thought, trying to ignore the unreasonable flash of anger that surged through her. She had immediately recognized the woman as Cissie Bergstrom, the singer Ralph had mentioned, which probably made this green-eyed enchanter Zack Dunham. Jamie eyed the woman coldly. She'd never thought much of the woman's voice, which seemed to her about as melodic as a cat screeching. It did match her face, though, which was sour and petulant as she studied the roses and drummed her thickly lacquered fingernails impatiently on the countertop. "It's too cutesy," she said. She pointed to the display case. "Give me the red carnations."

The man shrugged. "All right. Red carnations it is."

Jamie cast him a pitying look and started to pick up the roses to put them back. How did he ever get involved with a woman like that? Didn't he have any sense at all? No wonder his father was upset.

"No, wait," the man said. "I want the roses, too." He handed the bill to Jamie along with another melting smile. "The roses are for you," he added softly. "Somehow, they look just right for you."

At his words, Jamie's mouth went dry. The man's fingers touched hers as he pressed the money into her limp hand. She could feel a spark jump between them, as if she had touched a light switch on a dry winter day. Speechless, she stared at him, her mind whirling again. The woman's harsh voice brought her back to earth.

"Well, aren't you the regular Don Juan," she said, giving the man an icy glare.

"Never mind, Cissie," the man said, a hard edge of warning in his voice.

"I—I couldn't," Jamie gasped. She snatched up the rose bouquet quickly and returned it to the cabinet, then grabbed the carnations and set them in front of the woman with a loud clatter. "Sorry," she said, her cheeks red with embarrassment.

"Don't let it fluster you, honey," the woman said. "How much?"

"Uh, fifteen dollars," Jamie said, avoiding looking at the man, who was staring at her again.

"Pay the lady, Zack," the woman ordered, confirming Jamie's suspicion about his identity, as she picked up the bouquet and headed for the hotel lobby door.

Zack Dunham peeled off a twenty and thrust it at Jamie. "Keep the change," he said, "and take the roses home with you. I want you to have them. You do look like pink roses and baby's breath."

Jamie glared at him, then fumbled in her cash drawer and pushed a five- and a ten-dollar bill toward him. "No, thank you, Mr. Dunham," she said frostily. "That would not be appropriate."

Zack Dunham was now leaning with both elbows on the counter. "Tch, tch, you've been reading the gossip columns." He shook his head reprovingly. "You shouldn't believe that nonsense." He smiled that warm, engaging smile again. "You wouldn't be free later on, would you, Miss— It is 'miss,' isn't it?"

"Miss Exeter!" Jamie snapped. "And no, I certainly would not. You should be ashamed of yourself. It is incredibly rude of you to flirt with one woman while you're obviously escorting another, whether you're almost engaged or not!"

Zack laughed a deep, warm-sounding laugh. "How wonderful to meet a woman who really speaks her mind," he said. "I suppose I *should* be ashamed of myself, but I can't say that I am. How else could I still be here, talking to you?"

"You shouldn't be. Obviously your conscience needs some work," Jamie said tightly, wishing fervently that he would just take his change and remove his unsettling presence from her store. Having him so close was making little beads of perspiration break out on her upper lip. She pushed the bills closer to him. "I think you'd better go now."

Before Jamie could withdraw her hand, Zack captured it and carried it to his lips. "I hope you have a lovely evening, Miss Exeter," he said, grinning unrepentantly as Jamie tried vainly to pull free of his vise-like grip.

"And I hope you learn how to behave yourself!" Jamie countered. "Let go!"

"Not until you tell me your first name," he replied. "Miss Exeter sounds much too formal for someone I want to get to know a lot better."

"Well, I don't want to get to know you," Jamie fumed.

Zack laughed again, then looked around on the countertop. "Aha!" he said, spying the little plastic box of business cards next to the cash register and picking one up. "'Flowers from the Heart, Jamie Exeter, Proprietor,'" he read. "Jamie. I like that. It goes with pink roses and baby's breath, too." He pocketed the card, then pried Jamie's fingers open and kissed the palm of her hand. "Happy New Year, Jamie," he said softly. "I wish I didn't have to go to New York tomorrow, and then on to Africa, but I'll see you when I come back. You can count on it."

"Don't bother. I'm not even slightly interested in anyone as...as unreliable as you are," Jamie said, trying to ignore the tingling of her palm and the irregular palpitations in her chest.

For the first time, Zack Dunham's devil-may-care expression turned to a dark, serious frown. "Damned gossip columnists and their silly rumors," he growled. "I've had enough—"

"Zack, what in the devil is taking you so long?" demanded Cissie Bergstrom, poking her head back through the doorway, her scarlet lips set in a threateningly grim line.

"Coming," he said, making a wry face. He started to walk away, then suddenly turned back and bent across the counter toward Jamie. "From now on," he said softly, "don't believe anything unless I tell you it's true." He walked away, whistling softly.

Jamie watched him, again having that sense of unreality, almost expecting that both he and Cissie would cease to exist as he went through the door. Cissie's angry face, however, was perfectly real, and from the way her jaw was working it appeared that Zack was getting a thorough tongue-lashing. Jamie shook her head and sighed. From what she'd seen, that certainly didn't look like the love affair of the century. But then, some people seemed to enjoy fighting.

"I wouldn't trust that man as far as I could pitch an elephant," Jamie muttered as she put on her coat, gave the shop one last inspection and turned out the lights. Imagine him thinking she'd fall for that line about how he wanted to get to know her better! How gullible did he think she was? Jamie was just going through the lobby door on her way to the underground garage where her car was parked when she almost ran into a tall, gray-haired man. "I'm sorry," she said, giving him an apologetic smile and stepping to the side.

"Wait," said the man, putting his hand on her coat sleeve. "I'm Isaiah Dunham. Are you Miss Jamie Exeter? Was my son just in your shop?"

"Why, yes . . . and, uh, yes, he was, Mr. Dunham," Jamie replied, looking up and meeting two of the most penetrating steel-gray eyes she had ever seen. "Did he forget something?"

"Nothing he shouldn't have," Isaiah Dunham replied, those steely eyes whisking over Jamie so thoroughly she felt as if she were being subjected to a body search. His eyes met hers again. "To my great relief, Zack just told me he isn't marrying that Bergstrom woman, and when I asked him what changed his mind all he would say was that he'd just met you. I must admit, his taste seems to have improved, but naturally, I'm concerned that—"

"Just a minute, Mr. Dunham," Jamie interrupted, her temper rising as she caught the drift of his remarks. "I have no designs on your son. I wouldn't have him as a gift. In fact, I told him to get lost. I'm afraid he's playing games with you."

Isaiah Dunham's eyes narrowed fiercely, and for a moment Jamie regretted her rather tactless outburst. But before she could backtrack and apologize, the old man's face softened and he burst out laughing. "I was about to say I was concerned that he might be taking advantage of a naive little flower-shop owner, but I can tell he's met his match," he said, his eyes still twinkling. "Don't be too hard on the boy. He's not as bad as he seems, and you're just the kind of young lady he needs to see more of."

Jamie knew it would be stupid to make any more negative remarks about Zack to his father, but could think of nothing pleasant that wouldn't be insincere. She gave Isaiah Dunham a weak smile and said nothing, which made him laugh again.

"You're a rare young lady," he said. "Most people in your circumstances, knowing I'm going to own this hotel soon, would find all kinds of nice things to say about Zack. I appreciate your strength of character. I hope Zack's able to overcome the bad impression he made." He held out his hand to Jamie. "It's been a pleasure to meet you, Miss Exeter. I've already seen the ballroom, and your arrangements are excellent."

"Thank you, sir," Jamie said, shaking his hand rather dazedly and then exchanging wishes for a pleasant evening before he walked away. It suddenly hit her that she'd been absolutely insane to tell Isaiah Dunham that she wouldn't have his son as a gift. If she'd had her wits about her at all she probably *would* have said something reasonably nice about Zack. That man had really got under her skin. Usually she thought before she spoke. She'd been darned lucky that Isaiah took it the way he had!

Later that night, Jamie sat in her lounge chair with Cyrano on her lap, scarcely noticing the frantic celebration taking place on the television screen as the seconds ticked down toward midnight. Her mind kept squiggling back and forth between her encounters with Zack Dunham and his father. It had been so unnerving to have the man she had imagined the night before suddenly appear in front of her, that for a few wild moments she'd actually thought she heard those magical bells ringing. But Cissie Bergstrom had put a quick stop to that. It was a lesson she should definitely remember. Just because a man looked right didn't mean he was. Zack Dunham certainly wasn't. Not for her or any other woman with an ounce of self-respect. The Zacks of the world bounced from flower to flower like two-legged bumblebees—which was, after all, not her problem. She doubted he'd really come back. But if he did... His father seemed to want her to see Zack again, and Isaiah Dunham more or less controlled the fate of her shop. A difficult situation but, Jamie decided, totally irrelevant. She had enough character not to let that fact push her into a relationship she didn't want, and Isaiah would surely appreciate that. She doubted he'd do anything as unreasonable as cancel her lease if she didn't take up with his son. Not that she thought Zack really meant what he'd said about getting to know her better. She'd probably never see him again, and all her worrying would be for nothing.

A cacophony of horns and whistles called Jamie's attention to the fact that midnight had arrived. "Happy New Year, Cyrano," Jamie said with a sigh. "I hope tonight was the end of last year and not the beginning of this one. Worrying about Zack Dunham has worn me out more than the whole day at the shop!"

Chapter Two

JAMIE TURNED OFF the television and went into her bedroom. She had just taken her hair down from its usual tidy topknot and put on her pajamas when there was a loud knock at the front door.

"Must be the Breyers are out of ice already," she said to Cyrano as she slipped into her pink terry robe. Now that the TV was off, she could hear the sounds of a party upstairs. She hurried to the door, tying the robe around her as she went. Even though she was fairly certain it was a neighbor, she inched open the door without removing the security chain and peeked out. Seconds later, she slammed it shut again, her heart racing.

"It can't be," she muttered. "Now I am imagining things." Zack Dunham could not be standing outside her apartment door, wearing a tuxedo and a black trench coat, his hair and shoulders covered with melting snow.

The next knock was even louder, accompanied by a deep voice. "Jamie, let me in, please. I won't stay long."

With shaking fingers, she slid the chain free and opened the door. "What are you doing here?" she demanded of the very real Zack Dunham.

"I told you I wanted to see you again," he replied with an ingratiating smile, "and I decided I didn't want to wait until I got back from Africa, so I came looking for you." He paused. "May I come in?"

"Well, I—I guess so," Jamie said. He really did look cold and she doubted that he intended her any harm. She stepped back, letting him enter. "I didn't know it was snowing. Why on earth did you walk?"

"I like to walk. It didn't start snowing until I was almost halfway here," Zack said, removing his coat and holding it out somewhat gingerly. "This is pretty damp."

"Maybe we should take it into the kitchen," Jamie suggested. "I can hang it near the radiator." When Zack nodded in agreement, she hurried ahead of him, thinking as she went that this was certainly a strange way to begin a new year.

"I'm sorry if I got you up," Zack said, apparently noticing for the first time that Jamie was wearing her bathrobe.

Being reminded of that fact did nothing to calm Jamie's nerves. "I—I wasn't in bed yet," she said. She took Zack's coat, hanging it on the small clothesline she'd strung near the radiator and thanking her stars she didn't have the line full of underwear tonight. "There," she said, turning around, "that should dry pretty fast." Zack was watching her, and in the bright fluorescent light of the kitchen she could plainly see two red scratches on his left cheek. "Oh, so that's it," she said, looking at them pointedly. "Cissie didn't like it when you told her you weren't going to marry her."

"How did you know that?" Zack demanded. "Can't I make a move without some damned reporter—"

"Your father said you told him you weren't," Jamie interrupted, "so I assume you told her, too." She raised her eyebrows and gave him a cool look. "Is that why you're here? Because your father sent you?"

"Lord, no!" Zack said, more loudly than Jamie thought necessary. His voice lowered a little. "When did you meet my father? What did he tell you? Mind if I sit down?" He pulled out a chair at the kitchen table and sat without waiting for her answer.

"I met your father in the lobby," Jamie replied, giving Zack a brief account of their conversation. "I'm afraid I was pretty tactless," she concluded. "I really should apologize to both of you."

Zack groaned. "Actually, you handled Dad just right. He likes blunt people. *I'll* accept your apology, though. For what you said and for thinking I'm here because Dad sent me. I'm glad he's on my side this time, but I don't do his bidding. Never have, which is why we haven't got along very well." He gave Jamie a crooked smile and ran his hand over his wet black hair. "Now could we talk about something more pleasant? You, for instance?"

"I'm not sure that's more pleasant," Jamie said nervously. She wanted to believe Zack. He sounded sincere. But why, really, did he walk all the way to her apartment through the falling snow? Could he have had too much to drink before he left the hotel? He didn't look drunk at all, but she couldn't be sure. All she was sure of was that he filled her little kitchen with a kind of electric excitement she found very unnerving.

"I think you need a towel for your hair," she said, as he ran his fingers through it again, then shook the water from his hand. She scurried into her bathroom and returned with a thick, soft towel. "Do you need a comb?" she asked as she handed it over to him.

"Thanks. No, I've got one in my pocket." He rubbed his hair vigorously, ending up looking tousled and, Jamie thought, dangerously appealing—like a man who'd just got out of the shower.

While Zack combed his hair, Jamie cast frantically about for something prosaic to do to get her mind back on a safe track. "Uh, would you like something warm to drink?" she suggested. "Coffee or hot chocolate?"

"Hot chocolate sounds terrific, if it isn't too much trouble," Zack said with another of those engaging smiles.

"No trouble at all. I've got the instant kind," Jamie said, relieved at having something to do. She filled a kettle with water and set it on the stove to heat, then opened one of her crammed cupboards and pulled out the box of cocoa packets. She had to stoop to retrieve a box of raisins that tumbled to the floor. "I just don't have enough cupboard space," she muttered, as she shoved the raisins back into place. "My new house is going to have lots of cupboards."

"New house? Is there someone else in the picture?" Zack asked.

"No, I'm buying it myself," Jamie replied, glancing at him as she got out two mugs. His voice had taken on a growly note, and she wondered if maybe it wouldn't have been smarter to say there *was* someone.

"Seems kind of odd," Zack said, "a woman buying a house alone."

So that was it, Jamie thought. "In case you hadn't noticed," she said, "times have changed. You must still be suffering from the 'three bears' syndrome."

"The 'three bears' syndrome?" Zack smiled, his eyes crinkling with sparks of laughter that made Jamie devote close attention to emptying cocoa mix into the cups.

"Yes," she said. "Thinking every house is supposed to have a mama bear, a papa bear and a baby bear. I doubt more than half of them do these days."

"More's the pity," Zack said. "You're right, I think they should."

Jamie doubted that Zack was ever going to be a papa bear in a typical house, but decided it was probably not a good topic to pursue further. "You said you were going to Africa," she said as she stirred hot water into the cocoa mix. "That sounds interesting. I'll bet you're looking forward to it."

Zack chuckled. "You don't know much about me, do you?"

"No," Jamie said, frowning as she handed him his cup and sat down across from him. "Why should I? Contrary to what you thought this afternoon, I don't read the gossip columns. Someone told me you were involved with Cissie Bergstrom or I'd never have known anything at all."

"That's good news," Zack said, smiling. "I don't have to overcome too many false impressions. You already think I'm rude, tactless and unreliable. All of which are wrong."

He could melt a glacier with that smile, Jamie thought, looking down at her cocoa mug. "What about Africa?" she asked.

"I go there often," Zack said. "I run Fantastick Voyages, which is a branch of the Dunham empire. I personally lead about ten tours a year—to Africa, Alaska or the South Seas. If I were really rude, tactless and unreliable, I don't think we'd be the most successful tour business in the world, do you?"

"No, I guess you wouldn't," Jamie said, gazing at him with a new respect.

"I'll bet you thought I was some kind of good-for-nothing playboy," Zack teased. "Maybe now you won't jump to conclusions before you know the facts."

"I'll try not to," Jamie said, "but you probably know as well as I do that you have to try and figure people out by what you can see. Besides, being reliable in business doesn't always carry over into your personal life."

"Not always," Zack agreed. "I've made my share of mistakes." He cocked his head and studied Jamie seriously. "What about you? Why is a beautiful woman like you home alone on New Year's Eve? I really didn't expect to find you here, but I needed a walk to cool off and I was hoping you would be. I wanted to make sure my eyes hadn't deceived me this afternoon when I saw you. They hadn't."

"I started working at five this morning," Jamie replied, trying to ignore the little flush of pleasure his compliments gave her. "New Year's Eve is one of our busiest times. I'm not in any mood for a date after a day like that. All I want to do is sit down and put my feet up. Usually I doze off for an hour or so, but I was too wound up tonight to even do that." Which, she thought, was his fault, not that she would ever tell him so.

Zack glanced at his watch. "One o'clock. You've been up for over twenty hours. I'd better go and let you get some sleep before you get the impression that I'm inconsiderate along with everything else." He drained his mug and then stood. "Thank you for the hot chocolate and for rescuing me from the cold. And for being here so I could find out that you're real. I wasn't sure I hadn't dreamed you."

"Oh, you're . . . you're welcome," Jamie said, a little dazed by Zack's sudden decision to leave. Since his arrival, she felt as though time had taken a holiday, and they were floating along in some other dimension. "Is your coat really dry? Can I call you a cab?" she asked, suddenly wishing he wasn't in such a hurry to go. "I'm not sure it's safe to walk at this hour of the night."

"It's dry enough, and they've got extra patrols out on New Year's Eve," Zack said as he shrugged his broad shoulders into his trench coat, "but thanks for being concerned. That gives me hope. Who's this?" He looked down as Cyrano came yowling grumpily across the floor toward him.

"That's Cyrano," Jamie replied, "because of the way that spot makes his nose look too big. He's been asleep on my bed."

"Lucky cat," Zack said, reaching down and scooping the cat into his arms. "Hello, Cyrano. Can I count on you to see that no one else shares your mistress's bed from now on?"

"I don't do that sort of thing!" Jamie snapped, glaring at him. "Not that it's any of your business." She should have known a man with eyes like his would think about bedrooms.

Zack rubbed Cyrano's chin and looked at him thoughtfully. "If it isn't my business, why do you suppose she told me?" he asked the cat.

"Because I didn't like your insinuation," Jamie said coldly. "You're used to life in a lot faster lane than I am, so I suppose I should have expected it.

"I told you to stop jumping to conclusions about me," Zack said as he put Cyrano down.

"What were you doing about me?" she countered.

Zack straightened and regarded Jamie thoughtfully. There was a strange faraway look in his eyes, as if he was both seeing her and looking inside her. She felt a little chill skitter down her back, as if he had touched a nerve somewhere. She wanted to ask what he was thinking, if behind those beautiful green eyes he was wondering why on earth he'd ever come here tonight, if he was glad that he had. She knew, quite suddenly, that she wanted him to be glad. Finally he took a deep breath and smiled crookedly. "I think I was trying to tell you something," he said.

It had been so long since Jamie had asked her question that she'd almost forgotten what it was. For a moment she stared at him blankly, then, remembering, asked, "Tell me what?"

"I'm not quite sure," Zack answered. "Maybe that I could stand here forever looking at you and wishing that I knew more about what's going on behind those lovely blue eyes of yours. But I guess we'll have to save that for another time. I can see you're tired."

He bent down to give Cyrano a final pat, then started toward the front door. When they reached the living room, Jamie went over to the window, pushing the curtains aside to look out. "It's been snowing a lot," she said, turning to look at Zack. "Are you sure you don't want a cab? You aren't wearing boots or anything."

Zack shook his head. "No, I need the walk, even more than I did when I came here."

Jamie puzzled over that statement for a moment, then decided it was best not to comment. "Well, be careful," she said instead as she went to see Zack out of the door. "It's probably slippery."

"*Life* is slippery," Zack replied with a wry smile. "I never expected the year to start out this way."

"I guess I didn't, either," Jamie said, not sure what he meant, but knowing that she felt the same way. "I—I hope you have a nice trip to Africa."

"It's always beautiful, and interesting," Zack said, "but . . ." His voice trailed off and he stared at Jamie, his eyes suddenly so intensely green it almost took her breath away. When he reached up and touched her hair she held her breath. His hand caressed its silky length, and she could have sworn his touch generated the sparks of electricity running through her like wildfire. As his eyes wandered slowly down to her mouth, his lips parted. She knew he was thinking of kissing her, and she had to struggle to keep from moistening her own lips in response. Her pulse quickened while her mind raced in circles, first telling her that she shouldn't let him, then wishing he would. When he tucked his hand behind her neck, she stiffened, feeling near panic. He saw, and smiled gently, the warmth of his smile making Jamie's heart do a sudden skip and then begin to pound. "Will it frighten you so much if I kiss you?" he asked.

At that question, Jamie did lick her lips nervously, swallowing what felt like a grapefruit lodged in her throat. "Well, I—" she began, then gasped as Zack surrounded her with his arms, lowering his mouth to hers so swiftly that she had no time to say any more. When their lips touched she could have said no more even if she'd wanted to. A shock wave surged through her, leaving her feeling so dizzy that she grasped at Zack for support. In a mindless daze of sensations she could feel herself drawn closer and closer, as if they were melting together. Then, as suddenly as he'd begun, he drew back, still holding her close, his cheek resting against her hair. She could hear his breath coming raggedly, feel the tension in his muscular body and powerful arms. She could tell he was fighting strong emotions, and it occurred to her that she was no match for him if he should lose the battle and, if he were to kiss her again, she might not even put up much of a fight. Very carefully, she pulled away and looked up at him. To her surprise, he looked as dazed as she felt.

"Are you all right?" she asked.

Zack gave his head a little shake, then took a deep breath and smiled. "I guess maybe I shouldn't have had that last scotch at the party," he said. "For a minute there, I felt as if someone had hit me over the head. I was seeing stars and hearing bells."

Jamie frowned. "You really shouldn't walk back to the hotel."

"The cold air will do me good," Zack said. He put his hand on the doorknob, then paused. "I'll be in touch. Take good care of yourself."

Jamie nodded. "You, too."

"Always," Zack assured her, then opened the door and went out without a backward glance.

Jamie closed the door behind him, feeling terribly unsettled and suddenly very tired. What a strange man Zack Dunham was, she thought as she went toward her bedroom. She still wasn't sure why he'd come to see her, or what he thought of her now that he had. Maybe she never would know, and the idea made her feel a real physical ache inside.

"I think I like him," she said to Cyrano, who was staring at her curiously, his head cocked to one side. "He's much nicer than I thought at first." She stretched out and turned off the light. In the dark, an image of Zack's face floated before her, and in the warmth of the covers she pulled around her she could feel his arms holding her close. It made her feel wonderfully light and airy, as if she could float right up to the sky. "Maybe he *is* my dream man, after all," she mumbled as she drifted off to sleep.

Chapter Three

"I THOUGHT I WAS SEEING things, he looked so much like the man I imagined on the way home," Jamie said the next afternoon, describing her encounter with Zack in her shop as she watched Aunt Martha stuffing the turkey she was preparing to roast for their New Year's Day dinner. "He started flirting with me right away, and even when Cissie Bergstrom came in he kept right on flirting, even though it was obvious that she was madder than a hornet. It was terribly embarrassing. Then after she left, he told me I shouldn't believe the gossip columns about them getting engaged and asked if I was free later on. I told him I certainly wasn't, and not to bother me. After he left, his father showed up and said Zack told him he wasn't going to marry Cissie because he'd met me. I thought he was going to warn me off, so I told him I wouldn't have his son as a gift, and then—"

Martha Bellamy dropped her big metal spoon with a clatter. "You said that to Isaiah Dunham? Good heavens, child!"

"Oh, it was all right. Mr. Dunham laughed and said he thought Zack should see more of me. Then Zack showed up at my apartment after midnight, and—"

"Jamie, slow down!" her aunt commanded. "Bert, come and hear this!"

When Uncle Bert arrived in the kitchen, a questioning look on his face, his wife said, "You've got to hear what happened to Jamie last evening. Now, Jamie, start over and don't rush so. Tell us everything."

Jamie sighed and began again, this time going clear through Zack's visit but omitting the fact that he'd kissed her. She concluded by saying, "I tried to get him to let me call him a cab, but he wouldn't. He said he needed the walk."

Her uncle smiled and shook his head. "Poor fellow's got it real bad, I'd say. I remember what that was like." His eyes twinkled as he looked at his wife. "Like being hit with a club."

"Oh, come on, Uncle Bert," Jamie said. "Why would a man who's used to traveling all over the world with glamorous people be interested in me? I'm not in his league at all."

"Don't sell yourself short, dear," said her aunt. "You're pretty and smart enough to be in any league you want."

"Well, it doesn't really matter," Jamie persisted, "because there wouldn't be any future in getting interested in a man who's traveling most of the time. I'm certainly not going to give up my shop to chase after him."

"I can see that you're trying to talk yourself out of something," her uncle said with a smile. "Maybe instead you should think in terms of compromises. True love often requires compromises, doesn't it, Martha?"

"Quite often," her aunt agreed.

"You're jumping ahead of things," Jamie said. "Way, way ahead. I don't even know if Zack will be back again, or if I want him to be back."

"Of course you do, and I'd bet the farm he'll be back, if I had a farm," Bert Bellamy said.

Jamie shook her head, then gave him a warm kiss on the cheek. "I think you're crazy, but I love you, anyway. Time will tell, won't it?"

She tried to maintain that philosophical attitude all through January, but found it difficult. Valentine's Day, the day of lovers, was drawing near, and a steady stream of lovesick young men with glazed looks in their eyes came into her shop. They appeared to be in a state that was a combination of pleasure and pain, a state very similar to the way she felt. Thinking about Zack Dunham brought her a great deal of pleasure. But the fact she'd heard nothing from him was causing her a lot of pain. Pain, she told herself severely at least once a day, that was totally uncalled for. He'd only said he'd be in touch, which wasn't anything very definite and might have meant nothing at all. Besides, she rationalized, he was probably extremely busy, and communication from wherever he was wouldn't be easy. But she was forced to admit that if he'd really wanted to, he'd have found a way. She'd just have to adjust to the idea that she would probably never hear from Zack Dunham again.

Her adjustment was quickly undone when she was called into Isaiah Dunham's office to discuss her lease late on the Monday before Valentine's Day. Isaiah immediately told her that Zack was going to be in town in a few days to promote his tours. "You wouldn't mind if he called on you, would you?" he asked. "I'd appreciate it if you'd give him a second chance."

It took Jamie only a split second to realize that Zack must not have told Isaiah about his visit to her apartment. Well, it wasn't her place to fill him in on Zack's activities. "I guess I could do that," she said.

"Good, good!" Isaiah beamed at her. Then his expression turned serious. "Don't tell him I said anything to you. He'd be very angry, to put it mildly."

"Oh, no, of course not," Jamie agreed, thinking it would be funny, if it weren't so sad, how poorly Zack and his father communicated.

Isaiah nodded in apparent satisfaction. "Now, young lady, I'd like you to show me around your shop, and then we'll go up to my suite and discuss your lease over dinner. I've gone over your books, and they look pretty good. I'm going to want different terms than you've had before, but I think we can work something out."

Jamie wondered what those new terms might be, but she had little time to speculate. She needed to pay strict attention to Isaiah, who demonstrated his famous business acumen as he questioned her about everything from her advertising program to her inventory techniques. Finally he seemed satisfied, saying that it was time to go upstairs and discuss the details.

"I have a number of plans for this hotel that will require your close cooperation," he told her as they ate. He tossed out ideas almost nonstop—for planters, indoor gardens, a solarium. It was a dazzling opportunity, Jamie knew, and she did her best to come up with creative suggestions of her own. She had no idea how much she impressed him until, finally, he brought the discussion around to the new financial terms.

"You see, Jamie, I don't run my hotels in the usual way, and there won't be the usual kind of lease," he said. "The shops here are an integral part of the hotel, so I'll be drawing up profit-sharing agreements instead. That way, we all participate in the success or failure of the entire enterprise. I've found it's much more motivating, not that you seem to need any extra motivation. Would you be willing to consider that?''

"Why, yes, I would!" Jamie replied, almost unable to believe her ears. "Of course, I'd have to see the details..."

"Good, good," Isaiah said, beaming at her again. "I'll have my business manager go over the agreement with you and draw up your contract." He rose, and Jamie understood their discussion was over. She managed to take her leave graciously, in spite of feeling slightly woozy from trying to make her brain work so fast and simultaneously digest the information that Zack would be in town soon. The combination sent out alternating currents of elation and fear that left her dazed until she reached her car. Then, suddenly, she knew she had to talk to Aunt Martha and Uncle Bert right away!

"Good heavens, Jamie, what's happened?" Uncle Bert asked, as Jamie burst through their door, rattling the china in the cupboards in her haste.

"I had dinner with Isaiah Dunham," Jamie said, the words tumbling out in a rush, "and my shop is going to be an integral part of the hotel, and I'm going to share in the profits, and there's going to be a fountain in the dining room and flowers all over the place, and... Zack's going to be in town in a few days." She stopped, breathless.

"Did he finally call?" Aunt Martha asked.

"No, his father told me," Jamie said, relating the rest of her conversation with Isaiah. "Now I'm really sure he didn't send Zack that night," she said, "and pretty soon I'll know if Zack does want to see me again. If he doesn't call, I'll know I scared him off.''

"I don't think it's you that scared him," Uncle Bert said with a knowing smile. "A handsome fellow in his thirties who's used to playing the field is apt to panic when he discovers he may be really falling in love.''

"I'm not so sure that's his problem," Jamie said with a sigh. It had occurred to her recently that perhaps Zack wasn't interested in a relationship that stopped short of the bedroom.

"I'll bet there's no problem at all," Aunt Martha said. "He's just been busy. You let us know as soon as you hear from him.''

"I will," Jamie promised, but she didn't feel nearly as confident as her aunt and uncle. They, she knew, thought any man in his right mind would find her irresistible.

Fortunately the next three days, culminating in Valentine's Day, were frantically busy. Jamie had little time during working hours to think about anything except keeping her orders straight and everything running smoothly. In the evening, however, she had difficulty keeping her mind on even the most simple-minded sitcom, for one ear seemed tuned at all times to the sound of her phone.

The waiting and wondering began to get on her nerves. When the telephone rang just as she got home after a hectic Valentine's Day at the store, she tripped over Cyrano and banged her shin in her rush to get to it. "Hello!" she snapped, rubbing her throbbing leg.

"You sound cross as a bear," came Aunt Martha's voice. "Haven't you heard from Zack yet?"

"No, I haven't, and I'm cross because I just fell over Cyrano and hurt my shin," Jamie growled.

"Well, you should hear from him soon," Aunt Martha said soothingly. "He's in town. There's a picture of him in tonight's paper."

"Thanks for telling me," Jamie said dryly. "Now if he doesn't call I'll really feel miserable. Can I get back to you later? Cyrano's having a fit because he hasn't had his dinner."

"Yes, dear, I'll get off the phone," Aunt Martha said in knowing tones that made Jamie grimace as she hung up.

"I'm not sure anymore that I even *want* Zack Dunham to call," she told Cyrano, as he crunched his food with noisy gusto. "I think I'd rather just get over him. Not that there's anything to get over. It's not as if I was in love with him or anything." Cyrano gave her a glassy, contemptuous glance. "Don't *you* start in on me," she said, frowning at him, "or I'll buy that cheap food you don't like. Right now, I'm going to get the newspaper. It's time for some serious house-hunting."

Jamie hung up her coat, kicked off her shoes and went barefoot to retrieve her newspaper from the hall. She slid off the security chain, opened the door and then jumped back, gasping. There, just outside her door, stood Zack Dunham.

Chapter Four

"ZACK! WHAT are *you* doing here?" Jamie demanded as soon as she had regained part of her equilibrium. He looked so wonderful, his beautiful green eyes vital and alive in his handsome, tanned face. Once again she experienced that sense of unreality she had felt the first time she saw him. No real man had any business looking that perfect, she thought as she stared up at him. Sparkles of snow clung to his dark hair and to the fur collar of his leather bomber jacket, which was turned up around his neck. For several moments he looked at her intently, as if he, too, were not entirely sure that what he saw was real. Then, just as Jamie was beginning to wonder why he was staring at her like that, his lips slowly curved into a smile and his eyes took on the familiar warmth that Jamie had remembered so often.

"Hello, Jamie," he said. "You must be clairvoyant. I didn't even ring the bell." From behind his back he produced a soft, furry stuffed elephant with a big red bow around its neck. "I thought maybe you'd seen enough flowers for one day, and I'm kind of partial to elephants. Happy Valentine's Day."

Jamie stared from Zack to the elephant and back again. She wished she *were* clairvoyant. Having Zack appear before her so suddenly had hit her like the proverbial ton of bricks, leaving her feeling dizzy and breathless. She finally took the elephant, smiled and gestured vaguely with one hand. "Thank you. Thank you very much. This is a . . . surprise. Come in." She looked at the elephant more closely and gave it an experimental hug before setting it on her coffee table. "It's adorable. I'm partial to elephants, too."

"I thought you might be," Zack said as he closed the door behind him. He unzipped his jacket and shrugged it off. "I realize I should have written, but I didn't know what to say. I'm not a very good letter-writer." He smiled crookedly. "I guess that's not much of an excuse, is it?"

Jamie was so tense that she almost snatched the jacket from him. "I thought maybe you thought I wasn't very nice to you," she said as she crammed the jacket into her crowded closet. "I'm afraid sometimes I'm too blunt."

Zack shook his head. "No, I didn't think that. But New Year's Eve seemed almost unreal. I almost called you a dozen times, but I was afraid—" He stopped, staring at Jamie so intently again that she felt a quiver of excitement run through her. His eyes drew her like a magnet, and she took a few steps closer to him.

"Afraid of what?" she asked.

He held out both hands. "Come here," he said.

Jamie held her hands up for him to take hold of, her heart gyrating wildly as he grasped them tightly and pulled her even closer.

"I was afraid," he said, "that when I saw you again it wouldn't be the same, that I wouldn't feel as if I couldn't bear not to touch you, and that I wouldn't want so much to kiss you it made me ache all over. But I was wrong." He pulled Jamie closer still, his glance sweeping her face, then coming to rest on her eyes again. "I was very wrong," he murmured. He let go of her hands and slowly slid his arms around her slender waist.

Automatically, Jamie's arms encircled him. He smiled and quickly tightened his own embrace. Jamie was sure he could hear her heart pounding against him as she waited, breathless, for the kiss she knew was to come. She had no fear that it would be less wonderful than the last time. What Zack might think about her being so obviously willing, she didn't care. She would worry about that later. Then, suddenly, it happened. His arms crushed her to him. His mouth found hers with almost punishing force. Jamie felt as if a whole year's supply of fireworks had been set off at once.

She abandoned any attempt to hold on to rational thought. Her arms clung tightly to his broad, strong back. She wanted to feel his strength surrounding her, to savor every sensation that pounded against her reeling senses. There was the musky heather of his scent, the honeyed sweetness of his mouth, the magnificent firmness of his muscular shoulders beneath his soft sweater. The touch of his hands, eagerly caressing her back, sent tongues of fire surging through her. His lips moved delicately across her cheek and nuzzled next to her ear. "Oh, Jamie," he murmured, "I imagined this so often when I was away." His lips traveled back to hers at the same time as his hand slipped between their bodies.

The sensation of his delicate touch was so delectable that it was several moments before Jamie's mind registered what was happening. When it did, she tried to thrust herself away but Zack's embrace only tightened. "Don't!" she said, leaning back and wedging her arms between them.

Zack relented, but did not release her. He caressed her hair back from her forehead, his eyes searching hers in a combination of anger and frustration. "What are you afraid of, Jamie?" he asked.

"I'm *not* afraid," she denied hotly. "I just don't want you to touch me like that. Let go of me. Please."

"You *are* afraid," Zack said. He caught her face in one hand and held it tightly. "You're scared to death of finding out what it's really like to be a woman. I'll bet you've never—"

"That's enough!" Jamie snapped, jerking her head free.

"No, it isn't," Zack said. "Not nearly enough." He tilted his head back and looked at her through narrowed eyes, his black lashes casting deep shadows across their green depths. "You'll be mine sometime, Jamie," he said softly. "I want you, and you want me."

"I don't think so," Jamie said, a deep sadness replacing the euphoria of only moments ago. She should have known better than to keep on dreaming about a man like Zack, a man used to making love to glamorous, willing women. For her, it would never be enough to be simply the woman who shared his bed. She would want him to belong to her completely, and she doubted he ever would.

"It may take some time," Zack said confidently, "but you will." He sighed deeply and then released her. "I was going to ask you out to dinner. Would you like to do that?"

Jamie looked down at her bare feet sticking out from beneath her red slacks, and suddenly felt very tired. She would never be able to please Zack Dunham the way he wanted to be pleased. What was the use of going on? "I've had an awfully long day," she began tentatively.

"That's right, I almost forgot. It's Valentines Day and I'll bet you've been up since dawn," Zack said immediately. "How about phoning for a pizza? Do you have some wine? We can have a nice, restful party right here. You won't even have to put your shoes on."

For a moment, Jamie thought of sending Zack away. It would be much more sensible. But as she looked at his smiling face, the words got stuck somewhere between her brain and her lips. "That—that's a good idea," she said instead. "I have some chardonnay and some cabernet, I think. Which would you like?"

"The cabernet," Zack replied. "If you'll tell me where it is, I'll get it so you can rest your tired feet."

Jamie shook her head and started for her kitchen, trying to ignore the fact that she had probably let herself in for an evening of resisting Zack's advances while her heart told her one thing and her mind another. "You'd never find it," she said. "My kitchen is like one giant puzzle. Besides, the phone's out there. What kind of pizza do you like? I'm game for almost anything."

"Then let's get a big one with everything on it. I'm starved. I talked about Africa to a women's group today at lunch, and all they fed me was a dab of chicken in a pastry shell and a couple of sprigs of broccoli." Zack made a disgusted face. "Don't ever try to feed me broccoli. It tastes like something cows should eat."

Jamie shot a quick glance at him but said nothing. Why, she wondered, did Zack say that? She wasn't anticipating trying to feed him anything.

As soon as Jamie flipped on the kitchen light, Cyrano awoke with a *meroww* and stretched in his basket.

"Hey, there's that neat cat," Zack said, bending to pat him. "Hello, Cyrano. How's it going, old buddy? I'll bet you'd be impressed by some of the cats I've seen lately."

"I'll bet he would, too," Jamie said. "Now, let's see, where did I put that wine?"

"If you tell me where the phone book is, I'll call for the pizza," Zack said.

"There's the number of a good pizza parlor on the list beside the phone." Jamie gestured toward the phone by the wall. Then she dropped to her knees in front of a cupboard and began pulling out boxes of rice, cake mix, and assorted cans of vegetables. "I'm sure that wine is in here somewhere," she muttered.

Zack finished his call and crouched beside her to peer into the cupboard. "I think I see it in that far corner," he said.

Just as Zack started to reach into the cupboard, something small and gray shot out of the dark recesses. Jamie gave a shriek and lurched against Zack, who sat back suddenly and caught her. Cyrano leaped across them and caught the hapless mouse with one swift swipe of his paw. "Nice work," Zack said admiringly. "Quicker than a lion on a gazelle." He grinned at Jamie who was watching Cyrano administer the coup de grace, an expression of distaste on her face. "And I was afraid I might not get my arms around you for the rest of the evening," he said.

Jamie looked at him, startled, suddenly aware that she was almost sitting on his lap. His laughing green eyes were only inches away, and his arms were, indeed, around her. She tried to wriggle free, but Zack shook his head and tightened his grip.

"Oh, no, you don't," he said. "Providence sent that mouse, and I intend to take full advantage of it. You need more kissing, and I'm going to see that you get it. Don't worry, I'll be a perfect gentleman if it kills me."

"Don't—" Jamie began, but Zack's lips stifled the rest of her words. For a moment Jamie tried not to respond, then, as a surge of longing flooded through her, gave a deep sigh and answered the insistent pressure. How on earth, she wondered desperately, was she going to resist this man? Being in his arms made her feel as if every Christmas she had ever known was returning to delight her.

"This is where you belong, you know," Zack murmured against her ear, as his lips teased her with little kisses.

Lost in a swirling fog of conflicting emotions, Jamie could think of no answer until Cyrano, right beside them, let out several high-pitched demanding *merowws*. She pulled her head back and looked into Zack's eyes, warm and dark with passion. "Would you like to deal with a dead mouse?" she asked.

Sparks of mischief lighted Zack's eyes. "If you'll give me another kiss later," he said, then laughed as Jamie scowled at him. He snatched one last light kiss before he got up and helped her to her feet. "Where shall I dump it?"

"There's a big trash container in the back hallway," she replied, gesturing to the door. While Zack took care of the remains, she quickly retrieved the wine and put the rest of the items back into the cupboard. As she did, she thought that although Zack might have appreciated the mouse, he must think her a dreadful housekeeper, then wondered why she cared.

"Let's take this into the living room and get comfortable," Zack suggested, after Jamie, with a little less difficulty, found wineglasses and a corkscrew. He picked everything up and headed for the living room. Jamie followed, wondering if she'd ever be comfortable in the same room with Zack anymore. When he set bottle and glasses down on the coffee table in front of the sofa, she quickly sat a safe distance away in her reclining lounge chair and put her feet up.

Zack shook his head at her. "No, you sit right here," he said, pointing to the end of the sofa. "You can put your tired little feet in my lap and I'll give them a massage."

A tingle of anxiety scurried through Jamie's body and made her feel uncomfortably warm and cold at the same time. The idea of putting her bare feet in Zack's lap while his strong hands caressed them seemed terribly intimate. No doubt, she thought, exactly what he planned it to be. "I'm perfectly comfortable here," she said as calmly as she could. "This rests my feet just fine."

"Do I have to pick you up and put you there?" Zack asked, raising one eyebrow at her as he removed the wine cork.

"Don't try that macho stuff on me," Jamie said, frowning at him. "I don't like it."

"Then quit playing the timid, shrinking violet and move your cute little you-know-what over here," Zack retorted. When Jamie still didn't move, he put the wine bottle down and started in her direction.

"Bully," Jamie growled, but she got up and crossed to the sofa, sinking down into the far corner, her feet firmly planted on the floor.

Zack poured the wine, then sat down himself. He silently reached over, grasped Jamie's legs and lifted them, turning her so that her feet were on his lap. "There we are," he said, handing her a glass of wine. "Now, just relax. Tell me all about yourself. Tell me how you came to be a florist."

Jamie eyed him suspiciously. He'd certainly been trying to undermine her self-control. What was he up to now? "It's not a very fascinating story," she said. "I'd rather hear about Africa."

"All in due time," Zack replied. "I asked first. Start at the beginning." He began massaging her foot, pressing the arch upward, then stretching each toe.

Jamie sighed luxuriously. Zack looked over at her and smiled. "Feel good?" he asked.

"Heavenly," she admitted.

"See how useful I am to have around?" Zack said. "I can fix anything from dead mice to dead-tired feet. Okay, on with your story."

"All right," Jamie said, "you asked for it." She told him about growing up in a small white house in a middle-class neighborhood, an only child, a good student, who, until her father had died, had expected to go on to college. "Uncle Bert needed help in his shop, so I stayed with him and Aunt Martha and took a business course instead. I gradually assumed more and more responsibility, and he retired five years ago. Business has almost doubled since then. It's hard work, but I love it. I can't think of anything I'd rather do."

"You're lucky in that," Zack said. He cocked his head and studied her curiously. "No men in your life?"

Jamie shrugged. "Nothing serious. I've been too busy. Now tell me about yourself." She wanted to forestall any more personal questions. It had never bothered her before, but for some reason she was embarrassed to admit to this very sensual man that she had never had a serious romance.

Zack gave her a knowing look but said nothing, immediately launching into his life history instead. "I was born in Philadelphia thirty-five years ago next July," he said. "I have an older brother—" The doorbell rang. "Saved by the pizza," Zack said. "I'll get it."

While Zack paid the man, Jamie carried the big box into the kitchen, set it on the table, then got out some plates, thinking it would be a lot safer eating in the kitchen than sitting next to Zack on the sofa. She had an uneasy feeling that he was very, very skillfully edging his way into her life, almost into her very being, in an effort to make good his prediction that she would soon be his. She doubted if any other woman had been able to resist him for very long.

"Let's eat in the living room," Zack said, appearing in the kitchen moments later. "The wine's in there, and besides, I'd rather have you sitting next to me."

Jamie looked quickly away from his alluring smile and sat down in a kitchen chair. It was time, she decided, that she made it perfectly clear to Zack that she was not going to be led down his primrose path. "I feel safer here," she said, shaking her head. "I don't think you quite believed me that I'm not interested in...in the kind of relationship you have in mind."

Zack planted his hands on his hips and studied her intently. "Safer," he muttered, as if to himself. Then more loudly, he said, "I think you've spent entirely too much of your life feeling safe. Sometimes, safety is an illusion." With that, he bent down, tucked his hands beneath her arms, and flung her over his shoulder. Jamie gasped in surprise. "See what I mean?" he said.

"Put me down!" Jamie demanded, trying to kick and finding that Zack could control her legs with one arm. "Put me down right now, or I'll scream!"

"I wouldn't bother, if I were you," Zack advised, as he carried her rapidly into the living room. "I could easily convince anyone who came that you aren't in any danger. Just be quiet and listen."

"I am not going to listen to anything you have to say," Jamie said from between clenched teeth. "You are insufferable."

"No, I'm not," Zack said. "Now, this is an illustration of the way I would carry you out of the bush if you panicked and fainted at the sight of a charging rhinoceros. After I'd chased the rhino away, of course. I do my best to see that my clients don't find themselves in such situations, but sometimes, on a clear, starry night, they wander away from my camp, thinking it perfectly safe out there. It isn't." He stopped, swung Jamie into the curve of his arm and sat the two of them down on the sofa in one fluid movement. "Sometimes on the Serengeti," he continued softly, his face only inches from hers, "there are more stars in the skies than there are in your eyes. It's so still that it seems you're all alone in the world, safe on your own private planet. Then, suddenly, there it is, right in front of you, the thing you feared most." Zack stopped talking, his arm tightened around Jamie's shoulders, and his lips found hers.

Jamie had been staring at him, her lips parted. Her anger had subsided as he spoke, changing first to a kind of reluctant admiration for his inventiveness, then to fascination with the brilliant intensity of his clear green eyes. She could almost imagine seeing the vast plain of the Serengeti reflected in them. She realized she had been very skillfully outmaneuvered, but felt no real anger, merely a rush of excitement flooding through her. The current that flowed between them was too intense, quickly erasing everything but the awareness of his presence. He folded his arms around her, this time covering her mouth with his in a more demanding kiss, seeking her innermost secrets with devastating persuasiveness. When at last he pulled away, there was a triumphant gleam in his eyes.

"And you say you're not interested," he scoffed. "Why are you so determined to deceive yourself?"

"I am not deceiving myself," Jamie said, taking a deep breath and trying to slow her racing pulse. "I'm not denying I'm physically attracted to you. I am. But I am not interested in joining the list with Cissie Bergstrom and heaven only knows how many others before her. When I give myself to a man, it will be a permanent thing, and quite frankly, Zack, I don't think I'd trust you to make that kind of commitment. Not with the way you travel all over the world with all kinds of glamorous people."

At first Zack looked as if he was about to make an angry retort, then one corner of his mouth quirked into a little smile. "So," he said, "the gauntlet has been flung down. This should be interesting."

"It wasn't meant to be a challenge," Jamie said sadly, "it was meant to be goodbye. Why don't you take the pizza with you and go now? I'm not hungry.''

"The hell I will," Zack growled. "You asked me to tell you about myself and my work, and that's exactly what I'm going to do. You stay right where you are. I'm going to get the pizza and you're going to eat some of it. You're too damned thin already." He whirled and walked away.

"Darn!" Jamie said, pounding her fist into the sofa and blinking back tears of frustration. She should have known better than to agree to let him stay. Apparently his sole aim in life was to conquer every woman he took a fancy to. Well, she would listen to his story and then put him out of her life forever. And she was not going to eat any pizza!

Zack reappeared with the pizza and the plates. He took several slices himself, then held one up under Jamie's nose. "How does it smell?" he asked. When Jamie only pursed her lips together and did not answer he smiled. "Open your mouth. You're starving, and you know it."

Jamie groaned and took a bite. "Why are you doing this to me?" she complained mushily.

"Because you need it," Zack said calmly, handing Jamie a plate loaded with three large slices of pizza. "You aren't nearly as self-sufficient as you think you are. Now then, where was I? I grew up in Philadelphia with an older brother and a younger sister, the poor little guy in the middle. My father doted on my brother, who always did what he was supposed to, and my mother led my sister through the debutante ranks. I just got into mischief. As a result, when I finished college my father informed me either to do something useful for the Dunham empire or kiss my share of the family fortune goodbye. By then I had a pretty good idea of what I'd like to do, which was to become a wildlife biologist, but I also knew the value of money. I figured that in the long run I could do more for wildlife with my share of the fortune than I'd ever accomplish without it. I compromised by talking my father into starting the tour business. He gave me five years to make a success of it, and much to his surprise, I did. I think he still resents the fact.'' Zack took a rather vicious bite from his pizza and frowned.

"I should think he'd be proud of you," Jamie said, puzzled. "What makes you think he isn't?"

"He still waves that same old threat around, as if he's just waiting for me to do something foolish," Zack replied. He made a wry face. "I guess old habits die hard."

"You mean something foolish like marrying Cissie Bergstrom?" Jamie asked. "I heard he was dead set against it."

Zack nodded. "I never had any intention of marrying her, but he believed the gossips, so I let him. If he hasn't figured out yet that I'm smarter than that, that's his problem."

"That wasn't very nice," Jamie said. "And Cissie must have had some idea you were serious, judging by what happened on New Year's Eve."

"Not from anything I said," Zack said, giving Jamie a strangely intent look. "She believed what she wanted to believe."

"I'd say you could have done a lot better at communicating with both of them," Jamie said, returning his gaze levelly. "Are you sure it isn't your own old habits that aren't dead yet?"

Zack's eyes widened, then, very slowly, a smile spread across his face. "You do have a way of getting right to the heart of things, don't you?" he said. "You're right, I *should* reform."

"Do that," Jamie said, thinking that Zack had understood what she'd meant, and taken her criticism better than she had expected. Whether he would act on it was quite another thing. "Tell me about Africa," she suggested, as Zack munched thoughtfully on another slice of the rapidly disappearing pizza. "Is it really as beautiful as it looks in pictures?"

"More so," Zack said quietly. "You really should come along and see for yourself. I'd love to show it to you."

"Maybe sometime," Jamie said noncommittally. "Where do you go?"

"I'll describe one of my usual itineraries." Zack leaned back comfortably, gazing into space as if visualizing the places he was talking about. "We leave from New York in the evening, stop over the next day in Switzerland, and go on the next evening to Nairobi. After a day there to get over jet lag, we head for the Amboseli Game Reserve..."

Zack talked and Jamie listened and asked questions for more than an hour. At the end of that time, she was thoroughly impressed with his knowledge of African wildlife and his deep concern for its preservation. "You sound more like a wildlife biologist than a tour guide," she commented. "I think you've done a wonderful job of combining two careers."

"That's the nicest thing you've ever said to me." Zack flashed a brilliant smile. "You should come along on my next tour. I haven't even begun to tell you everything you'd be able to see and do."

Jamie sighed. "I must admit you make it sound almost irresistible, but I'm not set up right now to get away from my shop for that long." And, she thought, she would have to think long and hard before she went off for three weeks in Africa with the almost equally irresistible Zack. It might be more than she could handle.

"You should get someone you can turn part of the load over to, anyhow," Zack said frowning. "You work too hard." He glanced at his watch and sighed heavily. "I suppose I'd better be going. I have to catch an early-morning flight and I expect you have another busy day ahead of you."

"I'm afraid so," Jamie said. Suddenly she was sorry that he was leaving again so soon. If only he would stop looking at her as a prospective conquest, they might get along very well. It might be less than they both wanted—for different reasons—but it would be better than nothing. She retrieved his jacket and watched silently as he shrugged it over his broad shoulders and zipped it up.

"Where are you going from here?" she asked when he stood by her door, apparently struggling for something to say before he took his leave.

"New York," he replied. "I have to meet with the people who handle the business end of the tours. That's the dull part." He stared at Jamie intently for a moment, then took her face lightly between his hands. "Jamie," he said seriously, "I hope I didn't come on too strong tonight. I'd hate to leave with you thinking my only interest in you is getting you into bed. You're a...very special person. I don't want you to get the idea I'm some kind of hopeless degenerate that you never want to see again. I think that would—" he paused and smiled crookedly "—break my heart."

Jamie searched his face, unsure of whether she dared believe he really cared that much. The ache in her own heart told her how much she wanted to believe. "I don't think that at all," she said. "I do think that maybe... maybe we could be good friends."

Zack's eyebrows shot upward. "Friends?"

He looked so surprised that Jamie couldn't help smiling. "It does happen, you know. Men and women can be friends."

"*We* can't," Zack said, shaking his head. "Sooner or later we'd both go crazy, you ought to know that."

Jamie frowned. "I don't know any such thing. Besides, you know where I stand. I don't see what else is possible."

Zack looked at Jamie intently again, his face working as if a great many thoughts were going through his mind that he dared not voice. Suddenly he made a sort of growling sound and crushed her against him, kissing her with such passion that Jamie felt as if the floor were swaying beneath her feet. Then he drew back, tossing his head back defiantly. "Listen to your heart," he said. "It's beating like a drum. What does that tell you?"

Jamie could feel her heart pounding, telling her that Zack's kisses affected her as no other man's ever had, that she wished he could stay and they could get to know each other, and that then maybe something even more wonderful might happen. She could also feel the strong, heavy beat of Zack's heart against her. Did Zack really know what his was saying? she wondered. "Maybe you should listen to yours," she suggested softly.

"What do you think I'm doing?" he asked.

"Maybe . . . listening to something else," Jamie replied.

Zack smiled, a slow, warm smile that sent chills down her back. "Maybe," he said, "and maybe not. Good night, Jamie. I'll call you soon." Then he went out the door and closed it firmly behind him.

For several minutes, Jamie stood with her fingertips touching her lips and stared at the closed door, then she reached for the security chain on her door and slowly slid it into place. *I wish I could put a security chain on my heart,* she thought. It felt as if it wanted to follow Zack Dunham out the door.

Chapter Five

"IS HE COMING to see you again when he gets back from Africa?" Bertram Bellamy asked the following Sunday, after Jamie had given her aunt and uncle as complete a description as she dared of her evening with Zack.

"I'm not sure," Jamie replied, although Zack had called the previous evening and told her he would do exactly that. She hated to be deliberately evasive, but she didn't want these two romantics urging on an affair she was sure was going nowhere.

"This is the first time I've ever actually dreaded one of these tours," Zack had said. "Now one of my best leaders is sick, and I've got to do two, back to back. Damn, but I wish you'd come along on at least one of them."

Jamie had called upon all of her reserves of common sense to try to persuade herself he was only being clever, softening her up for the kill, as it were, when he returned. "I'll be home on April first," he had told her, "the day after we land in New York. Don't make any other plans for that day. And stay away from the other men when I'm gone."

"You take care of your tours and don't worry about me," Jamie had advised him coolly. "You may meet someone far more interesting than a plain little florist. If you still want to see me when you get back, give me a call."

At that, Zack swore volubly. "I am going to go insane before April first," he said, and hung up the phone with a loud clunk.

Afterward, Jamie spent so long pacing the floor and muttering to herself that Cyrano became agitated and spun in circles, chasing his tail until he fell over, something he hadn't done since he was a kitten.

"That man is driving us both crazy," Jamie had said, picking up the dazed cat and stroking him soothingly. "Why on earth did he have to decide I'm such a challenge to his manhood?" She was still almost sure that her refusal to succumb to his charms was Zack's only reason for pursuing her. *And what if it isn't?* asked a little voice. *What if he's interested in something more permanent?* She tried to squelch that faint hope by reminding herself that Cissie Bergstrom had called him Don Juan. That precipitated a vision of Zack standing in an open-topped safari van, surrounded by bosomy females in skintight shirts, a vision that made Jamie feel slightly ill.

"I really don't want him to come and see me," Jamie said now to her aunt and uncle. "What future could I have with a man who travels all over the world all of the time?" Even if Zack did get serious, she'd reasoned as she'd paced her living room the night before, having him gone most of the time presented a huge problem.

"You could see it with him," Aunt Martha said brightly.

"My, how I'd love to see Africa before I die," Uncle Bert said with a sigh. "Maybe if you marry that rascal, he'll give us a discount on one of his tours."

"Rascal is right!" Jamie said vehemently. "I certainly hope you don't want me to marry him just to get you a cut-rate tour! And I definitely don't plan to give up my shop and follow him around just to keep an eye on him. No, indeed! Zack Dunham is not the man for me."

"You wouldn't have to give it up," her uncle said. "You could train someone to take over when you were gone."

"Yes, but that would be for more than half of the time," Jamie said, frowning. "I don't think I'd want to do that. It...it wouldn't really be mine any more."

"Some women get along quite well with their husbands gone a lot," her aunt said. "Think of the navy wives, with their husbands at sea. Of course, I was very glad when Bertie decided not to reenlist after the war. He had quite the roving eye in those days."

Bertram Bellamy looked taken aback. "How can you say that?" he demanded. "I never looked at another woman after I met you."

For one of the few times Jamie could remember, the two bristled at each other. Then they both laughed. "See?" Jamie said. "It wouldn't even have worked for you two."

She found herself thinking of that frequently during the week that followed, a week during which she also spent what she felt was far too much time wondering what Zack was doing, and with whom. "Imagine what it would be like if I was really in love with him," she said to Cyrano on Saturday night as she sat at her kitchen table eating a bowl of cereal for dinner. "I'd be sitting here wishing he was here instead of there and wondering if he'd call. That just wouldn't do. It really wouldn't."

"Meroww," Cyrano said.

"I'm so glad you agree with me." Jamie poured a little extra milk in her bowl and put it on the floor. "Finish that up. You're my pal. You're always right here when I need you." Not that she *needed* Zack Dunham. No indeed. Needing him would be like needing a bad case of poison ivy. Who on earth would want an itch like that?

Cyrano licked up the milk eagerly, pushing the dish under the table in his quest to get every drop.

"Good work," Jamie said, crouching down and reaching under the table to retrieve the bowl. At just that moment the telephone rang. Jamie straightened like a shot and banged her head against the edge of the table. "Owww!" she cried as stars danced before her and tears filled her eyes. Stunned, she staggered toward the phone, rubbing her head vigorously with one hand and reaching for the receiver with the other. "Flowers from the Heart," she said automatically.

"What? Jamie, are you all right?" came Zack's unmistakable deep voice.

"Oh! Zack! Hello!" A rush of adrenaline partially cleared Jamie's head and sent her heart racing.

"Don't you even know where you are?" Zack asked in amused tones. "I've heard of people bringing their work home with them, but that's ridiculous."

"It's not funny," Jamie said. "I was under the table when the phone rang and I hit my head. I didn't know what I was saying."

"Oh, precious. I'm sorry." Zack's tone was instantly contrite. "I wish I was there to hold you and kiss it and make it all better."

Jamie thought about that, imagining herself in Zack's arms, and several more tears trickled down her cheeks. "Well, you're not," she said. "Where are you?"

"In Nairobi," Zack replied. "It's four in the morning here. I couldn't sleep, so I thought I'd call you. What were you doing under the table, anyway?"

"Picking up Cyrano's milk bowl," Jamie replied. "Why couldn't you sleep? Is it hot there?"

"No, it isn't hot. I miss you," Zack said. "I thought I might feel better if I could hear your voice, but I'm afraid it's only going to make me feel worse. I wish I was there instead of here more than ever. Why are you doing this to me?"

Jamie frowned. "I'm not doing anything to you. I'm just going about my business as usual."

"That's the trouble," Zack said. "Your business is too damned far away from me. I need you here."

"First you wish you were here, then you wish I was there," Jamie said. "I think you're confused."

Zack muttered something unintelligible, then in a voice raspy with irritation, said, "No, I am not confused. I don't care who's where, as long as we're in the same place. Am I hoping for too much, or is it possible you wish that, too, just a little bit?"

"I guess maybe just a little," Jamie replied grudgingly. She didn't want Zack thinking he was making inroads in her defenses, but the thought of having him close was suddenly very appealing. Then, thinking of the problem that had been bothering her all week, she went on, "But it really doesn't help much to wish that, does it? I mean, your work keeps you away most of the time, and mine keeps me here. I don't expect we'll see very much of each other, do you?"

There was a long silence on Zack's end before he said, "Something obviously has got to change. When I get back there, you can bet your boots it's going to."

His tone of voice sent a warning tingle through Jamie. She hadn't actually signed her lease yet. And Zack, after all, was Isaiah Dunham's son. He'd better not get any ideas about interfering in their business arrangements. She wouldn't put up with that. For a moment she thought of telling him so straight out, but decided it might be better to wait and see what, if anything, happened first. She managed to say quite calmly, "There's not much you can do, short of shrinking the planet. Maybe we should talk about something else. Or maybe you should go back to bed."

"There wouldn't be much point in that," Zack said. "I'll have to start checking the gear in less than an hour. We're leaving after breakfast for the Amboseli Game Reserve."

"Oh, yes," Jamie said. "I remember you telling me about that. Elephants and rhinos and Mount Kilimanjaro in the background. If you see a baby elephant, say hello to it for me."

"Jamie," Zack said plaintively, "why do you say things like that?"

"What's wrong with that?" Jamie asked. "I love elephants. Baby ones are so cute. Can't you say hello to one for me?"

"I think I'd rather turn into one," Zack muttered. He sighed loudly, then went on in wry tones, "Of course I can. Any other message I can give them besides hello? They're highly intelligent animals. Maybe I could strike up a regular conversation."

"You're making fun of me," Jamie said reprovingly. "You think I'm silly for wanting you to say hello to an elephant."

"No, I don't!" Zack said with more vehemence than Jamie thought necessary. "I think you're... perfectly adorable. It makes me feel funny inside when you say things like that. You're the oddest combination—" He stopped, and Jamie could hear him suck in his breath. "Now, don't take that wrong, too. I like the combination."

"I really don't know what you mean, but I guess it's all right," Jamie said. It had made her feel funny inside, too, when he said he thought she was adorable. She had better watch out, or she'd begin to believe him.

"I'll try to explain it to you when I get it figured out," Zack said. "What time is it back there?"

"About seven-fifteen," Jamie replied. "Isn't this phone call costing you an awful lot of money?"

"*That's* what I mean," Zack said, sounding exasperated. "First you're sweet and whimsical, then you're so damned practical.... I guess I'm not making much sense, am I?"

"Not much," Jamie agreed. "After all, everyone's got more than one dimension, or they're pretty dull. How's your tour group? Are there some interesting people in it?"

"Some," Zack said. "There's the usual assortment of wealthy types just trying to relieve their own boredom, but there's an old college professor and his wife from South Dakota who are really sharp and interesting, and a pair of maiden ladies from Georgia who've saved up for years to make this trip. One's a retired bank teller and the other used to run a dress shop.

They're so sweet and soft-spoken. I'm hoping everything will be perfect, for them, if for no other reason. It's a really big event in their lives."

"Oh, Zack, that's nice," Jamie said. "I hope so, too." She felt ashamed to realize it hadn't occurred to her that Zack would be sensitive to something like that. It was unfair of her to assume his warm, wonderful smile was only surface charm, a trap for unwary women. Obviously, it could also reflect a warm and generous heart.

As if he had read her mind Zack said, "Why do I have the feeling you thought my only interest in these trips was in making a play for any attractive woman who might be here? You really *do* think I'm a hopeless degenerate, don't you?"

Although he was almost half a world away, Jamie blushed, remembering her speculations. "No, but I did think you were probably used to...you know," she said tightly. "You're awfully good at...being charming and seductive."

Zack groaned. "I've done everything wrong, right from the beginning, haven't I? How I wish I could go back and start all over with you."

A little glimmer of hope flickered in Jamie's heart. "Well, you can't, but I am willing to keep an open mind."

"Good of you," Zack said dryly.

"It's the best I can do," Jamie said. She couldn't very well forget that there had been lots of other women in Zack's life. The only thing she was sure of was that he wanted to make love to her. Maybe all he meant was that he wished he'd tried a different approach.

Zack sighed. "You know, most of the women I've met—"

He stopped, and was silent for so long that Jamie finally said, "What about most of the women you've met?"

"Nothing," Zack growled. "Most of them have no sense at all, that's all. You have more than enough."

"Maybe that's the only reason you're interested in me," Jamie suggested. There was another long silence, during which she began to wonder if she'd suddenly made him realize he really didn't need a woman with too much sense in his life—a thought that made a tight little knot in her stomach. "I'm sorry," she said in a small voice, "but that's just the way I am."

"Oh, for God's sake, Jamie!" Zack exploded. "I didn't mean it as a criticism. Well, maybe in a way, but...but only because you're...because I'm..." He took a deep breath. "Oh, what the hell. I want to marry you, Jamie."

Chapter Six

THE FLOOR SUDDENLY FELT as if it were swaying beneath Jamie's feet. "Y-you what?" she croaked, forcing the words past the lump in her throat. Never in her wildest dreams had she imagined Zack Dunham proposing to her. The image of his handsome, smiling face swam before her eyes and she sank to the floor, clutching the telephone receiver in clammy hands.

"I want to marry you," Zack repeated. "Oh, I know, you'll say it's too soon, that we don't know each other well enough, or something sensible like that. I suppose it'll take me years to convince you that marrying me is the sensible thing to do—but I'll manage it. So you can just forget buying that house by yourself, and if you so much as look at another man I'll tear him apart, so help me I will. My God, why am I so far away from you when I'm telling you this? I must have lost my mind. But I mean it. Every word."

Still almost unable to believe what she had heard, Jamie rubbed her forehead. Zack was right about one thing. It was too soon. "Zack," she said, "I'm honored, of course, but—"

"Just shut up, Jamie," Zack interrupted. "I don't want an answer now. I won't even listen to one. We'll talk about it when I get back. Meanwhile, spend your energy trying to figure out how to make it work instead of piling up reasons it won't. All right?"

Jamie swallowed hard. Thoughts zipped through her mind at a dizzying rate. Here was Zack telling her to figure out how to make their marriage work when she hadn't even said she'd marry him. Wasn't even sure she wanted to. Not that he'd indicated she had much choice in the matter. No, he had very plainly said that *his* mind was made up, and sooner or later she would say yes. Well, she wasn't so sure about that. It would be a while before she'd recovered enough from the shock to reason clearly. "You've given me an awful lot to think about," she finally replied.

To her surprise, Zack laughed, a very relieved-sounding laugh. "Thank God," he said. "I was afraid you were going to tell me to go and stand in front of a charging elephant. Listen, sweetheart, I have to go now. Duty calls. Close your eyes for a minute and pretend I'm there. I'm going to kiss you goodbye."

Jamie closed her eyes and heard Zack make a soft kissing sound.

"There," he said. "Take good care of yourself. I may not be able to call you for a few days, but I'll be thinking of you. Good night, Jamie."

"Good night, Zack," Jamie said softly. "You take good care of yourself, too."

After Zack hung up, Jamie continued to sit on the floor, staring into space, the receiver spinning idly beside her on the end of its cord. Everything was happening so fast, she thought. Much too fast. It made her feel all stirred up and breathless inside, halfway between laughing and crying.

Cyrano walked haughtily across her lap and began batting at the dangling receiver. With a sigh, Jamie got to her feet and replaced the receiver, then picked up Cyrano and hugged him tightly. "What am I going to do, baby?" she asked him. "I think maybe I'm in love with Zack. I've never felt like this before. But I'm not sure I want to be, because I can't see how it would ever work out, being married to someone who was away all the time. Can you?''

Jamie asked her aunt and uncle the same question the next evening, after a day when everything seemed to go wrong, from misplaced orders to smashed vases. "It's totally out of the question," she said, answering herself. "I've got to find some way to tell him. He's got me all upset, and I don't like being upset, especially when it interferes with my work.''

"I'm afraid being in love is like that," her uncle said, smiling at her benignly. "It can turn the most sensible person into a dazed, impractical dreamer."

Aunt Martha giggled. "Bertie forgot to put on his trousers one morning just after we'd met. He was clear to the sidewalk before he noticed. He didn't tell me about it until years later."

"You two are no help at all," Jamie moaned, scowling. "I need to know how to get out of this mess and get myself back on an even keel.''

"Might as well ask the sun to come up in the west," Uncle Bert said. "Start thinking of possible solutions. Then, when your young man comes back, you'll be ready to work something out."

"But there are no solutions," Jamie said, "short of one of us giving up our job, and I am definitely not interested in giving up mine. I've worked too hard to get where I am. Now I've got a nice, secure future, doing something I love. Why would I give that up for a man who's...who's..?"

"Exciting? Unpredictable? Handsome?" her aunt volunteered.

"Yes, exactly," Jamie said.

"I can't imagine," her aunt said, giving her husband a loving smile.

Jamie groaned. "I think I'll go and talk to Cyrano. He's more help than you romantics."

Between phone calls, Jamie would almost convince herself that life with Zack would be impossible. But then he'd call again and tell her in his deep, soft voice that he wished she was with him. "It's kind of lonely, spending all your time with people you barely get to know before they're gone again," he said.

Jamie thought momentarily of telling him that it would be like that for her, being married to him, but the huskiness of his voice stopped her. It hurt to think of his being lonely. Perhaps he'd finally realize that loneliness would become a way of life for both of them if they were crazy enough to attempt a permanent relationship. Instead, she steered the conversation to the marginally safer topic of where he had been and what he had seen. His charming account of the two southern ladies, squealing with delight at seeing their first giraffe and his whimsical description of his conversation with a baby elephant made her ache with a deep longing to see him. There was so much more to Zack than the shallow, flirtatious womanizer that she'd first assumed him to be. She wanted to know all there was to know about him. Could there possibly be a way to make their relationship work? Could she go with him?

Then, back at her shop again, after a day or two without a phone call, she was sure she couldn't. She loved her shop so much. It was like a child she had produced and nurtured. She couldn't possibly spend most of her time away from it, neglecting it. Whenever she made up her mind that she couldn't—

wouldn't—leave, Zack would call again and she'd find herself torn by conflicting emotions.

"I feel like I'm caught in the middle of a tug-of-war," she told Aunt Martha plaintively one Sunday afternoon only a week before Zack was due to return.

"Your head tells you one thing and your heart tells you another," her aunt said, nodding in understanding. "I wish I knew a simple answer to your problem, but I'm afraid there isn't any. You can't measure human love the way you can profits and losses."

"But I love my shop, too," Jamie said. "It's not just the money."

"No," her aunt replied, "but the money is a tangible result of the love and work you've put into the store. You're never sure what you'll get back if you love someone. After that first bloom of romance is gone, a marriage is work, too, in a way. Two individuals have to do a lot of adjusting to become one. I guess the question is, how much do you love Zack? How much adjusting are you willing to do?"

"I'm still not sure," Jamie said with a sigh. "I need to see him again. We haven't had much time together. Maybe we're both imagining something that isn't real at all."

Martha Bellamy smiled. "Oh, I don't think that's the case," she said. "Maybe I'm old-fashioned, but I still believe in love at first sight. And I also agree that you should take your time and make a wise decision. It's not like the old days when a woman's only choice was get married or be an old-maid schoolmarm."

"I almost wish it was," Jamie said. "It sounds a lot simpler."

For the next few days, Jamie tried valiantly to look at Flowers from the Heart objectively. Filled now with the brilliant colors of tulips and daffodils and the commingled scents of purple hyacinths and stark white Easter lilies, it looked and smelled like the embodiment of spring, concentrated in one small space. But was it enough to satisfy her for the rest of her life? She wasn't sure. She tried to imagine herself growing old in a house with only Cyrano, or his successor, for a companion. Would she like that? She wasn't sure. Then Zack called again.

"I'll be there on Monday morning. I've got a couple of tremendous surprises that might help you make up your mind to marry me a little sooner," he told her, his voice electric with excitement. "Can you meet my flight?"

"Of course. I'll get Barney to hold the fort," Jamie said, her heart beginning to race in anticipation. Suddenly, nothing seemed more important than once again finding herself in his arms.

There was the usual rush of holiday business leading up to the Easter weekend. A spate of dreary, drizzly weather seemed to make people especially eager for the cheer of bright red tulips, and Jamie was on the telephone, trying to locate an additional supply, when Isaiah Dunham appeared in her shop. Maybe, she thought, he was finally going to have her sign her contract, an event long overdue.

"Can I help you, Mr. Dunham?" she asked after hanging up the phone.

Isaiah Dunham nodded. "Come to my office," he said, then led her quickly across the lobby and closed his office door behind them. He sat down in the big swivel chair behind his massive desk and gestured to Jamie, who was standing nervously clenching her hands and wondering why Isaiah looked so serious.

Had she done something wrong? "Sit down, Jamie," he ordered brusquely. "I want to talk to you about Zachariah."

Little icy fingers of warning crept down Jamie's back. "Zachariah" definitely sounded serious. She sat on the edge of a chair, wondering just how much Isaiah knew about her relationship with Zack. Had Zack started communicating, or was Isaiah still guessing?

"Don't look so stricken," Isaiah Dunham said. "I'm not an ogre. I only have your best interests and my son's at heart."

Oh, lord, Jamie thought, as he paused and studied her closely, *here it comes.* "Best interests" definitely sounded like a father about to say something his children didn't want to hear. She tried to read Isaiah's steely gray eyes, but they gave nothing away.

"Zachariah tells me he wants to marry you, but that you haven't given him an answer yet," Isaiah said, interrupting Jamie's train of thought. "Is that correct?"

"Well, uh, yes," Jamie replied. So Zack had told him about the proposal. Judging from Isaiah's expression, he wasn't happy. Well, Zack might put up with his meddling, but she wouldn't.

"Do you love him?" Isaiah asked next.

Jamie blinked. Isaiah asking if she loved Zack? She hadn't expected that. Why did he care? So he could tell her she'd better forget it?

"Come, now, Jamie," Isaiah said irritably as Jamie continued to stare at him. "You must have given Zachariah some indication that his proposal would be welcome. Answer my question."

The confusion in Jamie's mind began to focus in on a little spot of anger. "I don't intend to answer any questions until I know just what you're driving at, Mr. Dunham," she said coldly. "That was a very personal question."

Isaiah's lips twitched into a little smile. "All right, Jamie, I'll lay it on the line. Zack wants to marry you. I want him to marry you. Therefore, I want you to marry him, and the sooner the better. That's why I asked if you love him. I'm trying to find out why you're dragging your feet. Is that plain enough?"

Isaiah Dunham's answer was so far from what Jamie expected that for several moments she wondered if she had heard him right. Even when she convinced herself she had, she still did not know what to say. Her own ambivalence of the past weeks left her with no clear-cut response to give him. "Th-that's not an easy question to answer," she said haltingly. "I—I can't just give you a list of reasons."

"Let's start back at the original question," Isaiah suggested. "Do you love him?"

"Well, I..." Jamie licked her lips nervously. Should she answer him? Did she *have* an answer? Neither she nor Zack had talked about love—not in so many words.

"You're not sure?" Isaiah asked, leaning forward and studying Jamie intently.

Suddenly Jamie remembered her vow not to put up with Isaiah's meddling. "That's between Zack and me," she said defiantly, "and so is the question of when and if I'll marry him. When *we've* decided, I'm sure you'll be one of the first to know."

For a moment, Isaiah looked angry, then he bowed his head and studied his fingertips thoughtfully. "Very well," he said, "but I have news for you, Jamie. For the first time in his life Zachariah has picked out a woman I approve of and I want to see him married to her before I die. So either you marry Zachariah or there'll be no contract for your shop. I'll give you a month to make up your mind."

Jamie's mouth quite literally fell open. "You wouldn't," she said, then as Isaiah gave her a chilly smile, she remembered his threats to Zack. "You would."

Isaiah nodded. "Believe it." He waved his hand dismissively. "Run along now and think about your options. I have work to do."

Numbly, Jamie got up and went out the door, still hardly able to believe what Isaiah Dunham had said. At first, she felt like crying, then anger began to rise within her. She contemplated going back and telling Isaiah that it would be a hot day in Antarctica before she married his son, but by the time she reached her shop, common sense prevailed. She needed to think first, then act.

"I'm going home," she told Barney. "I have to think something out."

"Something wrong?" he asked, looking concerned.

"Plenty," she said. "I can't talk about it now."

She drove home slowly, alternately feeling furious and depressed. How dared Isaiah Dunham back her into a corner like that? She wouldn't stand for it! But, if she defied him, she would lose both Zack and her shop, at least in its present location. She could move, of course, but she wasn't likely to find another spot nearly as good. And she might still lose Zack. For all she knew, Isaiah had told him he'd cut off his inheritance if he didn't marry her within a month. Maybe that was why Zack had talked of surprises that would hasten her decision. If so, why didn't he have the backbone to tell his father to mind his own business? Not that *she'd* had, when the chips were down. What on earth was wrong with Isaiah Dunham? Did he think he could browbeat everyone into doing his bidding?

"Oh, Lord, Cyrano, what am I going to do?" she asked when her four-footed friend greeted her at the door. "I do love Zack, but I'm still not sure that's enough to make a marriage work. He'd be gone most of the time, and I don't know if I could bear to leave my shop that often, or even if he'd want me to." She gathered Cyrano in her arms and went to sit in her lounge chair, staring into space, feeling as if a chill, gray pall had settled over her entire life. For several hours she weighed the alternatives, until she felt exhausted from the conflict. It was dark outside when she finally reached a decision—she loved Zack, but she couldn't marry him. Marrying him in a month would mean giving in to coercion of the worst kind. Marrying him any time would mean either being away from her shop or her husband most of the time. Neither option appealed to her. She would just have to move her shop. It would mean starting over again and not having a house of her own for a while, but she could do it. The hardest part was going to be breaking the news to Zack.

On Sunday at the Bellamys, Jamie managed to pretend her edginess was only anticipation of Zack's return. She didn't want to listen to her aunt and uncle clucking in distress over her problem, or telling her she'd made the wrong choice. She would tell them after it was all over. She spent Sunday evening and most of a sleepless night bracing herself to meet Zack. She wouldn't tell him right away, at the airport. She would take him back to her apartment, where she could explain everything as calmly as possible. He at least deserved that.

The next morning, as Jamie waited at the gate for Zack's plane to disgorge its passengers, she found herself trembling with nervous excitement. She had managed to whip herself into a state of anger toward both Zack and his father for trying to manipulate her. Nevertheless, when she caught sight of Zack's handsome, smiling face, felt his strong arms close around her and his lips soft and warm against hers, she felt weak and dizzy. Tears of frustration sprang to her eyes. Why did her body have to betray her like this? she wondered desperately.

"Oh, sweetheart, I'm so happy to be home," Zack said, crushing her close to him and burying his face against her hair. A sob Jamie couldn't suppress made him draw back and peer into her face. "What's the matter, little one?" he asked.

"N-nothing," Jamie choked out. "I'm just happy to see you, that's all. Come on, let's get out of this place. Have you any bags to pick up? Have you had breakfast?"

"No bags and not enough breakfast," Zack replied.

"We'll go straight to my apartment and I'll fix you something to eat," Jamie said. Doing something ordinary would, she hoped, give her a chance to gather her wits and her courage.

They walked rapidly, Zack keeping his arm around Jamie and pausing now and then to hug her and drop another kiss on her upturned face. The intense warmth of his beautiful green eyes almost undid her. When they reached her car, he stowed his carry-on inside and then put his arms around her, bending his head to kiss her.

"Don't," Jamie said, shaking him off. "Not now. I do have to be able to drive, you know."

"I never knew that my kisses were so intoxicating," Zack teased, flashing his bright smile with devastating effect.

"Terribly intoxicating," Jamie said. She was beginning to wish she'd taken a plane in the other direction last night, to some faraway location where she could begin life all over. Telling Zack what she had to tell him was going to be even more difficult than she had imagined, especially if he kissed her again. She thought of bolting straight for the kitchen when they reached her apartment, but had no chance. As soon as the door closed behind them, Zack dropped his bag and gathered her in his arms.

"Now," he said, devouring her face with glowing eyes, "I'm going to kiss you until we're both too drunk to drive or do anything else!"

As Zack's lips found hers, Jamie did her best to fan the flames of her anger, but it was futile. She melted against him, her arms finding their way around his broad back and holding him close. Her lips opened to his eager onslaught, and she complained not at all when somehow Zack managed to get both their coats off and carry her to the sofa, without once stopping the kisses that left her dazed and breathless. When his hands slipped beneath her sweater and set fire to her bare skin, she only sighed, wishing that just this once she could follow where Zack led. Become his lover...

But when his explorations became more intimate, she knew that she must not. For her, that would be the point of no return.

"Please, don't," she whispered, pushing his hand away. "It's not that I don't want to, but ... I don't believe in sex outside of marriage."

Zack drew in a ragged breath. "I know," he said, cradling her against him and dropping tiny kisses against her ear. "I'll try to restrain myself, but we'll have to get married very soon or I'll go crazy."

Jamie made no reply. She should tell him now, she thought, but the words stuck in her throat. Instead, she clung to him, blinking back bitter tears. Of all the men on earth, why did she have to fall so hopelessly in love with this man? she wondered. It wasn't fair. It wasn't fair at all. For several minutes she stayed silently in his arms, then, with a great effort, pulled away, avoiding his eyes as she said, "I think it's time I fixed you some breakfast. Would you like bacon and eggs, or pancakes?"

"Bacon and eggs would be great," Zack replied, "but before you go anywhere I have something for you. The first of the surprises." He went to his coat and took something from a pocket, then came back, one hand behind him, and sat beside Jamie again. "Hold out your hand," he said, smiling that slow, warm smile. Jamie's agonized heart lurched unhappily. She was afraid she could guess his surprise.

Obediently, she held out her hand and received a small, beautifully wrapped box. "Go ahead and open it. It won't bite," Zack said as she stared at it.

With icy fingers, Jamie removed the wrappings to reveal a little velvet jeweler's box. It had to be what she feared, she thought, swallowing a huge lump in her throat. Carefully, she opened the hinged lid. In spite of the fact that she had suspected a ring, she gasped at the sight of the huge diamond solitaire. "Oh, my," she breathed, looking from its dazzling depths to the equally dazzling lights in Zack's eyes.

"I think that must mean you like it," Zack said, smiling. "Go ahead, try it on."

Jamie stared at the incredible diamond for a long moment, then shook her head. "I can't, Zack," she said. "No, I—I really can't. This is too much. I didn't even say I'd marry you." She closed the box and put it back into his hand. "I can't take this, not now. You should have made sure first." Her mind was trying frantically to make her tell him, but as she looked at his bright, hopeful eyes, her heart wouldn't let her.

"I *am* sure, Jamie," Zack said with a crooked little smile. "I think you are, too, even though you don't want to admit it yet. So I'll keep the ring until you do. Because even you have to admit there's a magic between us."

A magic that was turning her into a miserable coward, Jamie thought bitterly. Maybe, if she waited just a little longer, a better opening would appear. "I need more time. I need to be as sure as you are," she said, trying to smile encouragingly. "Maybe I'm simply a little slow. Why don't you come into the kitchen and have some coffee while I cook us breakfast? But I have to tell you, after that diamond as big as a baseball, I'm almost afraid to find out what your other surprise is."

Zack laughed. "It's even bigger," he said, "and I know you're going to love it. Want to guess what it is? Twenty questions?"

Jamie's heart sank. She couldn't imagine anything bigger than that stone. "I'm not very good at playing guessing games. What am I supposed to ask—whether it's animal, vegetable or mineral?''

"That's right," Zack said, taking a sip of his coffee, "and I think the correct answer is all three."

By the time Jamie had breakfast ready, she'd ascertained that the object was far too big and heavy for her to pick up. "Does it move?" she probed, thinking of a car.

"Only with the greatest difficulty," Zack replied grinning. "Give up?"

"No, not yet," Jamie said. Now that their breakfast was ready, Zack might as well eat. It would give her a chance to muster her waning courage. Seeing him sitting at her kitchen table, his strong, masculine presence filling the little room, made her heart ache so painfully that she could almost believe it was breaking. "Is it here, in St. Louis?" she asked.

"Yes," Zack replied. "Say, you're a good cook."

"Anyone can make bacon and eggs," Jamie said. She couldn't think of any more questions. She couldn't eat. She could only sit watching Zack—wishing she hadn't reached a decision, wishing she didn't feel so sick inside. When he finished breakfast he asked again if she gave up. Now, she told herself, was the time to tell him. She took a deep breath, looked him straight in the eye and felt her heart melt once again. He looked like a little boy, bringing a wonderful Christmas treat. "Okay, I admit defeat. What is it?" she said, at the same time cursing her weakness.

"First I'll tell you," Zack said, standing up and holding out his hand to her, "and then I'll take you to see it. Actually, I haven't seen it yet myself, but I think we're both going to like it. It's a house, in case you haven't guessed by now.''

Jamie stared at him, stunned. "A—a house?" she squeaked. Of all of the things she might have guessed, that would have been the last. Suddenly, she *was* angry. Very angry. When Zack reached for her, obviously mistaking her surprise for pleasure, she backed away, shaking her head. "Don't touch me," she said, tears filling her eyes and rolling unchecked down her cheeks. "Whatever possessed you to buy a house without even asking me? And that—that ring! Don't I have anything to say about anything? You're just like your father. My God! First he tells me I can't have my shop in the hotel if I don't marry you within a month. And now you do this! Did he talk you into it, or are you just as stupid as he is? Not that it really matters, because I've already decided I can't marry you. I'm not going to leave my shop and go traipsing around the world after you, not after all the work I've put into my business! But I'll move it somewhere else if I have to, you just bet I will. No one's going to push me around like this! No one! Just go away and leave me alone.''

Zack paled. "I had no idea what my father was up to, but believe me, he isn't going to follow through on his threat," he said, his voice harsh with anger. "Don't you worry about that, sweetheart. And if you want to pick out your own house and ring, we'll do that, too. I can understand why you're upset, but just calm down. Everything's going to be all right. We'll work out something—''

"No! I can't marry you. I mean it. Just go away," Jamie sobbed, afraid that if he didn't leave soon she would give way completely.

"I don't know what to say," Zack said, his expression bleak as he started slowly toward the door.

"Don't say anything. Just go."

Zack put on his coat and then looked at Jamie thoughtfully for several moments. "You must really hate me, the way you let me go on and on, making a fool of myself." He put his hand on the doorknob. "The way it felt when we kissed, I thought you loved me. I guess I had everything all wrong."

With that, he went out the door, slamming it behind him so quickly he didn't see Jamie suddenly turn ashen and bend over double as she burst into bitter tears. "I don't hate you, Zack, I love you," she sobbed. "Dear Lord in Heaven, what have I done?"

Chapter Seven

JAMIE RAN TO THE WINDOW. Through a blur of tears she watched as Zack trudged off down the street, his head lowered and his hands thrust deep into his jacket pockets. For a moment she thought of going after him, but from the way he walked she knew he wanted to be left alone. Especially by her. She watched until he was out of sight, then buried her face in her arms and sobbed uncontrollably. She'd driven the man she loved away, probably forever. Probably made the rift between him and his father worse than ever. And she could tell from the way she felt inside that she had been wrong, wrong, wrong. Why in heaven's name had she done it, and what could she ever do to straighten out the terrible mess she had made?

She could find no answer as the day wore on, only going into fresh bouts of tears each time she remembered the stricken expression on Zack's face when she'd told him to go away. Finally she got into her car and drove slowly to her aunt and uncle's house. She hated to bother them with her problem, but she felt too depressed to spend the evening alone, brooding. She needed her family with her.

"Good heavens, child, what's the matter?" her aunt asked the moment she saw Jamie's pale face and puffy eyes.

"Zack's gone," Jamie replied listlessly. "I told him to go away."

"Why on earth did you do that?" her uncle asked. "Did he try to do something he shouldn't have?"

At that question, Jamie burst into tears again, remembering how understanding Zack had been when she had stopped his lovemaking.

Aunt Martha put her arm around Jamie. "You come into the living room and tell us all about it. Just take a few minutes to calm yourself while I fix you a nice cup of tea."

Jamie sank into a deep lounge chair and blew her nose vigorously, then waited until the tea was made and Martha and Bert Bellamy were seated across from her. Then she told them the whole story, beginning with Isaiah's threat. "I was so sure I couldn't fit Zack into my life," she concluded miserably, "but now I'd do anything to have him back. Maybe if we'd been together more..." She choked to a stop, then added, "He was so happy to see me and I hurt him so badly. Now he thinks I hate him. He'll never believe I love him. Why didn't I just keep quiet? Why?"

Jamie buried her face in her hands, sobbing bitterly. "There, there, pet, don't carry on so," her aunt said, hurrying to Jamie's side. "You were right about one thing. Things were happening much too fast. I don't know why Zack thought he ought to buy a house and a ring without consulting you—that was wrong."

"But I love him," Jamie said miserably, "and I don't want him to be gone."

"Ah, there we have it," said Uncle Bert. "You feel you made a mistake. But did you, really? Now, be honest. Could you have gone along with things the way they were going?"

"N-no," Jamie said, "but I could have been reasonable, couldn't I?"

Her uncle sighed. "Lovers seldom are. Look on the bright side. You and Zack are both doing some deep soul-searching and things will either work themselves out between you or they won't. Better before you're married than after.''

Jamie groaned. "I don't think I can stand this. Do you think there's any chance he'll come back?''

Martha Bellamy gave Jamie's shoulders a comforting squeeze. "If he really loves you, he will," she said. "I'm sure of it.''

"A real man doesn't give up," Uncle Bert said firmly. "He'll be back. Meanwhile, keep busy. You shouldn't have any trouble doing that.''

"Probably not," Jamie said. "After Isaiah hears what I did today I'm apt to be very busy, moving the shop. I doubt Zack will try to stop him.''

She wasn't surprised the next morning to find a note instructing her to see the hotel's business manager immediately, but *was* amazed to find her contract waiting. "When Mr. Dunham and his son went home last evening they left specific instructions for me to see to it that you executed this contract as soon as possible.'' The manager leaned forward confidentially. "I think the younger Mr. Dunham has finally persuaded his father to take a little vacation. Isaiah has been working terribly hard here for the past month, and his heart isn't in the best of shape. He's had several coronary bypass operations.''

"Oh, I didn't know that," Jamie said, the information making her feel even more bleak and depressed. Maybe Zack had a good reason for trying to rush her. Isaiah had said something about wanting to see Zack married to her before he died. She'd thought his words only a figure of speech, but maybe they weren't. The only bright spot was that Zack had apparently patched things up with his father. She signed the contract and returned it to the business manager.

"The younger Mr. Dunham left this for me to give you as soon as you signed the contract." The manager handed Jamie a sealed envelope.

Jamie took the envelope, but waited until she was safely in her shop to open it. When she read Zack's message, she ran to the back room and burst into tears. "I hope you and your shop will be very happy together," was the bitter note Zack left her. Uncle Bert had had the forbearance not to remind her about being married to her shop, but Zack had obviously seen the situation in exactly the same way.

As the days stretched into weeks, Jamie heard nothing at all from Zack. Not, she admitted to herself, that she'd really expected to, but she couldn't help hoping. His father's continued absence surprised her, however, until she learned he'd appointed another man to oversee the renovations at the hotel. Ordinarily, Jamie would have found it exciting to be consulted on the many planters to be installed, but the aching void in her heart destroyed most of the pleasure.

"Shouldn't I be getting over this by now?" Jamie asked Aunt Martha. Spring had turned to summer and she was still feeling so blue that she scarcely cared whether she ate or slept. "I'm not so bad when I'm at work, but when I'm home I think of Zack constantly. And now Cyrano's taken sick and won't eat, and the vet doesn't seem to know what's wrong with him."

"Maybe he's been watching you," Uncle Bert said. "Why don't you try eating with him? It might perk you both up."

"You mean from a bowl on the floor?" Jamie asked. When her uncle nodded, she smiled. "I guess it's worth a try. If anything happened to Cyrano..."

That night, Jamie lay on the floor and nibbled cereal from a bowl next to Cyrano's dish of cat food. Cyrano stared at her for several minutes with typical feline stoicism, then suddenly plunged his face into his food and began crunching away with gusto. Jamie laughed and burst into tears of happiness at the same time.

"That's the first time I've really laughed in months," she told her uncle when she called to report the good news. "You should have seen Cyrano eat. It was wonderful. But am I going to have to take my meals on the floor from now on?"

"I don't know," her uncle replied, "but if it gets you eating, too, I'm all for it." He paused and then went on, "Maybe it's time for you to do something about Zack, as well as Cyrano. A man has a lot of pride, you know, and you gave his a pretty thorough beating. You may have to swallow some of yours, along with those dinners you're eating on the floor."

"I think I'm ready for that," Jamie said. "I just hope Zack is, too—once I figure out what to do."

After she hung up, she lifted Cyrano and cuddled him while she paced the floor. Which would be better, she wondered, call Zack or try to discover where he was and go see him? "I think I'll find out where he is and go there," Jamie said to Cyrano, "even if he's on the other side of the world. I prefer face-to-face confrontations for something this important. First thing tomorrow, I'm going to track that man down." She had recently begun training Barney as assistant manager. He could easily take care of the shop for a few days.

In the morning, Jamie called Fantastick Voyages' New York office to inquire about Zack's whereabouts. "He's here in New York City right now, at his father's bedside," the secretary informed her. "His father was taken to the hospital yesterday. I believe his condition is listed as critical but stable."

"Oh, no!" Jamie cried. "Which hospital is he in?"

Moments later, Jamie hung up the phone, her mind in a dither. Zack must be terribly worried about his father. Would it help or only make things worse if she went to him now? And if Zack still wanted her, was she ready to marry him, no matter what?

It took fifteen minutes of frantic pacing for Jamie to decide that she would marry Zack if they could work out how to be together for at least half of the time. But first, she had better call him and tell him she loved him. If he didn't care anymore, none of the rest mattered. Her heart pounding, her trembling fingers icy as death, she put through the call, gave her name and held her breath. Maybe, she thought as the silence lengthened, Zack wouldn't even come to the phone.

"Hello, Jamie," came Zack's voice minutes later. "It's good of you to call."

The familiar sound of his voice, deep and soft and resonant, made Jamie's throat constrict so with unshed tears that she could scarcely speak. "H-how is your father?" she asked.

"Not doing very well, I'm afraid. He's hanging on, but the doctors say his heart's just worn out."

"Oh, Zack, I'm so sorry," Jamie said, her tears beginning to fall. The thought of bringing up the conflict between them seemed out of the question now. So she asked the usual questions and made the usual comments, all the while trying desperately to think of some way to tell Zack that she cared about *him,* too. Zack's own comments were so restrained and polite that she could get no clue as to how he would react, yet their stilted conversation went on and on.

"Have you been well?" Zack asked.

"Oh, yes, quite well," Jamie answered. "Cyrano was sick for a while, but he's better now."

"That's good," Zack said. "What was wrong with him?"

"The vet wasn't sure. He wouldn't touch his food. Then Uncle Bert suggested I eat on the floor with him, so I lay down with my bowl of cereal next to his dish and Cyrano started eating right away."

There was a long silence on the line, then Zack's voice returned, harsh with strain. "Jamie," he said, "there's something I have to tell you. I know you called to ask after my father, and you may not want to hear it, but I have to tell you, anyway. I love you. I love you so much I can't think about anything else but you most of the time. I was about to come and tell you when my father was stricken and..."

For a split second, Zack's declaration of love hung suspended in the air. Then, a rush of elation pulsed through Jamie's body, shattering the icy chill of fear and sending it flying. "Don't say anything more!" she shouted into the receiver. "Oh, Zack, I love you, too." She burst into tears of joy. "Zack," she sobbed, "that's what I wanted to hear more than anything in the world! I was afraid you'd never forgive me."

"Jamie!" Zack's voice vibrated with joy. "Oh, my darling...damn it all, here we go again! Too far apart, and I can't get away. I have to see you, I must! Could you possibly come—"

"Of course I can!" Jamie answered, dashing the tears from her cheeks. "I'll be there on the first plane I can get to take me."

"Call me back and let me know your flight number," Zack said. "I can meet you. I'm not doing much good here, and this miserable hospital is no place for our reunion."

It was only four hours later that Jamie's flight touched down at JFK International, the most interminably long four hours Jamie could ever remember. A single thought crowded everything else from her mind. She loved Zack and Zack loved her, and somehow they would work things out. When the door opened, she ran through the tunnel, her eyes searching the waiting crowd for only a moment before she spotted Zack. Seconds later she was in his arms, being kissed and kissed again, then spun around like a child, while Zack laughed, his green eyes shining with happiness. He put her down on her feet, held her briefly at arm's length while he gazed at her adoringly, then pulled her close again.

"Jamie, Jamie, Jamie," he murmured in her ear. "We're going to work something out so we're never apart again for a minute, not ever, even if I have to spend the rest of my life delivering flowers for your shop. I've been to hell and back these last few months."

"So have I," Jamie said, clinging to him, "but don't say anything rash. I want to see the world with you. Africa, Alaska, all of those wonderful places you know about. We can do it all, I know we can, and almost never be apart.''

"Of course we can," Zack agreed. "If we work on it together we can do anything. Shall we go visit my father now? He's eager to see you. Do you have a bag to pick up?''

Jamie shook her head a little sheepishly. "I'm ready to go with you anywhere, but I don't have anything with me but my purse," she told him. "When you said you wanted me to come, I forgot everything but getting here. I dropped Cyrano off at Aunt Martha's and headed for the airport.''

Zack laughed. "For once you weren't sensible," he said, "but don't worry, there are plenty of stores in New York." He tucked Jamie's arm into his and together they hurried to the waiting limousine. "It's my father's," Zack informed her. "I always stay at his apartment when I'm in New York. I'm here so seldom there's no point in getting a place for myself. There's plenty of room for you, too. I hope you're not planning on going back to St. Louis today." He raised his eyebrows questioningly and, Jamie thought, a little anxiously.

"I'm here for as long as you want me," she said, smiling and snuggling into the curve of his arm. "I bought a one-way ticket. Barney's minding the shop.''

Zack's anxious look faded into a smile so warm and happy that Jamie could feel it sending tentacles of joy curling around her heart. "Then you really are ready to make some plans," he said, kissing her upturned face. "We have a lot to talk about, after we've stopped in to see my father." He drew back and looked at Jamie seriously. "He was so pleased when I told him you were coming. He feels it was all his fault we ran into difficulties, even though I've explained over and over that the fault was really mine. At first I gave you the impression I only wanted an affair with you, even though deep inside I knew damned well I wanted more than that. That was the reason you were never quite convinced I was good husband material, especially the way I travel around with supposedly glamorous people. You were happy and secure with your shop, so why risk everything on someone you weren't at all sure of? It took me a while to see your side of that, and the house and the ring business, too, but once I did, I started kicking myself for being such a fool. I'm sorry about that note, too. Can you forgive me?"

"I think you're being far too hard on yourself," Jamie protested. "I'm the stupid idiot who needs forgiving. Uncle Bert told me a long time ago that I acted like I was married to my shop. My only excuse, and it's not a very good one, is that we weren't together enough. Everything happened so fast." She buried her face against Zack's shoulder and sighed deeply. "When I'm with you I feel as if the whole world's in bloom. Who needs a flower shop?"

Zack smiled and dropped a kiss on Jamie's forehead. "You do. You still love it, and you should. As long as you love me, too." He tightened his arms around her. "Do you know the first thing my father asked me when I went roaring in to see him that day? He asked if you knew how much I loved you. When I said I hadn't told you, but you must know because I asked you to marry me, he said some rather memorable things about my stupidity. That's another mistake I made."

"Do you think it may help him to know that we're going to be married, after all?" Jamie asked.

"Are you proposing to me?" Zack asked, feigning a look of great surprise.

"I guess so," Jamie said, "if the original offer isn't still open."

"Well, not in its original form," Zack said. "How about this, instead. Jamie, I love you, I adore you. Will you marry me? I'd get down on my knees, but that's mighty hard to do in an automobile."

"Oh, Zack, yes, of course I will," Jamie replied softly. She melted into his arms as he kissed her long and passionately. She was breathless when he at last released her. "Do you still have that beautiful ring?" she asked.

Zack nodded. "It's in the safe at my father's apartment. Do you really like it, or would you prefer—"

"Like it! It's the most beautiful ring I've ever seen!" Jamie interrupted. "I don't know what got into me to complain about it. I'll probably love the house, too. That is, if you actually bought it?"

"No, I just had an option on the place," Zack said, "but we'll find another one. Together. That will be a lot more fun. Maybe we should even take Cyrano along to make certain he approves."

Jamie laughed. "I'm not sure I want one with built-in mice. That's what he'd like best."

"I liked that mouse in your kitchen just fine," Zack said with a grin. "I'll vote with Cyrano." He looked out the window as the chauffeur slowed the limousine and turned into the driveway in front of a hospital building. "I should warn you that my father's hooked up to so many tubes and monitors that he scarcely looks human. It's not a pleasant sight."

Jamie braced herself, but still was taken aback by how Isaiah Dunham had faded from the vigorous and energetic man she remembered. His eyes brightened when he saw her, though, and he held out his hand.

"I can't begin to tell you how much it means to me to see Zachariah happy again," he said. "I'm afraid my well-meant meddling almost caused a disaster, but—" a little smile played around his lips "—I seem to have got my way, after all, don't I?"

"You were smarter than either of us," Jamie said. "Now promise you'll get better before the wedding. You have to do that, you know. I might not marry Zack if we can't provide a proper grandfather for our children."

"I'll do my best," Isaiah agreed, "but don't wait too long. Zachariah needs you."

"I could almost see him begin to improve," Zack said a short time later as they drove on toward the Dunham apartment. "You were absolutely perfect with him, Jamie, but then, you always are. Since I met you, I've thought about so many things I hadn't thought about before—my relationship with my father, what I really want to do with the rest of my life. I think the pain was worth it, now that you're back with me."

"What's all this about what you want to do with the rest of your life?" Jamie asked. "You don't plan to continue with the tour business?"

"Only part-time," Zack replied. "I'm training some others to take over so I can go back and get my doctorate in wildlife biology. I think as I get older I'll find that more rewarding, and it will provide us with a more stable home life to raise our family." His eyes twinkled mischievously. "I gathered from what you said to my father that we *are* going to have a family."

"You'd better believe it," Jamie said, hugging him close and kissing his tanned cheek. "I was kind of getting used to the idea of traveling, though. Maybe learning about exotic plants and doing botanical tours along with you. Of course, once we have children, well, they can travel, too. Think of what they'd learn. We'll teach them the rest ourselves. Why not?"

"Why not, indeed?" Zack said, smothering Jamie in another loving embrace. Then he chuckled softly to himself, and when Jamie looked at him questioningly, he said, "I was just thinking of you lying on the floor next to Cyrano, getting him to eat. When you told me about that, I couldn't keep silent any longer. I could picture you there, so sweet and warm and funny, so worried about your beloved pet. I'd wanted to wait until we were together before telling you I loved you, but I had to tell you right then. Did you know that was what did it?"

Jamie shook her head. "No, but I'm so glad it did. My cat's even more successful than the original Cyrano at bringing lovers together, isn't he?"

"So he is," Zack agreed.

The limousine drew up in front of a dazzling modern building where a uniformed doorman greeted them with a deferential salute. Zack took Jamie's arm and led her to the elevator, which soared with heart-stopping speed to the very top, then hurried her through the sumptuous apartment to a terrace, where planters filled with flowers gave the illusion of a garden in the sky.

"This is gorgeous," Jamie said. "What a magnificent view!"

Zack shrugged. "This is nothing compared to the plains of Africa or the wilderness of Alaska." He looked at Jamie intently. "Cities and fancy apartments don't do much for me. Are you sure you'll be happy with a man who'd rather be thousands of miles from all this, watching a herd of elephants come to a watering hole or an eagle soaring above a rushing river?"

"Very happy," Jamie said, blinking back the mist that suddenly came to her eyes. "I like cities, but I like seeing new things and learning about them even more. I think we're going to have a wonderful life together."

"So do I," Zack agreed. Then he took Jamie into his arms and kissed her until she felt as if she were ready to fly into the sky and join the wisps of clouds floating high above them. Zack Dunham was, she now knew, a very remarkable man, and one so complicated she might never understand him completely, but well worth the effort of trying.

"Oh, Zack," she murmured against his lips, "I love you so much." She looked up at him wistfully. "It may be quite a while before your father's well enough for a wedding."

Zack smiled at her tenderly. "I'm ready to get married any time you are. Maybe we should get married quietly, right away, and then have a big reception for everyone else later. I know my father would understand. He knows how frantic I've been. Would Aunt Martha and Uncle Bert accept that idea?"

"Those two lovebirds?" Jamie laughed. "They'd cheer us on." She gave Zack a passionate kiss and then smiled at him adoringly. "I guess there's an answer to most problems if you use your head, isn't there?"

"And if you listen to your heart," Zack agreed.

MY FUNNY VALENTINE

Debbie Macomber

A word from Debbie Macomber

I'm probably going to surprise a lot of faithful Harlequin readers by telling you that *My Funny Valentine* is based on an incident that actually happened to me last February.

No, I didn't bribe a man to take me to a Valentine banquet. I bribed *two* men. My sons. My husband was out of town and the church I attend, Port Orchard First Christian, was holding a banquet that promised to be fun. I wanted to go. I wanted to go so much that I was willing to pay my two sons to take me. For those of you who don't know me, I live with four teenagers. All sympathy cards may be sent to me care of Harlequin Books! In the past several years, I've learned (the hard way) that in order to deal with teenage children one must sink to their level. And sink I did.

Ted, my sixteen-year-old, unwittingly fell into my scheme. He needed his term paper typed at midnight the Thursday before the banquet. I was more than happy to type it for him—for a price. Escorting his mother to the banquet.

Ted, however, argued that he shouldn't have to bear this heavy burden alone. If he was going to be forced to attend a Valentine banquet with his *mother,* it was only fair his fourteen-year-old brother, Dale, tag along and keep him company.

Dale wasn't convinced. It took the swimsuit issue of *Sports Illustrated* and a pepperoni-and-sausage pizza to persuade him.

It's somewhat humbling to admit that I, a romance writer, was forced to lower myself to bribery in order to attend a church dinner, but from that experience *My Funny Valentine* was born.

I hope you enjoy reading it as much as I did writing it, and if this story has a ring of truth, now you know why!

Chapter One

DIANNE WILLIAMS had the scenario all worked out in her mind. She'd be pushing her grocery cart down the aisle of the local grocery store and gazing over the frozen-food section when a tall, dark, handsome man would casually stroll up to her and with a brilliant smile say, "Those low-cal dinners couldn't possibly be for you."

She'd turn to him and suddenly the air would fill with the sounds of a Rimsky-Korsakov symphony, or bells would chime gently in the distance—Dianne didn't have that part completely worked out yet—and in that instant she would know deep in her heart that this man was the one she was meant to spend the rest of her life with.

All right, Dianne was willing to admit, the scenario was childish and silly, the kind of fantasy only a teen-age girl should dream up. But reentering the dating scene after umpteen years of married life created a wealth of problems Dianne didn't want to consider.

Three years earlier, Dianne's husband had left her and the children to find himself. Instead he found a SYT (sweet young thing), promptly divorced Dianne and moved across the country. It hurt; in fact, it hurt more than anything Dianne had ever known, but she was a survivor, and always had been. Perhaps that was the reason Jack didn't seem to suffer a single pang of guilt about abandoning her to raise Jason and Jill on her own.

Her children, Dianne discovered, were incredibly resilient. Within a year of their father's departure, they were urging Dianne to date. Their father did, they reminded Dianne with annoying frequency. And if it wasn't her children pushing her toward establishing a meaningful relationship, it was her own dear mother.

When it came to locating Mr. Right for her divorced daughter, Martha Janes knew no equal. For several months, Dianne had been subjected to a long parade of single men. Their unmarried status however, seemed their sole attribute.

After dinner with the man who lost his toupee on a low-hanging chandelier, Dianne had insisted enough was enough and she would find her own dates.

This proved to be easier said than done. Dianne hadn't gone out once in six months. Now within the space of a single week, she needed a man. Not just any man, either. One who was tall, dark and handsome. It would be a nice bonus if he were exceptionally wealthy, too, but she didn't have the time to be choosy. The Valentine's dinner at the Port Blossom Community Center was Saturday night. This Saturday night.

From the moment the notice was posted six weeks earlier, Jason and Jill had insisted she attend. Surely their mother could find a date given that much time! And someone handsome to boot. It seemed a matter of family honor.

Only now the dinner was only days away and Dianne was no closer to achieving her goal.

"I'm home," Jason yelled as he walked into the house. The front door slammed in his wake, hard enough to shake the kitchen windows. He slapped his books on the counter, moved directly to the refriger-

ator, opened the door and stuck the upper half of his
fourteen-year-old body inside.

"Help yourself to a snack," Dianne said, smiling
and shaking her head.

Jason reappeared with a chicken leg clenched between his teeth like a pirate's cutlass. One hand was
filled with a piece of leftover cherry pie while the other
held a platter of cold fried chicken.

"How was school?"

He shrugged, set down the pie and removed the
chicken leg from his mouth. "Okay, I guess."

Dianne knew what was coming next. It was the same
question he'd asked her every afternoon since the notice for the dinner had been posted.

"Do you have a date yet?" He leaned his hip against
the counter as his steady gaze pierced her. Her son's
eyes were incredible. They could break through the
thickest of resolves, and cut through several layers of
deception.

"No date," she answered cheerfully. At least as
cheerfully as she could under the circumstances.

"The dinner's this Saturday night."

As if she needed to be reminded. "I know. Stop
worrying, I'll find someone."

"Not just anyone," Jason said forcefully, as though
he were speaking to someone with impaired hearing.
"He's got to make an impression. Someone decent."

"I know, I know."

"Grandma said she could line you up with—"

"No," Dianne interrupted emphatically. "I cate-
gorically refuse to go on any more of Grandma's blind
dates."

"But you don't have the time to find your own now.
It's—"

"I'm working on it," she insisted, though she knew she wasn't working very hard. She *was* trying to find someone to take her to the dinner, only she never dreamed it would be this difficult!

Until the necessity of attending this affair had been forced upon her, Dianne hadn't been aware of how limited her choices were. In the past couple of years, she'd met few single men, apart from the ones her mother had thrown at her. There were a couple of unmarried men where she was employed part-time as a bookkeeper. Neither, however, was one she'd seriously consider dating. They were both too suave, too urbane—too much like Jack. Besides, problems might arise if she were to mingle her social life with her business one. It was simply too risky.

The front door opened and closed again, a little less noisily this time.

"I'm home!" ten-year-old Jill announced from the entryway as she dropped her books on the floor and marched toward the kitchen. She paused on the threshold and planted both hands on her hip as her eyes sought out her brother. "You better not have eaten all the leftover pie. I want some too, you know."

"Don't grow warts worrying about it," Jason said sarcastically. "There's plenty for everyone."

Jill's gaze swiveled from her brother to her mother. The level of severity didn't diminish one bit. Dianne met her daughter's eye and mouthed the words along with her.

"Do you have a date yet?"

Jason answered for Dianne. "No, she doesn't. And she's got five days to come up with a decent guy and all she says is that she's working on it."

"Mom . . ." Jill's brown eyes filled with concern.

"Children, please."

"Everyone in town's going," Jill claimed as if Dianne wasn't already aware of the fact. "You've got to be there, you've just got to be. I told all my friends you're going."

More pressure! That was the last thing Dianne needed. Nevertheless, she smiled serenely at her two children and assured them both they didn't have a thing to worry about.

An hour or so later, while she was cooking dinner, she could hear Jason and Jill's voices in the living room. They were huddled together in front of the television, their heads close together. Plotting, it looked like, charting her barren love life. Doubtless deciding who their mother should take to the dinner. Probably the guy with the toupee.

"Is something wrong?" Dianne asked, standing in the doorway. It was unusual for them to watch television this time of day, but more unusual for them to be so chummy. The fact that they'd turned on the TV to drown out their conversation hadn't escaped her.

They broke apart guiltily.

"Wrong?" Jason asked, recovering first. "I was just talking to Jill, is all. Do you need me to do something?"

That offer alone was enough evidence to convict them both. "Jill, would you set the table for me?" she asked, her gaze lingering on her two children for another moment before she returned to the kitchen.

Jason and Jill were up to something. But what, Dianne could only guess. No doubt the plot they were concocting included their grandmother.

Sure enough, while Jill was setting the silverware on the kitchen table, Jason used the phone, stretching the cord as far as it would go and mumbling into the mouthpiece so there was no chance Dianne could hear his conversation.

Dianne's suspicions were confirmed when her mother arrived shortly after dinner. And within minutes, Jason and Jill had deserted the kitchen, saying they had to get at their homework. Also highly suspicious behavior.

"Do you want some tea, Mom?" Dianne felt obliged to ask, dreading the coming conversation. It didn't take Sherlock Holmes to figure out her children had called their grandmother in hopes she'd find a last-minute date for Dianne.

"Don't go to any trouble."

This was her mother's standard reply. "It's no trouble," Dianne replied.

"Then brew the tea."

Because of her evening aerobics class—W.A.R. it was called, for Women After Results—Dianne had changed and was prepared to make a hasty exit at a moment's notice.

While the water was heating, she took a white ceramic teapot from the cupboard. "Before you ask, and I know you will," she said with strained patience, "I haven't got a date for the Valentine's dinner."

Her mother nodded slowly as if Dianne had just announced something of profound importance. Martha was from the old school, and she took her own sweet time getting around to whatever was on her mind, usually preceding it with a long list of questions that hinted at the subject. Dianne loved her mother dearly, but there wasn't anyone on this green earth who could drive her crazier faster.

"You've still got your figure," Martha said, her look serious. "That helps." She stroked her chin a couple of times and nodded. "You've got your father's brown eyes and your hair is nice and thick. You can thank your grandfather for that. He had hair so thick—"

"Ma, did I mention I have an aerobics class tonight?"

Her mother's posture stiffened. "I don't want to be any trouble."

"It's just that I might have to leave before you say what you're obviously planning to say, and I didn't want to miss the reason for your unexpected visit."

Her mother relaxed, but just a little. "Don't worry. I'll say what must be said and then you can leave. Your mother's words are not as important as your exercise class."

An argument bubbled up like fizz from a can of soda, but Dianne successfully managed to swallow it down. Showing any sign of weakness in front of her mother was a major tactical error. Dianne made the tea, then carried the ceramic pot over to the table and sat across from her mother.

"Your skin's still as creamy as—"

"Mom," Dianne said warningly, "there's no need to tell me all this. I know my coloring is good. I also know I've still got my figure and that my hair is thick and that you approve of my keeping it long. You don't need to sell me on myself."

"Ah," Martha answered softly, "that's where you're wrong."

Dianne couldn't help it—she rolled her eyes. When Dianne was fifteen her mother would have slapped her hand, but now that she was thirty-three, Martha used more subtle tactics.

Guilt.

"I don't have many years left in me."

"Mom—"

"No, listen. I'm an old woman now and I have the right to say what I want, especially since the good Lord may choose to call me home at any minute."

Stirring a teaspoon of sugar into her tea offered Dianne a moment to compose herself. Bracing her elbows on the table, she raised the cup to her lips. "Just say it."

Her mother nodded, apparently appeased. "You've lost confidence in yourself."

"That's not true."

Martha Janes's smile was meager at best. "Jack left you, and now you think there must be something wrong with you. But, Dianne, what you don't understand is that he would have gone if you were as beautiful as Marilyn Monroe. Jack's leaving had nothing to do with you and everything to do with Jack."

This conversation was taking a turn Dianne wanted to avoid. Jack was a subject she preferred not to discuss. As far as she could see there wasn't any reason to peel back the scars and examine the wound at this late date. Jack was gone. She'd accepted it, dealt with it, and gone on with her and the children's lives. The fact that her mother was even mentioning her ex-husband had taken Dianne by surprise.

"My goodness," Dianne said, holding out her wrist. "Look at the time—"

"Before you go," her mother said quickly and grabbed her wrist, imprisoning her, "I met a nice young man this afternoon in the butcher shop. Marie

Zimmerman told me about him and I went to talk to him myself.''

"Mom—"

"Hush and listen. He's divorced, but from what he said it was all his wife's fault. He makes blood sausage and insisted I try some. It was so good it practically melted in my mouth. I never tasted sausage so good. A man who makes sausage like that would be an asset to any family.''

Oh, sweet heaven. Her mother already had her married to the guy!

"I told him all about you and he generously offered to take you out.''

"Mother, please. I've already said I won't go out on any more blind dates.''

"Jerome's a nice man. He's—"

"I don't mean to be rude, but I've really got to leave now, or I'll be late.'' Hurriedly, Dianne stood, reached for her coat, and called out to her children that she'd be back in an hour.

It wasn't until she was in her car that Dianne realized they'd been expecting her to announce that she had a date for the dinner.

Chapter Two

"DAMN," DIANNE MUTTERED, scrambling through the bottom of her purse for the tenth time. She knew it wasn't going to do the least bit of good, but she felt compelled to continue the search.

"Double damn," she said as she set the bulky leather handbag on the hood of her car. Rain drops spattered all around her, adding to her dismay.

Expelling her breath, she stalked back into the Port Blossom Community Center and stood in front of the desk. "I seem to have locked my keys in my car," she told the receptionist.

"Oh, dear, is there someone you can get in touch with?"

"I'm a member of the auto club so I can call them for help. I also want to call home and say I'll be late. So, if you'll let me use the phone?"

"Oh, sure." The young woman smiled pleasantly, and lifted the phone onto the counter. "We close in fifteen minutes, you know."

A half hour later, Dianne was leaning impatiently against her car in the community center parking lot when a red tow truck pulled in. It circled the area, then eased into the space next to hers.

The driver, whom Dianne couldn't see in the dark, rolled down his window and stuck out his elbow. "Are you the lady who phoned in about locking her keys in the car?"

"No. I'm standing out in the rain wearing a leotard just for the fun of it," she muttered.

He chuckled, turned off the engine and hopped out of the driver's seat. "I take it this has been one of those days."

She nodded, suddenly feeling a stab of guilt at her churlishness. He seemed so friendly.

"Why don't you climb in my truck where it's nice and warm while I take care of this?" He opened the passenger-side door and gestured for her to enter.

She smiled weakly, and as she climbed in, said, "I didn't mean to snap at you just now."

He flashed her an easy grin. "No problem." She found herself taking a second look at him. He was wearing gray-striped coveralls and the front was covered with grease stains. His name, Steve, was embroidered in red across the top of his vest pocket. His hair was neatly styled and appeared to have been recently cut. His eyes were a warm shade of brown and—she searched for the right word—gentle, she decided.

After seeing she was comfortable in his truck, Steve walked around to the driver's side of her compact car and used his flashlight to determine the type of lock she had.

Dianne rolled down the window. "I don't usually do things like this. I've never locked the keys in my car before—I don't know why I did tonight. Stupid."

He returned to the tow truck and opened the passenger door. "No one can be smart all the time," he said cheerfully. "Don't be so hard on yourself." He bent the seat forward a little and reached for a toolbox in the space behind her.

"I've had a lot on my mind lately," she said.

Straightening, he looked at her and nodded sympathetically. He had a nice face too, she noted, easy on the eyes. In fact, he was downright attractive. The coveralls didn't distract from his appeal, but actually suggested a certain ruggedness. He was thoughtful and friendly just when Dianne was beginning to think there wasn't anyone in the world who was. But then, standing in the dark and the rain waiting might make anyone feel friendless, despite the fact that Port Blossom was a rural community with a warm, small-town atmosphere.

Steve returned to her car and began to fiddle with the lock. Unable to sit still, Dianne opened the truck door and climbed out. "It's the dinner that's got me so upset."

"The dinner?" Steve glanced up from his work.

"The Valentine's dinner the community center is sponsoring this Saturday night. My children are forcing me to go. I don't know for sure, but I think they've got money riding on it, because they're making it sound like a matter of national security for me to be there."

"I see. Why doesn't your husband take you?"

"I'm divorced," she said bluntly. "I suppose no one expects it to happen to them. I assumed after twelve years my marriage was as sound as a rock, but it wasn't. Jack's remarried now, living in Boston." Dianne didn't know why she was rambling on so, but once she'd opened her mouth, she couldn't seem to stop. It wasn't like her to relate the intimate details of her life to a perfect stranger.

"Aren't you cold?"

"I'm fine, thanks." That wasn't entirely true—she was a little chilled—but she was more troubled about not having a date for the stupid Valentine's dinner than freezing to death. Briefly she wondered if Jason,

Jill and her mother would accept pneumonia as a reasonable excuse for not attending the dinner.

"You're sure? You look like you're shivering."

She rubbed her palms together and ignored his question. "That's when my mother suggested Jerome."

"Jerome?"

"She seems to think I need a little help getting my feet wet."

Steve glanced up at her again, clearly puzzled.

"In the dating world," Dianne explained. "But I've had enough of the dates she's arranged."

"Disasters?"

"Encounters of the worst kind. On one of them, the guy set his napkin on fire."

Steve laughed outright at that.

"Hey, it wasn't funny, trust me. I was mortified. He panicked and started waving it around in the air until the maître d' arrived with a fire extinguisher and chaos broke loose."

Dianne found herself smiling at the memory of the unhappy episode. "Now that I look back on it, it was rather amusing."

Steve's gaze held hers. "I take it there were other disasters?"

"None that I'd care to repeat."

"So your mother's up to her tricks again?"

Dianne nodded, "Only this time my kids are involved. Mom stumbled across this butcher who specializes in . . . well, never mind, that's not important. What is important is if I don't come up with a date in the next day or two, I'm going to be stuck going to this stupid dinner with Jerome."

"It shouldn't be so bad," he said. Dianne could hear the grin in his voice.

"How generous of you to say so," she muttered, crossing her arms over her chest. She'd orbited her vehicle twice before she spoke again.

"My kids are even instructing me on exactly the kind of man they want me to date."

"Oh?"

Dianne wasn't completely sure he'd heard her. Her lock snapped free and he opened the door and retrieved her keys, which were in the ignition. He handed them to her, and with a thank-you, Dianne made a move to climb into her car.

"Jason and Jill—they're my kids—want me to go out with a tall dark, handsome—" She stopped abruptly, holding out her arm as if to keep her balance.

Steve looked at her oddly. "Ma'am, are you all right?"

Dianne placed her fingertips to her temple and nodded. "I think so, but then again I'm not sure." She inhaled sharply and motioned toward the streetlight. "Would you mind stepping over there for a minute?"

"Me?" He pointed to himself as though he wasn't sure she meant him.

"Please."

He shrugged and did as she requested.

The idea was fast gaining momentum in her mind. He was certainly tall—at least six foot three, which was a nice complement to her own slender five ten. And he was dark—his hair appeared to be a rich shade of mahogany. As for the handsome part, she'd noticed that right off.

"Is something wrong?" he probed.

"No," Dianne said, grinning shyly—although what she was about to propose was anything but shy. "By the way, how old are you? Thirty? Thirty-one?"

"Thirty-five."

"That's good. Perfect." A couple of years older than she was. Yes, the kids would approve of that.

"Good? Perfect?" He seemed to be questioning her sanity.

"Married?" she asked.

"Nope. I never got around to it, but I came close once." His eyes narrowed suspiciously.

"That's even better. I don't suppose you've got a jealous girlfriend—or a mad lover hanging around looking for an excuse to murder someone?"

"Not lately."

Dianne sighed with relief. "Great."

"Your car door's open," he said, motioning toward it and looking as if he was eager to be on his way. "All I need to do is write down your auto club number."

"Yes, I know." She stood there, arms folded across her chest, studying him in the light. He was even better looking than she'd first thought. "Do you own a decent suit?"

He chuckled as if he found the question amusing. "Yes."

"I mean something really nice, not the one you wore to your high-school graduation."

"It's a really nice suit."

Dianne didn't mean to be insulting, but she had to have all her bases covered. "That's even better," she said. "How would you like to earn an extra thirty bucks Saturday night?"

"I beg your pardon?"

"I'm offering you thirty dollars to escort me to the Valentine dinner here at the center."

Steve stared at her as though he suspected she'd recently escaped from a mental institution.

"Listen, I realize this is a bit unusual," Dianne rushed on, "but you're perfect. Well, not perfect, exactly, but you're exactly the kind of man the kids expect to escort me, and frankly I haven't got time to do a whole lot of recruiting. Mr. Right hasn't showed up, if you know what I mean."

"I think I do."

"I need a date. You fit the bill and you could probably use a little extra cash. I realize it's not much, but thirty dollars sounds fair to me. The dinner starts at seven and should be over by nine. I suspect fifteen dollars an hour is about what you're earning now."

"Ah..."

"I know what you're thinking, but I promise you I'm not crazy. I've got a gold credit card, and they don't issue those to just anyone."

"What about a library card?"

"That, too, but I do have a book overdue. I was planning on taking it back tomorrow." She started searching through her purse to prove she had both cards before she realized he was teasing her.

"Ms...."

"Dianne Williams," she said stepping forward to offer him her hand. His long, strong fingers wrapped around her hand as his smiling gaze held hers, studying her for perhaps the first time. His eyes softened as he shook her hand. The gesture, though small, reassured Dianne that he was exactly the kind of man she wanted to take her to this silly dinner. Once more she found her mouth rushing to explain.

"I realize this all sounds a bit crazy. I don't blame you for thinking I'm something of a nut case. I'm not, really I'm not. I attend church every Sunday, do volunteer work at the grade school, and help coach a girls' soccer team in the fall."

"Why'd you pick me?"

"Well, that's a bit complicated, but you have nice eyes, and when you suggested I sit in your truck and get out of the rain—actually it was only drizzling—" she paused and inhaled a deep breath "—I realized you had a generous heart, and you just might consider something this..."

"...weird," he finished for her.

Dianne nodded, then looked him directly in the eye. Her defenses were down, and there was nothing left to do but admit the truth.

"I'm desperate. No one but a desperate woman would make this kind of offer."

"Saturday night, you say?"

Just the way her luck was running, he would suddenly remember he had urgent plans for the evening. Something important like dusting his bowling trophies.

"From seven to nine. No later, I promise. If you don't think thirty dollars is enough..."

"Thirty's more than generous."

She sagged with relief. "Does this mean you'll do it?"

Steve shook his head as though to suggest he ought to have it examined for even considering her proposal.

"All right," he said after a moment. "I never could resist a damsel in distress."

Chapter Three

"HELLO, EVERYONE!" Dianne sang out as she breezed in the front door. She paused just inside the living room and watched as her mother and her two children stared openly at her. A sense of quiet astonishment pervaded the room. "Is something wrong?"

"What happened to you?" Jason cried. "You look awful!"

"You look like Little Orphan Annie, dear," her mother claimed, her hand working a crochet hook so fast the yarn zipped through her fingers.

"I phoned to tell you I'd be late," Dianne reminded them.

"But you didn't say anything about nearly drowning. What happened?"

"I locked my keys in the car—I already explained that."

Jill walked over to her mother, took her hand and led her to the hallway mirror. The image that greeted Dianne was only a little short of shocking. Her long thick hair hung in limp sodden curls over her shoulders. Her mascara, supposed to be no-run, had dissolved into black tracks down her cheeks. She was drenched to the skin and looked like a prize the cat had dragged onto the porch.

"Oh, dear," she whispered. Her stomach muscles tightened as she recalled the odd looks Steve had given her, and his comment that it must be "one of those days." No wonder! She looked like a charity case.

"Why don't you go upstairs and take a nice hot shower?" her mother suggested. "You'll feel worlds better."

Humbled, for more reasons than she cared to admit, Dianne agreed.

As was generally the rule, her mother was right. By the time Dianne reappeared a half hour later, dressed in her thick terry-cloth robe and fuzzy pink slippers, she felt considerably better.

As she brewed herself a cup of tea, she reviewed the events of the evening. Even if Steve had agreed to attend the Valentine's dinner with her out of pity, it didn't matter. What did matter was the fact she had a date. As soon as she told her family, they would be off her back.

"By the way," she said casually as she carried her tea into the living room, "I have a date for Saturday night."

The room went still. Even the television sound seemed to fade into nothingness. Her two children and her mother did a slow turn, their faces revealing their surprise.

"Don't look so shocked," Dianne said with a light, casual laugh. "I told you before that I was working on it. No one seemed to believe I was capable of finding a date on my own. Well, that simply isn't the case."

"Who?" Martha demanded, her eyes narrowed and disbelieving.

"Oh, ye of little faith," Dianne said feeling only a small twinge of guilt. "His name is Steve Creighton."

"When did you meet him?"

"Ah..." Dianne realized she wasn't prepared for an inquisition. "A few weeks ago. We happened to bump into each other tonight, and he asked if I had a date for the dinner. Naturally I told him I didn't and he suggested we go together. It wasn't any big deal.''

"Steve Creighton." Her mother repeated the name slowly, rolling the syllables over her tongue, as if trying to remember where she'd last heard it. Then she shook her head and resumed crocheting.

"You never said anything about this guy before." Jason's gaze was slightly accusing. He sat on the carpet, knees tucked under his chin as he reviewed this unexpected turn of events.

"Of course I didn't. If I had, all three of you would be bugging me about him, just the way you are now."

Martha gave her ball of yarn a hard jerk. "How'd you two meet?"

Dianne wasn't the least bit ready for this line of questioning. She'd assumed letting her family know she had the necessary escort would have been enough to appease them. Silly of her.

They wanted details. Lots of details, and the only thing Dianne could do was make them up as she went along. She couldn't very well admit she'd only met Steve that night and was so desperate for a date that she'd offered to pay him to escort her to the dinner.

"We met, ah, a few weeks ago in the grocery store," she explained haltingly, averting her gaze. She prayed that would be enough to satisfy their curiosity. But when she paused to sip her tea, the three faces were staring expectantly at her.

"Go on," her mother urged.

"I . . . I was standing in the frozen-food section and . . . Steve was there, too, and . . . he smiled at me and introduced himself."

"What did he say after that?" Jill wanted to know, her young face eager for the particulars. Martha apparently shared her granddaughter's interest. She set her yarn and crochet hook aside, focusing all her attention on Dianne.

"After he introduced himself, he said surely those low-cal dinners couldn't be for me—that I looked perfect just the way I was." The words fell stiffly from her lips like pieces of cardboard. She had to be desperate to divulge her own fantasy to her family like this.

All right, she was desperate.

Jill's shoulders rose with an expressive sigh. "How romantic!"

Jason, however, was frowning. "The guy sounds like a flake to me. A real man doesn't walk up to a woman and say something stupid like that."

"Steve's very nice."

"Maybe, but he doesn't sound like he's got all his oars in the water."

"I think he sounds sweet," Jill countered, rushing to defend her mother by championing Steve. "If Mom likes him, then he's good enough for me."

"There are a lot of fruitcakes out there." Apparently her mother felt obliged to tell her that.

It was all Dianne could do not to remind her dear, sweet mother that she'd arranged several dates for her with men who fell easily into that category.

"I think we should meet him," Jason said, his eyes darkening with concern. "He may turn out to be a serial murderer or something."

"Jason—" Dianne forced a light laugh "—you're being silly. Besides, you're going to meet him Saturday night."

"By then it'll be too late."

"Jason's got a point, dear," Martha Janes said. "I don't think it would do the least bit of harm to introduce your young man to the family before Saturday night."

"I . . . he's probably busy. . . . He's working all sorts of weird hours and . . ."

"What does he do?"

"Ah. . ." She couldn't think fast enough to come up with a lie and was forced to admit the truth. "He drives a truck."

Her words were followed by a thick silence as her children and mother shared meaningful looks. "I've heard stories about truck drivers," Martha said, pinching her lips tightly together. "None I'd care to repeat in front of the children, mind you, but . . . stories."

"Mother, you're being—"

"Jason's absolutely right. I insist we meet this Steve. Truck drivers and cowboys simply aren't to be trusted."

Dianne rolled her eyes.

Her mother forgave her by saying, "I don't expect you to know this, Dianne, since you married so young."

"You married Dad when you were sixteen—younger than *I* was when I married," Dianne stated softly, not really wanting to argue, but finding herself trapped.

"Yes, but I've lived longer." She waved her crochet hook at Dianne. "A mother knows these things."

"Grandma's right," Jason said, sounding very adult. "We need to meet this Steve before you go out with him."

Dianne threw her hands up in the air in frustration. "Hey, I thought you kids were the ones so eager for me to be at this dinner!"

"Yes, but we still have standards," Jill said, siding with the others.

"I'll see what I can do," Dianne mumbled.

"Invite him over for dinner Thursday night," her mother suggested. "I'll cook up my stroganoff and bring over a fresh apple pie."

"Ah . . . he might be busy."

"Then make it Wednesday night," Jason advised in a voice that was hauntingly familiar. It was the same tone Dianne used when she meant business.

With nothing left to do but agree, Dianne said, "Okay. I'll try for Thursday." Oh, Lord, she thought, what had she got herself into?

SHE WAITED until the following afternoon to contact Steve. He'd given her his business card, which she'd tucked into the edging at the bottom of the bulletin board in her kitchen. She wasn't pleased about having to call him. She'd need to offer him more money if he agreed to this dinner. She couldn't very well expect him to come out of the generosity of his heart.

"Port Blossom Towing," a crisp female voice answered.

"Ah . . . this is Dianne Williams. I'd like to leave a message for Steve Creighton."

"Steve's here." Her words were immediately followed by a soft click and a ringing sound.

"Steve," he answered distractedly.

"Hello." Dianne found herself at a loss for words. She'd hoped to just leave a message and ask him to return the call at his convenience. To have him there, on the other end of the line, when she wasn't expecting it, left her at a disadvantage.

"Is this Dianne?"

"Yes. How'd you know?"

He chuckled softly, and the sound was pleasant and warm. "It's probably best that I don't answer that. Are you checking up to make sure I don't back out Saturday night? Rest assured, I won't. In fact I stopped off at the community center this morning and picked up tickets for the dinner."

"Oh, you didn't have to do that, but thanks. I'll reimburse you later."

"Just add it to my tab," he said lightly.

Dianne cringed, then took a breath and said, "Actually, I called to talk to you about my children."

"Your children?"

"Yes," she said. "Jason and Jill, and my mother, too, seem to think it would be a good idea if they met you. I assured them they would on Saturday night, but apparently that isn't good enough."

"I see."

"According to Jason, by then it'll be too late, and you might be a serial murderer or something worse. My mother found the fact you drive a truck worrisome."

"Do you want me to change jobs, too? I might have a bit of a problem managing all that before Saturday night."

"Don't worry. Now, about Thursday—that's when they want you to come for dinner. My mother's offered to fix her stroganoff and bake a pie. She uses Granny Smith apples," Dianne added, as though that bit of information would convince him to accept.

"Thursday night?"

"I'll give you an additional ten dollars."

"Ten dollars?" He sounded insulted, so Dianne raised her offer.

"All right, fifteen, but that's as high as I can go. I'm living on a budget, you know." This fiasco was quickly running into a big chunk of cash. The dinner tickets were fifteen each, and she'd need to reimburse Steve for those. Plus, she owed him thirty for escorting her to the silly affair, and now an additional fifteen if he agreed to this dinner with her family.

"For fifteen you've got yourself a deal," he said at last. "Anything else?"

Dianne closed her eyes. This was the worst part. "Yes," she said, swallowing tightly. The lump in her throat had grown to painful proportions. "There's one other thing. I...I want you to know I don't normally look that bad."

"Hey, I told you before—don't be so hard on yourself, you'd had a bad day."

"It's just that I don't want you to think I'm going to embarrass you at this Valentine's dinner. There may be people there you know, and after I made such a big issue over whether you had a suit and everything, well, I thought you might be more comfortable knowing..." She paused, closed her eyes and then blurted, "I've decided to switch brands of mascara."

His hesitation was only slight. "Thank you for sharing that. I'm sure I'll sleep better now."

Dianne decided to ignore that comment since she'd practically invited it. She didn't know why she should find herself so tongue-tied with this man, but then again, perhaps she did. She'd made a complete idiot of herself. Paying a man to escort her to a dinner wasn't exactly the type of thing she wanted to list on a résumé.

"Oh, and one more thing," Dianne said, determined to put this unpleasantness behind her, "my mother and the kids asked me several questions about...us. How we met and the like. It might be a good idea if we reviewed my answers so our stories match."

"You want to meet for coffee later?"

"Ah...when?"

"Say seven, at the Pancake Haven. Don't worry, I'll buy."

Dianne had to bite back her sarcastic response to his "generous" offer. Instead she murmured, "All right, but I won't have a lot of time."

"I promise not to keep you any longer than necessary."

Chapter Four

"ALL RIGHT," Steve said dubiously, once the waitress had poured them each a cup of coffee. "How'd we meet?"

Dianne told him, lowering her voice when she came to the part about the low-cal frozen dinners. She found it rather humiliating to have to repeat her private fantasy a second time, especially to Steve.

He looked incredulous when she'd finished. "You've got to be kidding."

Dianne took offense at his tone. This was her romantic invention he was ridiculing, and she hadn't even mentioned the part about the Rimsky-Korsakov symphony or the gently chiming bells.

"I didn't have time to think of something better," Dianne explained irritably. "Jason hit me with the question first thing and I wasn't prepared."

"What did Jason say when you told him that story?"

"That you sounded like a flake."

"I don't blame him."

Dianne's shoulders sagged with defeat.

"Don't worry about it," Steve assured her, still frowning. "I'll clear up everything when I meet him Thursday night." He said it in a way that suggested the task would be difficult.

"Good—only don't make me look like any more of a fool than I already do. All right?"

"I'll do my best," he said in the same dubious inflection he'd used when they'd first sat down.

Dianne couldn't really blame him. This entire affair was quickly going from bad to worse, and there was no one to fault but her. Who would have dreamed finding a date for the Valentine's dinner would cause such problems?

As they sipped their coffee, Dianne studied the man sitting across from her. She was somewhat surprised to discover that Steve Creighton looked even better the second time around. He was dressed in slacks and an Irish cable-knit sweater the color of winter wheat. His smile was a ready one and his eyes, now that she had a chance to see them in the light, were a deep, rich shade of brown like his hair. The impression he'd given her of a sympathetic, generous man persisted. He must be. No one else would have so readily agreed to this scheme, at least not without a more substantial inducement.

"I'm afraid I might have painted my kids a picture of you that's not quite accurate," Dianne admitted. Both her children had been filled with questions about Steve when they'd returned from school that afternoon. Jason had remained skeptical, but Jill, always a romantic—Dianne couldn't imagine where she'd inherited that!—had bombarded Dianne for details.

"I'll do my best to live up to my image," Steve was quick to assure her.

Planting her elbows on the table, Dianne brushed a thick swatch of hair away from her face. "Listen, I'm sorry I ever got you involved in this."

"No backing out now—I've laid out cold cash for the dinner tickets."

Which was a not-so-subtle reminder she owed him for those, Dianne realized. She dug through her bag and brought out her checkbook. "I'll write you a check for the dinner tickets right now while I'm thinking about it.''

''I'm not worried.'' He brushed aside her offer with a wave of his hand.

Nevertheless, Dianne insisted. If she paid him in increments, she wouldn't have to think about how much this fiasco would end up costing her. She had the distinct feeling that by the time the Valentine's dinner was over, she would've spent as much as if she'd taken a Hawaiian vacation.

After adding her signature, with a flair, to the bottom of the check, she kept her eyes lowered and said, ''If I upped the ante five dollars do you think you could manage to look . . . besotted?''

''Besotted?'' Steve repeated the word as though he'd never heard it before.

''You know, smitten.''

''Smitten?''

Again he made it sound as though she were speaking a foreign language. ''Attracted,'' she tried for the third time, loud enough to attract the waitress's attention. The woman appeared and refilled their near-full cups.

''I'm not purposely being dense—I'm just not sure what you mean.''

''Try to look as though you find me attractive,'' she said, leaning halfway across the table and speaking in a heated whisper.

''I see. So that's what 'besotted' means.'' He took another drink of his coffee, and Dianne had the feeling he did so in an effort to hide a smile.

''You aren't supposed to find that amusing.'' She took a gulp of her own drink and nearly scalded her mouth. Under different circumstances she would have grimaced with pain, or at least reached for the water glass. She did none of those things. A woman has her pride.

"Let me see if I understand you correctly," Steve said matter-of-factly. "For an extra five bucks you want me to look 'smitten.'"

"Yes," Dianne answered with as much dignity as she could muster, which at the moment wasn't a great deal.

"I'll do it, of course," Steve said, grinning and making her feel all the more foolish, "only I'm not exactly sure I know how." He straightened, squared his shoulders and momentarily closed his eyes.

"Steve?" Dianne whispered, glancing around, hoping no one was watching them. It looked as if he were attempting some form of Eastern meditation. She half expected him to start humming. "What are you doing?"

"Thinking about how to look smitten."

"Are you making fun of me?"

"Not in the least. If you're willing to offer me five bucks, then it must be important to you. I want to do it right."

Dianne thought she'd better tell him. "This isn't for me," she said. "It's for my ten-year-old daughter, who happens to have a romantic nature. Jill was so impressed with the story of the way we were supposed to have met that I . . . I was kind of hoping you'd be willing to . . . you know." Now that she was forced to spell it out, Dianne wasn't certain of anything. But she knew one thing—suggesting he look smitten with her had been a mistake.

"I'll try."

"I'd appreciate it," she said.

"How's this?" Steve looked toward her, cocked his head at a slight angle, then slowly lowered his eyelids until they were half closed. His mouth curved upward in an off-centered smile while his shoulders heaved in what Dianne suspected was supposed to be a deep sigh of longing. As though in afterthought, he pressed his open hands over his heart while making soft panting sounds.

"Are you doing an imitation of a Saint Bernard?" Dianne snapped, still not sure whether he was making fun of her or seriously trying to do as she suggested. "You look like a...a dog. Maybe Jason's right and you really are a flake."

"I was trying to look besotted," Steve insisted. "I thought that was what you wanted." As if it would improve the image, he cocked his head the other way and repeated the performance.

"You're making fun of me, and I don't appreciate it one bit." Dianne tossed her napkin on the table and stood. "Thursday night, six o'clock, and please don't be late." With that she slipped her purse strap over her shoulder and stalked out of the restaurant.

Steve followed her to her car. "All right, I apologize. I got carried away in there."

Dianne nodded. She'd gone a little overboard herself, but not nearly as much as Steve. Although she'd claimed she wanted him to give the impression of being attracted to her for Jill's sake, that wasn't entirely true. Steve was handsome and kind, and to have him looking at her with his heart in his eyes was a fantasy that was strictly her own.

Admitting as much, even to herself, was something of a shock. The walls around her battered heart had been reinforced by three years of loneliness. For reasons she wasn't entirely sure she could explain, this tow-truck driver made her feel vulnerable.

"I'm willing to try again if you want," he said. "Only..."

"Yes?" Her car was parked in the rear lot where the lighting wasn't nearly as good. Steve's face was hidden in the shadows, and she wasn't sure if he was being sincere or not.

"The problem," he replied slowly, "comes from the fact that we haven't kissed. I don't mean to be forward, you understand. You want me to wear a certain look, but it's a little difficult to manufacture without ever having had any, er, physical closeness."

"I see." Dianne's heart was pounding hard enough to damage her rib cage.

"Are you willing to let me kiss you?"

It was a last resort and she didn't have much choice. But she didn't have anything to lose, either. "All right, if you insist."

Heaving a deep breath, she angled her head to the right, closed her eyes tightly and puckered up. After waiting what seemed an inordinate amount of time, she opened her eyes. "Is something wrong?"

"I can't do it."

Embarrassed in the extreme, Dianne planted her hands on her hips. "What do you mean?"

"You look like you're about to be sacrificed to appease the gods."

"I beg your pardon!" Dianne couldn't believe she was hearing him correctly. Talk about humiliation— she was only doing as he suggested.

"I can't kiss a woman who looks at me like she's about to undergo the most revolting experience of her life."

"You're saying I'm...oh...oh!" Too furious to speak, Dianne gripped Steve by the elbow and jerked him over to where his tow truck was parked, a couple of spaces down from her own car. Hopping onto the running board, she glared heatedly down at him. Her higher vantage point made her feel less vulnerable. Her eyes flashed with fire; his were filled with mild curiosity.

"Dianne, what are you doing now?"

"I'll have you know I was quite a kisser in my time."

"I didn't doubt you."

"You just did. Now listen and listen good, because I'm only going to say this once." Waving her index finger under his nose, she paused and lowered her hand abruptly. He was right, she hadn't been all that thrilled to fall into this little experiment. A kiss was an innocent-enough exchange, she supposed, but kissing Steve put her on the defensive. And that troubled her.

"Say it."

Self-conscious now, she shifted her gaze and stepped off the running board, feeling ridiculous and stupid.

"What was it you found so important that you were waving your finger under my nose?" Steve pressed.

Since she'd made such a fuss, she didn't have any choice but to finish what she'd begun. "When I was in high school...the boys used to like to kiss me."

"They still would," Steve said softly, "if you'd give them a little bit of encouragement."

She looked up at him and found it necessary to blink back unexpected tears. A woman doesn't have her own husband walk away from her and not find herself drowning in self-doubts. Jack had gone and left her swimming in a pool of pain. Once she'd been confident and secure; now she was dubious and unsure of herself.

"Here," Steve said, gripping her gently by the shoulders. "Let's try this." Then he gently, sweetly slanted his mouth over hers. Dianne wasn't prepared, in fact she was about to protest when their lips met and the option to refuse was taken from her.

Mindlessly she responded. Her arms went around his middle and her hands splayed across the hard muscles of his back. And suddenly, emotions that had been simmering just below the surface rose like a tempest within her, and her heart went on a rampage all its own.

Steve buried his hands in her hair, his fingers twisting and tangling the thick length, bunching it at the back of her head. His mouth was gentle, yet possessive. She gave a small, shocked moan when his tongue breached the barrier of her lips, but she adjusted quickly to the deepening quality of his kiss.

Slowly, reluctantly, Steve eased his mouth from hers. For a long moment, Dianne didn't open her eyes. When she did, she found Steve staring down at her.

He blinked.

She blinked.

Then, in the space of a heartbeat, he lowered his mouth back to hers.

Unable to stop, Dianne sighed deeply and leaned into his strength, letting him absorb her weight. Her legs felt like mush and her head was spinning with confusion. Her hands crept up and closed around the knitted folds of his collar.

This kiss was long and thorough. It was the sweetest kiss Dianne had ever known—and the most passionate.

When he finally lifted his mouth from hers, he smiled tenderly. For a long moment he didn't say anything. "I don't believe I'll have any problem looking besotted," he whispered.

Chapter Five

"STEVE'S HERE!" Jason called, releasing the living-room curtain. "He's just pulled into the driveway."

Jill's high-pitched voice echoed her brother's. "He brought his truck. It's red and—"

"—wicked," Jason said, paying Steve's choice of vehicles the highest form of teenage compliment.

"What did I tell you," Dianne's mother said, stiffening as she briskly stirred the simmering stroganoff sauce. "He's driving a truck that's red and wicked." Her voice rose hysterically. "The man's probably a spawn of the devil!"

"Mother, 'wicked' means 'wonderful' to Jason."

"I've never heard anything so absurd in my life."

The doorbell chimed just then. Jerking the apron from her slim waist and tossing it aside, Dianne straightened and walked into the wide entryway. Jason, Jill and her mother followed closely, crowding her.

"Mom, please," Dianne pleaded, "give me some room here. Jason. Jill. Back up a little, would you?"

Reluctantly all three moved several paces back, allowing Dianne some space. But the moment her hand went for the doorknob, they crowded forward once more.

"Children, Ma, please!" she whispered frantically. The three were so close to her she could barely breathe.

Reluctantly Jason and Jill shuffled into the living room and sagged into the beanbag cushions near the television set. Martha, however, refused to budge.

The bell chimed a second time, and after glaring at her mother and receiving no response, Dianne opened the door. On the other side of the screen door stood Steve, a huge bouquet of red roses clenched in one hand and a large stuffed bear tucked under his other arm.

Dianne blinked as she calculated the cost of long-stemmed roses, and a stuffed animal. She couldn't even afford carnations. And if he felt it necessary to bring along a stuffed bear, why hadn't he chosen a smaller, less costly one?

"May I come in?" he asked after a lengthy pause.

Her mother elbowed Dianne in the ribs and smiled serenely as she unlatched the lock on the screen door.

"You must be Steve. How lovely to meet you," Martha said as graciously as if she'd always thought the world of truck drivers.

Holding open the outer door for him, Dianne managed to produce a weak smile as Steve entered her home. Jason and Jill had come back into the entryway to stand next to their grandmother, eyeing Dianne's newfound date with open curiosity. For all her son's concern that Steve might turn out to be an ax-murderer, one look at the bright red tow truck and he'd been won over.

"Steve, I'd like you to meet my family," Dianne said, gesturing toward the three.

"So, you're Jason," Steve said, holding out his hand. The two exchanged a hearty handshake. "I'm pleased to meet you, son. Your mother speaks highly of you."

Jason beamed.

Turning his attention to Jill, Steve held out the oversize teddy bear. "This is for you," he said, giving her the stuffed animal. "I wanted something extra special for Dianne's daughter, but this was all I could think of. I hope you aren't disappointed."

"I love teddy bears!" Jill cried, hugging it tight. "Did Mom tell you that?"

"Nope," Steve said, centering his high-voltage smile on the ten-year-old. "I just guessed you'd like them."

"Oh, thank you, thank you." Cuddling the bear, Jill raced up the stairs, giddy with delight. "I'm going to put him on my bed right now."

Steve's gaze followed her daughter, and then his eyes briefly linked with Dianne's. In that split second, she let it be known she wasn't entirely pleased. He frowned slightly, but recovered before presenting the roses to Dianne's mother.

"For me?" Martha cried, and placed her fingertips over her mouth as though shocked by the gesture. "Oh, dear, you shouldn't have! Oh, my heavens, I can't remember the last time a man gave me roses." Reaching for the corner of her apron, she discreetly dabbed her eyes. "This is a rare treat."

"Mother, don't you want to put those in water?" Dianne said pointedly.

"Oh, dear, I suppose I should. It was a thoughtful gesture, Steve. Very thoughtful."

"Jason, go help your grandmother."

Her son looked as though he intended to object, but changed his mind and obediently followed his grandmother into the kitchen.

As soon as they were alone, Dianne turned on Steve. "Don't you think you're laying it on a little thick?" she whispered. She was so furious she was having trouble speaking clearly. "I can't afford all this."

"Don't worry about it."

"I am worried. In fact I'm suffering a good deal of distress. At the rate you're spending my money I'm going to have to go on an installment plan."

"Hush, now, before you attract attention."

The way she was feeling, Dianne felt like doing a whole lot more than that. "I—"

Steve placed his fingers over her lips. "I've learned a very effective way of keeping you quiet—don't force me to use it. Kissing you so soon after my arrival might give the wrong impression."

"You wouldn't dare!"

The way his mouth slanted upward in a slow, powerful smile made her afraid he would. "I was only doing my best to act besotted," he said.

"You didn't need to spend this much doing it. Opening my door, holding out my chair—that's all I wanted. First you roll your eyes like you're going into a coma and pant like a Saint Bernard, then you spend a fortune."

"Dinner's ready," Martha shouted from the kitchen.

Tossing him one last angry glare, Dianne led the way into the big kitchen. Steve moved behind Dianne's chair and held it out for her. "Are you happy now?" he whispered close to her ear as she sat down.

She nodded, thinking it was too little, too late, but she didn't have much of an argument since she'd specifically asked for this.

Soon the five were all seated around the wooden table. Dianne's mother said the blessing, and while she did so, Dianne offered up a fervent prayer of her own. She wanted Steve to make a good impression—but not too good.

After the buttered noodles and the stroganoff had been passed around, along with a lettuce-and-cucumber salad and homemade rolls, Jason embarked on the topic that had apparently been troubling him from the first.

"Mom said you met at the market."

Steve nodded. "She was blocking the aisle and I had to ask her to move her cart so I could get to the Hearty Eater Pot Pies."

Jason straightened in his chair, looking more than a little satisfied. "I thought it might be something like that."

"I beg your pardon?" Steve asked, playing innocent.

Her son cleared his throat, glanced both ways before answering, then lowered his voice. "You should hear Mom's version of the way you two met."

"More noodles?" Dianne said, shoving the bowl forcefully toward her son.

Jill looked confused. "But didn't you smile at Mom and say she's perfect just the way she is?"

Steve took a moment to compose his thoughts while he buttered his third dinner roll. Dianne recognized that he was doing a balancing act between her two children. If he said he'd commented on the low-cal frozen dinners and her figure, then he risked offending Jason, who seemed to think no man in his right mind would say something like that. On the other hand, if he claimed otherwise, he chanced wounding Jill's romantic little heart.

"I'd be interested in knowing myself," Martha added, looking more than pleased that Steve had taken a second helping of her stroganoff. "Dianne's terribly close-mouthed about these things. She didn't even mention you until the other night.''

"To be honest," Steve said, sitting back in his chair, "I don't exactly recall what I said to Dianne. I remember being irritated with her for hogging the aisle, but when I asked her to move, she seemed apologetic and was quick to get her cart out of the way.''

Jason nodded, appeased.

"But when I got a good look at her, I couldn't help thinking she was probably the most beautiful woman I'd seen in a good long while.''

Jill sighed, mollified.

"I don't recall any of that," Dianne said, reaching for another roll. She tore it apart with a vengeance and smeared butter on both halves before she realized she had an untouched roll balanced on the edge of her plate.

"I was thinking after the dishes were done that I'd take Jason out for a ride in the truck," Steve said after a few minutes had passed.

"You'd do that?" Jason nearly leapt from his chair in his eagerness.

"I was planning to all along," Steve explained. "I thought you'd be more interested in seeing how all the gears worked than in any gift I could bring you.''

"I am." Jason was so excited he could barely sit still another minute.

"When Jason and I come back, I'll take you out for a spin, Dianne.''

She shook her head. "I'm not interested, thanks.''

Three pairs of accusing eyes flashed in her direction. It was as if Dianne had committed an act of treason and her family had no choice but to hand her over to the CIA.

"I'm sure my daughter didn't mean that," Martha said, smiling sweetly at Steve. "She's been very tired lately and not quite herself."

Bewildered, Dianne stared at her mother.

"Can we go now?" Jason wanted to know, already standing.

"Sure, if your mother says it's okay," Steve said, with a glance at Dianne. She nodded, and Steve finished the last of his roll and stood.

"I'll have apple pie ready for you when you return," Martha promised, quickly ushering the two out the front door.

As soon as her mother returned to the kitchen, Dianne asked, "What was that all about?"

"What?" her mother demanded, feigning ignorance.

"That I've been very tired and not myself lately?"

"Oh, that," Martha said, clearing the table. "Steve wants to spend a few minutes alone with you. It's only to be expected—so I had to make some excuse for you."

"Yes, but—"

"Your behavior, my dear, was just short of rude. When a gentleman makes it clear he wants to spend a few uninterrupted minutes in your company, you should welcome the opportunity."

"Mother, I seem to recall your saying Steve was a spawn of the devil, remember?"

"Now that I've met him, I've had a change of heart."

"What about Jerome, the butcher? I thought you were convinced he was the one for me."

"I like Steve better. He's a good man, and you'd be a fool to let him slip through your fingers by pretending to be indifferent."

"I am indifferent."

With a look of patent disbelief, Martha Janes quickly shook her head. "I saw the way your eyes lit up when Steve walked into the house. You can fool some folks, but you can't pull the wool over your own mother's eyes. You're falling in love with this young man, and frankly, I couldn't be more pleased. I like him."

Dianne frowned. If her eyes had lit up when Steve arrived, it was because she was trying to figure out a way to repay him for the roses and the teddy bear. What she felt for him wasn't anything romantic. Or was it?

Dear Lord, she couldn't actually be falling for this guy, could she?

The question haunted Dianne as she loaded the dishwasher.

"Steve's real cute," Jill announced. Her daughter would find Attila the Hun cute, too, if he brought her a teddy bear, but Dianne resisted the impulse to say so.

"He looks a little bit like Tom Cruise, don't you think?" Jill continued.

"I can't say I've noticed." A small lie. Dianne had noticed a lot more about Steve than she was willing to admit. Although she'd issued a fair number of complaints, he really was being a good sport about all this. Of course, she was paying him, but he'd gone above and beyond the call of duty. Taking Jason out for a spin in the tow truck was one example, although why anyone would be thrilled to drive around in that contraption was beyond Dianne.

"I do believe Steve Creighton will make you a decent husband," her mother stated thoughtfully as she removed the warm apple pie from the oven. "In fact, I was just thinking how nice it would be to have a summer wedding. It's so much easier to ask relatives to travel when the weather's good. June or July would be nice."

"Mother, please! Steve and I barely know each other."

"On the contrary," Steve said, sauntering into the kitchen. He stepped behind Dianne's mother and sniffed appreciatively at the aroma wafting from her apple pie. "I happen to be partial to summer weddings myself."

Chapter Six

"DON'T YOU THINK you're overdoing it a bit?" Dianne demanded as soon as Steve eased the big tow truck out of her driveway. She was strapped into the seat next to him, feeling trapped—not to mention betrayed by her own family. They had insisted Steve take her out for a spin so the two of them could have some time alone. Steve didn't want to be alone with her, but her family didn't know that.

"Maybe I did come on a little strong," Steve agreed, dazzling her with his smile.

It was better for her equilibrium if she didn't glance his way, Dianne decided. Her eyes would innocently meet his and he'd give her one of those heart-stopping, lopsided smiles, and something inside her would melt. If this continued much longer she'd be nothing more than a puddle by the end of the evening.

"The flowers and the stuffed animal I can understand," she said stiffly, willing to grant him that much. "You wanted to make a good impression, and that's fine, but the comment about being partial to summer weddings was going too far. It's just the kind of thing my mother was hoping to hear from you."

"You're right."

The fact that he was being so agreeable should have forewarned Dianne something was amiss. She'd sensed it almost from the first moment she'd climbed into the truck. He'd closed the door and almost immediately something pulled wire-taut within her. The sensation was peculiar, almost wistful—a melancholy pining she'd never felt before.

She squared her shoulders and stared straight ahead, determined not to fall under his spell the way her children and her mother so obviously had.

"As it is, I suspect Mom's been faithfully lighting votive candles every afternoon, asking God to send me a husband. Mostly she thinks God needs a little help—that's why she goes around arranging dates for me."

"You're right, of course. I should never have made that comment about summer weddings," Steve said, "but I assumed that's just the sort of thing a *besotted* man would say."

Dianne sighed, realizing she didn't have much of an argument. But he was doing everything within his power to make her regret that silly request. She couldn't possibly understand what had led her to make it; now she was living to regret every syllable.

"Hey, where are you taking me?" she demanded when he turned off her street onto a main thoroughfare.

Steve turned his smile full force on her and twitched his thick eyebrows a couple of times for effect. "For a short drive. It wouldn't look good if we were to return five minutes after we left the house. Your family—"

"—will be waiting at the front door. They expect me back any minute."

"No, they don't."

"And why don't they?" she asked, growing uneasy. This ride wasn't supposed to be anything more than a spin around the block. As it was, she'd had to be coerced into even that.

"Because I told your mother we'd be gone for an hour or more."

"An hour?" Dianne cried, as though he'd just announced he was kidnapping her. "But you can't do that! I mean, what about your time? Surely it's valuable."

"I assumed you'd want to pay me a couple of dollars extra—after all, I'm doing this to give the right kind of impression. It's what—"

"I know, I know," she interrupted. "You're only acting smitten." The truth of the matter was that Dianne was making a fuss over something that was actually causing her heart to pound hard and fast. The whole idea of being alone with Steve appealed to her too much. *That* was the reason she fought it so hard. Every time she was with him she found him more fascinating. Without even trying, he'd managed to cast a spell on her family, and much as she hated to admit it, one on her, too. Steve Creighton was laughter and magic. Instinctively she knew he wasn't another Jack. Not the type of man who would walk away from his family.

Dianne stiffened as the thought crossed her mind. It would be much easier to deal with the hand life had dealt her if she wasn't forced to associate with men as seemingly wonderful as this tow-truck operator. It was easier to view all men as insensitive and thoughtless.

Dianne didn't like the fact that Steve was proving to be otherwise. He was apparently determined to crack the hard shell around her safe, secure world no matter how hard she tried to reinforce it.

"Another thing," she said stiffly, crossing her arms with resolve, but refusing to glance his way. "You've got to stop being so free with my money."

"I never expected you to reimburse me for those gifts," he explained quietly.

"I insist on it."

"My, my, aren't we prickly. I bought the flowers and the toy for Jill of my own accord. I don't expect you to pick up the tab," he repeated.

Dianne didn't know if she should argue with him or not. Although his tone was soft, a thread of steel ran through his words, just enough to let her know nothing she said was going to change his mind.

"That's not all," she said, deciding to drop that argument for a more pressing one. She realized she probably did sound a bit shrewish, but if he wasn't going to be practical about this, *she'd* have to be.

"You mean there's more?" he cried, pretending to be distressed.

"Steve, please," she said and was shocked at how feeble she sounded. She scarcely recognized the voice as her own. "You've got to stop being so...so wonderful," she said finally.

He eased to a stop at a red light and turned to her, draping his arm over the back of the seat. "I don't think I heard you right. Would you remind repeating that?"

"You can't continue being so—" she paused, searching for another word "—charming."

"Charming," he repeated, as though he'd never heard the word before.

"To my children and my mother," she elaborated. "The gifts were one thing. Giving Jason a ride in the tow truck was another, but agreeing with my mother about summer weddings and then playing a game of basketball with Jason were above and beyond the call of duty."

"Personally, I would have thought having your mother measure my chest and arm length so she could knit me a sweater would bother you the most."

"That, too!" she cried.

"Would you mind explaining why this is such a problem?"

"Isn't it obvious? If you keep doing that sort of thing, they'll expect me to continue dating you after the Valentine's dinner, and, frankly, I can't afford it."

He chuckled at that as if she was making some kind of joke. Only it wasn't funny. "I happen to live on a budget—" she went on.

"I don't think we should concern ourselves with that."

"Well I am concerned." She expelled her breath sharply. "One date! That's all I can afford and that's all I'm interested in. If you continue to be so...so..."

"Wonderful?" he supplied.

"Charming," she corrected, "then I'll have a whole lot to answer for when I don't see you again after Saturday."

"So you want me to limit the charm?"

"Please."

"I'll do my best," he said, and his eyes sparked with laughter, which they seemed to do a good deal of the time. If she hadn't been so flustered, she might have been pleased he found her so amusing.

"Thank you." She glanced pointedly at her watch. "Don't you think we should be heading back to the house?"

"No."

"No? I realize you told my mother we'd be gone an hour, but that really is too long and—"

"I'm taking you to Jackson Point."

Dianne's heart reacted instantly, zooming into her throat and then righting itself. Jackson Point overlooked a narrow water passage between the Kitsap Peninsula and Vashon Island. The view, either at night or during the day, was spectacular, but those who came to appreciate it at night were generally more interested in each other than the glittering lights of the island and Seattle farther beyond.

"I'll take the fact you're not arguing with me as a positive sign," he said.

"I think we should go back to the house," she stated with as much resolve as she could muster. Unfortunately it didn't come out sounding very firm. The last time she'd been to Jackson Point had been a lifetime ago. She'd been a high-school junior and madly in love for the first time. The last time.

"We'll go back to the house in a little while."

"Steve," she cried, fighting the urge to cry, "why are you doing this?"

"Isn't it obvious? I want to kiss you again."

Dianne pushed her hair away from her face with both hands. "I don't think that's such a good idea." Her voice wavered, sounding more like her teenage son than herself.

Before she could think of an argument, Steve pulled off the highway and down the narrow road that led to the popular lookout. She hadn't wanted to think about that kiss they'd shared. It had been a mistake. Dianne knew she'd disappointed Steve—not in the kiss itself, but in her reaction to it. He seemed to be waiting for her to admit how profoundly it had affected her, but she hadn't given him the satisfaction.

Now he wanted revenge.

Her heart continued to hammer when Steve stopped the truck and turned off the engine. The lights sparkled across the water in welcome. The closest lights were from Vashon Island, a sparsely populated place accessible only by ferry. The more distant ones came from West Seattle.

"It's really beautiful," she whispered. Some of the tension eased from her shoulders and she felt herself start to relax.

"Yes," Steve agreed. He moved closer and placed his arm around her shoulder.

Dianne closed her eyes, knowing she was not going to find the power to resist him. He'd been so wonderful with her children and her mother—more than wonderful. Now it seemed to be her turn, and try as she might to avoid it, she found herself falling a willing victim to his special brand of magic.

"You *are* going to let me kiss you, aren't you?" he whispered close to her ear.

She nodded.

His hands were in her hair as he directed his mouth to hers. The kiss was slow and easy, as though he was afraid of frightening her. His mouth was warm and moist over her own, gentle and persuasive. Dianne could feel her bones start to dissolve and knew that if she was going to walk away from this experience unscathed, she needed to think fast. Unfortunately, her thought processes were already overloaded.

When at last they drew apart, he dragged in a deep breath. Dianne sank against the cushion and noted that his eyes were still closed. Taking this moment to gather her composure, she scooted as far away from him as she could, pressing the small of her back against the door handle.

"You're very good," she said, striving to sound unruffled by the experience, and knowing she hadn't succeeded.

He blinked, opened his eyes and frowned. "I'll assume that's a compliment."

"Yes. I think you should." Steve was the kind of man who'd attract attention from women no matter where he went. He wouldn't be interested in a divorcée and a ready-made family, and there wasn't any use in trying to convince herself otherwise. The only reason he'd even agreed to take her to the Valentine's dinner was because she'd offered to pay him. This was strictly a business arrangement.

His finger lightly grazed the side of her face. His eyes were tender as he studied her, but he said nothing.

"It would probably be a good idea if we talked about Saturday night," she said, doing her best to keep her gaze trained away from him. "There's a lot to discuss and . . . there isn't much time left."

"All right." His wayward grin told her she hadn't fooled him. He knew exactly what she was up to.

"Since the dinner starts at seven, I suggest you arrive at my house at quarter-to."

"Fine."

"I don't think we need to go to the trouble or the expense of a corsage."

"What are you wearing?"

Dianne hadn't given the matter a second's thought. "Since it's a Valentine's dinner, something red, I suppose. I have a striped dress of red and white that will do." It was a couple of years old, but this dinner wasn't exactly the fashion event of the year, and she didn't have the money for something new, anyway.

She looked at her watch, although there wasn't any chance she could read the hands in the darkness.

"Is that a hint you want to get back to the house?"

"Yes," she said.

Her honesty seemed to amuse him. "That's what I thought." Without argument, he started the engine and put the truck into reverse.

The minute they turned onto her street, Jason and Jill came vaulting out the front door. Dianne guessed they'd both been staring out the upstairs window, eagerly awaiting her return.

She was wrong. It was Steve they were eager to see.

"Hey, what took you so long?" Jason demanded as Steve climbed out of the truck.

"Grandma's got the apple pie all dished up. Are you ready?" Jill hugged Steve's arm, glancing up anxiously at him.

Dianne watched the unfolding scene with dismay. Steve walked into her house with one arm around Jason and Jill clinging to the other.

It was as if she were invisible. Neither one of her children had said a single word to her!

To his credit, Jason paused at the front door. "Mom, you coming?"

"Just bringing up the rear," she muttered.

Jill shook her head, her young shoulders lifting, then falling, in a deep sigh. "You'll have to forgive my mother," she told Steve confidingly. "She can be a real slowpoke sometimes."

Chapter Seven

"OH, MOM," JILL SAID SOFTLY. "You look so beautiful."

Dianne examined her reflection in the full-length mirror once more. At the last moment, she'd been gripped by another bout of insanity. She'd gone out and purchased a new dress.

She couldn't afford it. She couldn't rationalize the expense on top of everything else, but the instant she'd seen the flowered pink creation hanging in the shop window, she'd decided to try it on. That was her first mistake. Correction: that was a mistake in a long list of recent ones where Steve Creighton was concerned.

The dress was probably the most flattering thing she'd ever owned. One look at the price tag had practically caused her to clutch her chest and stagger backward. She hadn't purchased it impulsively. No, she was too smart for that. The fact that she was nearly penniless and it was only the middle of the month didn't help matters. She'd sat down in the coffee shop next door and juggled figures for ten or fifteen minutes before crumpling up the paper and deciding to buy the dress, anyway. It was her birthday, Mother's Day and Christmas gifts to herself all rolled into one.

"I brought along my pearls," Martha announced as she breathlessly bolted into Dianne's bedroom. She was late, which wasn't like Martha, but Dianne hadn't been worried. She knew her mother would be there before she had to leave for the dinner.

Martha stopped abruptly, folding her hands prayerfully and nodding with approval. "Oh, Dianne. You look..."

"Beautiful," Jill finished for her grandmother.

"Beautiful," Martha echoed. "I thought you were going to wear the red dress."

"I just happened to be at the mall and stumbled across this." She didn't mention that she'd specifically made the trip into Tacoma for the express purpose of looking for something new to wear.

"Steve's here," Jason yelled from the bottom of the stairs.

"Here are my pearls," Martha said, reverently handing them to her daughter. The pearls were a family heirloom and worn only on the most special occasions.

"Mom, I don't know..."

"Your first official date with Steve," she insisted as though the event were on a level with God giving Moses the Ten Commandments. Without further ado, Martha formally draped the necklace around her daughter's neck. "I insist. Your father insists."

"Mom?" Dianne asked, turning around to search her mother's face. "Have you been talking to Dad again?" Dianne's father had been gone for more than ten years. However, for several years following his demise, Martha Janes claimed they carried on regular conversations.

"Not exactly, but I know your father would have insisted, had he been here. Now off with you. It's rude to keep a date waiting."

Before leaving her bedroom, Dianne briefly closed her eyes. She was nervous. Which was silly, she told herself. This wasn't a *real* date, since she was paying

Steve for the honor of escorting her. She'd reminded herself of that the entire time she was dressing. The only reason they were even attending this Valentine's dinner was because she'd asked him. Not only asked, but offered to pay for everything.

Jill rushed out of the bedroom door and down the stairs. "She's coming and she looks beautiful."

"Your mother always looks beautiful," Dianne heard Steve say matter-of-factly as she descended the first steps. Her eyes were on him, standing in the entryway dressed in a dark gray suit, looking tall and debonair.

He glanced up and his gaze found hers. She was gratified to note his eyes rounded briefly.

"I was wrong, she's extra beautiful tonight," he whispered, but if he was speaking to her children, he wasn't looking at them. In fact his eyes were riveted on her, which only served to make Dianne more uneasy.

They stood staring at each other like star-crossed lovers until Jill tugged at Steve's arm. "Aren't you going to give my mom the corsage?"

"Oh, yes, here," he said, looking as though he'd completely forgotten he was holding an octagon-shaped plastic box.

Dianne frowned. They'd agreed earlier he wasn't supposed to do this. She was already over her budget, and flowers were a low-priority item, as far as Dianne was concerned.

"It's one for the wrist," he explained, opening the box for her. "I thought you said the dress was red, so I'm afraid this might not go with it very well." Three white rosebuds were fashioned between a froth of red-and-white silk ribbons. Although her dress was several shades of pink, there was a spattering of red in the center of the flowers that matched the color in the ribbon perfectly. It was as if Steve had seen the dress and chosen the flowers to complement it. "It's . . ."

"Beautiful," Jill supplied once more, smugly pleased with herself.

"Are you ready to go?" Steve asked.

Jason stepped forward with her wool coat as though he couldn't wait to be rid of her. Steve took the coat from her son's hands and helped Dianne into it, while her son and daughter stood back looking as proud as peacocks for having arranged the entire affair.

Before she left the house, Dianne gave her children their instructions and kissed them each on the cheek. Jason wasn't much in favor of letting his mother kiss him, but he tolerated it.

Martha continued to stand at the top of the stairs, dabbing her eyes with a soft tissue and looking down as if the four of them together were the most romantic sight she'd ever witnessed. Dianne sincerely prayed that Steve didn't notice.

"I won't be late," Dianne said as Steve opened the front door.

"Don't worry about it," Jason said pointedly. "There isn't any need to rush home."

"Have a wonderful time," Jill called after them.

The first thing Dianne noticed once they were out the door was that Steve's tow truck was missing from her driveway. She looked around, half expecting to find the red monstrosity parked on the street.

With his hand cupping her elbow, he led her instead to a luxury car. "What's this?" she asked, thinking he might have rented it. If he had, she wanted it understood this minute that she had no intention of paying the fee.

"My car."

"Your car?" she asked. He opened the door for her and Dianne slid onto the supple white leather. Tow-truck operators apparently made better money than she'd assumed. If she'd known that, she would have offered him twenty dollars for this evening instead of thirty.

Steve walked around the front of the sedan and got into the driver's seat. They chatted on the short ride to the community center, with Dianne making small talk in an effort to cover her nervousness.

The parking lot was nearly full, but Steve found a spot on the side lot next to the sprawling brick building.

"You ready?" he asked.

She nodded. Over the years, Dianne had attended a dozen of these affairs. There was no reason to feel nervous. Her friends and neighbors would be there. Naturally there'd be questions about her and Steve, but this time she was prepared.

Steve came around the car, opened her door and handed her out. She noticed that he was frowning.

"Is something wrong?" she asked anxiously.

"You look pale."

She was about to explain it was probably nerves when he said, "Not to worry, I have a cure for that." Before she realized his intention, he leaned forward and brushed his mouth over hers.

He was right. The instant his lips touched hers, hot color exploded in her cheeks. She felt herself swaying toward him, and Steve caught her gently by the shoulders.

"That was a mistake," he whispered once they'd eased apart. "Now the only thing I'm hungry for is you. Forget the dinner."

"I...think we should go inside now," she said, glancing around the parking lot, praying no one had witnessed the kiss.

Light and laughter spilled out from the wide double doors of the Port Blossom Community Center. The soft strains of a romantic ballad beckoned them inside.

Steve took her coat and hung it on the rack in the entryway. She waited for him, feeling more jittery than ever. When he'd finished, Steve placed his arm about her waist and led her into the main room.

"Steve Creighton!" They had scarcely stepped into the room when Steve was greeted by a robust man with a salt-and-pepper beard. Glancing curiously at Dianne, the stranger slapped Steve on the back and said, "It's about time you attended one of our functions."

Steve introduced Dianne to the man, whose name was Sam Horton. The name was vaguely familiar to her, but she couldn't quite place it.

Apparently reading her mind, Steve said, "Sam's the president of the Chamber of Commerce."

"Ah, yes," Dianne said softly, impressed to meet one of the community's more distinguished members.

"My wife, Renée," Sam said, absently glancing around, "is somewhere in this mass of humanity." Then he turned back to Steve. "Have you two found a table yet? We'd consider it a pleasure to have you join us."

"Dianne?" Steve looked to her.

"That would be very nice, thank you." Wait until her mother heard this. She and Steve dining with the Chamber of Commerce president! Dianne couldn't help smiling. No doubt her mother would attribute this piece of good luck to the pearls. Sam left to find his wife, eager to introduce her to Dianne.

"Dianne Williams! It's so good to see you." The voice belonged to Betty Martin, who had crossed the room, dragging her husband, Ralph, along with her. Dianne knew Betty from the PTA. They'd worked together on the spring carnival the year before. Actually, Dianne had done the majority of the work while Betty had done the delegating. The experience had been enough to convince Dianne not to volunteer for this year's event.

Dianne introduced Steve to Betty and Ralph. Dianne felt a small sense of triumph to note the way Betty eyed Steve. This man was worth every single penny of the thirty dollars he was costing her!

The two couples chatted for a few moments, then Steve excused himself. Dianne watched him as he walked through the room, observing how the gazes of several women followed him. He did make a compelling sight, especially in his well-cut suit.

"How long have you known Steve Creighton?" Betty asked the instant Steve was out of earshot, moving closer to Dianne as though she was about to hear some well-seasoned gossip.

"A few weeks now." It was clear Betty was hoping Dianne would elaborate, but Dianne had no intention of doing so.

"Dianne." Shirley Simpson, another PTA friend, moved to her side. "Is that Steve Creighton you're with?"

"Yes." She'd had no idea Steve was so well known.

"I swear he's the cutest man in town. One look at him and my toes start to curl."

When she'd approached Steve with this proposal, Dianne hadn't a clue she would become the envy of her friends. She really *had* got a bargain.

"Are you sitting with anyone yet?" Shirley asked. Betty bristled as though offended she hadn't thought to ask first.

"Ah, yes. Sam Horton has already invited us, but thanks."

"Sam Horton," Betty repeated and she and Shirley shared a significant look. "My, my, you are traveling in elevated circles these days. Well, more power to you. And good luck with Steve Creighton. I've been saying for ages that it was time someone bagged him. I hope it's you."

"Thanks," Dianne said, feeling more than a little confused by this unexpected turn of events. Everyone knew Steve, right down to her PTA friends. It didn't make a lot of sense.

Steve returned a moment later, carrying two slender flutes of champagne. "I'd like you to meet some friends of mine," he said, leading her across the room to where several couples were standing. The wide circle opened up to include them. Dianne immediately recognized the mayor and a couple of others.

Dianne threw Steve a puzzled look. He certainly was a social animal, but the people he knew... Still, why should she be surprised? A tow-truck operator would have plenty of opportunity to meet community leaders. And Steve was such a likable man, who apparently made friends easily.

A four-piece band began playing forties' swing, and after the introductions, Dianne found her toe tapping to the sound.

"Next year we should make this a dinner-dance," Steve suggested, smiling down on Dianne. He casually put his hand on her shoulder as if he'd been doing that for months.

"Great idea," Port Blossom's mayor said, nodding. "You might bring that up at the March committee meeting."

Dianne frowned, not certain she understood. It was several minutes later before she had a chance to ask Steve about the comment.

"I'm on the board of directors for the community center," he explained briefly.

"You are?" Dianne took another sip of her champagne. Some of the details were beginning to get muddled in her mind, and she wasn't sure if it had anything to do with the champagne.

"Does that surprise you?"

"Yes. I thought you had to be, you know, a business owner or something to be on the board of directors."

Now it was Steve's turn to frown. "I am."

"You are?" Dianne asked. Her hand tightened around the long stem of her glass. "What business?"

"Port Blossom Towing."

That did it. Dianne drank what remained of her champagne in a single gulp. "You mean to say you *own* the company?"

"Yes. Don't tell me you didn't know."

She glared up at him, her eyes narrowed and distrusting. "I didn't know."

Chapter Eight

STEVE CREIGHTON had made a fool of her.

Dianne was so infuriated she couldn't wait to be alone with him so she could give him a piece of her mind. Loudly.

"What's that got to do with anything?" Steve asked.

Dianne continued to glare at him, unable to form any words yet. It wasn't just that he owned the towing company or even that he was a member of the board of directors for the community center. It was the way he'd deceived her.

"You should have told me you owned the company!" she hissed.

"I gave you my business card," he said, shrugging.

"You gave me your business card," she mimicked in a furious whisper. "The least you could have done was mention the fact. I feel like an idiot."

Steve was wearing a perplexed frown, as if he found her response completely unreasonable. "To be honest, I assumed you knew. I wasn't purposely keeping it from you."

That wasn't the only thing disturbing her, but the second concern was even more troubling than the first. "While I'm on the subject, what are you? Some sort of...love god?"

"*What?*"

"From the moment we arrived all the women I know, and even some I don't, have been crowding around me asking all sorts of leading questions. One friend claims you make her toes curl and an-other...never mind."

Steve looked exceptionally pleased. "I make her toes curl?"

How like a man to fall for flattery! "That's not the point."

"Then what is?"

"Everyone thinks you and I are an item."

"So? I thought that was what you wanted."

Dianne thought she was going to scream. "Kindly look at this from my point of view. I'm in one hell of a mess because of you!" He frowned as she elaborated. "What am I supposed to tell everyone, including my mother and children, once tonight is over?" Why, oh why hadn't she thought of this sooner?

"About what?"

"About you and me," she said slowly, softly, using short words so he'd understand. "I didn't even want to attend this dinner. I've lied to my own family and, worse, I'm actually paying a man to escort me. This is probably the lowest point of my life, and all you can do is stand there wearing a silly grin."

Steve chuckled and his mouth twitched as though he were struggling to restrain his amusement. "This silly grin you find so offensive is my besotted look. I've been practicing it in front of a mirror most of the week."

Dianne covered her face with her hands. "Now...now I discover that I'm even more of a fool than I realized. You're this upstanding businessman and, worse, a...a playboy."

"I'm not a playboy," he corrected.

"Maybe not—I wouldn't know about that part, but I do know that's the reputation you've got. There isn't a woman at this dinner who doesn't envy me."

The whole thing had taken such an unbearable turn, it was all Dianne could do not to break down and weep. All she'd wanted was someone presentable to escort her to this dinner so she could satisfy her children. She lived a quiet, uncomplicated life, and suddenly she was the most gossip-worthy member of tonight's affair.

Sam Horton stepped to the microphone in front of the hall and announced that dinner was about to be served, so would everyone please go to their tables.

"Don't look so discontented," Steve whispered in her ear. He was standing behind her, and his hands rested gently on her shoulders. "The woman who's supposed to be the envy of every other one here shouldn't be frowning. Try smiling."

"I don't think I can," she muttered, fearing she might break down and cry. Having Steve casually hold her this way wasn't helping. She found his touch reassuring and comforting when she didn't want either, at least not from him. She was confused enough. Her head was telling her one thing and her heart another.

"Trust me, Dianne, you're blowing this whole thing out of proportion. I didn't mean to deceive you. Let's enjoy the evening."

"I feel like such a fool." Several people walked past them on their way to the tables, pausing to smile and nod. Dianne did her best to respond appropriately.

"You're not a fool." He slipped his arm around her slim waist and led her toward the table where Sam and his wife, as well as two other couples Dianne didn't know, were waiting.

Dianne smiled at the others while Steve held out her chair. A gentleman to the very end, she thought wryly. He opened doors and held out chairs for her, and the whole time she was making an idiot of herself in front of an entire community.

As soon as everyone was seated, he introduced Dianne to the two remaining couples—Larry and Louise Lester, who owned a local restaurant; and Dale and Maryanne Atwater. Dale was head of the town's most prominent accounting firm.

The salads were delivered by young men in crisp white jackets. The Lesters and the Atwaters were making small talk, discussing the weather and other bland subjects. Caught in her own churning thoughts, Dianne ate her salad and tuned them out. When she was least expecting it, she heard her name. She glanced up to find six pairs of eyes studying her. She hadn't a clue why.

She lowered the fork to her salad plate and glanced at Steve, praying he'd know what was happening.

"The two of you make such a handsome couple," Renée Horton said. Her words were casual, but her look wasn't. Everything about her said she was intensely curious about Steve and Dianne.

"Thank you." Steve answered, then turned to Dianne and gave her what she'd referred to earlier as a silly grin and what he'd said was his besotted look.

"How did you two happen to meet?" Maryanne Atwater asked nonchalantly.

"Ah..." Dianne's mind spun, lost in a haze of half-truths and misconceptions. She didn't know if she dared repeat the story about meeting in the local grocery, but she couldn't think fast enough to come up with anything else. She thought she was prepared, but the moment she was in the spotlight, all her resolve deserted her.

"We both happened to be in the market at the same time," Steve explained smoothly. The story had been repeated so many times it was beginning to sound like the truth.

"I was blocking Steve's way in the frozen-food section," she said, picking up his version of the story. She felt embarrassed seeing the three other couples listening so intently to the fabrication.

"I asked Dianne to kindly move her cart, and she stopped to apologize for being so thoughtless. Before I knew it, we'd struck up a conversation."

"I was there!" Louise Lester threw her hands wildly into the air, her blue eyes shining. "That was the two of you? I saw the whole thing!" She dabbed the corners of her mouth with her napkin and checked to be sure she had everyone's attention before continuing. "I swear it was the most romantic thing I've ever seen."

"It certainly was," Steve added smiling over at Dianne, who restrained herself from kicking him in the shin, although it was exactly what he deserved.

"Steve's cart inadvertently bumped into Dianne's," Louise continued, grinning broadly at Steve.

"Inadvertently, Steve?" Sam Horton teased, chuckling loud enough to attract attention. Crazy though it was, it seemed that everyone in the entire community center had stopped eating in order to hear Louise tell her story.

"At any rate," Louise went on, "the two of them stopped to chat, and I swear it was like watching something out of a romantic comedy. Naturally Dianne apologized—she hadn't realized she was blocking the aisle. Then Steve started sorting through the items in her cart, teasing her. We all know how Steve enjoys kidding around.''

The others shook their heads, their affection for their friend obvious.

"She was buying all these diet dinners," Steve supplied, ignoring Dianne's glare. "I told her she couldn't possibly be buying those for herself."

The three women at the table sighed audibly. It was all Dianne could do not to slide off her chair and slip under the table.

"That's not the best part," Louise said, beaming with pride at the attention she was garnering. A dreamy look stole over her features. "They must have stood and talked for ages. I'd finished my shopping and just happened to stroll past them several minutes later, and they were still there. It was when I was standing in the checkout line that I noticed them coming down the aisle side by side, each pushing a grocery cart. It was so cute, I half expected someone to start playing a violin."

"How sweet," Renée Horton whispered.

"I thought so myself and mentioned it to Larry once I arrived home. Remember, honey?"

Larry nodded obligingly. "Louise must have told me that story two or three times that night," her husband reported.

"I just didn't realize that was you, Steve. Just imagine, out of all the people to run into the grocery and I just happen to stumble upon you and Dianne the first time you met. Life is so ironic, isn't it?"

"Oh, yes, life is very ironic," Dianne answered softly. Steve shared a subtle smile with her, and she couldn't hold one back herself.

"It was one of the most beautiful things I've ever seen," Louise finished.

"CAN YOU BELIEVE that Louise Lester?" Steve said later. They were sitting in his luxury sedan waiting for their turn to pull out of the crowded parking lot.

"No," Dianne said simply. She'd managed to make it through the rest of the dinner, but it had demanded every ounce of poise and self-control she possessed. From the moment they'd walked in the front door until the time Steve helped her put on her wool coat at the end of the evening, they'd been the center of attention. And the main topic of conversation.

Like a bumblebee visiting a flower garden, Louise Lester had breezed from one dinner table to the next spreading the story of how Dianne and Steve had met and how she'd been there to witness every detail.

"I've never been so..." Dianne couldn't think of a word that quite described how she'd felt. "This may well have been the worst evening of my life." She slumped against the back of the seat and covered her eyes.

"I thought you had a good time."

"How could I?" she cried, dropping her hand long enough to glare at him. "The first thing I get hit with is that you're some rich playboy."

"Come on, Dianne. Just because I happen to own a business doesn't mean I'm rolling in money."

"Port Blossom Towing is one of the fastest-growing enterprises in Kitsap County," she said, repeating what Sam Horton had been happy to tell her. "What I don't understand is why my mother hasn't ever heard of you. She's been on the lookout for eligible men for months. It's something of a miracle she didn't—'' Dianne stopped abruptly, pinching her lips together.

"What?" Steve pressed.

"My mother was looking, all right, but she was realistic enough to stay within my own social realm. You're a major-league player. The only men my mother knows are in the minors—butchers, teachers, everyday sort of guys."

Now that she thought about it, however, her mother had seemed to recognize Steve's name when Dianne had first mentioned it. She probably *had* heard of him, but couldn't remember from where.

"Major-league player? That's a ridiculous analogy."

"It isn't. And to think I approached you, offering you money to take me to this dinner." She stiffened, as humiliation washed over her again, then gradually she relaxed. "One thing I want to know—why you didn't already have a date." The dinner had been only five days away, and surely the most eligible bachelor in town, a man who could have his choice of women, would have had a date!

"Simple. I didn't have a sweetheart."

"I bet you got a good laugh over my offering to pay you to escort me." Not to mention the fact she'd made such a fuss over his owning a proper suit.

"As a matter of fact, I was flattered."

"No doubt."

"Are you still upset about that?"

"You could say that, yes." *Upset* was putting it mildly.

Since Dianne's house was only a couple of miles from the community center, she reached for her purse and checkbook. She waited until he pulled into the driveway and stopped, before writing out a check and handing it to him.

"What's this?" Steve asked.

"What I owe you. Since I didn't know the exact cost of Jill's stuffed animal, I made an educated guess. The cost of the roses varies from shop to shop so I took an average price."

"I don't think you should pay me until the evening is over," he said, opening his car door.

As far as Dianne was concerned it had been over the minute she'd learned who he was. When he came around to her side of the car and opened her door, she said, "Just what are you planning now?" He led her by the hand to the front of the garage, which was illuminated by a floodlight. They stood facing each other, his hands braced on her shoulders.

She frowned, gazing up at him. "I'm fully intending to give you your money's worth," he replied.

"I beg your pardon?"

"Jason, Jill and your mother."

"What about them?"

"They're peering out the front window waiting for me to kiss you, and I'm not about to disappoint any of them."

"Oh, no, you don't," she objected. But the moment his eyes held hers, all her anger drained away. Then, slowly, as though he recognized the change in her, he lowered his head. Dianne knew he was going to kiss her, and at the same instant she knew she wasn't going to do anything to stop him....

Chapter Nine

"YOU HAVE THE CHECK?" Dianne asked once her head was clear enough for her to think again. It was a struggle to pull herself free from the magic Steve wove so easily around her heart.

Steve pulled the check she'd written from his suit pocket. Then, without ceremony, he tore it in two. "I never intended to accept a penny."

"You have to! We agreed—"

"I want to see you again," he announced, gripping her shoulders firmly and looking intently at her.

Dianne was struck dumb. If he had announced he was an alien, visiting from the planet Mars, he couldn't have surprised her more. Not knowing what to say, she eyed him speculatively. "You're kidding, aren't you?"

A smile flitted across his lips as though he'd anticipated her reaction. The left side of his mouth canted slightly higher in that lazy, off-center grin of his. "I've never been more serious in my life."

Now that the shock had worn off, it took Dianne all of one second to decide. "Naturally, I'm flattered—but no."

"No?" Steve was clearly taken aback, and it took him a second or two to compose himself. "Why not?"

"You mean after tonight you need to ask?"

"Apparently so," he said, stepping away from her a little. He paused and shoved his fingers through his hair with enough force to make Dianne flinch. "I can't believe you," he muttered. "The first time we kissed

I realized we had something special. I thought you felt it, too.''

Dianne couldn't deny it, but she wasn't about to admit it, either. She lowered her gaze, refusing to meet the hungry intensity of his eyes.

When she didn't respond, Steve continued, "I have no intention of letting you out of my life. In case you haven't figured it out yet, and obviously you haven't, I'm crazy about you, Dianne."

Unexpected tears clouded her vision as her gaze briefly shot up to his. She rubbed the heels of her hands against her eyes and sniffled. This wasn't supposed to be happening. She wanted the break with him to be clean and final. No discussion. No tears.

Steve was handsome and ambitious, intelligent and charming. If anyone deserved an SYT it was this oh-so-eligible bachelor. She'd been married, and her life was complicated by two children and a manipulating mother.

"Say something," he demanded. "Don't just stand there looking at me with tears in your eyes."

"Th-these aren't tears. They're..." Dianne couldn't finish as fresh tears scalded her eyes.

"Tomorrow afternoon," he offered, his voice gentling, "I'll stop by the house, and you and the kids and I can all go to a movie. You can bring your mother along, too, if you want."

Dianne managed to swallow a sob. She held out her hand, scolding him with her index finger. "That's the lowest, meanest thing you've ever suggested."

His brow folded into a frown. "Taking you and the kids to a movie?"

"Y-yes. You're using my own children against me and that's—"

"Low and mean," he finished, scowling more fiercely. "All right, if you don't want to involve Jason and Jill, then just the two of us will go."

"I already said no."

"Why?"

Her shoulders trembled slightly as she smeared the moisture across her cheek. "I'm divorced." She said it as if it had been a well-kept secret and no one but her mother and children were aware of it.

"So?" He was still scowling.

"I have children."

"I know that, too. You're not making a lot of sense, Dianne."

"It's not that—exactly. You can date any woman you want."

"I want to date you."

"No!" She was trembling from the inside out. She tried to compose herself, but it was hopeless with Steve standing so close, looking as though he was going to reach for her and kiss her again.

When she was reasonably sure she wouldn't crumble under the force of her fascination with him, she looked him in the eye. "I'm flattered, really I am, but it wouldn't work."

"You don't know that."

"But I do, I do. We're not even in the same league, you and I, and this whole thing has got completely out of hand." She stood a little straighter as though the extra inch in height would help. "The deal was I pay you to escort me to the Valentine's dinner, but then I had to go complicate matters by suggesting you look smitten with me and you did such a good job of it that you've convinced yourself you're attracted to me and you aren't, you couldn't be."

"Because you're divorced and have two children," he repeated incredulously.

"You're forgetting about my manipulating mother."

Steve clenched his fists at his sides. "I haven't forgotten her. In fact, I'm grateful to her."

Dianne narrowed her eyes. "Now I know you can't be serious."

"Your mother's a real kick, and your kids are great, and in case you're completely blind, I think you're pretty wonderful yourself."

Dianne's finger fumbled with the pearls at her neck, twisting the strand between her fingers. The man who stood before her was every woman's dream, but she didn't know what was right anymore. She knew only one thing. After the way he'd humiliated her this evening, after the way he'd let her actually pay him to take her to this dinner, make a total fool of herself, there was no chance she could continue to see him.

"I don't think so," she said stiffly. "Goodbye, Steve."

"You really mean it, don't you?"

She was already halfway to the front door. "Yes."

"All right. Fine," he said, slicing the air with his hands. "If this is the way you want it, then fine, just fine." With that he stormed off to his car.

DIANNE KNEW that her family would give her all kinds of flack. The minute she walked in the door, Jason and Jill barraged her with questions about the dinner. Dianne was as vague as possible and walked up the stairs to her room, pleading exhaustion. There must have been something in her eyes that convinced her mother and children to leave her alone, because no one disturbed her again that night.

She awoke early the next morning, feeling more than a little out of sorts. Jason was already up, eating a huge bowl of cornflakes at the kitchen table.

"Well," he said, when Dianne walked into the kitchen, "when are you going to see Steve again?"

"Ah, I don't know." She put on a pot of coffee, doing her best to shove every thought of her dinner companion from her mind. And not succeeding.

"He wants to go out on another date with you, doesn't he?"

"Ah, I'm not sure."

"You're not sure?" Jason demanded. "How come? I saw you two get mushy last night. I like Steve, he's fun."

"Yes, I know," she said, standing in front of the coffee machine while the liquid dripped into the glass pot. Her back was to her son. "Let's give it some time. See how things work out," she mumbled.

To Dianne's relief, her son seemed to accept that and he didn't question her further. That wasn't the case, however, later that same day, with her mother.

"So talk to your mother," Martha insisted, working her crochet hook as she sat in the living room with Dianne. "All day you've been quiet."

"No, I haven't." Dianne didn't know why she denied it. Her mother was right, she had been introspective.

"The phone isn't ringing. The phone should be ringing."

"Why's that?"

"Steve. He met your mother, he met your children, he took you out to dinner..."

"You make it sound like we should be discussing wedding plans." Dianne had intended to be flippant, but the look her mother gave her suggested she shouldn't joke over something so sacred.

"When are you seeing him again?" Her mother tugged on her ball of yarn when Dianne didn't immediately respond, as if that might bring forth a response.

"We're both going to be busy for the next few days."

"Busy? You're going to let busy stand in the way of love?"

Dianne ignored the question. It was easier that way. Her mother plied her with questions on and off again for the rest of the day, but after repeated attempts to get something more out of her daughter and not succeeding, Martha reluctantly let the matter drop.

THREE DAYS after the Valentine's dinner, Dianne was shopping after work at a grocery store on the other side of town—she avoiding going anywhere near the one around which she and Steve had fabricated their story—when she ran into Betty Martin.

"Dianne," Betty called, racing down the aisle after her. Darn, thought Dianne. The last person she wanted to chitchat with was Betty, who was certain to be filled with questions about her and Steve.

She was.

"I've been meaning to phone you all week," Betty said, her smile so sweet Dianne felt as if she'd stepped into a vat of honey.

"Hello, Betty." She made a pretense of scanning the grocery shelf until she realized she was standing in front of the disposable-diaper section. She jerked away as though she'd been burned.

Betty's gaze followed Dianne's. "You know, you're not too old to have more children," she said. "What are you? Thirty-three, thirty-four?"

"Around that."

"If Steve wanted children you could—"

"I have no intention of marrying Steve Creighton," Dianne answered testily. "We're nothing more than friends."

Betty arched her eyebrows. "My dear girl, that's not what I've heard. Why, all of Port Blossom is buzzing with talk about you two. Steve's been such an elusive bachelor. He dates often, or so I've heard, but from what everyone is saying, and I do mean everyone, you've got him hooked. Why, the way he was looking at you Saturday night was enough to bring tears to my eyes. I don't know what you did to that man, but he's yours for the asking."

"I'm sure you're mistaken." Dianne couldn't very well announce she'd paid Steve to look besotted. He'd done such a good job of it that he'd convinced himself and everyone else he was head over heels in love with her.

Betty grinned. "I don't think so."

As quickly as she could, Dianne made her excuses, paid for her groceries and hurried home. Home, she soon discovered wasn't exactly a haven. Jason and Jill were waiting for her, and it wasn't because they were eager to carry in the grocery sacks.

"It's been three days," Jill said. "Shouldn't you have heard from Steve by now?"

"If he doesn't phone you, then you should call him," Jason insisted. "Girls do that sort of thing all the time now, no matter what Grandma says."

"I..." Dianne looked for an escape. Of course there wasn't one.

"Here's his card," Jason said, taking it from the corner of the bulletin board. "Call him."

Dianne stared at the raised red lettering. Port Blossom Towing, it said, with the phone number in large numbers below. In the corner, in smaller, less-pronounced lettering was Steve's name, followed with one simple word: owner.

Dianne's heart plummeted and she closed her eyes. He'd really meant it when he'd said he had never intentionally misled her. He assumed she knew, and with good reason. The business card he'd given her spelled it out, only she hadn't noticed.

"Mom." Jason's voice fragmented her introspection.

She opened her eyes to see her son and daughter staring up at her, their young eyes, so like her own, intent and worried.

"What are you going to do?" Jill wanted to know.

"W.A.R."

"Aerobics?" Jason said. "What for?"

"I need it," Dianne answered. And she did. Dianne had discovered long ago that when something was weighing on her, heavy-duty exercise helped considerably. It cleared her mind. She didn't enjoy it exactly; pain rarely thrilled her. But the aerobic classes at the community center had seen her through more than one emotional trauma. If she hurried, she could be there for the last session of the afternoon.

"Kids, put those groceries away for me, will you?" she said, heading for the stairs, ripping the sweater over her head as she raced. The buttons to her blouse were too time-consuming, so she peeled that over her head the moment she entered the bedroom, closing the door with her foot.

Within five minutes flat she'd changed into her leotard, kissed the kids and was out the door. She had a small attack of guilt when she pulled out of the driveway and glanced back to see both her children standing on the porch looking decidedly woebegone.

The warm-up exercises had already begun when Dianne joined the class. For the next hour she leapt, kicked, bent and stretched, doing her best to keep up with everyone else. By the end of the session, she was exhausted—and no closer to deciding whether or not to phone Steve.

With a towel draped around her neck, she walked out to her car. Her cardiovascular system might have been fine, but nothing else about her was. She searched through her purse for her keys and then her coat pocket.

Nothing.

Dread filled her. Cupping the sides of her face with her hands, she peered inside the car. There, innocently poking out of the ignition, were her keys.

Chapter Ten

"JASON," DIANNE SAID, closing her eyes in thanks that it was her son who had answered the phone and not Jill. Her daughter would have plied her with questions and more advice than "Dear Abby."

"Hi, Mom. I thought you were at aerobics."

"I am, and may be here a whole lot longer if you can't help me out." Without a pause, she continued, "I need you to go upstairs, look in my underwear drawer and bring me the extra set of keys to my car."

"They're in your underwear drawer?"

"Yes." It was the desperate plan of a desperate woman. She didn't dare contact the auto club this time for fear they'd send Port Blossom Towing to the rescue in the form of one Steve Creighton.

"You don't honestly expect me to sort through your, uh, stuff, do you?"

"Jason, listen to me, I've locked my keys in my car, and I don't have any other choice."

"You locked your keys in the car? Again? What's with you lately, Mom?"

"Do we need to go through all this now?" she demanded. Jason wasn't saying anything she hadn't already said to herself a hundred times over the past few minutes. She was so agitated it was a struggle not to break down and weep.

"I'll have Jill get the keys for me," Jason agreed, with a sigh that told her it demanded a good deal of effort, not to mention fortitude, for him to comply with this request.

"Great. Thanks." Dianne breathed out in relief. "Okay. Now the next thing you need to do is get your bicycle out of the garage and ride it down to the community center."

"You mean you want me to *bring* you the keys?"

"Yes."

"But it's raining!"

"It's only drizzling." True, but as a general rule Dianne didn't like her son riding his bike in the winter.

"But it's getting dark," Jason protested next.

That was something that did concern Dianne. "Okay, you're right. In that case, the best thing to do is call Grandma and ask her to stop off and get the keys from you and then have her bring them to me."

"You want me to call Grandma?"

"Jason, are you hard of hearing? Yes, I want you to call Grandma, and if you can't reach her, phone me back here at the community center. I'll be waiting by the phone." She read off the number for him. "And listen, if my car keys aren't in my underwear drawer, have Grandma bring me a wire clothes hanger, okay?"

He hesitated. "All right," he said after another burdened sigh. "Are you sure you're all right, Mom?"

"Of course I'm sure." But she was going to remember his attitude the next time he needed her to go on a Boy Scout camp-out with him.

Jason seemed to take an eternity to do as she'd asked. Since the front desk was now busy with the after-work crowd, Dianne didn't want to trouble the staff for the phone a second time to find out what was keeping her son.

Forty minutes after Dianne's aerobic class was over, she was still pacing the foyer of the community center, stopping every now and again to glance outside. Then, on one such glance she saw a big red tow truck turn into the parking lot.

She didn't need to be psychic to know that the man driving the truck was Steve.

Mumbling a curse under her breath, Dianne walked out into the parking lot to confront him.

Steve was standing alongside her car when she approached. She noticed that he wasn't wearing the gray-striped coveralls he'd worn the first time they'd met. Now he was dressed in slacks and a sweater, as though he'd come from the office.

"What are you doing here?" The best defense was a good offense, or so her high-school basketball coach had advised her about a hundred years ago.

"Jason called me," he said, without looking at her.

"The turncoat," Dianne muttered.

"He said something about refusing to search through your underwear and his grandmother couldn't be reached. And that all this has something to do with you going off to war."

Although Steve was speaking in an even voice, it was clear he found this situation comical.

"W.A.R. is my aerobics class," Dianne explained stiffly. "You don't need to look so concerned—I haven't volunteered for the French Foreign Legion."

"I'm glad to hear it." He walked around to the passenger-side door of the tow truck and brought out the instrument he'd used to open her door the first time. "So," he said leaning against the side of her compact. "How have you been?"

"Fine."

"You don't look so good, but then I suppose that's because you're a divorced woman with two children and a manipulating mother."

Naturally he'd taunt her with that. "How kind of you to say so," she returned with an equal dose of sarcasm.

"So how's Jerome?"

"Jerome?"

"The butcher your mother wanted to set you up with," he answered gruffly. "I figured by now the two of you would have gone out once, maybe a couple of times." His words had a biting edge.

"I'm not seeing Jerome." The thought of having to eat blood sausage was enough to turn her stomach.

"I'm surprised," he returned. "I'd have thought you'd leap at the opportunity to date someone other than me."

"If I wasn't interested in him before, what makes you think I'd go out with him now? And why aren't you opening my door? That's what you're here for, isn't it?"

He ignored her question. "Frankly, Dianne, we can't go on meeting like this."

"Funny, very funny." She crossed her arms defiantly.

"Actually I really came here to talk some sense into you," he said after a moment.

"According to my mother you won't have any chance of succeeding. I'm hopeless."

"I don't believe that. Otherwise I wouldn't be here." He walked over to her and gently placed his hands on her shoulders. "Maybe, Dianne, you've been fine these past couple of days, but frankly I've been a wreck."

"You have?" As Dianne looked at him she thought she'd drown in his eyes. And when he smiled, it was all she could do not to cry.

"I've never met a more stubborn woman in my life."

She blushed. "I'm awful, I know."

His gaze became more intent as he asked, "How about if we go someplace and talk?"

"I . . . think that would be all right." At the moment there was little she could refuse him. Until he'd arrived she'd had no idea what to do about the situation between them. Now the answer was becoming clear. . . .

"You might want to call Jason and Jill and tell them."

"Oh, right, I should." How could she have forgotten her own children? She began heading for the building.

Steve stopped her. He was grinning from ear to ear. "Don't worry, I already took care of that. While I was at it, I phoned your mother, too. She's on her way to your house now. She'll make the kids' dinner." He paused, then said, "I figured if I was fortunate enough I might be able to talk you into having dinner with me. I understand Walker's has an excellent seafood salad."

If he was fortunate enough he might be able to talk her into having dinner with him? Dianne felt like weeping. Steve Creighton was the sweetest, kindest, handsomest man she'd ever met, and *he* was looking at *her* as if he was the one who should be counting his blessings.

Steve promptly opened her car door. "I'm going to buy you a magnetic key attachment for keeping a spare key under your bumper so this doesn't happen again."

"You are?"

"Yes, otherwise I'm going to worry about you."

No one had ever worried about her, except her immediate family. Whatever situation arose, she handled it. Broken water pipes, lost checks, a leaky roof—nothing had ever defeated her. Not even Jack had been able to break her spirit, but one kind smile from Steve Creighton and she was a puddle of emotions. She blinked back tears and made a mess of thanking him, rushing her words so that they tumbled over each other.

"Dianne?"

She stopped and bit her lower lip. "Yes?"

"Either we go to the restaurant now and talk, or I'm going to kiss you right here in this parking lot."

Despite everything, she was able to smile. "It wouldn't be the first time."

"No, but I doubt I'd be content with one kiss."

She lowered her lashes, thinking she probably wouldn't be, either. "I'll meet you at Walker's."

He followed her across town, which took less than five minutes, and pulled into the empty parking slot next to hers. Once inside the restaurant, they were seated immediately at a table next to a window overlooking Sinclair Inlet.

Dianne had just picked up her menu when Steve said, "I'd like to tell you a story."

"Okay," she said, puzzled. She put aside the menu. Deciding what to eat took second place to listening to Steve.

"It's about a woman who first attracted the attention of a particular man at the community center about two months ago."

Dianne picked up her water and took a sip, her eyes meeting his above the glass, her heart thumping loudly in her ears. "Yes..."

"This certain lady was oblivious to certain facts."

"Such as?" Dianne prompted.

"First of all, she didn't seem to have a clue how attractive she was or how much this guy admired her. He did everything but stand on his head to attract her attention, but nothing worked."

"What exactly did he try?"

"Working out the same hours as she did, pumping iron—and looking exceptionally good in his T-shirt and shorts."

"Why didn't this man say something to...this woman?"

Steve chuckled. "Well, you see, he was accustomed to women giving him plenty of attention. So this particular one dented his pride by ignoring him, then she made him downright angry. Finally it occurred to him that she wasn't *purposely* ignoring him—she simply wasn't aware of him."

"It seems to me this man is rather arrogant."

"I couldn't agree with you more."

"You couldn't?" Dianne was surprised.

"That was when he decided there were plenty of other fish in the sea and he didn't need a pretty divorcée with two children—he'd asked around about her and so knew a few details like that."

Dianne smoothed the pink linen napkin across her lap. "What happened next?"

"He was sitting in his office one evening. The day had been busy and one of his men had phoned in sick, so he'd been out on the road all afternoon. He was feeling more than ready to go home and take a hot shower. Just about then the phone rang. One of the night crew answered it and it was the auto club. Apparently some lady had locked her keys in her car at the community center and needed someone to come rescue her.''

"So you, I mean, this man volunteered?"

"That he did, never dreaming she'd practically throw herself in his arms. And not because he'd unlocked her car, either, but because she was desperate for someone to take her to the Valentine's dinner.''

"That part about her falling into your arms is a slight exaggeration,'' Dianne felt obliged to tell him.

"Maybe so, but it was the first time a woman had ever offered to pay him to take her out. Which was the most ironic part of this entire tale. For weeks he'd been trying to gain this woman's attention, practically killing himself to impress her with the amount of weight he was lifting. It seemed every woman in town was impressed except the one who mattered.''

"Did you ever stop to think that was the very reason he found her so attractive? If she ignored him, then he must have considered her something of a challenge.''

"Yes, he thought about that a lot. But only after he met her and kissed her he realized that his instincts had been right from the first. He was going to fall in love with this woman.''

"He was?'' Dianne's voice was little more than a hoarse whisper.

"That's the second part of the story.''

"The second part?'' Dianne was growing confused.

"The happily-ever-after part.''

Dianne used her napkin to wipe away the tears, which had suddenly welled up in her eyes again. "He can't possibly know that."

Steve smiled then, that wonderful carefree, vagabond smile of his, the smile that never failed to lift her heart. "Wrong. He's known that for a good long while. All he needs to do now is convince her."

Sniffing, Dianne said, "I have the strangest sensation that this woman has real trouble recognizing a prince when she sees one. For a good portion of her life, she was satisfied with keeping a frog happy."

"And now?"

"And now she's... I'm ready to discover what happily-ever-after is all about."

SOME
KIND OF HERO

Leigh Michaels

A word from Leigh Michaels

I met my major Valentine on my first day of work as a newspaper reporter, when the editor called the chief photographer into his office and told him to issue me a camera and make sure I knew how to use it. My picture-taking lessons were not terribly successful—he still carries the Nikon, and I just tell him what I'd like photos of—but we've been together for seventeen Valentine's Days now, and each one gets better.

He's a lot more creative with romantic gestures than I am—he has wonderful taste in flowers and jewelry—but some of my sharpest memories are the unromantic ones, like our first date.

He was a divorced father with custody of his son and daughter at the time we met. Probably we would never have had a first date at all if I'd been dry and dressed when he telephoned to ask me to come over for dinner. But I had just stepped out of the bathtub, and it was easier to say yes than to drip all over the carpet while I found an excuse.

His four-year-old son answered the door. Cute. Blond. Blue-eyed. Charming. Excited at having company. Eager to keep me entertained while Daddy finished up the meat loaf.

He was entertaining, all right. Within five minutes, this delightful child had slapped a set of handcuffs on me.

No problem, said his father. Except— hmm. Is that the set with the missing key?

It was. By the time he'd picked the lock, the meat loaf was cold, the ice was long broken, and I'd had a perfect opportunity to admire his hands—beautifully shaped, sensitive hands that are one of his best features. I think I was in love before the evening was over.

It hasn't all been sunshine and roses, of course. After that introduction, I should have known the household could only get zanier. But we're honestly best friends—and sometimes we even read each other's minds.

Last February, I was writing *Some Kind of Hero*. He hadn't read a word of it yet, but he came home on Valentine's Day with three pots of purple crocus. I laughed so hard at the irony that I hurt his feelings, and then had to explain why it was so funny—and why it was the most perfect gift I could have received.

But in fact, it wasn't. And the perfect gift isn't roses and diamonds, either. The best gifts from my Valentine are the laughter he brings to me and the fact that no day ever passes without him saying, "Have I told you today that I love you?"

So this story is for you, Michael William Lemberger. I'll have it framed, and you can hang it right next to the plaque with the handcuffs on it.

And by the way...have I told you today that I love you?

Chapter One

LAUREN LEANED into the display window and pushed at the crumpled sheets of red tissue paper that lined it. If she flattened an area at the corner, there would be room for a small velvet box to nestle comfortably, almost against the plate glass, where no passer-by could miss the ruby-studded ring it held. And then...should she put out that sterling-silver bracelet with the heart-shaped links, or would the window look better with only gold?

She drew back to study the effect. It was hard to tell from her position inside the store what the finished window looked like from the outside. From this angle, it was impossible to tell if the glorious diamond in the necklace that was the centerpiece of her display caught the spotlight and fractured it into a dazzling rainbow, or if it looked as dull as a rock instead. She glanced out to the street, her head to one side, and then looked thoughtfully over her shoulder at the girl who was straightening the trays of diamond engagement rings in the display case across the store. "Kim," she began, "could you give me a hand with this window?"

Kim didn't look up. "If you're going to suggest that I stand on the street and tell you in sign language when you've got each piece of jewelry at the right angle, don't even think about it."

Lauren laughed. "I wasn't—not exactly."

"Good. Because I'm not going out. Haven't you noticed? It's sleeting now."

She was right. The January wind had shifted, too, and pellets of frozen rain were rattling against the plate glass. Lauren shivered. "It's inside work," she said. "Just hand me things, will you? I can't keep crawling in and out, but I can't reach both the window and my supplies."

Kim locked the engagement rings into the display case and crossed the room. "Why can't you crawl in and out? It would certainly draw a crowd."

Lauren made a face at her. "Hand me that white leather glove. And the ruby dinner ring— No, not that one. The really exotic marquise with the baguette diamonds."

Kim picked up the glove and the velvet box from the assortment scattered over the top of the display case and looked thoughtfully out at the storm. "I may not go outside ever again. At least not till spring."

From the back of the display area, the owner of the jewelry store sniffed. "As long as you're not going anywhere," he said, "do you suppose you could manage to do some real work, instead of simply leaning on a display case looking decorative?"

Kim shrugged. "I can't sell things if there are no customers, Mr. Baines," she pointed out sweetly. The instant the man vanished into his office, she tugged hard at Lauren's sleeve. "I thought he'd never leave," she said in a rush, "and he might be back any instant, and I've been choking myself to keep from asking since I came in the door this morning. Ward got the tickets for you, didn't he? How can you be so calm about it?"

Lauren's hand trembled just a little as she slid the ring onto the proper finger of the glove, so it looked like the languid white hand of a ghostly lady, draped across the red tissue. But her voice was perfectly calm. She had known, of course, that this would happen, and she had rehearsed the conversation in the mirror. "No," she said. "He didn't."

Kim's mouth dropped open. "But he said—" It was practically a screech. "Some birthday! I thought Ward told you it was going to be a special celebration."

"He did. And it was. We had a very nice evening at his apartment, and he cooked steaks, and—"

"He didn't even take you out to *dinner?*"

"—gave me a book I've been longing to read, and—"

Kim dismissed the book with a gesture that verged on obscene. "How perfectly romantic!" she said dryly. "You were counting on those tickets, Lauren. What a horrible thing to do to you. Aren't you just furious at him?"

Lauren had to swallow hard to keep from agreeing, but admitting that to Kim would only encourage her to continue, and Lauren wasn't sure her pride could take much more.

If only Ward had not told her that he wanted to keep his plans for the "very special celebration" of her birthday a surprise, she might not have let herself hope so much. She had been a fool, perhaps, but after that buildup, how could she help but be disappointed by an ordinary dinner and an ordinary book? Oh, the food had been wonderful, and she would genuinely enjoy the book, but how could things like that compare to the much-coveted tickets to the Hunter Dix concert?

The biggest trouble with Ward, she thought, was that there was not a single romantic bone in his body. If there had been, he would appreciate Hunter Dix's music—the most touching love songs anyone in the world was singing today—and he would not have to be told why his concert tonight was so important to Lauren.

"He knew how much you want to go," Kim wailed. "How could he *not* get you the tickets?"

Lauren had practiced the answer to that, and it came out sounding rather flat. "The same way you and I missed out on getting them. There just weren't enough to go around, and they were snapped up by the members of the group that's sponsoring the whole event."

"A bit selfish of them, I'd say," Kim said unforgivingly. "Just because we're not alumni of the college doesn't mean we're the dirt under their feet. They could have given us ordinary people a chance to buy them. But Ward knows enough of those people. Surely he could have talked a couple of tickets out of one of his doctor friends."

"Apparently not. The few that aren't held by fans are in the hands of the scalpers, and they want a fortune. I can't blame Ward for not wanting to spend so much money on a single evening's entertainment."

Kim didn't believe a word of it, and Lauren had to admit it sounded rather unconvincing. But how was she supposed to convince Kim when she wasn't convinced herself? she thought rebelliously. Kim was right; she was absolutely livid at Ward. She would walk on ground glass to be able to go to that concert, but just because Ward didn't happen to like Hunter Dix and his kind of music, he wouldn't ask his friends if they had extra tickets. He wouldn't do even that much for her....

"Ward is a jerk," Kim said, under her breath.

The comment startled Lauren back into sanity. "No, he's not," she said soberly. "He's a very nice guy who just doesn't understand that this is the best chance I'll ever have to see Hunter Dix in person—" She stopped and bit her lip, and went on in a very small voice, "The best chance I'll ever have to actually see and hear the best singer in the world."

"Well, you'd better think twice before you marry him," Kim said unsympathetically, "or you'll never have a chance to go anywhere or see anybody."

Lauren looked at her in surprise. "Who said I was going to marry Ward?"

Kim shrugged. "Everybody on the street thinks you're practically engaged. And you certainly act like it. You never date anyone else."

That was true enough, and Lauren thought about it while she finished trimming the window, scattering pink marshmallow hearts and red silk roses among the jewelry. She had been dating Ward for months, and oh so slowly she'd stopped seeing anyone else. She almost hadn't noticed the change, for Ward had filled her time, and she liked him better than anyone else she had ever dated. So much better, in fact, that only yesterday it wouldn't have bothered her to know that everyone along the close-knit little street assumed that someday they would marry.

Whereas today... today it bothered her a lot.

BY MIDAFTERNOON it was almost dark, the wind had come up, and the sleet had turned to steady snow. The small flakes whipped against Lauren's face with cutting force as she walked slowly down Poplar Street toward the pharmacy. It wasn't that she really wanted to go there, but the pharmacy's snack counter was the only place in this small retail district to have lunch or get a cup of coffee. And she couldn't help the fact that Ward owned the pharmacy. She certainly wasn't trying to avoid him, was she?

Alma, the motherly woman behind the snack counter, had a cup and saucer already out for her when Lauren sat down. "Coffee or tea today, Lauren?" she asked. "Or hot chocolate? I made it from scratch. Ward will be right down— I made sure he knew you were here."

"Thanks," Lauren said dryly. She remembered hearing much the same words on a dozen other occasions, but they had never grated on her quite this way before. "Tea, please."

She sat dunking her tea bag in the hot water and looking at nothing. Kim was right, then. Everybody on Poplar Street did assume that she and Ward had some sort of private understanding about their future—together.

But the fact was, they did not. Until today, it hadn't occurred to her to wonder about it, but now that she gave it some thought, the question made her feel almost queasy. Surely if Ward was serious he would have said something by now—not a proposal, perhaps, but something that indicated his intentions. And since he had not, in all these months, did that mean that he was contented to leave things just as they were? Birthday dinners, movies, pleasant Sunday afternoon drives—going on straight into the indefinite future?

A big hand brushed gently over her hair. It was typical of Ward's greetings; in public, there would be a restrained touch and a private smile, but never a kiss. Funny, she thought, that it had not occurred to her before. It wasn't that he had a distaste for physical contact, she knew, for last night, when she had arrived at his apartment, he had kissed her so long and thoroughly that she'd been practically smoldering by the time he'd finished. So what caused this hesitation now? Was it simply that he didn't want to commit himself in public?

"Sorry," Ward said briskly as he sat down beside her. "Everybody in the whole town has the blasted flu, and I'm an hour behind on filling prescriptions. I can't even stop for coffee."

She didn't lift her eyes from the surface of her cup. "That's certainly good for business."

"Yes, but if I had my choice... Are you trying to drown that poor tea bag?" he asked, with a hint of laughter. "Lauren..."

She looked up, then, into his face. His eyes were deep set and a wonderful shade of coffee brown, especially when they were lit by a smile, as now, and he had the world's longest lashes. It was a pleasant face, well put together, though not exactly handsome. His nose had character; his mouth was generous; his ears were a little large—or did they look that way only because of the sternly conservative cut of his dark hair?

She had teased him once about his haircut, and he had confided the advice he'd been given by the previous owner of the pharmacy, who had warned him that people found it hard to trust a man who looked too young, no matter how solid his qualifications. "I can't exactly make myself look wrinkled and stooped," Ward had finished, "but I can be careful about my haircut and my clothes and the way I talk and act, so that I look solid and trustworthy and not like some harebrained kid."

Lauren had listened, straight-faced, and then solemnly recommended that he have half of his hair surgically removed and the remainder dyed gray. That was when she first discovered the dimple lurking at the corner of his mouth, just waiting for him to laugh, and she had promptly forgotten haircut and all in her fascination with that improbable little dent in his cheek.

It was so fascinating, in fact, she told herself, that she hadn't ever noticed how stubborn his chin was, and how unyielding the line of his jaw.

That wasn't fair, she told herself. After all, no two people can agree on everything, and if they did it would make life pretty boring.

But still... Ward didn't even seem to know how much she had been hoping for those tickets! He hadn't any idea, despite all her hints, how important it was to her. He obviously hadn't wanted to get the message. She wondered what he would have said if she had come straight out and told him how much she wanted to go to that concert?

He was watching her, too, and his eyes were twinkling. "For an older woman," he teased, "you're holding up really well—"

"Ward," she said abruptly, "could you try once more to get just two tickets?"

He sighed. "Are we back to what's-his-name again?"

"Don't worry," she said grimly. "I'm not asking you to come along. The tickets are for Kim and me."

"Lauren, there just aren't any."

"If the price is right, someone will sell. You certainly know enough people who have tickets, Ward. And you don't need to be concerned about what it costs. I'll pay you for them."

He said quietly, "It's that important to you."

It was not a question, but she nodded, anyway. "Ward, please." It was a bare whisper.

"All right," he said, his voice still quiet. "I'll try. But—"

"Thank you." It was cool.

Ward pushed himself off the stool. "I'd better get back to work, or I'll be two hours behind." His hand flicked over her hair again, and revealed the sparkle of diamonds on her earlobe. "New earrings?" he asked casually.

Lauren nodded.

He tucked a windblown blond lock of hair behind her ear, and studied the inch-long curve of glittering stones, half a carat's worth in each ear. "They're pretty. I'll let you know what I find out."

"I'll be at the store until six."

She didn't watch him go. Alma came to clear away the mess, and eyeing the earrings, said, "I'd be afraid to wear that sort of thing myself. I'd be petrified of losing one."

"No big deal. They're insured." Lauren paid for her tea and went back to work. Her hopes were no better about the odds of getting a ticket, but at least she had done the best she could.

Mr. Baines was arranging a new shipment of pearls in the velvet-lined case. "Did anybody notice the earrings?" he asked eagerly. At Lauren's nod, he beamed. "I knew having you wear them would be a good idea—those perfect earlobes of yours make a great advertisement. Wear them for a week or so, all right?" He didn't wait for an answer, but went off toward his workroom, whistling.

"Perfect earlobes," Kim muttered, on her way to the door for her own afternoon break. "You've got perfect hands, too, long and slender and just right to show off dinner rings. And that throat . . . We should all be so lucky."

Lauren grimaced at her. "I thought you weren't ever going outside again."

Kim let her coat slide off her shoulders and gave it a backward kick into an out-of-sight corner. "Not right now, I'm not."

Lauren looked at the cast-aside wrap with concern; it wasn't like Kim, the clotheshorse, to mistreat her things like that. But Kim's face was rapt as she stared out the window, and instead of saying anything, Lauren followed her gaze and found herself looking at a long white car that had pulled up just in front of the jewelry store. "What on earth?"

"You might as well ask," Kim said. "That, my friend, is a limousine. A Cadillac limousine."

"I know a limousine when I . . ." Lauren's voice trailed off.

"But how many people do you know who might be riding around this city today in one?"

A man in a dark uniform and a gold-braided cap got out of the driver's seat and opened the limousine's rear door for his passengers.

"That's Hunter Dix," Lauren whispered, as the famous profile came into view. "And he's coming in here."

THE UNIFORMED DRIVER climbed back into the car, and Hunter Dix turned toward the jewelry store. The two burly men with him wore very dark glasses.

What a hoot, Lauren thought. As if they needed protection from brilliant sunshine instead of the gray gloom of a winter storm.

One of the men came in, glanced around the store and then jerked his head to the other, who held the door for Hunter Dix and followed him in.

Of course, Lauren thought. They were bodyguards, and the dark glasses allowed them to look around without it being obvious what they were looking at. Bodyguards—she hadn't thought, before, about the need for them. Hunter Dix probably couldn't go anywhere without them, for fear of being mobbed by fans.

Across the store, Kim fiddled with her glasses and said nervously, "Mr. Dix...can I help you find something?"

He glanced at the display of engagement rings and matching wedding bands in the glass case in front of her and said, with a wry smile, "Not that sort of thing, I'm afraid."

His voice was softer than Lauren had expected, but then she'd only heard it amplified and recorded; of course it would be different in person. It was more intimate, somehow, and it seemed to sweep around her in waves and tickle in her ears.

He turned toward Lauren. "Now that's the kind of thing I'm looking for," he murmured, and crossed the store, silent footed, looking straight into her face. His eyes were big and icy blue and magnetic, and he did not blink.

Lauren swallowed hard. He was not as tall as she had thought he would be—not even as tall as Ward—and that surprised her. The oversize trench coat he wore was belted but not buttoned, and its bulk made him look thinner than she had expected. His hair was longer than in most of his photographs; it rested, curling softly, on his collar. And his face—it, too, was subtly different, for no photograph could possibly capture the intensity of his eyes and the charm of his slightly crooked smile as he studied her face....

"Now that's the kind of thing I'm looking for," he repeated softly, and then added calmly, "Gold chains, that is."

Lauren turned to the case at her elbow and unlocked it. "Of course," she said. "What else?"

He laughed delightedly. "So you're not impressed with me, are you." It was more a statement than a question.

"Impressed?" Kim had found not only her tongue, but her feet, for she appeared at Lauren's elbow. "Of course she's impressed. You're her hero."

Lauren ignored Kim and began laying out chains on a black velvet background. "What sort of thing are you looking for, Mr. Dix? Do you prefer fine gold, or something that is a little less pure but more durable? And is it for yourself, or is it a gift?"

He stretched out a hand and picked up a diamond-cut rope. "For myself," he said.

"Is it true, then?" Both of Kim's elbows were propped on the case. "What the tabloids said, that she left you? The actress, I mean."

Seemingly undisturbed by such blatant curiosity, he smiled ruefully. "Don't remind me. For once they got it right, yes."

"And she broke your heart." Kim sighed. "I'm so awfully sorry that it almost breaks my heart, too."

He looked startled, and then a light that was almost amusement sprang into his eyes. "Does it? How lovely of you. And what about your modest friend, hmm?" He swung the chain and watched it catch the light, and then laid it down, leaned on the counter and looked into Lauren's eyes. "So I'm your hero? What's your name? I'll sing a song for you tonight."

She couldn't quite get a full breath. Just being so close to him was putting clamps around her chest, and the idea of a song, just for her... "I—I'm afraid I won't be at the concert. I couldn't get tickets."

He frowned. Then he raised his hand from the gold chain he'd been caressing and snapped his fingers. "Two passes," he said, without even looking over his shoulder, and one of the bodyguards pulled an envelope from the inside breast pocket of his jacket.

Kim started to shriek, then clapped her hands over her mouth. Mr. Baines rushed out of the workroom, his mouth open in shock and his jeweler's eyepiece still firmly over one eye. The combination made him look vaguely like a trout. "Is there a problem?" he said.

Lauren imagined Mr. Baines thought his tone sounded menacing; it came out with a waver, instead. "It's all right," she managed. "I think Mr. Dix has found a chain he'd like, that's all."

Hunter Dix snapped his fingers again at the bodyguard who had handed him the passes. "Take care of this," he said. "I'll take this one...this one...and this one...and this one..." The guard picked up the selected chains with surprisingly delicate fingers until his hand was almost full.

"But the prices," Lauren said helplessly as she watched her inventory being rapidly depleted. "I didn't even tell you the prices."

"I hate being bothered with things like that," Hunter Dix murmured. "I'd much rather hear your name."

But it was Kim who obliged, and eagerly. The singer filled out the passes himself and signed them with a flourish. "These will get you backstage, too, so do come and say hello. And there will be a song for each of you tonight," he promised lavishly as he wrapped Kim's fingers around her pass. But when Lauren reached for hers, he caught her hand and raised it to his mouth, lingering over her fingertips, kissing each one.

Mr. Baines was writing up the bill, looking less distressed by the moment. The guard fingered one of the chains and said, "Hey, it's an honor to you to have Mr. Dix wearing your product. How about giving him a break on the price since he's buying so many?"

"Alec," Hunter Dix said between gritted teeth, "you idiot, not *here*." He smiled at Lauren and murmured, "Brains so seldom go with size, you know."

The bodyguard scowled and began peeling bills off a sizable roll into Mr. Baines's hand, and then Hunter Dix and his retinue were gone, a mere memory except for the two bits of cardboard that Kim was waving over her head as she did a joyful jig in the middle of the store.

It had really happened, Lauren told herself blankly. He had really been here. *And I'm really going to the concert.*

Well, she thought. That should put Ward in his place—but good.

THE REST OF THE AFTERNOON was a loss; every time one of them caught the other's eye, Lauren and Kim were off in a spasm of delighted giggles, and Mr. Baines would make a snide remark about their attitude toward work. Even he couldn't be too annoyed, however, considering Hunter Dix and the gold chains and the infusion of cash into the register that afternoon, and so he finally left them alone and retreated to his workroom.

Kim was leaning against a case, holding out the hand that the singer had caressed and studying it, when a longtime customer came in to have Mr. Baines check a loose stone in her diamond ring.

"I will never wash this hand again," Kim was vowing as Lauren came back from the workroom with the finished ring. "Never. I swear."

"You'll look pretty funny with one grubby hand," the customer said. "But it's more than most of the fans will have. Too bad about the concert, isn't it?"

There was nothing save good humor in her voice, but Lauren's throat closed up. "What do you mean, the concert?"

"Hadn't you heard? It's been canceled. The wind is up to gale force now—so strong that the airport's had to close, and that means Hunter Dix's backup musicians are stranded in Chicago. Since they can't get here, he can't perform. That's that."

Lauren thought for an instant that the floor had dropped out from under her.

"It's kind of funny, really," the customer's relentlessly cheerful voice went on. "All the talk about this exclusive concert, and now it'll never happen. All those uppity, educated people at the college, and they didn't have enough sense to schedule a thing like that for some other time than the last day of January. Ought to have known Mother Nature wouldn't cooperate. Thanks, Lauren.'' She slid the ring back onto her age-spotted hand and gathered up her shopping bags.

Lauren peered out the window and watched her walk down the street. The woman hadn't been kidding about the wind, for she was bent almost double as she struggled against it.

"I think I am going to kill myself," Kim said. "Diamonds cut glass. I wonder if they'd cut my wrists."

Lauren didn't even answer; the lump in her throat was far too large. She could live without going to the concert, she thought. But to have the damned pass in her hand—not just a ticket, but a personal backstage pass!—and then to have the whole thing snatched away... It was too much to bear.

Mindlessly, automatically, she went through the routine of closing the store, putting the most valuable of the merchandise in the huge old double-locked safe, closing out the cash register, putting the afternoon's receipts in the bank bag to be dropped off on her way home. Only the familiarity of the routine saved her; if someone had asked whether she had done the work, she would not have known.

She was not surprised when Ward came up behind her at the night-deposit drop at the bank; the pharmacy closed at six, too, and she frequently saw him there. It was where they had met, actually. One evening last summer she'd forgotten to zip the bank bag and then had stumbled and dropped it at his feet, letting change bounce in the gutter and checks flutter off in the breeze, and he had helped her chase it all down....

But she didn't want to think about that, tonight, and so she said, rather formally, "I hope you didn't go to much trouble over the tickets this afternoon."

He nodded. "I heard you'd managed it yourself, after all. Poplar Street has been buzzing about the visit all afternoon." There was an odd overtone to his voice. Was it a note of warning?

She knew it was foolish to be angry at Ward; it wasn't his fault that the weather had gone foul. But she heard herself saying, "I suppose you're happy the concert has been canceled!"

"Of course I'm not happy. Lauren, I really did try my best. I just didn't realize, before, how strongly you felt about it."

She didn't answer.

After a moment he said, "It's too cold to stand here, that's for sure, and I have to go back to the store, anyway— I have another batch of prescriptions to get ready before the delivery van comes back. How about later? Would you like to go to a movie?"

She shook her head silently.

Ward's eyebrows shot up. "I see," he said quietly. "You'd rather just go home and feel sorry for yourself."

Lauren didn't feel cold anymore; the heat of anger started clear in her toes and swept over her like a wave. "That is the most heartless thing anyone has ever said to me!"

He said quietly, "I'm sorry, Lauren. You've got a right to be disappointed. Well, see you tomorrow, then." He turned back toward the pharmacy, his long stride consuming the distance. Within three steps he had been nearly swallowed by the gloom. If it hadn't been for his height and his broad shoulders, he would have vanished altogether.

She almost called him back, but she swallowed the words and turned toward the parking lot instead. She didn't need any more lectures or sermons tonight, that was certain. And if she wanted to go home and sit by the fire and think of what could have been, what business was that of Ward's?

She didn't hear the limousine until it pulled up beside her and the darkened rear window slid down. "Lauren Hodges," said a voice that there could be no mistaking, and her heartbeat started to quicken. "You've no idea how lucky I feel to see you. Will you take pity on a stranger in your town—an unemployed stranger, at that—and let me take you to dinner?"

She thought about it, for five endless seconds. Having dinner with Hunter Dix was the chance of a lifetime, but—as he'd said himself—he was a stranger; a wise woman did not get into a car and go off with a man she didn't know. Ward would be absolutely livid at the idea, she thought.

She stepped over the hump of snow at the edge of the street and into the limousine without another thought.

Chapter Two

SHE WAS VAGUELY disappointed by the back of the limousine, but she couldn't have said just why. It was nicely lined with butter-soft black leather, and fitted out with a television, a tape player, a telephone and a refrigerator.

So what on earth more had she expected, Lauren asked herself with a jeer. A full-fledged bar, complete with bartender? A pint-size hot tub surrounded by bathing beauties? If that had been so, Hunter Dix wouldn't have been looking out the window!

"The people at the hotel recommended Marconi's," he said. "So unless you have a better suggestion..."

She sank down beside him; the bodyguards were occupying the facing seats. "That's the best place in town." Then, a bit too late, she saw the trendy rip in the knee of his jeans, and swallowed hard. Marconi's was the town's premier restaurant, and it had a dress code to match. But surely they wouldn't throw Hunter Dix out, no matter what. Would they?

The maître d' looked askance at his famous guest, but the ripped jeans and the lack of a jacket and tie seemed to fade as one of the bodyguards murmured in the man's ear and warmly pressed his hand. From the sudden smile that dawned on the maître d's face, Lauren judged it must have been a sizable banknote that had slipped from palm to palm.

The maître d' held her chair, and Hunter Dix seated himself opposite her. Lauren glanced over at the bodyguards, three tables away, and raised her eyebrows.

"The poor guys get tired of looking at me," the singer said, and that engagingly crooked smile lit his face. It seemed to light a candle in her heart, and she relaxed. Why should she be so concerned about his clothes? There was nothing really wrong with his appearance, now that the rip had disappeared under the table. And what did the rules matter, after all? Certainly they didn't seem to trouble him.

Ward, now, would never have dreamed of walking through the Marconi's front door in ripped jeans. He didn't have the self-assurance that Hunter Dix had, Lauren thought, and—she smiled a little to herself— he probably didn't even own a pair of ripped jeans. Last fall he had helped her clean up her lawn and get it ready for winter, and even after a full day of digging up flowerbeds and pushing the mower he had looked cool and unsmudged and almost *neat,* for heaven's sake. She had been tempted to push him into the compost pile just to see what he'd look like with dirt all over him, except that he'd probably have dragged her in, as well.

"You are a beautiful lady," Hunter Dix whispered.

There were steel bands around her chest, keeping her from breathing right. "Mr. Dix—"

"I'm Hunter, to my friends." He reached for her hand, and held the curve of her fingers to his cheek. "Your hair looks as if it's been kissed by starlight—it has the strangest silvery glow."

Ward had told her once that her hair looked almost dusty under certain lights— Dammit, Lauren told herself, I am not going to think about Ward again!

"Tell me what that was all about this afternoon, when the old guy came flying out of the back room," her companion prompted.

The waiter arrived with champagne, somewhat to Lauren's surprise. Had it even been ordered? Hunter tasted it and shook his head, and the waiter retreated, silently, with the bottle.

"The old man," Hunter prompted again. He was stroking the back of her hand with his fingertips, and it took an effort to pull her mind back to his question.

"Mr. Baines?" she said. "Oh, well, just think about it. It's his store. He hears a shriek from one of his staff, and the first thing he sees is two big bruisers in dark glasses, looking as if they're ready to haul the safe away, to say nothing of everything in the display cases."

Hunter was shifting his grip on her fingers from one hand to the other. He frowned a little, as if he was preoccupied.

"I just meant," Lauren said hesitantly, "that I wondered myself for a second if your bodyguards were getting ready to rob the place."

He smiled then. "I suppose I've gotten too used to having them around to think about what other people see," he said, and she laughed.

The second bottle of champagne arrived; this one was satisfactory, and the waiter was filling their glasses when a teenage girl fluttered up to the table to ask for an autograph. Before she could get all the words out, a bodyguard materialized beside her and urged her gently away. Lauren would have liked to kick the bodyguard in the shin; the girl looked so disappointed, and it would have taken such a little time and effort to grant her request.

Hunter intercepted her glance and shrugged. "If I start," he said rather sadly, "they'll be standing in line, and I'll never have a minute to eat."

"Oh. Of course." She was faintly embarrassed. "I hadn't thought about that."

The singer snapped his fingers at the other bodyguard and murmured something to him, and then settled back in his chair with the stem of his champagne flute between two fingers. "I'd be going on stage just about now," he said thoughtfully.

"Are you sorry to miss the concert?"

His eyes narrowed a little as he studied her. "And miss this? What do you think, Lauren Hodges?"

The bands around her chest tightened just a little. "How did you happen to get separated from your backup band, anyway?"

He shrugged. "I made a side trip. They stayed an extra day in Chicago. Damn charter jets, anyway. You can't ever count on them."

"It's hardly the airplane's fault that the storm blew in."

He looked at her for a long moment, and then laughed softly and reached over to turn her face up to his. "You're an earnest little thing, aren't you? Tell me about yourself, sweet Lauren."

She smiled and shook her head. "There's nothing much you'd like to know, I'm sure."

But it seemed there were a great many things he wanted to hear about, as many as she wanted to ask of him, and their leisurely dinner was gone before all the questions had been answered. It hardly seemed possible, she thought in astonishment, that they had talked the hours away so easily, that a man like Hunter Dix could have been so interested in the way she had lost her mother the year before, and in the question of whether she should keep the house where she had grown up, or sell it for the freedom of an apartment, now that she was alone.... She hadn't shared that particular concern with anyone before; indeed, she hadn't really thought it out completely for herself until she had started to tell Hunter about it. It was so natural, so perfectly effortless, to share things with him. It was unlike any first date she'd ever had—

Whoa, she told herself sternly. *First date?* Don't be an idiot, Lauren Hodges. Don't set yourself up for grief; just hold on to the treasure you already have. No one can take this night away, this special few hours all alone with your hero. For all you know, he was just politely listening to you babble, doing his best not to yawn, and not really hearing you at all!

She looked around when she heard the scrape of the bodyguard's chairs, and was surprised to see only empty tables around them. "It's gotten so quiet," she said a little nervously. "Even with a storm I've never known Marconi's to be so empty."

Hunter smiled a little. "That's because I bought it out for eight o'clock on, so you wouldn't be disturbed by autograph hounds."

The candle flame in her heart steadied, then grew. She'd known he was special, she thought. But she'd had no idea...

"I wouldn't say the food was worth it," Hunter went on thoughtfully. "But the company certainly was."

She hastily picked up her coffee cup for a last sip.

"Don't rush," he said. "The boys will take care of the bill and get the car." He leaned forward and, letting his fingertips rest along the line of her jaw, kissed her, very softly, his mouth warm and mobile against hers.

It was like a benediction, she thought. The perfect ending to a perfect evening.

He raised his head. "I don't suppose you're the kind of girl who would accept an invitation back to my hotel?"

Her eyes must have dilated in shock.

He laughed a little. "I'm sorry. I guess you just sort of overwhelmed me, Lauren. I've never felt this.... Well, just forget I said anything, all right?"

Never, Lauren thought humbly. *This supreme compliment I will never forget...*

The bodyguards discreetly turned their backs when Hunter walked her to her door. He touched her face, then kissed her hungrily, and Lauren fought a battle between her own desires and what little was left of her common sense.

You can't just go to bed with a man you've known such a short time, she thought.

But I feel I know him so well....

He'll be gone tomorrow, and you'll never see him again!

Exactly. And it would be a night to celebrate the rest of my life....

"Don't forget me, sweet Lauren," he whispered.

"I couldn't," she tried to say.

"I won't let you." He grinned at her in the cold shadows. "After all, I owe you a concert!"

And then he was gone, without another word. He might have called goodbye, but if he had the wind whipped it away. She watched the white limousine speed off, gleaming under the streetlights despite the falling snow.

When the car was out of sight and she went inside, the first thing Lauren did was to take the useless pass and slip it into the corner of the big gilt mirror in the front hall. Not that she needed a reminder. This evening had been so much better than any concert could have been. How could any detail of it ever fade from her memory?

I owe you a concert! What on earth had he meant by that?

THE MORNING BROUGHT another cold gray sky; the wind had died, and the snow had stopped, but the day was even drearier for Lauren than yesterday had been, because she knew that the brilliance that was Hunter Dix was gone from the city. There were people waiting for him somewhere else—she hadn't had time to ask where he would be going next.

Business was slow, because the streets had not yet been thoroughly plowed. Even walking was difficult; most of the snow had been shoveled away, but the sleet had stuck stubbornly to the concrete walks, and now the surface was uneven, as well as slick. Lauren picked her way cautiously up Poplar Street to the pharmacy to get Mr. Baines's morning coffee. It looked to be a quiet day, he had said, and it would be the perfect time to bury himself in the delicate repair and finishing work that took so much time when it was constantly interrupted by customers. And since there was little to do in the front of the store, if Lauren would just bring his coffee...

She could hardly refuse. For months now she had eagerly seized any opportunity to run down the street, because she might see Ward. And now that she suddenly didn't care to see Ward . . .

But it wasn't that exactly, either, she told herself. There was no reason to avoid him. She certainly wasn't feeling guilty this morning; she hadn't violated any vows to Ward by spending the evening with Hunter Dix, because she had never *made* any vows to him. She had no apologies to make.

And nothing had changed, when it came right down to it. She'd had a pleasant evening, that was all. Not even Ward could begrudge her that.

But she was uneasily aware, even as she said it, that it was not true. Something *had* changed—Lauren herself. She was no longer quite the same woman she had been just yesterday. For she had discovered that there were men in the world to whom romance was not a foreign concept; men to whom complimentary words came easily; men who knew the good things in life, and enjoyed them.

Well, one man at least, she told herself.

The pharmacy was busy, of course, despite the aftermath of the storm. It nearly always was; people were always getting sick, and though Ward had a part-time assistant, as well as several employees who took care of all the other departments, the largest part of the drug dispensing fell on him. Lauren supposed he must like it that way, for he even lived in the apartment above the store, as if he couldn't bear to be far from his business. If he'd wanted, he certainly could have hired another pharmacist so that he could be free more often—to take up a hobby, or have a day off, or just to go for a walk in the snow.

She wondered if Hunter liked to walk in the snow, and she was smiling softly, thinking about it, when she bumped into Ward in the aisle and had to juggle Mr. Baines's large foam cup to keep from spilling the contents down the front of Ward's immaculate long white lab coat.

"Take-out coffee this morning?" he mused. "Am I supposed to read a message into that?"

That annoyed her. Was he so self-centered that he took her actions personally? "No message," she said tartly. "I can't imagine why you'd think I need to play that sort of game, Ward."

His eyes darkened, and the dimple that had been playing hide-and-seek at the corner of his mouth disappeared. He thrust his hands into the pockets of the lab coat. "I begin to see," he said levelly. "One of my employees saw you getting into the limousine, you know."

"What business is it of yours?" Lauren said tightly.

"And of course she noticed that your car was still in the lot this morning...."

Lauren bit her lower lip and stared at the precise center of his tie, so that she didn't have to look up into his eyes. She had paid off the taxi at the end of Poplar Street this morning rather than in front of the jewelry store, thinking that there was no need to advertise the fact that she had never come back for her car. And now he was making it look sordid, when it had been so very innocent. So very beautiful...

"You know that you're playing with some rough customers, of course," Ward went on quietly. "A local photographer tried to get a picture of your hero yesterday, and his camera was smashed into the street by one of his goons."

"Well, what do you think bodyguards are for? If he was threatening—"

"By taking a picture?" Ward scoffed. "Come on, Lauren, you don't know what you're dealing with."

She squared her shoulders. "For your information, and certainly not because I owe you any explanations—"

"Hey," Ward said. "Lauren. If you'll stop a minute, you'll notice that I didn't ask for any explanations, either. I'm worried about you, that's all. I'm—"

"Well, you don't need to be. Hunter took me to dinner, and then home, and that's all. And we were chaperoned all the time by those 'goons,' as you call them, and nothing happened, and—and I wish it *had,* you miserable, suspicious creep! But it's all over, so you don't need to make it sound like a one-night-stand, which it wasn't, and I'm only telling you this so the rumor doesn't take over the whole street by the end of the day—"

"Are you going to stop for a breath, or keep right on for the rest of the morning?" Ward asked calmly.

She glared at him.

"All right," he said hastily, "I owe you an apology. I'll freely admit it— I suspected the worst, and I should have known better than to think you'd lose your head. You're too solid and sensible for that."

Solid? *Sensible?* She was furious. Was that what Ward considered a compliment? And as for his apology, it was hardly the most gracious she had ever received, but she knew better than to hold her breath and wait for an improvement. Ward, she thought mockingly, was too solid and sensible to abase himself! So she nodded stiffly. There was nothing else she could do.

Ward's eyes softened a little, but she never found out what he might have said then, for there was a sort of scuffle at the back of the store, and a voice called his name. There was a note of urgency in it, almost of panic, and Ward moved off briskly without another word to her.

Lauren peered around the corner of the aisle. She could see a man stretched out on the floor with a frantic woman at his head; then Ward knelt beside him and her view was blocked.

"Has someone called an ambulance?" she asked.

The cashier who was standing beside her nodded. "He's a sweet old man—he had a heart attack last year. This looks like another one. I hope he doesn't die. But Ward's there now, so it will be all right."

"Oh, absolutely," Lauren said dryly. "Nothing bad can possibly happen as long as Ward's there."

The woman nodded.

She didn't even hear the irony in what I said, Lauren marveled. What was there about the man, she wondered as she walked back to the jewelry store, that had inspired his staff to such worship?

SHE HAD BEEN HOME barely a quarter of an hour that evening when the flowers came, two dozen glorious creamy-white roses, with Hunter's name on the card. He had thought of her this morning, even on his way out of town, she realized, and her heart nearly burst with quiet gladness.

She kicked the front door shut and stood there hugging the huge box, with almost the same enthusiasm as if he himself had returned to her. She was breathless with delight. Roses—what luxury! And these were the most beautiful ones she had ever seen, with enormous blossoms still studded with water droplets, the velvety petals just starting to unfold....

She pulled a single rose out of the bundle and whirled around the room with it as if it were a dancing partner. Then she put it back with its fellows and buried her face in the green tissue that cushioned the blooms, taking long deep breaths of their fragrance until her head swam with the heavy, drugging scent.

She had forgotten all about dinner and was still arranging the flowers—trying out new combinations and filling vases for her bedroom, the kitchen, the mantel—when the telephone rang.

"Hello, sweet Lauren," said the throaty, intimate voice, and she almost dropped the telephone.

"Hunter!" She twisted around to see the kitchen clock. "But it's concert time!"

He laughed. "Oh, my innocent, it's two hours earlier on the West Coast, so I'm supposed to be getting rested and ready. But I couldn't rest. I can't close my eyes without thinking of you. Did you get the roses? I hope you like white ones. I think red ones are prettier, but they just wouldn't have been right for you."

"Oh, yes, I got them. Thank you! They're beautiful. I've never known such luxury."

"You poor child! Does no one ever send you flowers?"

She stopped herself abruptly. Was he laughing at her? There had certainly been a hint of humor in his voice, and her words *had* been awfully naive. "I mean, of course I get flowers," she said primly. "Just never two dozen roses at one time. I hardly know what to do with them all."

Now he was certainly laughing. "Oh, don't spoil it, darling! You're so preciously innocent and sincere, sweet Lauren, don't try to be sophisticated. That's why I sent white roses, you know—for your purity and innocence and earnestness. I've never met anyone like you."

She clutched the telephone in a hand that was suddenly damp and shaking. With anticipation? With fear? With shock? Yes, last night he had implied that he had found her attractive—more than attractive. But . . .

"Most of the girls I meet are such a cynical lot," he went on very quietly. "They seem to think it's the only way to impress a man these days. No one would send them white roses, that's for sure—not with a straight face, at least. But you . . . I never thought I could feel this way again, sweet Lauren."

She swallowed frantically, trying to get her heart back to its proper anatomical location. It seemed to be permanently lodged in her throat.

The husky, sexy murmur gave way to a more vibrant tone. "I've shocked you, haven't I? Perhaps I'd better not pursue that any further—just now. We'll take it up on Valentine's Day."

"Valentine's . . ." she said uncertainly. "What . . .?"

"How could I have forgotten to tell you the good news? I've arranged it all with my manager, and we've rescheduled last night's concert."

"For Valentine's Day?" *I will see him again,* her heart was singing. *I will see him soon . . .* "That's wonderful! But how is it you don't already have a concert then, Hunter? I mean, you sing love songs! Doesn't everyone in the world want a concert on Valentine's Day?"

She could hear the smile in his voice. "The day for lovers? Plenty of them do, yes. I'd kept it free, you see, for... well, we won't talk about the woman who used to be in my life. That's all over now. And since now I have a new Valentine—" the husky twinge was back in his voice. "—I do, don't I, sweet Lauren? I can't be the only one who felt that instant attraction."

"You're not the only one," she whispered. It felt almost like a vow.

"Do you have one of those roses handy?" His voice was a little unsteady.

"Right here. Why?"

"Give it a kiss," he whispered. "And pretend it's me."

THE NEXT MORNING when Lauren told Kim about the rescheduled concert, Kim dropped a tray of rings that she had just taken out of the safe. Gold and precious stones spilled and rolled and scattered across the floor.

Lauren stopped wiping glass cleaner off the top of a display case and plunged to her knees to help grab up the rings before Mr. Baines could see what had happened.

Once the rings were safely corralled, however, Kim began to look concerned. "If I were you, Lauren, I don't think I'd say much about the concert until the newspaper announces it," she advised. "There's no reason to have everybody on Poplar Street asking how you were the first to know."

"Oh, for heaven's sake. You can't mean you believe the nonsense that's running up and down the street, Kim!"

"Of course I don't think you spent the night with Hunter Dix. But I'm warning you, plenty of people do."

A customer came in just then, and Kim began showing him earrings for his girlfriend's Valentine's Day gift.

Lauren caught herself chewing on a perfectly manicured nail, and took it out of her mouth. Glass cleaner tasted awful, she thought. Or was it the gossip on Poplar Street that had left such a bitter aftertaste on her tongue?

She hadn't finished the display cases yet, and Kim's customer was still working his way through every pair of earrings in the store and shaking his head over each one, when Ward came in. Lauren saw him coming down Poplar Street and watched as he tried to dodge between the random droplets of melting snow that fell from the awnings, and thought, *Just what I need this morning!*

"Spring is on the way," he announced with a brilliant smile. "At least it looks like it on a morning like this, with the sun out and the mess starting to melt." He set a bag down on the case right in front of her. "And here's a little bit of springtime for indoors." He began to unbutton his wool topcoat.

"If it's so nice," Lauren said, "I'm amazed you bothered with a coat. It's only three doors down."

"I didn't say it was warm, exactly, just that the groundhog saw his shadow this morning, so there are only six weeks of winter left."

Lauren put her elbows down on the glass case and propped her chin in her hands. "And do you know what happens if he didn't see it? It means we have a month and a half, instead."

"You're certainly a pessimist this morning," Ward said. "Did somebody steal the hole out of your doughnut at breakfast, or something?"

Lauren couldn't help but laugh; she couldn't be gloomy, even about the certainty of more snow and cold to come, after last night's good news—the concert, the phone call, the roses...

A warm, almost mischievous gleam sprang into Ward's eyes. "Besides," he said, "now you don't have to wait even another day for spring." He waved an inviting hand at the bag.

Lauren unfolded the top and peeked in, a bit warily, at a shallow clay pot full of crocus bulbs. The leaves were already fully developed and brilliantly striped in grassy green and white, and tiny buds were just beginning to peek up from the base of the plants. She thought she saw a hint of purple on one of them. "They look quite healthy," she said.

He nodded. "The shipment just came into the store this morning. And of course they can be transplanted to your garden after it warms up, and then they'll bloom every spring."

He sounded very proud of himself. Wasn't that just like Ward, she thought. He was so efficient himself that even when he gave a girl flowers, he expected them to do double or triple duty!

That wasn't fair, she told herself. He knew she liked things like crocus—he saw that last fall when he'd helped clean up the flowerbeds in her back yard for winter. His gift might not be glamorous, but it was thoughtful.

She bit her lip. "Look, Ward," she said softly, "I shouldn't have said those things yesterday. I can't even remember what I called you, but I know it wasn't very pleasant...."

He winced a little. "Let's not try too hard to recall it, shall we? And I'm sorry to have been so abrupt—walking away from you like that."

She set the crocus next to the cash register and said carelessly, "Oh, that's all right. You had other things to worry about. How is the patient?"

"He'll be fine." He didn't enlarge on the topic. "Lauren, that movie is still on. Would you like to go?"

She didn't want to refuse him, yet something inside her shivered away from accepting any invitation whatever; it wouldn't be fair to encourage him just now. And besides, what if Hunter called again and she wasn't there? "Oh, here comes Mrs. Schuyler," she said quickly. "That will take care of the morning—you know what a talker she is."

Ward seemed to accept her changing the subject as a refusal. "I'd better get back to the store—no doubt there are people waiting in line for me already." He patted her hand and, with one well-groomed fingertip, turned the sapphire ring she was wearing until it caught the light perfectly, then smiled and went out just in time to hold the door for Mrs. Schuyler. If he'd been wearing a hat, Lauren thought, he'd have tipped it.

It was almost noon before she and Kim were alone again. Lauren was counting the excess money out of the cash register so she could make a bank deposit on her lunch hour. Kim was studying the sturdy buds of the crocus. In the warmth, one of them was already pushing aggressively upward, as if it was eager to see its new surroundings.

"Poor Ward," Lauren said, glancing at the crocus. "He tries so hard, and it just never quite comes off." Crocus, she was thinking. Ward would never dream of blowing money for two dozen roses. He would think so many all at once was a waste.

Kim didn't look at her. "I was thinking it was awfully nice of him."

Lauren stopped counting cash for a moment. "Correct me if I'm wrong, but aren't you the one who called Ward a jerk?" Her fingers began to move again, efficiently rippling through the twenties.

"I didn't mean it exactly. I was just disappointed about the tickets, and you know how I say things sometimes without thinking." Then Kim added, "That guy's heart had stopped yesterday, at the pharmacy. Ward saved his life. The paramedics said so."

"That's wonderful, but what does it have to do with the crocus?"

Kim shrugged. "Nothing, I suppose. But give Ward some credit. He could be telling everyone what a hero he is."

"Perhaps he realized that bragging about it wouldn't be the way to impress me."

"I don't think he wants to impress you. Ward's trying to bail you out of trouble, Lauren. Why do you think he brought those flowers down here, anyway? He knows that everyone on the street is watching, and if he were to turn his back on you now..."

Lauren said with frost in her voice, "Are you implying that he's trying to patch the tatters of my reputation back together? Well, isn't that thoughtful of him!"

Kim gave the clay pot a push. "That's not what I meant, Lauren. Not exactly. I just, well, I'm confused. And I'm surprised at you, I suppose."

"Because I'm too solid and sensible to lose my head like this? That's no compliment as far as I'm concerned." Lauren slammed shut the cash drawer. "Have some crocus, Kim," she said on her way out the door. "I certainly don't want them."

Chapter Three

THE DAYS THAT FOLLOWED would have been pure magic if it hadn't been for the head cold that attacked Lauren over the weekend. She must have picked it up from running to the bank without her coat on Groundhog Day; she'd been so furious at Ward, and at Kim, that she hadn't felt the need of a wrap to keep her warm, and now she was paying the price.

Hunter loved what the cold did to her voice; he teased her about her sexy little whisper, especially the night he called just after finishing a concert in Honolulu and woke her at three in the morning when she had only just managed to fall asleep. But she couldn't be annoyed for long, because he began to confide in her about the problems attacking his tour from all sides. An inept advance team had booked him into a series of inadequate concert halls and uncomfortable hotels. And it was impossible to get anything decent to eat. Only her soft voice and common sense could make things feel right again, he declared.

"If it wasn't for having you to talk to, sweet Lauren, I'd cancel the whole tour. It's a disaster. But of course," he added, with self-deprecating humor, "we performers have to make the little people happy."

It made her feel sad; he was always on stage, in a sense, no matter where he went—always surrounded by fans, each wanting a piece of his attention, a piece of his heart.

Her cold gave her a good excuse to stay at home; she played a lot of solitaire that weekend while she waited for the telephone to ring. Ward stopped by on Sunday afternoon with the newest issue of her favorite magazine and a jigsaw puzzle, and he stayed to help her put it together. She was glad of his company, even though every time she sniffled she was reminded of her annoyance at him. Trying to preserve her good name on Poplar Street, indeed, when she hadn't done a single thing to injure it in the first place! Still, his company was a lot better than being alone. Her thoughts strayed often to Hunter; she knew he was on his way to Tokyo that afternoon.

She was looking forward to getting back to work on Monday, but overnight her cold became worse. Her cough deepened into a bark that threatened to rip her ribs apart, and so she dragged herself to the doctor's office, instead, only to be told that she had developed bronchitis.

"Go home and go to bed," the doctor ordered. "And don't worry about your antibiotics. I'll have the pharmacy deliver them to you before the day is out."·

She went home, but she didn't have enough strength to get herself to bed; she collapsed in her living room and woke to early-evening darkness with a neck so stiff from being propped against the arm of the couch that she thought her head might never turn again.

When the doorbell rang, she groaned and actually thought about lying still and not bothering to answer it. But it pealed a second time, followed by a fist hammering against the door, and then she remembered the pharmacy's delivery van, and her promised medicine. It had certainly taken long enough.

It wasn't the delivery boy, however, but Ward himself who stood on the small front porch, with a white bag in his hand and huge snowflakes drifting down around his head, sticking in his dark hair and clinging to the shoulders of his coat. There was even one enormous crystal flake caught in his eyelashes, and he blinked and flicked it away with a gloved finger just as she opened the door.

It wasn't fair, Lauren was thinking. A mere man shouldn't be allowed to possess the world's longest, darkest and curliest eyelashes. Especially a man who didn't have the slightest idea how to use them to best advantage.

"Come in," she started to say, and had to stop till her coughing spell relaxed. Ward almost pushed her back into the house, away from the cold sweep of outside air, and he supported her with an impersonal arm around her shoulders till the spasm had passed.

"Sit down," he ordered, "and I'll get your first dose. It should have been here hours ago, but my delivery boy got sick, too, and went home to bed."

She sank onto the couch, weak from the coughing spell, and he brought her a glass of water and dropped a huge red-and-white capsule into her palm. Lauren swallowed it with difficulty—her throat was sore, too—and looked up at him with a grateful smile. "Take your coat off," she said.

Ward shook his head. "I can't. I have a dozen more deliveries to make."

Disappointment shot through her; she felt abandoned. But she couldn't blame Ward. He was busy, and why on earth would he want to hang around her, anyway—red-nosed, croaking, stringy-haired and laden with germs? She lay back on the couch with an achy little moan.

From her almost flat position, Ward looked incredibly tall as he studied her, his forehead wrinkled with concern. "You'll be all right, now? You'll be able to rest?"

"Sure. I'm in great shape." Tears crept into her eyes; she couldn't even manage irony. Ward looked awfully tired, too, she thought. He needed a rest himself, from the sound of that sigh. Having to do all the deliveries himself, on top of everything else...

"Your cough syrup is in the bag," he said, "and I brought a decongestant, in case you need it. If your nose isn't stuffy tonight, it will be by morning. Don't get up— I'll let myself out."

Then he was gone, and silence closed around her again. Lonely, chilly silence.

"You have two minutes to wallow in self-pity," Lauren told herself aloud, "and then you are going to get up and find something to eat. You're miserable because you've been by yourself all day, and it isn't very pleasant to be alone when you're ill, but feeling sorry for yourself certainly isn't going to make you less wretched. So you're going to get up and do something to help yourself feel better."

But the pep talk didn't do much good. Thinking about a mug of hot soup was one thing, but actually getting up and making it was something else when every muscle in her entire body ached. So she dozed off instead, and she dreamed that Ward returned with something that smelled delightful—was it possible for anything to smell so good, even in a dream?—and stooped over to kiss her temple. Tears stung the corners of her eyes....

"I brought chicken soup," Ward said cheerfully. His fingertips brushed the rumpled hair back from her face.

"You did come back!" She turned her cheek into his palm. It was blessedly cold against her hot skin.

She saw his eyes darken, and she sat up hastily. "I mean," she croaked, "you got your deliveries all finished?" It was stupid, she thought, to feel so grateful just because he was here.

He nodded. "I'm done for the evening, thank God. Have you had anything at all to eat today?"

Lauren shook her head tiredly. "I don't think so."

He said something under his breath that she didn't quite catch, because her ears were plugged, too, and went out to the kitchen. Lauren put her head back down with a sigh of relief.

The first thing he brought her was a tall, frosty glass full of orange juice and tiny chips of ice that slid refreshingly down her burning throat, soothing as they went. Between sips she said, "I don't know why you're taking a chance with my millions of germs."

Ward shook his head. "I think I must be immune to this one. I've obviously had a hundred chances to get it."

"Well, I must say I'm awfully glad you're here. Sorry I'm not up to offering you a game of gin rummy or something—unless you'd like an awfully easy victory, that is."

He smiled. "I'll wait till you're mended enough to be a worthy opponent. I brought a movie, though, from the rental place, if you'd like some entertainment."

"As long as it doesn't require me to think. But if it's something deep and foreign with subtitles..."

"Pure fluff."

"I can handle that. Did you say something about chicken soup a while ago?"

"It's warming. I'm not promising that it's gourmet quality, but it was the last quart the deli had." He brought in two bowls on a tray. "They seemed to be doing a booming business in the stuff."

"Chicken soup from the deli?" she teased. "You mean it's not homemade?"

He smiled again. "I see you're starting to feel human again."

Lauren sat up experimentally and stirred her soup; it was steaming gently and smelled divine. So she hadn't been dreaming, after all. "Almost human," she decided. "Except for my neck. I think my head's going to be at this angle permanently."

He moved to the couch beside her, and his fingers moved gently over the vertebrae. "Where does it hurt?"

"Right there. Ouch," she muttered as his thumb dug with certainty into the protesting muscle. But it was a healing discomfort, one that brought warmth and relief to the painful spot, and within minutes the tightness had relaxed and her neck turned easily again. She tipped her head back and looked up at him through narrowed eyes.

"You're awfully good at this," she said. "Where did you learn it? Did you have a summer job as a masseur, or something?"

Ward laughed. "Nothing that exotic, I'm afraid."

Of course it hadn't been exotic, she thought. It was impossible to think of Ward and exotic summer jobs in the same breath.

His arm was lying about her shoulders now. It was warm and pleasant, and she was too comfortable to move. There was no point in moving, anyway; she could see that her soup was still too hot to eat.

His mother had probably liked to have her neck rubbed, that was all, she thought. "Don't worry," she said lazily. "Your dusty little secret is safe with me."

He smiled a little at that, and his arm tightened, just a fraction. His fingertips were drawing slow circles on the curve of her shoulder, still massaging the aching muscles even as he pulled her gradually closer.

She really should sit up this minute, Lauren thought. It really wasn't fair to Ward to let this go on. It wouldn't be very flattering to him for her to be in his arms, letting him kiss her while she was thinking of Hunter. Pretending he *was* Hunter....

But there was something almost hypnotic about the motion of his fingers, and so she didn't move. Instead, she warned in a soft almost-whisper, "You'll get my germs, Ward."

He said huskily, "It's worth it."

And then it was too late to move, to sit up, to call a halt. His big hand came up to cup her face. His fingertips caressed her jaw and the soft hollow beneath her ear, and his palm rested warmly over her throat. His thumb brushed the point of her chin as softly as his mouth touched hers, like the kiss of a butterfly's wing.

But the caress did not remain tentative for long: The gentleness remained, of course—Ward could never be anything but gentle—but there was certainty in it now, and confidence, and sure knowledge.

I had almost forgotten, Lauren thought, *how very beautifully he does this.* His kisses were never smothering, never grinding or demanding, like so many men's were. Ward's kisses could go on forever, and a woman would never feel suffocated or assaulted, just elated and uplifted and practically delirious with delight....

Her eyelids drooped as if her brain had ordered them to, closing out all other information so it could better concentrate on this supreme sensation. Her thoughts became nothing more than a senseless swirl.

No wonder he'd never kissed her—or anyone else, she'd bet—where other people could see. It wouldn't be fair not to give a woman a chance to recover a bit from this kind of sensual uproar before exposing her to curious bystanders. And Ward was, above all, a gentleman. Yes, a very decent sort of man....

She knew, with a sort of detached sense, that his heart was pounding, and realized that her fingertips were resting on the pulse point just below his ear. She didn't even remember reaching up to hold him.

He raised his head and said almost hoarsely, "Lauren..." and she waited, without anxiousness, to see what it was he wanted to say. She wasn't even curious—she was incapable of curiosity, for she was still floating on that seductive cloud he had so masterfully created.

The telephone rang beside her. It might be Hunter, she thought, and in a fraction of a second crashed off the cloud and back to cold, solid earth. She had lain here in Ward's arms and allowed him to kiss her, and had not even once thought of Hunter. How on earth had she allowed herself to lose control like that? It was a compliment to Ward's technique, that was all—but he certainly wouldn't hear about it from her!

Guiltily she pulled away from him and reached for the telephone.

"Dammit, Lauren, let it ring," Ward said, his voice a little rough, but she had already picked it up.

The first thing she heard was muted swearing. "I did it again, didn't I?" Hunter said ruefully. "Woke you in the middle of the night? I couldn't remember how many blasted hours different Tokyo is, and I thought it was worth a chance...."

Beside her, Ward abruptly got to his feet, picked up her orange-juice glass and vanished into the kitchen.

"No, of course you didn't wake me. It's only—" Lauren peered into the clock on the mantel "—half-past eight, that's all." She tried to see around the corner in the kitchen. Ward couldn't be leaving, she thought; his coat was still draped over the back of a chair in plain view, and he certainly wouldn't walk off without it. Not Ward. Not when a snowstorm was going on outside.

"Well, you sound as if you just got out of bed," Hunter said. He sounded a bit disgruntled.

She could feel the warm flush of embarrassment rise in her cheeks. "Oh... that's only my cold. It's gotten worse, I'm afraid, and now I'm really croaking."

"Aren't you over that yet?" Hunter asked. "Your special concert is a week from tonight, and you have to be well by then."

My special concert, she thought, with the lift it always gave her. *A Hunter Dix concert just for me.* "Oh, I wouldn't miss the concert, no matter what!"

"Well, you'd better get over this disease of yours so you don't infect me with it."

"Hunter!"

"I'm only teasing," he said hastily. "You know that, sweet Lauren. You wouldn't like it if I couldn't sing at all, would you?"

She relaxed. "Of course I know you're teasing. And I'll be well by then, really I will. I'll probably be back at work tomorrow." She reached out, half-consciously, and touched the rose in the vase on the coffee table. It was the last survivor of the two dozen, and it, too, was drooping now, its creamy-white petals withered and crumbly and slightly brown along the edges. It looked a little like she felt, Lauren thought ironically. As if she was on the verge of dying, and should be carried upstairs and put to rest between two heavy things, to be preserved forever... But this wouldn't last. She would be better tomorrow.

"I've been writing your song," Hunter said. He sounded almost shy about it.

"My song? You're writing me a special song?"

"Well, you're a special girl, aren't you? And it's a special concert. And I promised you a song."

"But one all my own—just for me?" She could hardly breathe, she was so deeply touched. "Oh, Hunter—"

"I woke up at an ungodly hour this morning with it running through my head. It, and thoughts of you."

"Sing me a bit of it now, please!"

"Oh, no. That wouldn't be fair to the song. I want you to hear it the first time in all its glory—not over a phone line sung by a worn-out old hack singer who's still hoarse from last night's concert."

"A hack singer?" she said indignantly. "Don't you dare run yourself down that way, Hunter Dix!"

There was a laugh in his voice. "That's my sweet Lauren, keeping me on the straight and narrow. Don't you want to hear about the concert last night? Tokyo turned out in droves. I wish..." His tone dropped. "I wish you could have been with me to see it."

To share it with him, to experience the adulation of the crowd as he received his well-earned acclaim. How she would have loved being there. "That would have been wonderful!" she said.

"I wish you'd been here with me last night after the concert, too," he went on huskily. "I needed your warmth last night."

"After all that adoration? Surely you didn't need one more fan."

"Not just one more fan. I needed *you,* sweet Lauren. Adoration is fine until you come home alone," he confessed, and there was a tremor in his voice that startled her.

"Hunter . . ." she began uncertainly.

The tremor gave way to urgency. "And I need you right now, too, when I've got a long day on an airplane stretching out ahead of me, and only a band and a bunch of backup singers for company."

"I miss you a lot, too—"

"Dammit, it's more than that, and you know it. How about it, sweet Lauren? You're coming with me next week, aren't you?" There was a sudden harsh note to his voice, as if he couldn't stand the waiting, the not knowing, any longer.

"Coming with you? I don't—"

"Yes. Coming with me. Sharing with me. Making it all worth doing. Surely you know that's what I want, what I've been wanting for a week. I was a fool to leave you there. A fool."

What he was saying was too much for any heart to hold; Lauren thought hers would crack open from the strain of being overfull with happiness. The difficulties of a world tour that he had described to her—the less-than-perfect hotels, the long flights, the occasional troublesome fan, the arrangements that sometimes went wrong—would all be bearable if he had her beside him.

If he has me, she thought humbly. *Me—ordinary Lauren Hodges...*

"We'll be in New York next month," he cajoled. "And then London. And after that, Paris..."

The real world reasserted itself for a moment. "It can't all be Paris," she reminded him. "I'm sure there will be plenty of boring little cities like this one in between the glamorous spots."

She could almost see the careless wave of his hand as he dismissed the objection. "Yes, there always are. But with you beside me, not even the little towns will be so bad. You'll see. It's settled, then."

A tremor ran through her. "I don't know," she heard herself saying. "This is so sudden."

"Dammit, it's not sudden." His voice had a hard edge to it. "You know it as well as I do—and you knew it that first night, too. You don't have any more doubts than I do, so don't be coy about it!"

"Hunter, there are things here that I can't simply walk away from—"

"What things? A job? A house? You don't need them, Lauren."

"I can't just leave—"

"Yes, you can. Maybe I shouldn't have asked you like this over the telephone. I should have waited till I could hold you, and kiss you, and convince you with all the right trappings, but I'm too impatient for that, sweet Lauren. You don't have to answer me now. You don't have to say anything at all. And I'm not going to bring it up again, because there's nothing more to discuss. Just be prepared to come with me on Valentine's Day—because that's what you want, just as much as I want it.''

And with that, he whispered a goodbye, and he was gone. Once more he was half a world away, unreachable.

Lauren replaced the receiver slowly. He was so sublimely sure of her, she thought, as if she would have no objections, as if there were no barriers standing in the way of their being together. But it wasn't fair. He could not dismiss her job and the question of the house so lightly—or could he? She certainly would not need employment if she went with him. And the house, well, she'd been thinking of selling it, anyway, and he knew it.

He was so superbly self-assured...but what woman in her right mind could turn down the promise of New York, London, Paris, with Hunter Dix at her side? And even if there were only the multitude of tiny nameless cities, well, the sophisticated cities weren't really what Lauren wanted, anyway. Nor was it Hunter Dix the famous singer, either. It was Hunter Dix the man, the lost little boy she had gotten to know that first night over dinner at Marconi's. As long as she was with Hunter, she would have the best of all the world, no matter where they were to go.

And if she didn't seize this chance now, it might never come again. When they were half a world apart like this, there were too many things to interfere, to pull them away from each other. They might never be able to recapture the perfect harmony they had known that night at Marconi's. Already the frustration of having only a telephone link between them was showing on him, and perhaps on her, as well.

''Your soup has gotten cold,'' Ward pointed out.

"Oh." She pulled herself back with an effort. She hadn't even heard him return. "It doesn't matter. I wasn't really hungry, anyway."

He looked down at her, his hands in his trouser pockets. She noticed—why hadn't she realized it before?—that he was still in his working garb—dark trousers, striped shirt, tie. He'd left the long lab coat at the store, of course, and he'd loosened his tie, but that was all. Didn't the man ever relax?

He looked as if there was a great deal he'd like to tell her, but instead he said mildly, "I'll put it in the refrigerator, in case you want it later."

"That's fine. Thank you."

She put her head back against the couch cushions, and her eyes were closed a couple of minutes later when he returned. "You look exhausted," he said. "It takes a lot of energy to put on a performance like that, doesn't it?"

She sat straight up. "What is that supposed to mean? What performance?"

Ward shrugged. "Just that you certainly came back to life when Hunter called, and now look at you. Worn to a thread."

"If you'd think about what you just said, Ward, it's not at all hard to understand." She curled up.

"Oh, I don't have any trouble understanding that you wanted to impress him. What I don't quite see is why. Does he think getting bronchitis is a moral weakness, or does he just disapprove in principle of anything that keeps you from giving him your full attention?"

She opened her eyes and glared at him. "Hunter is a very sweet man who's absorbed right now in a draining world tour. It would be a miracle if he wasn't tired out and short-tempered sometimes, so I try not to weigh him down with my problems. And of course he tries to stay away from colds and things like that. His voice is his profession, and he can't afford to take chances with it.''

"Of course." His tone was faintly mocking.

"I wouldn't expect you to sympathize, but he's a very lonely person, really," Lauren said.

"Lonely? Perhaps. Also spoiled, selfish, cynical, rude, manipulative..."

She was getting annoyed. She wasn't surprised that Ward felt jealous, even though he had no real right to be. But this vindictiveness was completely unlike him. This was not the Ward she knew. Certainly he was no Pollyanna—he could see the shadowed side of things—but he usually didn't attack people without reason, and he didn't call them names. "What's the matter with you?" she asked. "You've got no right, just because I let you kiss me tonight, to carry on like this!"

There was no hint of a dimple now at the corner of Ward's mouth; instead a muscle twitched tensely. "He's quite possibly abusive," he went on levelly, "and he's certainly—"

She got shakily to her feet. "That's enough. I don't know where you got your ideas, but they're wrong, Ward. Dead wrong. Hunter is like a gentle, lonely little boy. Oh, you must know the kind I mean. They have a bigger allowance than most kids, and so the ones who don't have as much make up to them and use them, and they never know who their real friends are."

Ward shook his head. "The little boys with money that I knew were never like that. They were the users and the bullies, and they didn't care whether they had any friends at all.''

She stamped her foot. "Would you stop twisting my words? You're taking something beautiful and making it sinister, and I won't let you do it! I don't have to listen to this!''

There was a long silence. Lauren sat down again, because her knees were trembling. And she was cold, all of a sudden, as if every nerve had suddenly been rubbed with ice.

Ward's voice softened. "You think he loves you, don't you, Lauren?''

She said peevishly, "I think I'm certainly a better judge of that than you are.''

"And you're actually thinking of going with him when he comes back?''

"Yes,'' she said. Her voice was very low, as if saying it aloud made it somehow more real—even though it was only Ward, not Hunter, she was telling. "Yes,'' she repeated, more firmly. "I am going with him.''

The silence in the house could not have been more complete.

"What's holding me here, anyway?'' she said at last, like a child parroting what she had been told. "I have no family. The house, well, it's only a place to live, after all. And as for my job, Mr. Baines won't mind all that much, because it's the start of the slow season. After the Valentine's Day rush, Kim can handle the store by herself most of the time. Mr. Baines will probably be happy to have one less on the payroll, to tell the truth, and he'll have plenty of time to train someone new before the store starts to get busy again next fall.''

"Who are you trying to convince, Lauren? Me? Mr. Baines? Or yourself?"

She turned her back. "Please don't feel that you have to stay here and lecture me." Her tone was icily polite. "I'm certain you have more important things to do tonight."

"You're a fool, Lauren."

"You don't have any right to judge me."

There was a rustle; when she looked over her shoulder he was putting on his topcoat. "I suppose that's so," he said quietly. "I don't have any rights at all, when it comes down to the bottom line. I'm terribly sorry I bothered you this evening."

"Don't forget your movie," she said childishly. "I don't think I'll be watching it."

He took the videotape box from her hand and shoved it into his pocket. "You'll be too busy humming your song, I suppose—the one he's writing for you. If you want my advice—"

"I don't."

"—you should learn it by heart, and substitute it for where you used to say your prayers. Perhaps you'll be lucky, and it will help to keep you warm at night after you realize what a terrible mistake you've made."

She slammed the door behind him, then struggled up the stairs and almost fell into her bed, too drained even to straighten the crumpled sheets she had crawled out of that morning.

And she was not surprised when it was Ward who stalked her fevered, restless sleep. Ward, and the way he had behaved tonight, was the stuff of nightmares. When she began to feel better, then she would be able to dream once again of Hunter, and the lovely days to come.

Chapter Four

MORE ROSES ARRIVED the next day—another two dozen long-stemmed, creamy-white beauties. They must have been wired the moment Hunter set foot back on American soil, and Lauren buried her face in them and thought, *Six more days and I'll be with him. By the time these roses fade...*

Then she drew back and looked at the flowers a little sadly. Two dozen glorious roses, and she couldn't even enjoy their heavy, sultry fragrance, because she couldn't smell a thing. "They'll last," she whispered. "I'll smell them later. It's all right. I can wait." Her words sounded like a vow, made in the cathedral-like silence of her living room.

Six more days...

Each hour passed with infinite slowness. The time dragged even more because there was no one to share Lauren's excitement, her anticipation, her joy. For she had decided not to tell anyone of her plans.

She knew she ought to tell Mr. Baines, at least, but she just couldn't bring herself to do it. He hated having his neat time schedules upset, and Lauren knew that he simply wouldn't understand why she wasn't giving him the full month's notice she should. If she was going to leave him in the lurch, anyway, she might as well really be a rat, she told herself, and avoid the trouble that honesty would bring. For if she told him she was leaving in less than a week, things would be mighty unpleasant around the store, and the details would inevitably leak out to the rest of Poplar Street.

Ward's reaction to the news had made her wary of letting anyone else have a chance to comment. While she didn't think that many people would dare to say the things Ward had—at least to her face—she knew they would talk about it and shake their heads, up and down the length of Poplar Street. She would be the subject of gossip once she was gone, of course; that was inevitable. But to face it in person, to have to keep her chin up while people covertly pointed her out and discussed behind her back, to have to pretend calmness when guilty silence fell as she walked into a room or met a group on the street ... No, she couldn't face that.

At least, she didn't have to bring it upon herself, she thought. Ward might not keep her secret, of course. All he had to do was to let a word drop, and it would unleash a firestorm of talk. But, she told herself with a mental shrug, that was completely out of her hands; she could not prevent him from talking. If Ward wanted to soothe his masculine pride by making her appear to be some sort of dreamy-eyed star-chaser, he could do it easily enough. The people on Poplar Street would be easily convinced that she was truly the dizzy blonde of legend, off on a mad whim. They simply wouldn't comprehend the sort of instant understanding that she and Hunter had found, and Lauren knew it would be senseless to try to explain to them that she wasn't acting on some crazy self-destructive impulse, but that this was a true and lasting love.

It still brought faint pink to her own cheeks, to think of the magic of loving Hunter, so how could she hope to explain it to these people, who didn't know the real man?

Only Kim seemed to understand at all, and even she wavered now and then—or perhaps it was just her habit of saying whatever she was thinking. One day a customer brought in the latest tabloid and, with a malicious smile at Lauren, murmured, "I'm sure you've already seen this, since it has Hunter Dix on the front page. But I thought you'd like an extra copy." And as soon as the customer had left, Kim buried her nose in the paper.

Lauren sighed and turned back to her sketches of a window display for St. Patrick's Day; it was a display she would certainly never be arranging herself, but to ignore the window would raise suspicion, and she supposed Kim would appreciate the suggestions when the time came. "Enjoying yourself?" she asked finally.

Kim tossed the tabloid across the display case. "You might like to see this."

It sounded like a warning. Lauren glanced at the front page. HUNTER TAKES HONOLULU! the headline shrieked. SEXY SINGER SETS THE TOWN ON FIRE AFTER CONCERT...

The headlines went on, in banks of descending size, but Lauren stopped reading. "What nonsense," she said. "I know perfectly well what he was doing after that concert. He was in his hotel room talking to me on the phone."

Kim reached for the paper. "There are pictures inside—"

"Haven't you ever heard of faked photographs? Oh, Kim, you know the press will go to any lengths to get a juicy new story. You even heard Hunter himself say that they just aren't ever right."

Kim shook her head. "What he said was, they were right about his actress friend leaving him."

"Well, it would have been difficult for anyone to mess those facts up, don't you think?" Lauren held her sketch out at arm's length. "Do we still have those ceramic leprechauns in the back room? I think with a little of that sticky wax they could each hold a ring, don't you?"

"Only if you promise to clean the wax off afterward," Kim said.

Lauren almost smiled, and then stopped abruptly, as the realization sank in that she certainly would not have to worry about the wax. She had always enjoyed decorating the windows, coming up with new ideas as the season passed, refining and changing them each year. And now she wouldn't ever be doing this again. No more collecting unusual little objects at flea markets, just because they might fit into a display someday. No more gathering up odd trinkets from her friends' castoffs. There were boxes of things like that at the house; what on earth would she do with all of them?

Throw them away, she told herself firmly. She should go home and put them in the garbage tonight. She certainly wouldn't need that kind of junk anymore. She'd have much more important things to do than decorate windows, and just because she didn't know yet exactly what those things would be, certainly didn't mean that she wouldn't enjoy them just as much—even more, because they would involve Hunter. She'd always had sort of a knack for public relations. Maybe she could—

Kim was still studying the tabloid. "Lauren, I think you should at least look at these pictures."

"What? No, I won't, Kim. I won't dignify that rag by looking at it anymore. The pictures are bound to be retouched or airbrushed or whatever they do to make people look as if they're in compromising situations—"

"How did you know that they're compromising pictures?" Kim asked quietly. "I didn't say they were."

"Aren't they always? For all I know, they could even have used a double. I've heard of them doing that, when they can't get real dirt on someone." She took the paper by the corner and dropped it into the nearest wastebasket.

"You're probably right," Kim said. "Doubles, hmm? Still—" But she stopped there, and she didn't say any more about the tabloid.

Neither of them said much at all, in fact, and Lauren was glad when the time came for her afternoon break. Not even the pharmacy snack counter could be worse than silence.

At least, it hadn't been yet. On the first day that her cold had allowed her to go back to work, she had taken her courage very firmly in hand when it was time for her break. What if Ward thought that her mere presence in his store was an invitation to take up his lecture again precisely where she had called a halt to it before?

He wouldn't do that, she told herself. Not in public. Not Ward, who always thought about appearances.

But it wasn't until her coffee was in front of her and she was aimlessly stirring it that she realized that an argument was not the only sort of conduct that would draw attention. If Ward simply ignored her, that would be equally curiosity-provoking. And, she realized, it would be far more soothing to his ego than would an embarrassing fight. It would look, if he simply paid no attention to her, as if she was pursuing him. As if he had jilted her and not the other way around.

But of course he hadn't done that. Not Ward, the perfect gentleman. On that first afternoon, he had simply come down from the glass-walled cubicle at the back of the store to have his cup refilled, as he always did when she came in. And if this day, he had perched for barely half a minute on the stool beside hers and talked only about the suddenly warmer weather, well, who would notice, really? He was obviously busy; that was enough to account for the brevity of their chat and the fact that he hadn't even touched her hair, or commented about the silver-dollar-sized opal in the new necklace she was wearing.

And so it had continued as the days dragged slowly by. Sometimes he came down and sat beside her briefly; sometimes he only waved when she came in and then turned back to his work. She was grateful to him for not making a scene.

Alma refilled Lauren's cup. "Don't let it get you down," she recommended.

Lauren was so startled that she burned her tongue on her coffee.

"Ward, I mean," the woman went on. "With this bug that's going around, he's so busy he doesn't know if he's coming or going these days. It's nothing for you to worry about, dear."

"I'm sure it isn't," Lauren managed to say.

Alma smiled a little. "Trying to put a good face on it? I understand. He's a little impatient these days, himself. Just don't fret. As soon as the rush dies down he'll be the same old Ward. I understand you've had this bad cold, too?''

Lauren nodded, and got out of the pharmacy as soon as she could. The next day she didn't go back. There was no sense, she told herself, in making things more difficult for both of them.

The experience left her feeling a bit somber. For the first time, she had gotten a glimpse of what it was going to be like for Ward after her Valentine's Day departure. If everyone on Poplar Street was as sympathetically understanding of his feelings as Alma was, well, it wouldn't be easy on him, once everyone knew that Lauren had tossed him aside for Hunter Dix. In fact, for a man like Ward, that sympathy would not only grate, it would be close to unbearable.

At least he knew the truth, she reminded herself, so it wouldn't come as a nasty shock to him at the same moment the rest of Poplar Street found out. But there was nothing much else she could do to lessen the blow, and she felt guilty about leaving him to face the inevitable gossip.

Ward didn't deserve this kind of pain, that was sure. But someday, she knew, this would all be behind him, and he'd be happy again. Someday Ward would make some woman a wonderful husband. All he had to do, Lauren thought, was find a purely practical woman, one who would be happy with the things he could give her. A woman who understood that Ward was frosty orange juice and chicken soup and crocus bulbs in a pot, and who would be content with that. A woman who didn't have a romantic streak, and so didn't long for champagne and caviar and white roses by the dozen.

She hoped it didn't take long, for she hated to see him hurt like this and know that she had been the cause of it.

VALENTINE'S DAY dawned clear and unseasonably warm, and Lauren greeted it with the boundless, breathless joy of the sort she could recall feeling as a child on Christmas mornings when her feet scarcely touched the stairs as she hurried down to see what Santa had brought. Her heart was like a hot-air balloon, struggling to be free, and even doing the final things could not tug it back within earth's sober gravity again. The final things—cooking the last breakfast, cleaning out the few remaining perishables from the refrigerator, telephoning to stop the newspaper delivery, running across the street to drop off the extra key with the neighbors who always kept an eye on the house when she was gone—all those things she had done before, when she was leaving for a week or two. It would not truly sink in on her for days, perhaps, that this was the very final time.

She put the last few things in her suitcases, which lay stretched open on the bed in the guest room, but she did not close them up. Hunter hadn't been very clear about the exact schedule of the day, and so she thought they'd probably get her things after the concert. There was no sense in letting everything be mashed for longer than necessary; she could close the bags in a minute, when it was time.

And then there were the boxes to deal with—quite a pile of them, really, containing the sentimental things she simply could not let go. Family photo albums, her own baby book, her father's proudly framed law degree, that sort of thing. The boxes would have to go into storage for a while, she supposed; she certainly couldn't drag them around the world with her. The rest—the furniture, the dishes, the odds and ends of living—could be auctioned. That was the simplest way. The real-estate people could handle that, she supposed, before she actually put the house up for sale.

She felt a little disloyal for not having done so already; after all, she would not be coming back. But that news would have been very hard to keep quiet, so she had decided to wait till after Valentine's Day. The necessary papers could be mailed, and by that time, Poplar Street would have so much to talk about, the house wouldn't matter.

She made a last tour, pausing to rub a hand over her mother's oak hutch in the dining room with its precious Haviland china so carefully arranged on the shelves. She sat for a moment in the leather chair behind her father's walnut desk, and looked at the books that lined the shelves in his study.

"No," she told herself. "You must be reasonable, Lauren. You cannot take everything."

But perhaps she could take some extra things later. She would have to talk to Hunter about that, of course. If he had a house, there would surely be room for the hutch and the desk, at least, and for the precious memories they represented. There simply hadn't been time to talk to him about details like that.

The bronze mantel clock that had been her grandmother's told her that she had to go now, or she would be late for work. She turned the thermostat down and drew the curtains in the living room, then paused in the front hall. It was silly, but she could have sworn that something—the house itself, perhaps—had whispered goodbye. It was an almost mournful sound.

She gathered up her things from the hall table—her gloves, her handbag and the sealed envelope that held her resignation letter. She would leave it in the safe tonight for Mr. Baines to find tomorrow morning, after she was gone....

Tomorrow morning, when she would truly be beginning her new life, with Hunter.

"Oh, Hunter," she whispered. "To have you always! How did I deserve to be so lucky?"

THE POT OF CROCUS was still on the counter next to the cash register. Lauren hadn't touched them, but she knew that Kim had watered them faithfully, and she had been rewarded with a burst of cheerful, satiny, deep-purple blooms. This morning, even the prosaic crocus brought joy to Lauren's heart, and she was sniffing a particularly beautiful bloom when Kim came in. "You're actually here?" Kim said in disbelief. "I thought sure you'd be waiting for Hunter at the airport."

"No." Lauren tried to pull discreetly away from the crocus; she'd practically had her nose buried against the secret orange center of that flower! "He asked me not to, because there will be fans all over the place. He said he'd rather see me privately, later."

"Privately? I suppose that means he'll turn up at the store, white limousine, bodyguards and all?"

"Kim, what's happened to you? I thought you admired him!"

Kim shrugged. "I don't know. It was different somehow, looking up to him when he was untouchable. He was so glamorous and so perfect, he wasn't like a real person at all. Then when it turned out he's human after all . . .''

"Then it's even more wonderful," Lauren said.

Kim sighed. "I guess I like my heroes to stay on their pedestals, that's all.''

Lauren shook her head sadly. "It makes it very difficult on the heroes—trying to live up to all their admirers' illusions.''

"There's nothing wrong with illusions," Kim said flatly, "unless you get confused about what's real.'' Then she changed the subject firmly.

Lauren was glad. She knew that Kim must suspect what she was going to do, and it wasn't a thing she wanted to argue over—or even to talk about. She wanted only pleasant memories to take with her when she left tonight.

That was why she almost groaned when she saw Ward coming down Poplar Street late in the afternoon. She had deliberately avoided taking her coffee break, so she didn't have to go to the pharmacy and face him. And so he had come to her—to try one last persuasive argument? Or simply to say goodbye? Either would be less than comfortable, with Kim in the room and Mr. Baines within hearing.

Ward leaned on the counter and touched a fingertip to the satin petal of a crocus bloom. "They've done well, haven't they? It's hard to believe that such beautiful blooms can come from such tiny bulbs.''

Lauren said a little stiffly, "It was very thoughtful of you.''

"It's too bad . . ." he began, then turned a little pink, as if the words had slipped out despite his best intentions.

Lauren knew what he was thinking—that the crocus would have only a brief life, since they would never
be planted in the garden he had intended them to
grace. It hurt her, too, now that she thought about it.
It was not the crocus' fault, after all. They shouldn't
get a death sentence out of it.

"I suppose..." It was a bit awkward. "Well, Kim's
been taking care of them. It's up to her, really."

Kim looked at her oddly and opened her mouth as
if to ask why Lauren would be giving her credit—and,
incidentally, telling Ward that she had given his
flowers away to someone else!

Lauren hurried on. "There's a little patch of dirt by
the street lamp." She waved a hand toward the front
of the store. "Maybe they could go there, and help
make the street pretty next year, too." She touched a
glossy petal and bent over quickly to sniff the bloom.
"They *are* too beautiful to waste, and the fragrance... I'm only now beginning to be able to smell
again, after my cold, so I hadn't noticed before."

You're babbling, she told herself. Why can't you
just shut up, and let Ward say whatever he came in for,
and then he'll go away and leave you alone? It's almost the end of the day....

And Hunter has not come, the demon in the back
of her brain reminded. His plane landed hours ago,
and you have not had a word.

As if in answer, the white limousine pulled up in
front of the store and double-parked, blocking a
traffic lane. The chauffeur did not appear, and the
rear door opened from the inside. One of the bodyguards got out with a package in his hands.

Lauren's heart felt as if it had bounced on the floor.
No Hunter, then. Why not?

The bodyguard came into the jewelry store without a look to either side and set the package down in front of Lauren. "Mr. Dix wanted me to deliver this, Miss Hodges," he said in a near monotone. "And to tell you that the limousine will pick you up here before the concert tonight."

Lauren nodded, and after he was gone she looked down at the heart-shaped, cellophane-wrapped box. Chocolates, she thought helplessly.

"Well, I guess candy is the obvious thing for the day," Ward said. "Too bad, of course, that you're allergic to chocolate. Doesn't he know that? Or doesn't he care?"

Lauren bit her lip, but she was determined not to let her disappointment show. "I guess the subject just never came up," she said mildly, and reached for the nearest pair of scissors to slit the cellophane. When she lifted the lid off the box, two slips of cardboard fluttered out—new, signed backstage passes for tonight's show. She handed one to Kim with an almost ceremonial bow.

Underneath was a single layer of rich, moist candies, each in a dark paper cup, each identified by shape and color and the professional swirl on the surface. They were obviously good quality, but they were still chocolates, and she couldn't eat even one of them or she would break out into a gigantic case of hives— her whole body would turn red, and puff up and itch. And Ward would have to go rushing down to the pharmacy for an antihistamine to get it under control again.

He sends me roses I can't smell and candy I can't eat, she thought. But it wasn't fair to blame Hunter for not considering her stupid allergy; how could he have known? And lots of people wouldn't have thought about her stuffy nose and the roses, either.

"Well, would you look at that!" Kim said breathlessly. "What brand are these chocolates? I think I'd have Mr. Baines take a look at it, Lauren. It might be like the prize in a box of breakfast cereal."

Lauren looked at her in astonishment. "If you'd take your nose out of the box so I can see what brought on this torrent of enthusiasm, Kim . . ."

It was a ring, propped between two chocolate-coated butterscotch-crunch candies in the very center of the box. It had fallen to one side, which was why Lauren hadn't seen it right away; the stone had nestled against the side of a caramel, and only the gold glint of the band had drawn Kim's attention.

Lauren plucked the ring out of the box. A ruby winked back from between her fingers—a large, heart-shaped ruby, at least a full carat in size. On each side of it were mounted three tiny diamonds.

Lauren stood there and held it, and wondered why she was feeling just a little sad. Then she knew. Hunter had promised that when he returned she would have all the trappings of romance, and in her mind's eye she had seen a pleasant little dinner with champagne and caviar and candlelight. And afterward, in some private little spot, Hunter would kneel and formally ask her to marry him, and then he would put a very special ring on her finger. . . .

Well, there simply wasn't time for that, she told herself stoutly. There were demands that couldn't be put aside. There wasn't time for a leisurely dinner before the concert, and it was stupid to be annoyed at him for not wanting to wait until afterward to present her ring!

Besides, she thought, it was a rare woman who had a personal concert on the evening of her engagement. It *was* her concert tonight, devoted entirely to her. How much more romantic that was than any mere dinner could ever be.

And the ring—yes, it was a very special ring. Nothing could have been more appropriate than a heart-shaped ruby. And if Hunter couldn't be here himself to put it on her finger... Well, she was sure that later tonight he would bless it with a kiss.

She slid the ring onto her left hand. "Isn't it beautiful?" She stretched out her hand on the top of the display case and studied the effect of the blood-red stone. A heart-shaped ruby. She hadn't seen many of those.

Ward touched the stone with the very tip of his finger, turning the ring to face the light. It moved easily; it was a little large for her tiny hand. But that could be fixed easily enough, Lauren thought. Perhaps even this afternoon, if Mr. Baines had time...

Ward was extremely cautious to touch only the ring and not let his hand brush against her skin. She stayed very still, her hand almost frozen against the glass top of the cabinet, until he pulled away.

"I hope both of you will have a good time at the concert of the century," he said, and Lauren knew what he was really saying.

She drifted over to the window and watched as he walked down the street and stopped to chat with a customer and her little boy. And she told herself that it was foolish to feel sad because there hadn't been a chance to say a real goodbye. Very foolish, indeed. For what, really, was there to say?

Chapter Five

KIM OBVIOUSLY INTENDED to enjoy herself; the moment that the chauffeur ushered the two of them into the back of the limousine, she began playing with the buttons—turning the television on and off, tinkering with the telephone, and in general driving Lauren mad. Finally she settled back against the leather seat with a contented sigh. "May I look at your ring again?"

"It depends," Lauren said dryly. "Are you admiring the ring, or checking to see if my finger has turned green yet?"

Kim grinned. "That tabloid had me worried, you know. I really thought Hunter was just giving you a rush and that you were an idiot to fall for it. I never dreamed he was serious." She was studying the ruby in the glow of one of the reading lights when Lauren grabbed for the switch and turned it off. "Wait a minute," she protested. "I wasn't finished!"

"That's the convention center ahead," Lauren said, "and look at the crowd waiting. With the lights off, they can't see into the car."

"She learns fast, doesn't she?" Kim said to no one in particular.

Lauren glanced at the tiny clock built into the limousine's entertainment center. It was later than she had thought, and on the stage inside the convention hall, the opening band would already be performing. Yet there was an incredible number of people still standing outside, jamming the walks and pressing against the police barricades that had been set up to keep the street clear.

Even inside the quiet car, Lauren and Kim heard the shout that went up when the limousine was spotted, and Lauren could feel the color draining from her face as people began to leap the barricades almost into its path. It was not fear of what they might do that made her turn white, but fear for their safety as the car swept through the crowd without reducing its speed. Once past the barricades, it dropped down the ramp to the hidden, protected parking area beneath the building.

Kim's eyes were wide, and she was clutching at the edge of her seat. "So this is the way things will be from now on? I guess you won't be going to the grocery store very often, will you?"

Lauren laughed a little shakily. She had known intellectually that this sort of thing was likely to happen. But she hadn't really understood how it felt to be the pursued, and the experience had rattled her a little.

They thought it was Hunter in the car, she told herself; that's why the commotion was so great. I'm sure I'll get used to it eventually.

One of the bodyguards met the limousine and opened the door for them. Then he hurried them up another ramp to the main part of the building. "There's a special box reserved for you just off stage," he said. "I'll take you there right now—the concert has already started and Mr. Dix is getting ready to go on, so he'll see you at intermission."

But Lauren wasn't listening. She had managed to peek around his bulk, and in the wide hallway ahead she saw Hunter. He was leaning against an untidy pile of unrecognizable stage gear, and he was talking to a man a head shorter than he was.

He looked so different, she thought involuntarily. The tour had taken its toll.

He was thinner, and there were heavy lines almost slashed into his face, and his color was terrible—or was that only the stage makeup? It had to be harsh and garish, Lauren told herself, to stand up under the tremendously powerful lights he would face on stage. But he looked . . . awful. That was the only word for it. As if he needed a rest.

And he sounded worse. She didn't catch every word of what he said, but she got the substance of it. He was announcing that he detested the fans who were waiting for him to perform tonight, stupid fools that they were. He was tired of being at the beck and call of every pimply teenage girl who had the price of admission. . . .

"Hunter," she said in a voice that was little more than a whisper.

He didn't hear her, but the man with him did, and he put an elbow in Hunter's ribs. Hunter frowned at him and turned and called, "Sweet Lauren!" He came toward her, his arms outstretched. "My precious girl. You're shocked at me, aren't you?"

"You sound so cynical. . ." Her throat almost closed up.

"You mustn't fret, sweet Lauren. Of course I don't mean it. It's stage fright, you see. I have to do this every time I face a crowd, or I'd never get my nerve up to go through that door when the curtain rises. But with you here now to give me courage. . ." He reached for her hands, and when he saw the ruby on her finger something in his face changed. Before she could move, his arms were tightly around her, and his mouth was hard against hers till she couldn't get her breath, and her lips felt bruised. She tried to protest, but his tongue probed deep into her mouth, eager and demanding. She felt almost violated at the very public nature of that kiss, and she had to tell herself quite sternly that of course he was a little exuberant tonight. He hadn't seen her in two weeks; the man had a right to a kiss from the woman he loved, the woman who wore his ring. If he had gone a little overboard, that was understandable, and flattering, in a way.

And after all, the bodyguard hadn't seemed to notice anything unusual, and the man in the hallway had just walked away as if nothing had happened.

Kim gave Lauren a sidelong look as they settled into the draped private box at the side of the stage, but she didn't say anything. It was impossible to talk, anyway; the opening act was already well into its performance, and the hall was too noisy for conversation. Or for thinking, Lauren told herself; this group of performers certainly didn't agree with Hunter on what music was supposed to be.

People were still coming in, the ones, perhaps, who had been waiting outside, not caring about the first act, in the hope of seeing Hunter. They hadn't seen him, only the limousine, but they were happy. They didn't know it had been only illusion.

The band finished with an earsplitting roar, took its bows and left the stage, and a crew moved in, crawling over the stage like so many giant ants as they tugged the equipment into new positions. The work went incredibly fast, and less than five minutes later the lights changed, the crew vanished, and the anticipation began to build as Hunter's band members came on stage one by one and began a heavy, pounding, rhythmic theme that grew slowly and steadily into a crescendo of sound. And then, at the height of it, two spotlights snapped on and intersected at center stage on Hunter. The crowd was on its feet, and over the screaming, he began to sing.

It had been the stage makeup that had made him look so odd, Lauren thought. From her seat almost in the wings, he looked tanned and rested.

Another illusion, she thought.

He sang about the joy of coming back, and when the song was done he swept them all a bow, and began to talk to the "girder people"—the ones crammed into the very top of the house, almost against the steel rafters—telling them how important they were, and how delighted he was to be there to sing for them.

And that, too, Lauren thought, was illusion. For she knew, in the depths of her heart, that what she had overheard backstage had been the truth. He had meant every word of what he had said then. This charming Hunter, here and now, was the act—the one who was false.

But why should she be so surprised? He was a performer—a creator of illusion. That was what these people had come to see; they weren't disappointed.

But if all that was only a performance, she found herself wondering, then how much of what she had seen in Hunter was real, and how much was . . . just illusion?

It was almost as if each of Lauren's nerves had been rubbed with sandpaper and sensitized to falsehood, for she could hear it now in his voice. Even in songs she had loved for years, in lyrics she could quote entirely from memory. Tonight she was hearing a man who thought himself at the center of the universe and saw no reason that everyone else should not agree.

She glanced over at Kim, who was leaning forward, sometimes almost singing along, her eyes rapt. Obviously she didn't hear the egotistical undertone in this well-loved voice.

Was she being fair? Lauren asked herself. Any performer—any star—had to be certain of himself. How could anyone get up on that stage and bare his soul without that sort of self-confidence? Was she suddenly seeing him clearly for the first time, or was she just suffering from a case of cold feet?

She tried to swallow her confusion and simply enjoy the concert—her concert!—but she knew that the first half was almost over, and he was expecting her backstage at intermission.

Kim punched her in the ribs, and Lauren's attention snapped back to the stage.

"...a new song," Hunter was saying, "for a very special lady on Valentine's Day, to close out the first half of the evening..."

It was a beautiful melody, and the haunting lyrics spoke of love coming back into his life after he had thought his life was forever empty.

It was very good, Lauren thought, this song he'd written for her. It would be a hit, for it was enough to bring tears. Kim was crying. She would cry herself— if she still believed.

Perhaps Kim was the wise one after all, Lauren mused. *I like my heroes to stay on their pedestals,* she had said. Perhaps she too, should have left him there—a hero on a pedestal.

Kim stayed in the box at intermission, still sniffling and fumbling for her handkerchief. "You're one lucky girl," she said with a gulp, when the bodyguard came to get Lauren.

Lauren hugged her and smiled. Yes, she thought, she was. For she could see it all clearly now. That beautiful love song wasn't about her at all, but about him; her feelings and her desires had never entered his mind when he wrote those lovely words. And she could see now that the passionate kiss tonight had nothing to do with her, but with the need to conquer. And the urgency of his plea that she come with him tonight—why was it so important, after all, that it be now? *Because once I was away from the familiar, I would be dependent on him. And there are lots of other women who would have done just as well.*

The things he said and did had not been an expression of his love, but of his selfishness. There had been signs of it all along, now that she looked for them— the telephone calls at hours convenient only to him, the list of complaints of the way he was being treated on the tour, the way he had belittled the bodyguards. He obviously thought that rules—like restaurant dress codes—did not apply to him, and also that cash was a tonic to be applied to solve any problem.

But she had excused those things, overlooked them, ignored them, and concentrated on the romantic gestures instead—the champagne and the roses and the ring—things that in the end were meaningless. How much thought did it take, really, to tell a bodyguard to wire two dozen roses? And what did a ring mean, when it was delivered without a word about love or commitment—indeed, without any word at all?

She did not feel angry at him for betraying her, or for villainously plotting this entire scheme. She had asked for it, after all, and eagerly marched along to the tune he had sung. Besides, she thought that his self-centeredness was so complete that Hunter himself was incapable of realizing when he was using other people.

No, she was not angry. She was conscious of nothing but a soul-deep relief that she had come to her senses in time.

Backstage, Hunter moved to seize her for another kiss, but she sidestepped him.

He looked startled, and then he said, "I see. A little more privacy?" and started to draw her into a dressing room nearby.

Lauren shook her head. "That's not necessary. I came backstage to thank you for my concert, Hunter." She pulled the ruby ring off her finger and dropped it into his palm. "And to return this. I'm not sure what it meant, but I'm certain you didn't intend it to be an engagement ring. Did you?"

He was still stammering—it was an interesting phenomenon, Lauren thought, Hunter Dix without words!—when a tall redhead in elaborate makeup and a very short skirt sauntered up beside him and slipped her arm through his. "You're in wonderful voice, darling," she murmured.

"Who the hell let you in?" Hunter said roughly.

"You don't think I'm going to tell you, do you? You'd fire the poor soul." But the woman wasn't looking at him; she was surveying Lauren through narrowed eyes. Lauren recognized her. So the tabloids hadn't had all the details right about his actress friend leaving him, after all, for here she was....

"Who is *she?*" the woman asked. "Honestly, Hunter, not another groupie. I swear, every time you go on tour—"

"I'm no one you need to worry about," Lauren said gently. "Goodbye, Hunter."

It was busy backstage, and easy to slip through the crowded hallways and out to the street, where the air was fresh. There were still a few people hanging about outside the convention center. One was a girl, clutching a promotional poster and a pen, waiting patiently for a moment with her hero—

Some kind of hero he had turned out to be, Lauren thought. She realized that her backstage pass was still in her hand, and she considered giving it to the girl. Then she shredded it into the gutter instead, for she could not square it with her conscience if she helped to feed someone else's hero-worship.

It was cold but not bitter, and as she walked away from the glow of the convention center's lights, the stars appeared, gleaming in the clear sky. Her heart was soothed a little, and when she saw a cab she hailed it and gave the driver her home address. She sank back against the ripped vinyl and began to think of the peaceful quiet of her own living room, and of the work that awaited her—putting back in place all the pieces of her life she had ripped apart in the past couple of weeks. The clothes, the photograph albums, the sentimental memories—the friendships.

It was too late, she told herself. She'd been such a fool—rude, obnoxious, stupid. How could any man forgive being called a miserable, suspicious creep? To say nothing of the other things she'd called him, the way she'd acted, the nincompoop she'd been.

Still . . . she had to try, didn't she? She could at least say she was sorry, and clear her conscience, even if Ward didn't care to accept her apology.

She sat up straight and said to the driver, "I've changed my mind. Take me to Poplar Street instead, please."

"Nothing's open there this time of night, miss."

"I know," she said. "That's why I want to go."

The cabbie shook his head at the craziness, but he changed direction. Lauren had a sudden twinge of apprehension as the blocks went by. Bursting in on Ward like this might not be such a good idea.

Well, she told herself firmly, it was better than just turning up tomorrow at the pharmacy. He might say anything, then. And she couldn't apologize in public—not the way she should apologize. She probably couldn't tell him all the things she should, anyway. She certainly couldn't say that she was an idiot for not knowing what love really was!

But why couldn't she? she asked herself. It was the truth.

It was like waking from a nightmare, drenched with sweat, relieved to find that the bogeyman wasn't real, but finding that the whole world had assumed a greater clarity—every noise, every ray of light, every thought...

She'd let herself be so blinded by illusion, she thought, that she couldn't see reality. She'd fallen so hard for an image that she couldn't recognize real love when she saw it.

When she had been sick, Ward had been there, quietly doing what needed to be done. He had brought her food, and stayed with her, and risked her germs, and made sure she was cared for. How much easier it would have been for him to go back home, kick off his shoes, call the shop down the street and send her a bunch of flowers!

Romance isn't just a word, she mused, it's an attitude. It isn't lavish gifts, it's thoughtful ones. Sometimes it's not caviar, but chicken soup. And roses are beautiful, but crocus lasts forever, and renews itself each spring.

Why had she never seen Ward's gifts in that light before—in the light of love?

But was that truly what it was, she asked herself, or only what she wanted it to be? *Don't kid yourself, Lauren; he's never said a word about loving you.* And he had all the time in the world to tell her before Hunter ever came along. And he hadn't done a thing for her that he wouldn't have done for half of his customers.

There was a dim yellow glow in the windows of his apartment above the pharmacy. She stared up at the front of the building for a long moment, and then paid off the cab.

It was funny, she thought as she turned toward the stairs. At the convention center, she didn't feel a bit as if she'd burned all her bridges. Now, she did. What if she went up there and told Ward that birthday dinners at home and movies and Sunday afternoon drives were important to her, after all, even if that was all she'd ever have—and he said that he didn't want even that much anymore?

Ward opened the door six inches and stopped. There was no warm gleam in his eyes. "To what do I owe this pleasure?"

She ducked her head. What did she expect, she asked herself miserably. Arms thrown wide in welcome? She had treated the poor man like dirt.

"Surely the concert isn't over yet, Lauren."

She concentrated on the second button of his shirt. "It's over for me."

He didn't move. After a moment, he said, "And since you didn't want to be alone with your self-pity, you came here for comfort?"

She looked up in surprise. "No. Not at all. I came to tell you I've been temporarily insane, and I'm sorry."

His eyes closed for a moment as if in pain, and Lauren's heart twisted. She thought, *He does know how to use those incredible eyelashes to good effect!* Or perhaps it was just that he didn't have to manipulate people, and so didn't use them....

He stepped back then, and she followed him into the living room, cheerfully cluttered with books and records. There was a volume facedown on the coffee table, as if he'd put it hastily aside to answer the door.

Lauren took her coat off, and then didn't quite know what to do with it, for Ward made no move to take it from her. She sat down finally with the coat folded awkwardly in her arms, and Ward perched on the edge of a chair across from her. "He didn't jilt me, you know," she said, with a note in her voice that was almost a challenge.

Ward sighed. "I suppose that's my cue to ask what *did* happen. If it's all the same to you, Lauren—"

"I told him goodbye," she said simply. "I told him..."

He did not move, or respond, and Lauren's eyes filled with tears. *It's too late,* she thought. She couldn't say that she blamed him for it, after the way she'd treated him. If he ever did love her, it was certainly gone now.

"Well, I'm proud of you." Ward got to his feet. "Thanks for letting me know, so I wouldn't think I was seeing a ghost when you came in for coffee tomorrow."

"Do you have to be so mean and stubborn?" Lauren asked in fury. Then the anger died with a hopeless little gasp. What good would that do, now? "It was obviously a mistake for me to come here," she said stiffly. "May I use your phone to call a cab?"

He waved a hand toward it without a word, and she fumbled with the telephone book, trying to find the number.

"You said I was a fool," she said, "and I came to tell you that you were right, you know. More than that, I was an idiot. You know that song he was writing for me?"

"Lauren—"

"Remember the old story about the guy who called up girls and asked them out for a day on his boat? 'It's a very special boat,' he'd tell each one. 'I named it after you.' And when they got to the dock, sure enough, there on the stern of the boat was painted two words— 'after you'. That's what my song was like. It'll be a hit, and I'm sure Hunter knew exactly what he was doing. Any woman can pretend it's all about her."

Ward took the telephone receiver out of her hand and hung it up just as the dispatcher answered. Then he put his arms around her. "Lauren, I'm so sorry."

"Dammit, don't you see that I don't want you to be sorry?" Her words were indistinct, between sobs, but they were the best she could do.

He led her over to the couch and held her while she cried tears of anger, frustration, fear and happiness all mixed in together. For nothing could be completely wrong when she was in his arms like this. He hadn't thrown her out. That was something, wasn't it?

Eventually he dried her face with his handkerchief and said, "Better?" and smiled down into her eyes, a sad sort of smile. "I'll take you home."

It was oddly final. So, all those loving things he'd done for her, she thought hopelessly, had been just friendship, after all. She'd been fooling herself; now that she had finally decided that he was what she wanted—the man she loved—he only wanted to get rid of her.

"No," she said forlornly. "I'm not better." It didn't hurt her pride to admit it, for she had none left to be hurt.

"Lauren, what is it you want from me?"

She had started to cry again, silently and torment-edly. "I want you to *care,* that's all."

"Care that you're hurting? Or course I—"

"No. I want you to care about *me.*" It was so quiet that he had to bend his head to hear.

His voice was husky. "Oh, I care, all right. Too much. It ripped me up to watch you these past two weeks, and know what a horrible mistake you were making, and that there was not one thing I could do to stop you. If I'd said something before he came along, but I couldn't, and so—"

"Couldn't?" That was an odd way to put it, surely. She mopped futilely at the tears on her cheeks. "Why couldn't you?"

For a moment she thought he wasn't going to answer at all. "What have I got to offer you?" he said quietly. "I'm not talking about his kind of money...but the things you've got already that I could never afford, the things your parents left you. I'm up to my eyebrows in debt after buying the pharmacy, Lauren. Someday I'll be out of it, but it isn't fair to drag you down with me in the meantime."

"It certainly—" she began.

"I can't take on the upkeep on your house—and I won't ask you to give the place up. I love you too much to ask you to make sacrifices like that."

There was a little glow in her midsection. She had been right about one thing, at least. He was awfully stubborn. No, perhaps not actually stubborn, but he was firm in his beliefs. A woman would always know where he stood, and she could be certain that it was safe to lean on him, to trust him.

"Oh, hell, honey," he said ruefully, "I might as well be honest. I can't even afford your earrings, and I won't ask you to give up pretty things for the sake of..." His fingers brushed softly across her hair, pulling it back to expose the simple costume pearl in her earlobe.

"They were ten dollars," she said, "with my employee discount."

"What happened to the diamond ones?"

"Those belong to the store. And since I wasn't planning to go back, I left them in the safe tonight, along with the opal necklace and the sapphire ring. Oh, Ward, how could you have thought I owned all that stuff? There was something new every week!"

"I know," he said simply. "And I added it up and it didn't fit very well in my budget. And I couldn't afford the kind of ring that would coordinate with all that glitter, so—"

"Ring?" she said demurely. "What sort of a ring are we talking about?"

But for a long time after that they didn't talk about much of anything, except some whispered bits between kisses. And Lauren reflected—in the odd spaces when she could think at all—that if they gave a prize for knowing how to make a woman feel loved, and cherished, and adored, that Ward would surely win it....

It was a great deal later when she said, with a twinge of wry humor, "Good heavens, I forgot to say goodbye to Kim. I just walked out on her at intermission."

"Kim can take care of herself," Ward said mildly.

"Oh, I'm not worried, exactly. She was going to take a cab home, anyway, since we didn't want to risk upsetting Hunter's plans for after the concert—" Then, as she abruptly remembered that it might not be a good idea to mention Hunter's name, she looked up at Ward warily.

He was smiling. "I'd say you did a pretty good job of that all by yourself." He stretched. "Kim will get a surprise tomorrow, that's all—it will be good for her. I think I've got a bottle of champagne somewhere. If you'd like to celebrate, that is."

"Oh, I'd certainly like to celebrate." She hesitated, and then said firmly, "But I'd rather have orange juice."

"Orange juice? Lauren, that's the craziest—"

She silenced him with a finger across his lips, and then with a kiss. She'd explain it someday, she decided.

And she knew Ward would understand that some things were just too important to toast with mere champagne.

HARTZ & FLOWERS

Peggy Nicholson

A word from Peggy Nicholson

It happens frequently. Learning I'm a romance writer, some single man sidles up to me at the cocktail party, dinner, whatever. He lowers his voice. "I've been wondering," he murmurs, "where you get your ideas? Are they based on, ahem! ah... experience?" Being a typical male, this man has probably never read a romance, but he thinks he knows what they're all about.

Depending on my mood—and his looks—I assume a haughty, incredulous stare, or I bat my eyelashes and give him my mysterious wouldn't-*you*-like-to-know smile.

But experience does, in fact, feed the writing muse, and bits and pieces of me show up in everything I write—how could they not? In *Hartz & Flowers,* you'll find several of my recurring themes. For instance, the love of animals. This time it's a miniature pet pig and a lop-eared rabbit, neither of which I was lucky enough to own as a kid. But on my family's one acre "farm" on the outskirts of Houston, Texas, we kept two horses, two goats—the first goat was my eleventh-birthday present from my whimsical mother, and the second was a bonus because goat one was pregnant—one calf, one hamster, one rat, a ton of turtles, the odd snake, a canary, an alligator, three cats, four dogs, some vile-tempered Egyptian geese... Well, you get the picture.

My delight in whimsical men and the crazy gifts they bring is another theme you'll find here. No man has given me a coat like the one Duncan brings Joanna, but some of my own most treasured gifts are a duck phone—quacks instead of rings—and a Hell's Angel tank top, which I sometimes wear for writing inspiration.

An actual experience is the basis for Duncan's tale of his first date. I was the awkward girl who didn't know how to receive a small, heart-shaped box of Valentine chocolates in the spirit in which it was offered. (Pickle, wherever you are, I apologize. You were a doll, and I'd date you again in a minute.) And now, enough of confessions. I hope you enjoy Joanna Hartz's show, and here's wishing you a Valentine's Day that, in Duncan's words, curls your toes and leaves a silly grin on your face!

Chapter One

TEN MINUTES TO AIRTIME. Joanna Hartz gulped a deep breath to slow her panting, pasted a smile of brisk composure on her face and opened the unmarked door that led to a back corridor of the NBS network studios.

Her crew was waiting, of course. Susan and Tasha pounced, while in the background, Art, the number-one cameraman, shook his clasped hands at heaven in thanks for prayers answered. "There you are!" Susan cried.

"What happened?" Tasha demanded. The makeup artist caught Joanna's chin to study her flushed face, then shook her head in despair.

"Truck jackknifed on the Cross Bronx Expressway into Manhattan. Blocked every lane. No one was really hurt, thank goodness," Joanna told them as they wheeled and marched toward the makeup room. She smiled at Art as he hugged the wall, standing on tiptoe in mock terror of the women's high heels as they clattered past. "Everyone's made up and ready to go?" The Joanna Hartz morning talk show started at nine, and seven million viewers would be waiting. The familiar excitement and dread rippled through her stomach.

"Joanna, which do you want first? The good news or the bad?" Susan Hadley, Joanna's capable young senior producer, had a pale complexion at the best of times.

This morning the blonde's face almost matched her celery-green shirtwaist, Joanna realized as her head snapped around. "The bad," she said automatically, then staggered as Tasha pulled her sideways into the makeup room.

Susan squared her shoulders, then delivered her speech in one machine-gun burst. "The bad news is that your pig lady canceled. She said her porky pet— what's his blasted name?—Munchems—has, and I quote, 'a wee case of indigestion this morning.' She thinks maybe it's stage fright."

The miniature pet pig didn't know what real stage fright was, Joanna thought savagely, as her own stomach stepped out an imaginary plane door and dropped into a free-fall. Without Evelynn Weatherby and her Munchems, the show would be a disaster. The mayor of Evelynn's town and her landlord couldn't carry it by themselves. They had only been invited to supply some fireworks—the mayor in particular, who was prone to bellowing. But what use was it in debating the zoning laws that prevented people from keeping pet pigs in their apartments in Winston, Pennsylvania, if she couldn't supply exhibit A—the oh-so-winsome and impeccably house-trained Munchems himself?

"Give me the good news," she pleaded, as her knees gave out and she dropped onto the stool in front of the mirror. She turned her face one way then the other automatically, as Tasha powdered it.

"The good news is that I've found you a *fabulous* replacement," Susan assured her with the soothing heartiness of a life-insurance salesman. Reflected in the mirror above Joanna's shoulder, she flushed a becoming shell pink. "I interviewed him yesterday, and I was going to recommend that we book him for some time in May, if we could possibly fit him in...."

A warning bell tolled somewhere in the back of Joanna's whirling brain. "You interviewed a prospect on a *Sunday?*"

Susan's blush deepened a shade, but her chin lifted defiantly. "Over brunch. And he happened to ask me for a ticket to your show for today. So when the pig finked out on us, I went out in the audience and—"

"Seven minutes to air," tolled the gloom laden baritone of the show's assistant director from out in the hallway.

"Who is he?" Joanna prodded.

"Duncan Flowers."

To be a successful talk-show host is to be a generalist, crammed to the gills on every subject from the politics of drift-net fishing to the art of Balinese shadow puppetry. A drawer in Joanna's mental file cabinet slid open with an ominous clang. "Flowers, the ex-English professor from Harvard? Best selling author of *How to Make Your Book a Bestseller (Even if It's a Bowwow)?*"

"That's him," Tasha cut in with an earthy chuckle. "And believe me, *he's* no bowwow!" She picked up a powder puff lying on the table in front of the mirror. "I'm retiring this pad I used on him. It lives under my pillow from now on."

"But that's the book he wrote two years ago," Susan said, ignoring the glint in Joanna's eye. "That's not what he wants to talk about today. He—"

"No. He wants to push his latest, doesn't he?" Joanna snapped her teeth together and stretched a taut smile while Tasha applied a rich red lipstick that would not bleach out under the stage lights.

"Four minutes, Joanna—let's move it!" the assistant director called.

"Yes, he does, and here it is." Susan dropped a book in Joanna's lap, then beat a hasty retreat from the room.

While Tasha pulled a brush through her red shoulder-length hair, Joanna stared down at the books' garish cover in disgust—*101 Ways To Win The Woman Of Your Dreams* the title blared. Its subtitle declared it The Modern Man's Guide to Romance. She had not read it yet, but she'd certainly heard about it. Her friend Liza Janak had been lambasting it only yesterday at a cocktail party in Greenwich. What had she said? Cynical, trite, manipulative and insulting to any woman with a brain. And bound to be a raging bestseller.

That's where she came in, of course. Duncan Flowers plainly meant to use her and her show as a platform from which to launch his latest bowwow at the bestseller list. "We'll see about that!" Joanna growled as she headed for the door. "We'll *just* see." She swung back as Tasha spoke.

"Joanna? It'll go great. The audience will love him." She winked and gave a thumbs-up. "Just don't let him blow you off the stage."

With ninety seconds till air, Joanna stepped out onto the dais. As always, the audience's roar of approval sent a surge of adrenaline sweeping through her. She felt as if her mane of red hair were standing on end. Her palms turned to ice and her stomach to a sickening whirlpool. But she'd forget all that once the show started. Ignoring the man who sat waiting in an armchair beside her stage desk, she sketched a cocky salute at the crowd, then glanced down at her watch. Seventy seconds.

As she approached her desk, Duncan Flowers rose to meet her—and kept on rising. Unfolded to full height, he topped her own five-foot-ten-in-heels by a good five inches. But this was no string bean. With those shoulders, the overall effect was Great Wall of China on the hoof. *High, wide and handsome,* she thought derisively as she met his eyes.

Bam. It was like running into a wall—they stopped her cold, her wheels still spinning. These were eyes of heavenly blue with a gleam of pure devilment. One eyelid, fringed in silver-tipped gold, came down in a lazy wink as he held out his hand.

Usually the guest waited for *her* to make the first move. Tossing his book on the desk, she smacked her hand into his a little too briskly.

A hint of a dimple shadowed his left cheek. His fingers curled around hers, her hand disappearing entirely into a place of warmth and almost frightening power. Then he just stood there. Looking down at her.

Showtime. They were playing her intro. On screen, the TV viewers would see but not hear her and her guest for the next thirty seconds, their live images overlaid with the name of her show. Was this clown going to let go of her hand, or would she have to wear him for the next sixty minutes? "Hi," he said in a rumbling undertone.

"Do you *mind?*" she whispered.

"Huh...oh!" He glanced down, then released her hand.

"One question before we go audible, Mr. Flowers." Joanna detoured around his bulk to reach her chair. "What did you pay Evelynn Weatherby to stay home?"

His grin was absolutely wicked—teeth and dimple flashing all at once, his golden head tipping back in a silent yelp of laughter. And his eyes crinkled at the corners, she noticed in disgust. Probably he'd had plastic surgery to create the effect. It was too good to be true.

"Nice guess," he murmured and pulled her chair out for her. "I paid her five thousand, and Munchems settled for a box of Valentine candy. Evelynn says to tell you thanks very much, anyway, and that she's using the money as a down payment on a condo outside the city limits where they take pigs. Munchems said to tell you 'oink.'"

Five thousand! Joanna shut her mouth with a snap and slipped into her chair. But that was peanuts to spend on promotion, she calculated swiftly. If his book made the bestseller list, he'd earn that much back overnight. He assisted her in easing her chair close to the desk, and she glanced over her shoulder at him. Fifteen seconds till the intro theme ended. "Nobody uses me, Mr. Flowers." She'd promised herself that the night Jason walked out on her—had held to it come hell or high water, the past three years.

His blue eyes widened guilelessly. "Who's talking about using, Ms. Hartz? I always pay my way."

"Oh? And what are you going to pay me for hijacking my show?"

A lock of her hair must have been trapped between the chair and her back. It pulled suddenly—the sensation was that of someone tweaking it gently. But that was unthinkable. Even this man wouldn't dare.

"Your reward will be the most talked-about show you've had all year," Flowers assured her.

Why, the egotistical, insufferable...! "Thanks," she growled, "but I preferred the—"

Airtime. In the control room, the sound engineer threw a switch.

"—pig!" Her last word was picked up by the mikes. It resounded through the hushed studio like a smack in the face.

Flowers clapped one hand to his breast in mock pain and collapsed in his chair, wounded to the quick. The audience tittered nervously, except for one man way in the back, who had a guffaw like a donkey's bray. Flowers jerked his head toward the sound, his face miming comic disbelief. He actually shielded his eyes with one hand, as he tried to spot the source of the outburst. The audience laughed louder.

Don't let him blow you off the stage. He was the class clown grown up, Joanna realized grimly as she waited for the noise to die down. With the wit and the charm and the sheer, good-looking charisma to steal the class right out from under the teacher, if she wasn't on her toes. And he had caught her empty-handed. She didn't know beans about his book.

Except for one thing. She was already sure she loathed it. She cut smoothly into the laughter as it trailed off. "Good *morning,* and welcome to The Joanna Hartz Show. For those of you in the studio audience, let me say thanks for braving the sleet and snow to be with us today. Those of you at home, believe me, there's no place you'd rather be than cuddled up in front of a warm TV. And if everybody's not cozy enough already, we have a guest who *claims* to have written a book to warm your heart." Beside her, Flowers caught the note of skepticism in her voice and swung around to study her instead of the audience. "At the very least," Joanna continued silkily, "it should inspire some heated debate."

She continued her intro, outlining Flowers's professional credits and emphasizing his previous success with a book that had become a primer on media manipulation for authors and politicians alike. "And now, perhaps Mr. Flowers will tell us something about his latest effort?" She turned her smile on him. His blue gaze touched hers, and the sensation brought back memories of the fencing class she'd taken once—that tiny rasp of steel crossing steel for the first time.

"Be glad to. My book's about courting women..." Flowers rose, picked up his portable mike and sauntered away from her, talking as he went. Dumbfounded, Joanna stared after him. He was upstaging her beautifully. He stopped on the second wide step down from the dais, one hand in his pocket in a casual, just-between-you-and-me folks pose that was probably as rehearsed as it was effective.

And his action torpedoed her original plan. She'd meant to stay at her desk for this interview, using its cover to sneak peeks at his book in the intervals while he spoke. Instead she rose and stalked after him. "Mr. Flowers," she purred, "your last book outlined an approach for making any book a bestseller, even if it was a 'Bowwow.' But with this new book, aren't you simply trotting out another tired old dog for the American public? Why is a book on wooing women even needed? People seem to have been meeting and mating without your help for the past fifty thousand years or so."

"They have, Ms. Hartz," he admitted cheerfully. "But have they had *fun* while they were doing it? Believe me, for the average American male, the dating-and-mating scene is no day at the beach. It's scary. It's tough on the ego. Sometimes, when you're rejected, it's...heartbreaking."

If he was looking for sympathy, he'd come to the wrong place. There wasn't a woman in the audience who could conceive of this blond hunk being rejected—ever. Lifting her arms and grinning wickedly, Joanna played an imaginary violin for him, and the audience joined in gleefully with an extended "Aw-w-w!"

But he wasn't rattled. He laughed at them all, then said, "I'm serious! We men were dropped here on earth without operating manuals. Our instinct tells us to chase women, but it doesn't tell us how."

"You need any lessons, *I'll* show you how!" called a sexy contralto from the audience.

Joanna put a finger to her lips and looked stern, while Flowers pressed on. "Sure, the average American male knows the basics—me Tarzan, you Jane. But he doesn't know the *fine* points of how to melt a woman's heart. And because he doesn't know how to romance a woman, how to woo her, he strikes out. Too often."

"So this book is to help men *score*. It's not for women at all." Joanna lifted her thick red-gold brows and looked out at her mostly female audience with weary significance. *Men!* her look said.

"No." This time Flowers turned and addressed her directly. "No, this book is to help people *connect*—and I'm talking hearts, not bodies." He swung back to the audience. "I'm saying a romance should spark. It should sizzle. It should curl your toes and leave a silly grin on your face. It should be funny and tender, and it should leave you with memories that'll warm your poor old heart when you're ninety." His voice had dropped to an intimate drawl—he was playing them like a violin, now. He held up his book, angled slightly toward the correct camera. "That's the kind of love affair every woman should have at least once in her life. And this book shows a man how to give it to her."

He was good with words, so good. Joanna could feel them tugging at her the way the moon tugs the tide. The women in the audience were practically falling chin first out of their chairs as they yearned toward him. But this was nothing but a sales pitch. She had to regain control.

As Joanna opened her mouth, Flowers appealed directly to the audience. "What do *you* all think? Is there enough romance in your lives?"

"No!" It was a full-throated feminine chorus, laughing and rueful and plaintive.

Joanna gritted her teeth. This was *her* audience—he had no right to talk to it directly. Just who was the host here and who the guest?

"Would you like your date, or your lover, or even your husband to polish up his romantic techniques?" he prompted them.

"Yes!" they thundered, then broke into a storm of applause.

She had lost them completely. It had never happened before. She felt like a jilted woman, watching her lover dance away with his new love. Her eyes stung, and she widened them fiercely. Flowers had raised his book even higher—he was obviously about to say that, in that case, everyone should buy his book. She cut in neatly. "Well, that's emphatic enough. And now I think we'll take a short break. Back in a moment."

Lowering his book, Flowers gave her a lopsided smile. She returned it with one sweet enough to gag a honeybee and turned toward her desk. Now was her chance to scan his book for ammo. But his hand closed on her arm.

"Why are you so mad at me?" His voice was a husky growl.

"I've told you, I've got better things to do than promote your book for you. And I used up my whole weekend, slogging through *Swine in Prehistoric and Modern Times*. I read municipal zoning laws until I could have wept with boredom. Then I came up with twenty questions for Evelynn and her pig. And now you barge in and throw it all away!'' She looked pointedly at the big fingers creasing her winter-white silk suit.

He didn't take the hint. ''I'm sorry, but look at it this way. You didn't have to do one minute of prep for this show, so it evens out, doesn't it?''

''But you haven't got Munchems' stage presence,'' she assured him and twitched her arm. He grinned and let her go.

After the commercial, they were both seated again, and Joanna returned to the attack. ''Mr. Flowers, your book is structured in the form of tips—number one, two and so on. For instance, tip number eight suggests that the man give his 'target' a dozen red roses. Now, does anyone really need to *pay* for advice like that? Are all your tips that trite and obvious?''

Flowers looked soulful. ''What's wrong with being obvious? Red roses promise passion—you're right, my suggestions aren't wishy-washy, they go straight to the point. But is there anything nicer, sexier, more *romantic* than a man telling you he wants you? No gesture can ever be corny if it comes from the heart,'' he said, touching his chest. ''That's my point exactly.''

The audience burst into applause, and Joanna steamed. He was such a phony, couldn't they see? But if he wasn't genuine, he was fast. Each time she jabbed, he parried with a grin, or a diversion, or an appeal to the doting spectators. And after the third commercial break, when she accepted questions from members of the studio audience, things only got worse. They were all on his side. One woman, obviously having read the book, asked him to demonstrate tip six. He went down into the audience and kissed her hand with all the swashbuckling flair of

Errol Flynn. Joanna wanted to throw up her hands and storm off the stage.

But she hadn't earned her own talk show by being a quitter. "If the methods you recommend are as foolproof as you guarantee, Mr. Flowers, then couldn't this book be misused?" she cooed.

His eyes sparkled wickedly, but he answered her with a straight face, turning back to the camera as he spoke. "You're absolutely right, Ms. Hartz. In the wrong hands, my book could be shamelessly exploited. And this is a good time to say something." He pointed a stern finger at the audience. "Men, I don't want you buying my book if you're not going to use it with discretion. It wouldn't be fair to turn these tips loose on a married woman."

Joanna snorted. "Mr. Flowers, that's utterly obnoxious! You're claiming that, using your 101 tips, a man could steal a contented wife from her loving husband? That's not only asinine, it's absurd!"

"But unfortunately, it's true," Flowers insisted humbly. He lowered his shaggy gold brows at the camera. "So I'm telling you, men, it's okay to use my book on Miss Universe, or Playboy's Miss February. They're not taken. But stay away from Kathleen Turner. I hear she's happily married. Same goes for Maggie Thatcher."

Rolling her eyes, Joanna announced a break for a commercial. Although, come to think of it, that's all her show had been today—one long commercial. But the ordeal was nearly over.

After the break she took phone calls from the home audience. Two of the callers were men demanding to know where they could buy the book. The third was a woman with a breathless baby-doll voice, who offered Flowers her phone number. The control room censors cut her off just in time.

The show cut to the final commercial and the laughter was stemmed. Joanna stalked back to her desk, while Flowers signed autographs for the women in the front row of the studio.

A few questions from the audience should finish the fiasco off, Joanna thought. She had a raging headache, and she hated to think of the ragging she'd take backstage after this. "Questions?" She chose a young black man in the second row who was waving his hand frantically.

He stood and accepted her microphone. "Mr. Flowers, you said your tips would work on any woman. But Ms. Hartz here doesn't seem to like you so much. Do you think you could woo *her* successfully?"

"Certainly," Flowers said immediately.

Joanna snatched back her mike. "Certainly *not!*"

"How'd you go about it?" the young man called.

"Well..." Flowers flipped open his book and studied a page thoughtfully. "To make my first approach, I might use number five, and tell her what gorgeous green eyes she has." He glanced up at her with a grin. "But I bet she's heard that before." Thumbing through his book, he descended the steps, and in spite of his casual approach, Joanna felt the hairs at the nape of her neck prickle. The man moved like a sleepy tiger.

"Or," Flowers drawled as he stopped beside her, "I might try number fourteen." He cocked his head consideringly at her, while she racked her brains for a clue to what number fourteen said. Was that the one about serenading her with a guitar?

"But I'd probably do number twenty-one," Flowers decided with a little nod of decision. "So...first I do this." He hooked his free arm around her waist and dipped her expertly backward, tango-style.

Joanna squeaked and grabbed for his shoulders. She could see laughing blue eyes, a swath of silky gold and the ceiling tiles. Then, as his mouth came down on hers, her senses spiraled inward, noting lips that were as soft as his arms were hard, a hint of mint tooth-paste on his warm breath, the pounding of a heart against her breast. There was a roaring in her ears, but whether that was the audience or just her having a stroke, she couldn't have said.

His lips brushed a line of fire across her cheek as he turned his head toward the audience and the book he held. "And then I say...I say... Darn, I lost my place."

Still bent like a willow, Joanna turned to see the maniac flipping the pages with one hand.

"Ah, I say..." He turned to smile down at her. "*Gosh,* I've been dying to do that ever since I first met you!" Gently he brought her back to the vertical. "And then *she* says—"

"You cynical clown!" Her palm connected with his cheek in a resounding smack.

The audience booed—they'd never booed her before in her life! Hurt layered itself on top of her outrage and confusion.

"Wait a minute!" One hand to his reddening cheek, Flowers consulted his book. "Is *that* what she says?" He read for a second, then looked up indignantly. "You're not supposed to say that."

She was shaking all over, but somehow her voice came out steady. "I guess that proves how effective your methods are." She turned to the audience. "I'd advise everyone to save their money."

"Not at all," Flowers insisted. "My methods are one hundred percent effective. But they don't always work immediately. Sometimes they take a little time."

She spun back to glare at him. "Flowers, your methods wouldn't work on me if you took forty years!"

"Want to bet?" His voice dropped to an electric whisper.

It stopped her cold, that or the sparkle in his eyes. "Uh...I..."

"What's the matter, Ms. Hartz?" he taunted, advancing a step. "Are you scared to bet? Scared to let a little romance into your heart?"

"Not at all!" Joanna whipped her ruffled hair back from her face with one hand and stood her ground. "I'm just choosy."

"Fine," he agreed in a rumbling purr. "But I'm saying that, even though you're choosy, I could make you choose *me,* in fourteen short days. All I have to do is apply the methods outlined in my book."

"Not a snowball's chance in Hades, *Mr.* Flowers." In spite of herself, she retreated a step as he prowled even closer.

"So we've got a bet?" he pressed.

"Bet him!" the audience yelled. "Bet him! Come on, Joanna! Bet! *Bet!*"

He had planned this, damn him! Herded her toward this moment from the first word of the interview.

His eyes were no longer playful. They blazed with an almost scary intensity. "I'll make it formal," he said, and the audience hushed. "Ms. Hartz, I bet I can win your heart by Valentine's Day."

He had planned it—down to the perfect timing of ending her show with his dare. But she didn't care. She was going to show the clown—show him up in public for the clown he was. Thrusting her face into his (that was the picture that would appear in the papers the next day) she jabbed a slim finger into his brick-hard chest. "You're on!" she snarled.

And the audience cheered.

Chapter Two

FLAT ON HER BACK on the hearth rug, long legs propped up on her favorite wing chair, Joanna held the phone to her ear and stared at the ceiling. She'd been doing her prep for the next day's interview while lounging in front of a roaring fire, when her best friend Liza called. "The worst of it was, everybody loved the clown! We got the biggest phone-in response we've ever had—all favorable. And then Morton Stern, head of promotion, called. He told me I was brilliant, that this was the best stunt I'd ever thought up!"

Liza chuckled. "You didn't set him straight, did you?"

"I bit my tongue," Joanna admitted with a little groan of despair. "But I *hate* this, Liza."

"Hey, can it really be that bad, being chased until Valentine's Day by an attractive bachelor?" Liz teased. "I mean, I should be so lucky!"

"I said Flowers was handsome. I didn't say he was attractive." Joanna turned her face to stare blindly at the fire. "He leaves me cold." The fire's caressing warmth on her face brought back the memory of warm lips, soft against her own. She scowled and rolled away. "He had this all planned from the start, Liza. He's a user. Just another smiling user."

"Sure you're not seeing a Jason behind every bush?" Liza inquired gently. She knew all the gruesome details about Joanna's marriage at twenty to a charming young cameraman at the television station where she'd got her first job.

Jason, as Joanna's business manager, had ridden her comet all the way to the top. When it came time for a renewal of her three-year contract, he'd done the negotiations. The deal she'd signed had also guaranteed him a top-salary job in production—with the network's West Coast office. It was only when he'd left that she realized, in return for the job he wanted, Jason had traded the pay raise due her. And if that hadn't cost her enough, the property settlement she'd had to pay him . . . She grimaced. "No, Flowers is the same kind. I can spot 'em a mile away now."

"Will you see him again, then?" Liza asked.

"Have to. That was one of the conditions of the bet that Susan and he worked out after the show. I can't avoid him. He says his wonderful tips don't work through locked doors. And I can't read his book. That was the other agreement. Not that that will be any hardship."

"Wants to surprise you, does he?" Liza chuckled again. "Well, look at it this way. If he keeps you hopping for the next two weeks, you won't have time to miss Benjie. Oops, I said his name. Sorry."

Joanna sighed. "Doesn't matter. I never stop thinking about him." Her seven-year-old son was visiting his father during winter vacation. That was surely why, tonight, her heart felt as empty as the old birdhouse that stood on a pole in the front yard of her Connecticut farmhouse. She sighed again. "And now I've got to get back to work, my friend. I've got three members of Mothers against Motorcycles, and two Hell's Angels tomorrow."

Liza laughed. "Should be interesting."

But the only thing that seemed to interest anyone the next day was her bet with Duncan Flowers. Her staff wanted to know if she'd heard from him and looked disappointed when she said no. One of the MAM ladies—a seventy-year-old who admitted she was actually a Grandmother against Motorcycles—asked if that nice Mr. Flowers had tried tip seventeen yet, and then blushed. One of the Hell's Angels offered on camera to show Joanna how a *real* man kissed, and then there were the questions from the audience.

"Who's winning the bet?" a young man asked with a knowing grin.

"Mr. Flowers has been most notable for his absence the past twenty-four hours," Joanna said coldly. "Now about motorcycles?" She chose a middle-aged woman sporting the black lace and leather of a die-hard female biker.

"That's tip number four!" the woman cried and held up a copy of Flowers's book for the camera. "He says to chase hard and then back off for a while. Keep the girl guessing."

Joanna fought off an impulse to brain the woman with her mike. "Right now, I'm guessing that Mr. Flowers paid you to push his book. Would that be correct?"

"Not at all," the woman said with great dignity. "I'm his mother." She sat down as the audience roared.

That was Tuesday. By Wednesday, when she'd still seen no sign of Flowers, Joanna began to hope that the worst was behind her. Flowers had probably shot his bolt. Just making the bet with her had won him national attention. He didn't have to worry about winning it. Win or lose, he'd won already.

Still, when it came time for questions, she scanned the audience warily. In the fifth row aisle seat, a man raised his arm. It was the first sign of life he'd shown, as he'd spent the entire show apparently snoozing, with his curly gray beard propped on his broad chest and his Stetson hat pulled down over his eyes. Dragged here by his wife, Joanna had long since concluded. He probably wanted to ask if he could go now. Still she walked down and held out the mike obligingly. "Yes, sir?"

His other hand swung into view, and he held out one exquisite, long-stemmed red rose. "I've been thinking about you," he said huskily.

"It's *him!*" a woman shrieked from behind Joanna.

How could she have been so stupid? Even shadowed by the brim of his hat, she should have recognized the laughter in those wicked blue eyes. He stood up and took the mike out of her limp fingers, addressing her guest while he passed Joanna the rose. "Chief Seconset, you say that your tribe welcomes this landfill, but have you conducted a referendum to be sure of that?"

It was a good question—she'd meant to ask it herself if no one else did. Still she didn't need Flowers's help. While the chief blustered, she balanced the rose neatly in the crease of Flowers's ridiculous hat. "I haven't been thinking about you!" she snapped, then retreated back up the aisle.

But after the show, he was lounging against the wall outside her private exit. Straightening, he held out a dozen red roses.

She sniffed and sailed past him. "Who told you about this door?"

"I've got my sources." He fell into step beside her.

With those long legs of his, she certainly couldn't outwalk him. Striding in amiable silence, he followed her on her roundabout route through the building and into the elevator that led down to the parking garage. "You really skewered that old fraud," he said at last. "It was a good show."

"No thanks to your interruption!"

"When do you get your weekly Nielsen ratings?" he asked. He'd removed the false beard, and his dimple dinted the cheek nearest her shoulder.

She knew what he was getting at. "Mr. Flowers—"

"Duncan," he interjected mildly.

"*Mr.* Flowers, there's something I treasure more than Nielsen points. It's called peace of mind." The elevator doors slid wide, and she hurried out.

"Then I'm getting to you?" He looked ridiculously pleased.

She wanted to say no, but knew somehow that those penetrating blue eyes would see the lie if she did so. She walked faster, scowling at the big rawhide cowboy boots he'd worn to complete his disguise. The boots stopped suddenly. Automatically she stopped and swung to look at him.

"Do me a favor?" He held out the roses. "Tell me what's wrong with these. They smell funny."

Anything to get rid of him. Closing her eyes with exaggerated patience, she inhaled. But to her they smelled heavenly, redolent of languid summer days. She looked up over the roses to find him surprisingly near. "Smell fine to me." It was just another of his tricks, and a good one. For she wanted to bury her face in that fragrance, rub her nose on the velvety petals.

He didn't remove the flowers. "Do that again," he commanded.

She did, filling herself with the scent. If love had a smell, this was it. She opened her eyes to find he'd leaned closer.

He sighed and gave her a little lopsided smile. "When you do that, your lashes sort of shiver, like a butterfly's wings. It's nice."

"Pay her compliments. What tip number is that?" In removing the beard he'd missed a small smear of adhesive at the angle of his jaw. She had the irritating urge to reach up and snatch it off.

His furry golden brows drew together as he considered the question. "Guess I'd file it under number one—know what you like." His eyes moved over her face, as if he was cataloging her freckle by freckle. "But I brought you the wrong flowers, I'm afraid. They should have been sunflowers. Or marigolds."

She pushed his bouquet away and started walking again, faster. "Then give 'em to your mother."

He laughed. "I caught holy heck for that one! My mother called me last night. I had to promise to print a retraction in my next book. Something like 'My mother is not, repeat not, a Hell's Angel and never has been.'"

"Serves you right." Joanna pushed through the door that led into the parking garage. Her reserved space was only a few feet from the exit. She snatched her keys out of her shoulder bag and unlocked her car.

"Joanna."

Folding her legs in after her, she would have shut the Saab's door. But he held it open. "Joanna, take the flowers. You want them."

She let out a weary sigh. "Mr. Flowers, I can buy myself all the roses I'll ever want."

"Sure you can." He set the bouquet gently in her lap. "But it's not the same as someone giving them to you, is it?"

He turned and left her, moving with that long, supple stride of his. Slumped in the seat, Joanna watched him go. He was right, damn him, he was so right. She'd trade an interview with...with the president for a man who'd bring her flowers for love. "But not for publicity!" she whispered after him. She closed her door, and the smell of roses filled the car.

Chapter Three

THE BABY SEAL had been staring directly at the camera when its picture was taken. Its soulful brown eyes reminded her of Benjie's. With a little sigh Joanna set the photo down on the bed beside her notes for the next day's show and glanced at the bedside clock radio. Ten p.m. Jason's maid had said that Benjie and his father would return about seven, California time, and that she would remind Benjie to call his mother when he came in. But perhaps the maid had forgotten to deliver the message?

She jumped as the phone rang, then reached for it with a smile. "I was just thinking about you, sweetie," she said, laughing into the receiver.

"You mean it's working already?" an all-too-familiar voice rumbled in amusement. "I expected you to put up more of a fight than that, Joanna."

She flopped back against her pillows and felt her jaw tighten. "How did you get this number, Mr. Flowers?" It was unlisted, of course.

"Call me Duncan, if you want an answer," he teased.

She growled a little wordless sound of disgust and slid further down on the pillows. "Duncan, who the holy heck—" She stopped as she remembered that that was *his* phrase. "Who had the ill-advised audacity to give you my private number?"

"Can't tell you," he answered promptly. "Got to protect my sources. Ask me anything else—my pec measurements, time in the last marathon... Who's sweetie?'' he continued when she snorted but didn't speak.

Odd to have his voice right in her ear, as close as if they were sharing a pillow. She hunched her shoulders nervously. ''Benjamin,'' she muttered. Perhaps if he thought she had a lover, he'd leave her alone?

''Your son,'' he said with no hesitation at all.

Joanna jerked herself upright and gripped the receiver harder. *''Who told you that?''* He sighed in her ear, and she went on before he could refuse to name his source again. ''Duncan, if you knew what I've gone through to keep his name and picture out of the media. I swear if you mention Benji's name in public, I'll—I'll—''

''Hey, whoa, calm down,'' he soothed, and there was no smile at all in his voice now. ''I wouldn't do that. Never. It was just a fact I came across when I was doing my research.''

''On me,'' she said bitterly.

''On you,'' he agreed. ''It's more fun to research books than write 'em, so you tend to learn a lot more than you'll ever need or use. Gets to be a habit. For instance, I know your favorite color is forest green.''

Joanna looked down at her forest-green bathrobe and shivered. He might as well have been sitting on the bed beside her, she felt so pinned by his knowing blue gaze.

''But the flip side of knowing a lot is discretion,'' he rumbled on when she didn't speak.

It had better be. ''I mean it, Duncan. If you ever mention Benjie—''

''Who?'' he asked innocently.

She sighed in exasperation, then breathed a helpless little laugh of surrender and shook her head at the ceiling. ''Okay, okay...thanks.''

''Anytime...''

Neither spoke for a while, which should have been awkward but somehow wasn't. She could hear him breathing, could almost feel his breath on her cheek. Their minds were linked as closely as two hands. They were simply being together—Joanna, Duncan. Breathing.

"How are my roses doing?" he asked comfortably at last.

Joanna glanced at the vase on her bedside table. "They seem to feel right at home." She reached to stroke a petal of velvety crimson.

"That's good." His voice lost a shade of its usual self-assurance. "I...guess I called to say...thanks for taking them."

"Haven't you got that backwards?" She lifted a rose out of the vase and, bringing it to her nose, shut her eyes as she inhaled.

"I suppose...but whenever I give a woman something, seems I always remember the first time. Greta Hoffman, my first real date. Ninth grade." A note of rueful laughter shimmered behind his words.

Ninth grade. Had he reached his full height by then? she wondered. He'd have gone through a shambling, big-footed, bean-pole stage some time in high school and before that had probably been a small, quick, very blond and clever child—a junior wise guy. "What happened?" she murmured.

"I had a notion you were supposed to bring a date a gift of some sort. It was a few days after Valentine's Day, and I found a leftover box of chocolates at the drugstore—the heart-shaped box, you know. I thought it was perfect. She was blond and to die for—she sure had *my* heart."

"She didn't like 'em?"

He chuckled. It was a sound of such bittersweet forgiveness that Joanna found herself smiling.

"Looking back, I think she didn't know how to take it. Maybe no boy had ever brought her a gift before, and she was embarrassed. She made some wisecrack about stale chocolates, and if I could've sunk through the floor..." He laughed again, shrugging off the ancient and tiny hurt. "Anyway, thanks for taking my flowers."

"Thanks for giving them." Joanna inhaled deeply, let the rose fragrance out on a sigh, then said, "And now, Duncan, I *am* expecting a call from the man in my life...."

"Right," he said promptly. "Tell what's-his-name 'hi' for me." And he was gone, the phone clicking softly in her ear.

Joanna stared at it for a long moment. He'd gone from her so suddenly, she almost expected air to rush in and fill the vacuum he'd left with a little *pop*. With a sigh she set the phone down, then lay there listening to the silence. The old house creaked in the wind. She brought the rose to her face and stroked it across her cheek, shutting that empty sound out of her heart—then jumped as the phone rang. "Benjie!" she cried into the receiver.

"Sorry, sweet, it's Liza."

"My night for mistakes," Joanna admitted and told her about the previous one, finishing with Duncan's anecdote. "You know, Liza, he almost seemed human tonight. Maybe I've been judging him too harshly."

"Wait a minute, wait just a minute..." The sound of flipping pages came faintly over the line. "I bought his book today. Figured if you couldn't read it, I could.... Yeah! I thought I remembered something like that. Listen to this." Liza cleared her throat. "'Tip number fifteen: Show vulnerability. Women are the natural nurturers of the race. Contrary to what you may think, your quarry isn't looking for a man of steel. She wants someone who's human. Someone who needs her sweet sympathy. So don't try to hide it when you take a pratfall, fellows—exploit it! Tell her about the time the boss hurt your feelings. Tell her about—'''

"I get the picture," Joanna cut in bleakly. "The manipulative, conniving... He seemed so genuine." And it had worked like a charm on her for a minute, hadn't it? She looked down at the rose in her hand, grimaced and stuffed it back in the vase. "So much for letting down my guard."

AND SHE WAS STILL ON GUARD the next morning. When she walked out on stage, she swept her audience with a searching, suspicious glance. But if Duncan was there, she didn't spot him. And once the telecast started, she had other things to worry about—like preventing bloodshed on camera.

The subject was fur coats. On one side of the question stood guests Joe Pasternak, raccoon trapper, and Anton Furzz, owner of Furzz for My Lady, New York's biggest discount furrier, and an indignant fur-coat owner. In glowering opposition were two members of the militant animal rights group, Fight for Fuzzies! And by the end of the fourth commercial, all pretense at civilized debate was gone. The gloves, synthetic or fur lined, were off, and the brass knuckles showing.

"This is America!" yelled the trapper. "I wanna grow up to be president, I can—God willing—be president. If I wanna paint myself blue and sashay down Madison Avenue in nothing but a lynx coat, I got a right to do that. This is America, and it ain't hurting anybody!"

"You tell 'em!" screamed a woman from the audience.

"Isn't hurting anybody?" the president of Fight for Fuzzies!, barely a hundred pounds, with a braid to her waist and bulging eyes behind round wire rims, shot to her feet. "Isn't hurting anybody? How'd *you* like to be skinned? I've got this nice, sharp Swiss army knife here—"

"I believe you said you were a pacifist, Ms. Rivers?" Joanna cut in. She turned to the gorgeous young model, whose ten-thousand-dollar sable coat had been spray-painted at the Metropolitan Opera last month, but she was no help. She seemed to be quietly hyperventilating. Joanna nodded instead to Anton Furzz, who looked relatively rational. He stood and jabbed a finger at Leo, the long-haired, ex-pro wrestler and national secretary of the Fight for Fuzzies!

"All right, Leo, if you're such a bleeding-heart Bambi lover, what about meat? You eat hamburgers, right? Am I right?"

Jerking at his droopy handlebar mustache, Leo scowled and started to speak, but Furzz rode right over his attempt. "Sure you do, ya big muscle head! You didn't gain all that lard eating bean sprouts. Well, where do you think meat comes from? From cows— that's where. You ever look a calf in its big brown eyes? Cows are cute. Cows are fuzzy. You wanna talk animal rights, first you stop eating cows!"

"First you shut your little weasel mouth and let me speak!" roared Leo as he surged out of his seat—all six and a half feet of him. Rather than sitting down, Anton Furzz bristled like a bantam rooster, but at least he shut his mouth. Leo tugged thoughtfully on a lock of his gleaming black hair. "Now Rome wasn't built in a day. So we gotta start somewhere—"

"Ah-ha, I was right!" Furzz crowed. "You admit it. You wanna take our furs away today, our hamburgers tomorrow. How do you like that, America? What are we supposed to eat? Polyesterburgers?"

"We gotta take a stand somewhere," Leo insisted. "So this is what we say: No killing for vanity!"

"Right on!" cheered half the audience, while the other half booed.

"We say, you want a pretty fur, then grow your own." Leo lifted his beefy arms and wrenched his skintight T-shirt with its Save the Fuzzies! slogan over his head. Tossing it aside, he flexed his biceps and puffed out his massive chest for the audience and the cameras.

He was the most awesomely hairy man Joanna had ever seen, bar none. The audience roared its delight as Leo rotated to display his curly pelt, front and back. Not to be outdone, his companion was ripping the ties off her braid and shaking it out, lashing the trapper in the face as she did so.

And someone else was entering the fray. Joanna whirled to see Duncan Flowers mounting the steps to the stage. In his arms he held a long, rectangular, glossy white box with the emblem of a well-known New York City furrier on its side. The audience went raptly silent, and even the guests turned to stare at him.

"Funny you should mention furs," Duncan said cheerfully as he leaned in close to Joanna's mike. "That's one of the tips in my book, *101 Ways to Win the Woman of Your Dreams*. Tip number nineteen— Give your lady a fur. It's the sure way to turn that tiger into a pussycat. So..." He handed the box to Joanna with a flourish.

She didn't need this! He was bringing matches to a gasoline-tanker wreck, a spare rope to the lynching.

She tried to thrust the box back at him, but Duncan grinned and clasped his hands behind his back.

"Brute," yelled the female Fuzzie. "Barbarian!"

"Open it," urged Duncan, blue eyes dancing.

She should call for a commercial, but if she cheated her home audience of this one, they would never forgive her.

"Open it!" yelled Anton Furzz and the trapper.

"Open it!" begged the audience.

Out of the corner of her eye, Joanna saw the president Fight for Fuzzies! whip a can of red spray paint out of her kaftan. Anton Furzz whirled to grapple with her. It was open the box, or call the security guards, or both. Joanna ripped open the box.

A tiny, gray rabbit hunched lower in his nest of hickory chips, his dark eyes wide and frightened.

"Aw-w-w!" crooned the audience.

"Oh-h-h!" cooed Leo. Furzz and the female Fuzzie forgot the spray paint and turned to gape at the rabbit.

Duncan put a finger to his lips in a warning *shh!* then lifted the bunny out of its nest. Its outsize ears drooped over his big hand. He smoothed the rabbit's ruffled fur, then handed the animal to Joanna. "For you, my sweet."

Soft as dandelion down, the rabbit's fur caressed her palms as her hands cupped the little creature. Duncan had done it again, upstaged them all with half a pound of lop-eared rabbit and impeccable timing. She wanted to glare at him, but she looked down at the bunny and grinned instead. Its nose was twitching irresistibly. She held the little guy up for the cameras and said, "And now it's past time for a commercial. We'll b-b-be right back, folks." She turned to scold Duncan and found that he was halfway down the aisle to the back exit, without a backward glance.

After that the show sailed amiably to its conclusion. No one could compete with Duncan's gift. The Fight for Fuzzies! members were smugly righteous. How could anyone deny that the fur looked best *on* the bunny? Anton Furzz tried to prove he was a rabbit lover with the best of them, and got a hole nibbled in his silk tie for his troubles. With that Joanna closed the show.

BUT BY THE TIME she stepped out her private door, the bunny nestled in a small box that one of the technicians had found for her, Joanna was no longer smiling. Duncan had done it again. Used her and her show for his own ends. The man was a master manipulator. And though she had to admire his sheer talent for using people, she didn't have to like it. Or him.

"There you are," he said, falling into step with her near the elevator. A large mesh cage swung from one hand. Inside it a small booklet entitled *Rabbits as Pets* slid back and forth, bumping a bag of rabbit feed.

She sniffed and punched the elevator button.

"You do want him, don't you, Joanna?"

"What, would you feel rejected if I didn't?" Like the chocolates. She bet he'd made that story up.

He gave her a puzzled frown from under his lowered gold brows, and stepped into the elevator with her. "I'd be upset if you gave him away. I promised Alistair a good home. So if you don't want him, I want him back." He tapped the box she cradled to her stomach. "Hear that, Al? She doesn't like you. Guess I should have bought her the rabbit earmuffs, after all."

"I didn't say I didn't like him." Did Duncan really care what kind of home the rabbit went to, or was he just faking vulnerability again to charm her?

"So, do you want to keep him?" he insisted as they stepped out of the elevator and walked to her car. "If you don't, just say the word, and me and Al will hit the road."

Did she need a bunny in her life? Remembering its softness in her hands, she knew how Benjie would vote. "I'll keep him," she said grudgingly.

"Whew!" He grinned down at her as she opened the lid to her trunk, and he put the cage inside. "I was really sweating it. I don't think Al would like my condo in Stamford. And taking him on book tours..."

"Would be difficult," Joanna agreed.

He held the box for her as she got into the car, and she looked up to find he'd cracked open the lid to peek inside. "Catch you later, buddy," he said solemnly, then handed the box over. He looked down at her, not quite smiling, the dimple dinting one lean cheek. "You, too, Joanna." He flicked her shoulder with a fingertip, then shut her door and strolled away.

"Tip number fifteen again," Liza said that night when Joanna had told her the latest. "*Oozing* vulnerability. Grown men don't like rabbits, except for the top-heavy Playboy kind. So call his bluff. Next time you see him, tell him you cooked Al for Sunday brunch—lapin avec champignons. I bet he doesn't turn a hair."

Joanna saluted the pun with a groan and looked down at the rabbit snuggled in her lap. "I expect you're right." Which was a shame. If she ever did find a man who could fall for a bunny...

After she and Liza had said good-night, Joanna sat there, stroking Al's velvety ears. Outside a gust of wind splattered rain against the pane. Another wet and lonesome night.

The phone rang again. She breathed a sigh of relief and reached for it. She'd settle for any human voice tonight, a telemarketer, a wrong number.

"Joanna." Duncan's laughing baritone answered her greeting. "How's Al?"

It was frightening how good it was to hear his voice. It only underlined her emptiness, this welcoming a call from a man who was patently using her. Disgust for her own weakness followed, smothering the glow his voice had kindled. "Duncan, I was just wondering how to tell you," she said, one hand resting on the bunny's head. "I lost Al. I took him out for a nibble of grass and—"

"You lost him? Outside? On a night like this? Good Lord, Joanna! That's a cage-bred bunny! He'll freeze to death, or an owl will snap him up in no time. *Damn* it!"

"Er...actually..." So he did care. But how to apologize and still keep her dignity?

He didn't give her a chance. "I'm coming right over. Be there in twenty minutes." The phone slammed in her ear.

"Hoo, boy!" She lifted the rabbit and brought his quivering nose to her own. "I've done it now, Al, buddy, haven't I?"

Chapter Four

GUILT MADE Joanna walk down the long drive to meet Duncan. With her intercom and security system, she could have let him through the electric gate from her house. But he'd still have to walk from his car to her front door in the cold rain. So it seemed the least she could do.

But that wasn't the only reason she waited, huddled in her trench coat under a dripping umbrella, just inside the high black iron gate. For this was the best place to make her apologies and her stand. This was as close as she wanted Duncan to come to her personal sanctuary. She looked up as headlights outlined the wet iron in ragged silver. Rain beading on its lovingly waxed curves, an old Jaguar sedan turned into the drive.

She slipped through the gate just as Duncan switched the lights off and swung out of the car. "Get back in and stay dry!" she called as she hurried to meet him. But perverse as ever, he ignored her order. "Darn!" she muttered in frustration and brought the umbrella over his head.

He caught her wrist to steady the umbrella against a gust of wind. "You've been out looking already?" he demanded. He was dressed for the search, in jeans and a waterproof jacket that made him loom even larger than usual. A long flashlight was tucked in one pocket. "Any sign of him?"

"Duncan, I've a confession to make." She peered up at him, trying to see his eyes in the umbrella's shadow. "I lied. Al didn't escape. He's snug in his hickory chips this second." She gave him a brisk smile that she hoped he could see. "So I do apologize—I don't know what got into me. But you're not needed now. You can go home. I'm sorry," she added in a smaller voice when he simply stood there, his fingers tensing on her wrist.

"You know the problem with lies?" As the wind gusted again, he lifted the umbrella out of her hand and centered it over her head. "The problem with calling wolf—or rabbit—is that then I don't know what to believe. How do I know that this isn't the lie? That you lost poor Al, and now you're just trying to make me feel better by claiming he's safe?"

"I wouldn't do that." But guilt at what she had done robbed her voice of conviction.

"Prove it, Joanna." His free hand touched her arm, and he urged her toward the gate. "Show me the rab, if you've really got him."

"Darn it, Duncan!" She dug in her heels then flinched as his hand moved to her waist. To escape that touch, she started walking.

"Darn it yourself, Red. I was lounging in the hot tub when I called you. After hauling me out of there, the least you can do is reassure me." He maneuvered them and the umbrella through the heavy gate, then hooked his arm firmly around her waist.

"Okay, okay!" She tried to stiffen her body against the enticing heat of his side and thigh, but that made it hard to match his strides—he wasn't giving her an inch of clearance. But then he winced as a ribbon of rain sluiced down his cheek, and she felt guilty all over again. The umbrella wasn't wide enough for them both, and he was giving her the lion's share.

"You know," he murmured after they'd come out of the pine trees that encircled her property and they could see the lights of the old farmhouse at the top of the hill. "There are easier ways to get my company than scaring me half to death. You could have just said, 'Come on over, I'm lonesome.' That would have worked just as well."

She glared up at him. "I wasn't lonesome." Not for this arrogant, manipulative man—who didn't want his rabbit left out in the rain.

"No?" he taunted her softly. "You were having the time of your life all by your sweet lonesome on a night like this?"

She didn't answer, but didn't try to pull away, either, when he snugged her closer with his arm. The wind roared in the pines, the blood roared through her veins, the lights of the house loomed nearer. It would be a mistake to take him inside, when she was feeling like this. She especially didn't want to meet his eyes in a well-lit room. She had the feeling he could see her too clearly already. *Most people think I've got everything I could desire,* she thought bleakly. *How does he know?* And why did it have to be a man like this who knew her? Because for all he'd said about his discreet use of knowledge, she didn't believe him. He was a user, whatever else he might be. And no one was going to use her again, if she could help it.

They mounted the steps to the wraparound porch, but at the front door, she turned within the crook of his arm to face him. "Al's really inside, Duncan."

"Yes, I know." He collapsed the umbrella and handed it to her without setting her free.

But if he did know, then why had he...? She took a steadying breath. "And I don't want to invite you in." Though by every right she owed him at least a cup of hot coffee. But not this man. Her breath came faster at even the thought of letting him inside.

"I know that, too." His free hand rose slowly to span her bare throat. Warm fingers smoothed up its damp, slender length to cup her chin and raise her face higher. "So I guess this is good-night, Jo."

There was no way to back away from his kiss, held as she was. No way she could have done so even if she were free. Closing her eyes, she gave herself up to the sensation of warm lips slowly exploring her own, to the feeling of a sun rising deep within, to a strength that was irresistible by its very gentleness. With a little shivering gasp she arched on tiptoe to meet him, felt his arm tighten around her ribs in response. And then he wrenched his mouth away and dropped his arm.

They stood for a moment, simply staring at each other, then his lips curved. "Sleep tight, Joanna." His low voice was even huskier than usual. He turned and started down the steps.

"Duncan," she called breathlessly.

And he spun on his heel. "Yes?"

But his face wore such an expression of masculine triumph that her words—whatever they would have been—died in her throat. She swallowed convulsively. "Take my umbrella," she told him and held it out.

His face went absolutely blank for a second, then his head tipped back to the rain and he laughed. "No, thanks, Joanna. I never use 'em." He took a step backward down the stairs.

"Don't be an idiot, Duncan."

Laughter quivered in his voice as he shook his head. "Against my principles. Man's got to draw the line somewhere." Tossing her a salute, he turned and strode off jauntily through the rain.

As he broke into a long-legged jog, something about the set of his broad shoulders told her that he was still laughing—at them both—while she didn't know whether to laugh or cry. At last she settled for a rue-ful smile. She shook her head and slipped inside.

BUT HER AMUSEMENT didn't survive her conversation with Liza a half hour later, after Joanna had stopped touching her lips and started to think. "Is there any-thing in Flowers's book about walking in the rain with a woman?" she asked the instant Liza picked up her phone.

"Sure is," Liza said briskly. " Around tip thirty five—what he calls the middle game. I could look it up, but . . . let's make it later, okay?"

"Oh, sorry. You've got company, haven't you?"

"Hazel eyes and a smile to die for," Liza agreed in a chuckling undertone. "New neighbor. He stopped in to borrow something—I forget what. Talk to you later?"

"Uh, sure." But she'd learned all that she needed to know and more than she'd wanted. She switched off the lights and left the kitchen. In the hallway she brushed by the rabbit cage. Alistair scrabbled rest-lessly through his hickory chips as if he, too, was searching for something that he desperately desired and could not find. Hugging herself hard, she hur-ried up the stairs to bed.

FRIDAY. All her staff were wearing their Friday smiles, but somehow Joanna couldn't join in this morning. Maybe it was the thought of the weekend without Benjie. Or the fact that she'd slept badly the night be-fore, and awakened from wistful dreams that faded even as she reached for them. Whatever, she was in no mood for any of Duncan's shenanigans today.

Two minutes before show time, Art, the camera-man, stopped her in the corridor. "Word to the wise, Joanna. You want to change your shoes."

"I do?" She looked down at the green suede heels that went with her forest-green coatdress, then up at his mischievous grin.

"You do, trust me."

When Art said that, he was either to be believed, or one was being set up for another practical joke. But this time Joanna thought the joke might be on someone else. So she carried the suggested change of footwear on stage in a paper bag, then slipped them on at her desk while her intro played.

Luckily Friday's was the kind of interview she could do sitting down. It was a case of celebrity palimony. With the aging, white-toothed, suntanned movie star on one side of her desk, and his erstwhile lover, very pretty, very pregnant and all of twenty-two, on the other, Joanna felt as if she were at a pro tennis match. She and the audience simply swung their heads to follow each claim and smashing counterclaim.

"I gave up my career as dog walker to the stars to take care of you! I was earning fifty thousand a year!"

"You weren't earning five! You couldn't help an Afghan find a tree in an arboretum. If I hadn't taken you in, you'd have gone to the dogs, all right. And this is what I get instead of gratitude?"

"I deserve compensation. You promised..."

It wore thin pretty quick, but the participants were too engrossed to let her move the debate onto more general grounds as she'd intended. This wasn't a discussion of rights and responsibilities within a relationship. It was a mud-slinging match, which continued at peak volume even through the commercials. After the final break Joanna rubbed her aching temples and sighed with relief. Four minutes to go. If this was love, she'd stick to children and rabbits. The final straw came when she looked out into the audience and saw a familiar figure rise from a chair in the back row.

Duncan swept off the dashing fedora that had disguised his bright hair, tucked it under one elbow and sauntered down the aisle to meet her. He held a brown bag that appeared to contain a large bottle.

Her guests stopped in midyammer and turned to glare. Duncan plucked the mike out of the actor's hand and turned to the audience. "Seems like on a Friday, it might be nice to end on a positive note," he said in that laughing, confidential tone of his. "For every romance that goes sour, you want to remember that two more couples marry. So if you still believe in the institution after today, here's another recommendation from *101 Ways to Win the Woman of Your Dreams.*"

As Joanna came around the corner of her desk, Duncan looked her way and pulled a bottle of champagne out of his bag. A ripple of giggles spread across the audience as they spotted Joanna's shoes. Missing the source of their amusement, Duncan turned back to them with an engaging grin. "What you want to do is prove your devotion. And you want to do it dramatically. I recommend tip number forty—the traditional approach."

Ah, so that was what he was up to. Bless Art. She would give him a raise. Demurely she let Duncan lead her to the front of her desk.

"So, Joanna, if you'll just sit here." Duncan passed the champagne to the dumbfounded movie star. "Pop that for me, will you, buddy?"

Swinging his attention to Joanna, who had seated herself on the desk edge, legs elegantly crossed, he knelt beside her. Which brought him level with the shoes Art had recommended—her grungiest, oldest pair of sneakers, which she kept in her office for occasional games of racquetball. Washed—some time last fall. Duncan's jaw slowly dropped as the champagne cork popped, and the audience broke into a roar of delight.

"To..." His composure was starting to crack, too, as he looked up past the ghastly sneakers to her triumphant grin. "To show her how...*ardent* you are, I recommend toasting her from her own dainty slipper. But I didn't know it'd take *this* much devotion." Catching her ankle with one hand, he slipped off her sneaker with his other. His fingers tickled the back of her ankle, then he released her and stood up. He held out the shoe to the smirking movie star, who filled it with champagne to its frayed shoelaces.

With a grimace Duncan held the shoe up to Joanna. "Here's looking at you, kid," he rasped in a lovely imitation of Bogart. Tipping back his head, he chugged it down, a ribbon of silvery liquid trickling down his tanned throat. The audience whooped their applause, and the show was over.

Duncan lowered the shoe, wiped his grin with the heel of his hand and demanded, "Who told you?"

"I never reveal a source," she assured him, then retreated while the movie star slapped Duncan on the shoulder. Looking back from the curtain, she saw the two men laughing as they shared the last of the bubbly straight from the bottle. *They're birds of a feather,* she thought with a sudden tumble from the peak of her triumph. Both performers in their own way, neither of them with a clue to what love really was.

But then, did they even need to know? They were doing very well without it, weren't they?

And then, as if to underscore that the whole scene had been a performance, nothing more, Duncan didn't meet Joanna on her way to her car when she left the studio. Even though she lingered by the elevator until she felt like a silly fool.

SHE'D JUST FINISHED her shower that night when the phone rang. Clutching her towel, she scurried for the phone in the bedroom. "Hello."

"What are *you* doing there?" a familiar voice demanded.

He'd expected Alistair to pick up the phone? "I live here, Duncan," she said with exaggerated patience. "Where else would I be?"

"Oh . . . out on a date?"

She grimaced and sank onto the bed. "Not tonight."

"Why not?"

She let out a little hiss of exasperation. "Not that it's any of your business, but I haven't found anyone I've wanted to date lately."

"Then you can't have been looking very hard. There's got to be plenty of men who want to date you."

"Maybe they want to, but the only ones who ask are the ones with overgrown egos." If she wanted to hear "me, me, me" all evening long, she could take herself to the opera.

Duncan chuckled sympathetically. "I guess it does take a pretty healthy ego to ask you out."

"I don't mind a healthy ego, Duncan. I've got one myself. It's these windbags who define themselves by the thickness of their wallets, or whether they rate the best table at Elaine's, or . . . you know the type." The type who could talk all night without once asking a woman a question about herself. The type who wanted to be seen with her for the same reason they drove a Ferrari or wore a custom-fitted Saville Row suit.

"So what *do* you do on a weekend?" he persisted.

She leaned back against the headboard and curled her feet under her. "If Benjie were here..." They would have gone to a movie tonight. Or sometimes they rented a film and watched it at home. She had her next week's programs to prepare for, groceries to be bought, meals to be cooked and frozen. She'd probably do some planning for the garden she meant to plant this spring. Maybe coffee with Liza. As she told him, she absently rubbed the towel between her breasts, catching the drops of water that dripped from her wet hair.

"And tomorrow night?" he wondered. "Saturday night was always the big date night in my hometown."

The sense of warm, encircling peace into which she'd been drifting ended suddenly. What was she doing, confessing her loneliness to this man as if he cared? Why tell him she had nothing on for tomorrow, nor for Sunday? That unless she made some special effort, it would be all too easy not to see another human face till she went back to work Monday morning. "I haven't decided yet," she said, her voice growing cooler. "Now, was there some reason you called?"

"Not really," he said easily.

She wanted to believe him but wouldn't let herself. He wasn't stupid. He surely must know that by now her ears were tuned for the phone's ringing each evening. For there was some sort of comfort in a habit, even a bad one like Duncan Flowers. *Even a temporary one,* she reminded herself. He wouldn't be a habit for long. Once their bet was over, less than ten days from now... "Well, in that case..." she murmured.

"In that case, good night, Jo. Sleep well." He hung up before she could think of anything to say, to keep him there a little longer.

Slowly she set the receiver down, then sat staring out her windows at the dark. When she was growing up, the little girls on her block played a game called Red Light, Green Light. The object was to sneak up to the person who was *it* and touch her, but not get caught moving.

When *it* yelled "Green light!" and covered her eyes, the other players would scurry toward her. When she yelled "Red light!" and opened her eyes, any player caught in motion had to return to the starting line. The game had always scared her as much as it excited her. Each time you opened your eyes, your frozen pursuers were looming closer, ever closer.

That was how Duncan made her feel. She never caught him moving, but each time she looked up, he was closer. Shrugging off that notion with a jerk of her shoulders, she went in search of a bathrobe and a cup of warm milk.

Chapter Five

"DOMINO'S PIZZA," insisted the boy's voice over the intercom. His car radio was screeching something about undying love, and he sounded as if he was speaking around a wad of chewing gum.

"But I didn't order one," Joanna repeated in rising exasperation. Though come to think of it, pizza sounded better than the cottage cheese and toast she'd intended to have for Saturday supper.

"Hartz, rural route two, that's you, lady, i'n'it?"

This was a joke, she decided suddenly. No doubt there was a tip in Duncan's book—send your quarry a pizza on Saturday night. "Okay, okay, come on up," she told the kid and hit the gate button.

But when she opened the door to a knock a few minutes later, there was no delivery boy on her doorstep. Just Duncan Flowers, with a wide boyish grin, holding a brown grocery bag. "I lied," he said immediately.

"So I see," she said, trying to catch her breath. She'd backed up a step at the sight of him. Mistake two. He took a giant step through her entrance before she could consider slamming the door, then looked around approvingly. "It's not a Domino's," he continued absently. "It's a Flowers extra special deluxe pizza. Or it will be when I make it. The kitchen's through here?"

"Duncan, I'm not in the mood for this," she said, following him into the kitchen. Or she hadn't been, till a moment ago. It had been a gray day emotionally, as well as weatherwise. She'd spent it slogging through her research for the coming week. She'd just decided to take a break when he'd pulled his gate-crashing trick. "I don't feel like talking to you."

"Good, because I don't, either. To me or to you." He set his bag on her counter as he spoke. "I just want to put my feet up, munch pizza and watch a video. Have you ever seen *Doctor Zhivago?*" He handed her a tape.

"I missed that one." She should run him out of here this minute. But he looked about as movable as her big, old-fashioned stove, and just as much at home in her kitchen.

"You want to open the Chianti while I roll out the dough?" he asked, seemingly intent on dusting flour over her butcher-block counter. There wasn't a hint of a smile on his face, although his lone dimple was showing. "And then we'll need a skillet to sauté the mushrooms."

Whatever Duncan had promised about not talking, it was impossible to share a kitchen with him and not talk. By the time they'd constructed a monster pepperoni, green pepper and mushroom pizza on superthin whole-wheat crust, they'd covered half a dozen topics, from whale watching to ancestral sourdough starters to the economy of the Pacific Rim. But as interesting as Duncan was on any topic, he was confining himself to the strictly impersonal tonight, Joanna realized. He seemed to know by instinct just how far he could advance on her and when to back off. Having breached the defenses of her house tonight, he apparently was not going to invade her inner privacy with questions or comments.

"Twenty minutes to heaven," Duncan said and slid the pizza into the oven. "Just time enough to get a good fire going."

They ate the pizza by firelight while they watched *Doctor Zhivago,* and slowly Joanna began to relax and enjoy herself. The movie was superb, and Duncan was still respecting the careful three-foot gap she'd established between them on the sofa when she'd first sat down. The only move he'd made so far was to go get Alistair during the wolf-howling scene. "He's probably scared out of his fuzzy wits," Duncan said.

But the bunny had ignored the video wolves in favor of the belt loops on Duncan's jeans. And when Joanna had drawn up her legs to sit Indian fashion, Alistair settled in the crook of her knee. Eyes glued to the screen, she drew out one of his long ears between her fingers in an absent caress, dropped it, then repeated the motion. Her hand bumped into something warmer and smoother than bunny fur, and she glanced down to see that Duncan was playing with the rabbit's other ear. With a little smile she went back to watching the movie. But sometime near the end of the love story the pressure increased on her knee. Still holding the rabbit's ear, Duncan's hand now rested on the side of her leg. From the corner of her eye, she studied Duncan warily, but he wasn't looking at her.

She returned her gaze to the movie, but now it was harder to concentrate. A little harder to breathe steadily. Warmth spread out from that simple contact point in slow shock waves of awareness. She wanted to shift in her seat, but the weight of that big hand seemed to have pinned her to her place. Alistair solved the problem at last by sitting up, shaking his ear loose from Duncan's grip and trying to hop down from the sofa.

"No, you don't," said Duncan as he captured him. He hit the video control and froze the picture. "Guess it's back in the cage for you, buddy."

When he returned, he found Joanna curled into a tight, neat bundle, her arms firmly clasped round her shins, her chin propped on her knees. She felt him studying her as he sat, a little closer this time, but he didn't try to touch her again, if indeed he'd been trying to before.

They watched the rest of the movie in silence. The ending was both heartbreakingly tragic and joyful. Zhivago never regained his beloved Lara, but their daughter inherited his gift for music. With the final words of the story, Joanna dissolved in a torrent of silent tears.

"Hey." A big hand smoothed across her wet cheek. "Hey, Jo, it's a movie, remember?" Sliding an arm around her shaking shoulders, he wiped her lashes with a fingertip. "Wow, that hit you, huh?" When she nodded, trying to smile, unable to speak, he gathered her in, turning her face into his shoulder. "That's okay, feels good to cry sometimes, doesn't it?"

She laughed through her tears and burrowed closer. How would he know? He didn't look as though he'd had a good cry since he was five. But all the same he was right; it did feel good to cry—and have someone hold her. She inhaled a deep breath, trying to get a grip on herself, and was suddenly aware of the clean, masculine smell of him. Of the solidity of the shoulder her face was pressed against. The arms wrapped around her.

Duncan Flowers—well on his way to winning his bet with her. Spreading her fingers against his chest, she pushed herself upright.

"You okay?" His fingertips stroked lightly across her back, raising a flurry of goose bumps in their wake.

"Of course." Joanna sprang to her feet and retreated to the bathroom. She scowled at her wet-eyed reflection in the mirror. *Less than two weeks to Valentine's Day, you idiot. Why do you think he's doing this?* Well, if he thought that was all it took to seduce her—a love story and a great pizza—he had another think coming.

But when she stepped out of the bathroom, eyes pink and face scrubbed, she found Duncan in the kitchen, packing up his supplies. He looked up with a smile. "Rest of the pizza's in the fridge, Joanna. You can eat it for breakfast." He picked up his bag and advanced on her.

He was going? Just like that? Without an argument, without the fight she'd thought she'd have to provoke to push him out the door? He touched the tip of her nose lightly, then traced a line down to her lips. "No more tears. It was just a movie."

"A good one." He wasn't going to even kiss her?

"The best," he agreed. He wasn't. His hand fell away, and with a funny half smile he moved on past her.

Dazed, still not quite believing what was happening, she followed him to the front door. He was really leaving?

He was. "Lock this," he warned her lightly. And then he was gone, shutting the door behind him. She heard the sound of his feet on the steps, light and quick for such a big man, then the slamming of the Jag's door.

"Darn it!" she whispered, turning to prop her back against the door. Her eyes blinked once, then blinked rapidly, as she fought off another bout of foolish tears. The room couldn't have looked emptier, not if Duncan had taken every last stick of her furniture with him.

SUNDAY BROUGHT a warmer, sunnier day to cheer her, and the *New York Times,* which Joanna always read, front to back, in her perpetual search for interesting show topics. By eleven, she'd worked her way through half of the newspaper and talked on the phone with Benjie while he ate his breakfast on a patio in Beverly Hills. Next Sunday night he'd be home again.

Buoyed by the thought, she headed for the old barn that had been converted to a garage. She'd drive into town for groceries, maybe see if she could coax Liza out for a cup of coffee . . . She stopped and frowned. The garage door was up. But surely she'd lowered it?

She couldn't remember. Perhaps a thief? But her car still sat there, and no one could get past the estate fence she'd had installed after Jason left. So it followed that she was the one who had left the door open.

But even with that conclusion, she moved on rapid tiptoe to the car, swung into it and jammed the key in the ignition. The sooner she backed into the daylight, the better, she'd— She jumped like a scalded cat at the sound of metal clanking nearby. Glancing around wildly, she could see no one as she twisted the key and the engine roared to life.

"Hey!" The man's yell came faint but frantic, and a pounding racket exploded from beneath her. Someone was hammering on the underside of the Saab!

With a squeak of terror Joanna killed the engine and shoved open her door. If she could just get to the house, phone the police— She put a foot to the garage floor, then shrieked as a hand shot out and caught her ankle. Her knees gave out, and she collapsed to the concrete floor beside the car.

"Joanna!"

Duncan's voice! At the revelation, relief surged through her veins in a burning flood. "Oh...thank God!"

"Holy heck, what were you trying to do? Squash me flat?" Using her ankle for leverage, Duncan squirmed halfway out from under her car to give her an upside-down scowl. A smudge of grease decorated one cheek like a slash of war paint, and he looked as if he was in a scalping mood—or maybe a bashing mood, judging by the wrench in his other hand. "Don't you use your eyes—or your brain? You could have killed me!"

With relief, her fright gave way to an adrenaline rush of pure outrage. "I could have killed *you?* You nearly gave *me* a heart attack. What do you think you're doing under my car?"

Duncan squirmed out a foot farther, then stopped, his head pillowed against her other calf. His lips quirked, straightened, then curled irresistibly. "Tip number forty-four. Show her you care," he recited. "Check her tires and change her oil." He laughed under his breath. "Wish I'd put a disclaimer on that one. First guy that gets run over by the woman of his dreams, I'm going to get sued for sure. You didn't see the cans of oil I brought on the other side of your car?"

"No, I didn't, and how the heck did you get over my fence?" He was practically lying in her lap. She yanked her foot away from his fingers, eased her leg out from under his head and scrambled to her feet.

"Climbed out on a branch of a tree, then dropped. Won't work the other direction, of course."

"No problem, I can just let you out the gate," she said grimly.

"First I've got to finish changing your oil." He squirmed back the way he'd come.

"Don't bother, Duncan. I have a mechanic for that."

"Could've fooled me. Your oil's filthy," he said from under the car. "Anyway, it's too late now. I've drained it already. I was putting the plug back in when you tried to kill me."

"I wasn't trying to..." She gave up. He was humming to himself, something so wildly off-key that she couldn't identify the tune. So she waited in fuming silence while he finished under the car, crawled out on the far side where there was more room, then poured several quarts of oil into the crankcase. "You climbed a tree carrying all that oil," she said finally.

He stopped humming to flash her an absent smile. "In a backpack." He jerked his chin at the camouflage-colored pack propped against the garage wall, then returned to scanning her engine.

The picture of Duncan, weapons of wooing stashed in his backpack, dropping over her fence like a commando of love was irresistible. She fought back a giggle. "Does insanity run in your family?"

He considered. "My father collects butterflies, and a great aunt won the Capetown-to-Kinshasa motorcycle race back in 'thirty-seven."

"I thought as much."

He looked vaguely flattered, his blue eyes somehow catching light in the garage's dimness. "Where were you going?"

"On errands."

"Want some company?"

Yes. But not just for the morning. Not just till Valentine's Day. Surely she wasn't such a fool that she'd take him seriously, when clearly there wasn't a serious bone in his body? "Yes." It was little more than a whisper.

"Good," he said with quiet satisfaction, and lowered the hood.

He was a magic man, Joanna decided that day. He had twice the charm that Jason had ever had, and he turned it on for everyone they met, teasing the woman behind the bakery counter, a child they met in the candy aisle, the man at the fish market. And Joanna loved it. She was used to being the uneasy center of attention wherever she went, was used to people asking, "Aren't you Joanna Hartz?" So she found it delightful to fall back in Duncan's shadow and let him steal the show if he wanted it.

And today he wanted it, she realized. His spirits were rocketing, for whatever reason. Duncan Flowers was acting as if he were literally walking on air and wanted everyone to join him three feet off the ground. "No, I'm *not* going to eat that in the middle of the parking lot!" she said, laughing as Duncan waggled a chocolate eclair in front of her nose.

She tried to back off, but he'd laid a forearm across her shoulders, and now he simply flexed his muscles to keep her there. With a wicked grin he brought the eclair into eye-crossing proximity. "You want it, Joanna, you know you do. You're getting hungry. Very...very...hungry. You can't wait till you get home."

"Can." She put a hand to his chest as he pulled her closer, and she was surprised to find his heart slamming beneath his sweater.

"Can't." He brushed her lips with the pastry, leaving a smudge of soft chocolate across her upper lip.

Automatically she licked her lip clean, and his arm jerked. "Mmm," he said, almost purring, his eyes going from blue to black. "Do that again." He stroked the pastry across her mouth.

"See, what'd I tell you, it *is* them!" a woman's voice squealed from nearby.

Joanna turned to see two women bearing down on them.

"Joanna Hartz and Duncan Flowers!" the woman announced to the world at large. She stopped beside them, beaming nearsightedly through a pair of horn-rim glasses, a dumpling of a woman in her quilted down coat, grocery bag clutched tight. Her older friend hung back, looking as embarrassed as Joanna, who was trying to lick her lip clean. "I was going to ask who was winning the bet, but that's as plain as the nose on your face, isn't it?" The woman giggled. "I'm going to run right out and buy that book for my husband. Maybe there's hope yet." She thrust her grocery bag at Duncan. "Mr. Flowers, I don't have any paper, but could you autograph this?"

While Duncan obliged, Joanna loaded her own groceries into her car. Then it was her turn to sign the woman's bag, and then they were free. The woman's bubbly wishes for their future bliss followed them out of the parking lot as Joanna made a beeline for the blessed quiet of the countryside.

"Bite of eclair?" Duncan asked and held the pastry below her nose.

"No, thank you." From the corner of her eye she could see him bite into the eclair. The incident hadn't taken *his* appetite away, she thought resentfully, but the sweetness of the afternoon had turned as bitter as baking chocolate for her. So, how she was beginning to feel about Duncan was as plain as the nose on her face, was it? She was that transparent? Her hands tightened on the wheel until her knuckles went white. She had to get a grip on herself. Had to remember that this was a game, not reality. Duncan's attention would last till Valentine's Day, not a minute longer.

But my feelings for him, how long will they last? She bit the inside of her lip until she winced. *Come on, Joanna, you're tougher than that. You can't let yourself care for somebody who's just using you.*

And the bet was paying off for him already, wasn't it? That woman would buy his new book, and a hundred thousand people like her would buy it, too. *How to Make Your Book a Bestseller,* she reminded herself. *Just make Joanna Hartz fall head over heels for you in front of seven million amused viewers.* And would they all send her condolence cards when her romance dried up and blew away the day after Valentine's Day?

The car rounded the bend, and her driveway came into view, with Duncan's Jaguar pulled off to one side of the gate. She stopped her car beside it. "Goodbye, Duncan." She turned to give him a stiff but pleasant smile, the same smile she reserved for interviews with the Ku Klux Klan and other newsworthy creeps. "Thanks for your help today."

"Joanna . . ." He shook his head, not returning her smile.

"I have lots of work to do, Duncan." She could feel tears gathering behind her lashes. She had to get him out of here before they fell.

"All right, then," he agreed after what seemed an endless time. "But in that case, can I ask a favor in return for the oil change?"

Anything to get him out of here. "Sure." She reached up to the visor to press the button that controlled her gate and watched it slowly open.

"I need a new suit to wear for an interview that's coming up. Could I get some advice on buying one?"

"Now?" She flashed him a stricken glance. She simply couldn't sit here right now, discussing lapel widths and fabrics.

"No, later. In a day or so." He opened his door halfway, then stopped, looking back at her.

She took a deep breath. "All right." That was later, and this was now. And right now, she'd promise anything to get him out of the car.

"Great." He leaned over, kissed her ear, then swung out of the car before she could react. The door shut behind him. He patted her car's moving flank, then stood watching as the gate closed behind her.

Rubbing her ear dazedly, Joanna drove on. *I won't fall for a user. I will not.*

Yet in spite of her resolution, she checked her phone twice that night to see if it was really working. But when it finally rang, it was Liza. "Did you see the *Times Book Review?*" she asked Joanna immediately.

Joanna had not. She'd spent the rest of her day preparing questions for the next day's interview.

"Flowers's book made number eight on the best-seller list," Liza informed her. "What do you bet he's in the top five by next week?"

But Joanna wasn't betting anything. She'd made one bet too many already.

Chapter Six

By Monday Joanna had rallied her will to fight. The weekend had simply been that—a temporary weakness brought on by her loneliness for Benjie and her social isolation in general. But if it was company she needed, she could do better than a con man like Duncan Flowers. *I haven't lost that bet yet,* she reminded herself as she walked out on stage.

But now that she was in the mood to fight, true to form, Duncan had danced out of punching range. Instead of coming to see her, he sent a corsage of marigolds as vivid as her hair, but a little golder. It arrived via a smirking messenger boy just as she was asking for questions from the studio audience. With a taut smile she opened the box, then pinned on the corsage while the audience watched in rapt silence. A woman raised her hand and Joanna brought her the microphone. "Who's winning?" the woman wanted to know.

"I am," Joanna assured them all. She stroked the corsage on her shoulder defiantly. "But that doesn't mean I don't like flowers." She realized the double entendre as the audience laughed. "Flowers with a *small* f," she clarified. "Now who has a question for our guest?"

An elderly white-haired gentleman stood and fixed her with beady black eyes. "I hear you saw him this weekend," he said on a note of accusation.

"I . . . how did you know that?" she blurted then could have kicked herself. No doubt he was a shill for Duncan and had it straight from the horse's mouth.

"Tell . . . tell . . ." chanted the audience gleefully.

"There's nothing to tell." She glowered at them all. "Mr. Flowers is pursuing his ridiculous bet, and I'm simply counting the days till the ordeal is over. Now, since no one else has a question—Mr. Crumpet, could you tell *me* why you think the light you saw was a UFO? Wasn't the moon full that night, and didn't it rise at roughly the same time you noticed this apparition?"

She came offstage after the show, feeling as if her hair was standing on end like the ruff of an outraged Persian cat. Duncan had disrupted her show yet again, while for all she knew, he was half a world away, touting his book in Hong Kong.

But he wasn't. He was waiting for her outside her private door when she left the studio. "What do you want?" she growled and kept walking.

"An hour of your time. I want to buy that suit today."

"You expect me to go shopping with you?" After what he'd done today? And it didn't help her temper one bit to have just learned that her Nielsen ratings for the previous week were her highest ever. Besides, Duncan dressed beautifully when he felt like it. So this was simply another one of his despicable tips, she realized and gritted her teeth. Make the little woman think her advice is indispensable. Let her help you pick out a tie. Or a suit if you're rich. *And brave,* she thought, as inspiration struck.

"You said you would." He punched the elevator button, then followed her into it as the doors slid open.

No, she hadn't. But if it was shopping advice he wanted . . . She bit down on a smile and looked at him coolly. "All right, Duncan. I know a place in the garment district that discounts designer labels."

He blinked. "I was thinking that a store like Brooks Brothers would—"

She shook her head decisively. "Not the style you want for an interview. I'll find something that suits you, Duncan. Trust me."

A short while later Duncan stuck his head around the curtain of the shabby dressing room that occupied a corner of the vast fashion warehouse. "You sure you didn't like that last one?"

Joanna solemnly shook her head. He'd chosen the first three suits himself, with her murmured approval, and his choices had confirmed her suspicion. His taste was impeccable, though more conservative than that of most executives in the television industry.

All the same, she'd found something wrong with each one of his choices when he stepped out of the dressing room. He'd looked positively breathtaking in the navy-blue wool suit, but she wasn't about to admit it. Holding on hard to the laugh that fluttered inside her, she held out two suits to him. "I think these are more like it."

His hand reached for the suits then stopped in midair. "Um..." His eyes swung back to her face. "You really think...?"

She thought that if she let one giggle escape, she'd never stop laughing, he looked so dismayed. She put the purple, orange and green Italian-check creation, with its flaring lapels and the pegged pants that went with it, in his unresisting hand, then followed it with a three-piece suit in sleazy, silvery sharkskin, which was tailored snugly enough to set off a claustrophobic attack in anyone with the tendency.

"No fair!" he protested, starting to laugh.

"You wanted my advice, Duncan Flowers, you've got it. Wear it and weep." She hugged herself with glee and did a little victory spin on her high heels. "Try the check one first, will you? I can't wait."

"Why, you sadistic little—" He caught her forearm and pulled. Off balance, she stumbled against him, and his arm hooked around her waist to keep her there. The flimsy curtain was draped across Duncan like a rayon toga, from shoulder to opposite hip, and she suddenly realized that, although he wore his dress shirt, he was between pairs of pants.

"Hey!" she protested. "Wait just a—"

The rest of her protest was swallowed by his kiss. And this wasn't a tender kiss like their last one on the porch. This was a Duncan Flowers show-her-who's-boss kiss, a laughing conquest of a kiss that took her the way a child takes a Christmas present—she was opened and owned before she could think to resist. She was responding to his lips and tongue and hard, overarching body with an eager obedience that would have frightened her if she'd had time to think—would shame her later when she did think. But now... now there was only Duncan's lips, Duncan's heartbeat slamming against her splayed fingers, Duncan's warmth enfolding her—and the sound of a throat being cleared.

Duncan brought her down off tiptoe and held her away from his body. The throat cleared again with theatrical disapproval. Dazedly Joanna looked around. With suits draped over both forearms, an elderly gentleman stood waiting for the dressing room. His eyebrows were raised to meet his snowy white hair, and one polished wing-tip shoe tapped impatiently.

"Be out of here in a minute," Duncan called over her shoulder.

"Take your time, take your time," the man said, meaning no such thing.

Duncan's gaze switched back to Joanna's lips, then to her eyes. "You're really going to make me buy one of these?" He nodded at the suits he'd dropped sometime during the kiss.

He was making her do so many things, feel so many things she'd not wanted to feel. Surely she deserved one small victory over him. "I am."

With a groan he let her go and picked up the suits. "I'm going to get you for this!" he warned.

Not if she could help it. But with her whole heart and body fighting on his side against her common sense, did she even stand a chance? She gave him a breezy grin that she hoped concealed her fear. "Start with the check suit," she purred, "while I go pick out a tie."

HE PAID HER BACK the very next day by attending her show. Joanna spotted him the moment she came out on stage. He was hard to miss in his purple, orange and green checks. And the extra-wide tie with its pattern of life-size bananas stood out with hideous clarity.

The audience hadn't missed him, either. Their eyes switched expectantly back and forth from Joanna's grim stare to the smirk that was all you could see of Duncan's face—the rest of it was hidden behind a pair of red-framed sunglasses he'd added to her ensemble.

Duncan let their expectations build for most of the show. He simply sat there grinning, while Joanna did her best to keep her own mind and those of the audience on the issue of water rights for a small western Rhode Island river. But even the trout fishermen and the public-affairs chief of the hydroelectric corporation that wanted to dam the river seemed more intrigued by the issue of Hartz versus Flowers than by their own dispute. Finally one of the fishermen stopped in middiatribe. He jerked a thumb at Duncan. "You know, we ain't gonna get anywhere while everybody's thinking about Mr. Day-Glo, Joanna. Why don't we let him get it off his chest, whatever he's come to say, then maybe we can talk fish."

Joanna sighed and crooked a finger at Duncan, then watched him stride down the aisle to meet her. He didn't walk as if he was wearing a geek suit. He moved like a baseball slugger with a .348 average stepping up to the plate. If he could have bottled his self-confidence and sold it, he'd have never needed to write another bestseller in his life.

He jammed his hands in his jacket pockets, ruining whatever lines the suit pretended to have, and leaned down to speak into Joanna's mike. "I don't think I covered the issue of trout in my book *101 Ways to Win the Woman of Your Dreams*, but maybe I should have. So my off-the-cuff tip is, if you want to show the lady of your dreams that you've got poetry in your soul, take her trout fishing. Don't take her on a tour of the local hydroelectric plant." Ignoring the agonized squawk of the public-affairs chief, he grinned out at the audience as they applauded.

A young black man stood—the same one Duncan had planted in the audience to help him pose his bet in the first place. "Where'd you get those gosh-awful turkey feathers?" the man yelled, loud enough for the mikes to pick up.

"Where'd I get this?" Duncan preened his lapels. "I tried tip number fifty-seven from my book yesterday. I asked Joanna to go shopping, help me pick out some clothes. And she made me buy this. So I just have one question—do you think she's playing fair?"

"No!" the audience thundered gleefully.

"That's all I wanted to know." He flipped a cheerful salute to the audience, punched Joanna's arm in a feather-tap farewell. "Gotcha!" he whispered before bounding down from the stage.

"Time for a commercial," Joanna said firmly. "Then it's back to fish." She turned to soothe Mr. Hydroelectric's feelings, and the next time she looked up, Duncan was gone.

And he stayed gone the next day. Nor did he call that night, although Joanna stayed up an hour past her usual bedtime, puttering around the house and glaring at the silent phone when she couldn't help herself. Not that she wanted to hear from him...

Which was just as well, because he didn't show up for her Thursday show, either. "Where is he?" one of her audience demanded.

"I neither know, nor do I care," Joanna said and took the mike back. "Questions for our *guest?*" she said, emphasizing the word, then handed the microphone to a grandmotherly sort who was fluttering her fat little hand.

The round, tiny woman stood up and gave a nervous gulp. "Joanna, I know he's a clown and he's driving you crazy, but I think you should take him seriously. It's the ones who really get to you, who get to you." She sat down with the finality of a Delphic oracle, while the audience cheered.

Joanna didn't know whether to laugh or to cry with frustration. And she still didn't know after the show, when Susan Hadley brought her a telegram that had just arrived from the West Coast.

"I miss you," was all it said, with not even a signature. Trust the arrogant so-and-so to assume she'd known it was from him. As if there was no other man in the world who might be missing her—or whom she might be missing. Reading the slip of paper for the twentieth time that night, she looked up to stare at the phone as if she could will it to ring—then she jumped when it did. "Hello!" she cried too eagerly.

"So he hasn't called tonight, either?" Liza asked.

Joanna felt her jaw tighten at the note of sympathy in her friend's voice. "Nope," she said lightly, "but he did send a telegram from out of town. What tip number would that be?" She narrated Duncan's message, then waited while Liza flipped through his book.

"I can't find anything about that," Liza reported at last. "Looks like he's departing from his own script. What do you think that means?"

Joanna didn't dare say what she hoped—wished— that meant. All she knew was that she missed him, too, clowning and all.

So when she looked up in midinterview on Friday to see Duncan approaching the stage, her first response was a wide, happy smile.

Her next response was dismay. What did he mean to do with that bottle of avocado oil he was carrying?

Bob Kirby, oldest of the Texan World Champion rodeo triplets by eight minutes, was showing her and the audience how to bulldog a steer, using his identical brother Billie, the calf roper, who was down on all fours, as the luckless steer. Baxter, the youngest and the bull-riding champ of the trio, was sitting on the couch beside Joanna, whooping encouragement.

Duncan waited politely while Bob grabbed Billie by his ears—since he lacked horns—and twisted his head until poor Billy flipped neatly onto his back. Then, under cover of the audience's laughter, Duncan bounded up the steps to kneel at Joanna's feet. "Hi!" he whispered, as he caught her ankle and slipped her left shoe off.

"Duncan!" she whispered furiously.

"Now just a minute there, what's going on?" demanded Baxter, leaning forward over his snakeskin boots. His brothers had realized that they no longer held center stage, and they, too, were coming over to see.

Duncan pulled Joanna's mike into talking range but left it in her hand. "Considering this is my last day on the show to work on Joanna before Valentine's Day, I decided I'd better pull out all the stops. So this is tip number sixty-six from my book. Give her a foot massage, and she'll follow you anywhere." He propped Joanna's foot on his knee and opened the bottle of avocado oil.

"Hey, boy, I believe the lady was interviewing us," Bob pointed out.

"No problem," Duncan assured him. "Keep right on talking. I promise I won't say a word, and I'm sure Joanna will muffle her moans of ecstasy."

"Duncan!" Joanna tried to swing her leg away, but his hand clamped around her ankle.

"Darn, you're wearing nylons—I didn't think about that," he said. "Guess I'll just have to replace 'em." He poured a tablespoon of oil over her squirming foot.

"Duncan!" Joanna cried just as Baxter bounced to his feet.

"Ain't nobody bothering a lady while I'm around," he declared, pushing up his sleeves. "Bill, Bob, what say we show the audience how we hogtie a calf?"

"No, *please!*" Joanna called, but it was too late. Baxter caught Duncan by the shirt collar and hauled him to his feet. Duncan came up smoothly, transferring his grip from Joanna to the cowboy's boot as he rose.

Baxter sat down with an *ooof!* of surprise. Duncan caught Joanna's microphone. "Joanna, folks, I apologize. I'm causing a disturbance, so I'll just mosey—" He dropped the mike in Joanna's lap as Bob spun him around. He ducked the first punch and stepped back from the second, his palms upraised. But although he smiled placatingly, his blue eyes had narrowed.

"Security," Joanna said in a bored voice that belied what her heart was doing, and looked up to see the guards halfway across the stage already and coming fast.

Bob tried a third roundhouse swing, grunting with the effort, but he kept on twirling as Duncan caught his wrist and spun him like a top.

"Gentlemen, if you'll just sit down," Joanna called soothingly over the yells of her audience. "Mr. Flowers is leaving."

Perhaps faster than he wanted to. The two security guards closed in on Duncan from either side. And that's when Bill, the silent one of the triplets, took his first swing. Duncan stepped back from it, bounced off the burly guard behind him and rebounded into the right hook that followed. The solid *thok!* resounded throughout the studio, and with a rueful little smile Duncan sagged toward the floor. The guards caught him neatly by the elbows and frog-marched him off the stage.

"Dang!" Bill murmured. "I didn't mean to hit him that hard."

"No, I'm sure you didn't," Joanna said, her voice shaking. "Now if you'll sit down, gentlemen, it's time for a commercial break." And then she'd have another five minutes of show to endure before she could get to Duncan.

Somehow she stumbled through it. Duncan had exposed another side of frontier mentality with his idiotic stunt, and in spite of the quaver in her voice she couldn't control, she explored her guests' rough-and-ready gallantry with a few well-chosen questions. Then the show was over, and she dashed backstage.

Tasha, Susan and one of the secretaries were fluttering over Duncan in the makeup room. "He won't let me put any ice on it," Tasha complained, showing Joanna the plastic bag of melting ice she held.

"He'll take what we give him," Joanna declared as she snatched the bag. By now her fright had turned to fury. Pushing past Susan to where Duncan sat, his head in his hands, she knelt before him and slid a hand around the back of his neck. "You big goof!" she growled and put the ice to his purpling eye. He tried to recoil, but she held him there, her hand tightening on his nape, his soft hair tickling her palm.

"I'm sorry, Joanna, that was all my fault," he said, looking at her with his good eye. "Ouch! Take it easy."

"Sit still," she snapped. "Yes, it was your fault, and you got just what was coming to you. Don't mess with Texas." But despite her irritation, as if it had a mind of its own, her hand gentled on his neck. It massaged the taut muscles there, played with his silky hair. She stopped it just as it tried to sneak down to explore his broad shoulders.

"Feels good," he murmured gratefully.

"Hmph," she sniffed, not sure if he meant the ice or the massage. Lifting the bag of ice, she inspected his eye. "You're going to have some shiner, boy."

"Yeah." As she put the bag back to his face, he turned his head, bringing his lips to her wrist. "I'm really sorry about this, Joanna."

"You darn well should be." But if *she* couldn't accept his apology, her fingers could. They caressed the back of his neck, brushed his ear....

"Joanna." Susan Hadley touched her shoulder. "Morton Stern just phoned. He'd like to see you upstairs."

The head of network promotions. Joanna winced.

Duncan caught her wrist. "Joanna, if I've caused any trouble for you . . ."

She shook her head as she pulled away. "Knowing Morton, I'm sure he wants to congratulate me. He was pea green with envy when Geraldo was punched out on camera." Catching Duncan's hand, she pulled it up to hold the ice pack in place. "Will you be here when I come down?"

"'Fraid not. My editor's taking me to lunch. Got to meet her in half an hour."

"Let her buy you a filet mignon for that eye." No doubt she'd be delighted to do so, Joanna reflected as she hurried away. Duncan's stunt wouldn't hurt his book sales any more than it would her ratings. Her mouth twisted wryly. Used again? And yet throughout the day, her hand remembered the softness of his hair beneath her fingers, the warm, hard curve of his neck.

That night, when the buzzer sounded for her electronic gate, still it remembered. Not that she was expecting anybody, but she'd fast learned to expect the unexpected since Duncan Flowers had stormed into her life. Taking a deep breath, she flicked on the intercom. "Yes?"

"Joanna, it's Duncan. May I come up?"

"Yes," she said, her voice a mixture of resignation and delight. She stepped out onto the porch to wait for him. The northeastern states were enjoying one of those strange, late-winter thaws, and the weather was almost balmy tonight. Huge silver-edged clouds scudded across a full moon, and a faint breeze lifted her hair. Headlights winked beyond the pines.

It wasn't the Jag coming along the driveway, it was a white stretch limo. It drew to a ghostly halt below the porch, and Duncan stepped out a rear door of the vehicle and bounded up her steps. Dressed in a tuxedo, he carried a dark garment over one arm, a bottle of champagne in the other.

"Insane," she murmured ruefully, as he bent to kiss her cheek. He was mad as a hatter, but he looked marvelous in a tuxedo. And it matched his black eye.

"Mad about you," he agreed.

"And what are you up to tonight?" she half whispered, smiling up at him.

"Magic, if you'll play along."

Did she have a choice? Putting a hand to the dress he held, she touched the electric softness of velvet. With a helpless little laugh that caught in her throat, she nodded and stepped backward. Duncan followed her into the house.

Chapter Seven

"WHERE ARE we going?" Joanna asked, leaning back into the limo's cream-puff embrace with her second glass of champagne.

She'd sipped her first while she'd dressed in the velvet gown. Duncan had lounged in the doorway of her bedroom, gallantly not peeking, sipping from his own glass while he told her of his lightning trip to the West Coast for an appearance on a late-night talk show. There'd been something so right about his being there while she dressed, the intimate, laughing rumble of his voice from across the room, that Joanna could feel the enchantment closing around her already.

And then there was the velvet gown that enfolded her like a dream, with its low cut, fitted bodice, its sweeping skirt and the black elbow-length gloves that went with it. And the way Duncan's eyes had gleamed when at last she let him turn around.

A big hand smoothed across her cheek, bringing her back to the present. "You're not even listening," Duncan laughed, "but the answer is wait and see."

So she did, contenting herself with watching the moon fade and flare as the clouds marched by, and teasing Duncan that his black eye balanced the dimple on his other cheek. And somehow, when the limo stopped in the middle of nowhere, she was not surprised. She'd flown right past surprise tonight—somewhere to the left of the moon and the right of delight. So she stood on the road while Duncan spoke to their driver, and she was not surprised when he turned and she saw him holding a boombox.

As the limo glided away into the night, Duncan offered her an arm. "If madam would accompany me to the top of the hill?"

Madam would and did, although the going was rather slow in high heels. But it was worth it. At the top, they stood on the highest point of a hilly golf course, the manicured lawns stretching away like rough velvet as the moon stepped from behind its veils. "We're going to golf?" She giggled.

"Nope." Duncan set the boombox down and pressed a button. A lilting melody spun out on the pearl-bright air. Strauss. "We're going to waltz. The only catch is, you'll have to take off those heels, my lady."

So she did, and Duncan took off his shoes. "To keep you company,' he said. And then, there on the moonlit hilltop, they waltzed.

At first they laughed like children. Giddy with champagne and moonlight, icy grass tickling her bare feet, she couldn't seem to find her rhythm. She stepped on his foot. "Oops, sorry!"

Duncan sighed under his breath and pulled her closer. "Come here." She came willingly. The softness of her breasts brushed his hardness and he murmured a wordless pleasure as his arm tightened to keep her there. His lips brushed the hair at her temple as they turned, her skirt belled out, and suddenly the music caught her. He knew the way, and she could follow—couldn't help but follow wherever he led.

They were one. One moonstruck creature, one blissful spirit, spinning and dipping to music like liquid silver on top of a silver world. Their breath plumed white in the luminous air. Unvoiced laughter lay silver between them. That and one exultant word. *Yes.*

Then the lights went out as the clouds overwhelmed the moon. Now they were shadows, spinning as one in the heart of darkness. But tonight, Joanna didn't fear the cold and lonely dark. Turned inward to their reflected warmth, their arms forming a magic circle, they turned their backs on the darkness. All that mattered lay between them. With that knowledge, silver washed their world again. And the waltz ended.

They swayed to a stop and stood, eyes holding each other. Slowly Duncan's hands slid around her and up to span her back. Slowly they leaned into each other until their bodies kissed from breast to thigh. So slowly, her head tipped back as his lips came down. She closed her eyes, and he kissed the left one, then the right, then, just as she smiled, her mouth.

What she was feeling, it had a name. A name she didn't yet dare to even think. She shivered. Because if one cared and one did not . . .

"Cold?" he murmured, stroking her throat with the backs of his fingers. When she shook her head, he smiled. "Then one more?"

"Oh, yes." The spell held while they danced one more waltz, but by the end of it she was shivering in earnest. She didn't care. "Another one," she begged, her voice muffled against his shoulder.

He shook his head, his chin caressing her hair as he did so. "That's the other thing about magic," he murmured ruefully. "Got to use it sparingly." So they walked hand in hand down to the road and found the limo waiting.

On the way home, with her head nestled in the curve of Duncan's shoulder, she had time to think. What had he said on her program the first time? That a love affair should make some memories to warm your heart when you were ninety? Well, he'd made a memory for her tonight that would last a lifetime. Was she greedy to want more than that?

Was she crazy to hope that, tonight, Duncan had made a memory for himself as well? That by some miracle they'd moved beyond his silly bet into an enchantment that would last longer than the lovely buzz from champagne, would last when moonshine gave way to light of day?

They walked in silence to her door. Duncan unlocked it, then glanced back at the limo. *Doesn't want to kiss me good-night where the driver can see,* she told herself as he followed her inside. And yes, the moment the door closed, he took her in his arms again.

But his kiss wasn't one of farewell, although it made her weak to the knees. His lips lifted, then hovered just beyond kissing range. "Joanna, will you have me?" he whispered.

For a night, or forever, which did he mean? "I ..."

He kissed her parted lips, a quick, fierce kiss. "Don't say anything, if you can't say yes." He smiled, but now his face looked hard. Or maybe it was strain that made it seem so. "That's another thing about magic," he said lightly. "You should never stop to think. It breaks the spell."

And that's what she needed to know. Would this spell break by morning? Because if it didn't, if by some miracle—

"Damn!" Duncan exclaimed and whirled to her window. Beyond his head she saw the glow of headlights as they swept across her yard and away from the house. "I guess he thought I wasn't coming out again."

Or Duncan had told him to leave? He was a man who made his own magic, after all. She came to stand at the window beside him and watch the taillights disappear into the pines. "Doesn't matter," she said mildly. "You can borrow my car."

His snort told her he was more amused than grateful. "Tell you what I'd rather borrow, Joanna—your couch. Is that okay? I guess I'm jet-lagged. It's starting to feel like crash-and-burn time."

Was that the truth or only an excuse to stay? She didn't know, only knew that she wanted him near, sleeping under the same roof. *And maybe, if I still feel this way in the morning* . . . she thought, when she left him standing at the foot of the stairs, a wry little smile on his face and his arms stacked high with blankets. *In fact, no maybes about it.*

"Hey, Jo," he called softly from below.

"Hmm?" She turned to smile down at him.

He looked for a second as if he was going to say something serious, but then he must have thought better of it. "Sleep tight." He blew her a kiss, then vanished into darkness as she nodded and switched off the light.

The red light was gleaming on her answering machine when Joanna entered the bedroom. It could wait till morning, she decided, then changed her mind. It might be Benjie.

Instead it was Susan Hadley. "Have I got a coup for you!" her recorded voice exulted. "A renewal of wedding vows tomorrow in Miami, between—get this!—a couple who're celebrating their sixtieth wedding anniversary. And they were married on Valentine's Day, Joanna. They're perfect! I've got the crew rounded up to fly to Florida, and we'll meet you at Kennedy Airport at 7 a.m. Call me to confirm whenever you get in, okay?"

Joanna sighed. Susan was right. A tape of that wedding-vow renewal would round out the program she had scheduled for Valentine's Day perfectly. But of all times for the opportunity to arise!

Five years of putting her program before her personal desires won out, of course. At 6 a.m. Joanna tiptoed past the couch where Duncan gently snored. Only the golden top of his head showed above the blankets. She had to fight the urge to kneel and kiss his silky hair. There was no use waking him when she couldn't stay. Instead she tucked a slip of paper into his shoes. She wouldn't be back until late that night, the note said, but perhaps he could call her then? Or perhaps, although she didn't suggest it, he would even wait for her here rather than taxi to his apartment? She felt her heart turn over at the prospect of coming home to him, then she shook her head sternly at the wish and hurried out the door.

But all day, while Joanna interviewed the Bowmans and her crew filmed the simple but lovely ceremony by which the couple renewed their wedding vows, it was Duncan she thought about. What would it be like to stand in a church and say those ancient words of promise and surrender to him? Could last night's magic be spun out like a thread of gold, fine and strong enough to withstand the test of time, as had the Bowmans' love? Would Duncan ever give her children? Might they stand hand in hand someday at the center of a family as vibrant and loving as the four-generation Bowman clan that had gathered to celebrate this sixty-year-old love affair?

Stop dreaming! she kept chiding herself. She was an idiot to be building a marriage out of a moon dance. Crazy to be in love with a man she'd only just met. Why, for all she knew, her first impression of him was the correct one. Although she was almost too head over heels to see it, he might still be a user, manipulating her and her emotions strictly for his own gain.

Please, don't let him be that, she prayed, hugging herself and shivering under the hot Miami sun. *I don't believe he's that.* But there was only one way to be sure. Valentine's Day was only two days away now. If his courtship ended with his bet, then clearly, his interest had been self-interest, not genuine love at all. But if it continued . . .

She'd forgotten how terrifying it was to want something so badly, she reflected as she drove the last few miles from the airport to her home in Greenwich that evening. Because to hope and then to lose . . . *I'll still have Benjie,* she reminded herself. But Duncan's raffish smile, Duncan's tender arms, had reawakened a terrible yearning in her that Benjie's companionship could not satisfy. She had been fooling herself these past few years, telling herself she was content. *Oh, Duncan, don't be just using me. Please don't.*

But the unlit windows of her old farmhouse seemed to mock that plea as she drove up the driveway. He had not waited for her. *Doesn't prove anything,* she told herself. He had better things to do than sit waiting for her like a pet dog. But perhaps he'd left a note?

He had. But her eager smile faded to a bewildered frown as she read it:

Benjie arrived a day early, care of some stewardess (pal of your ex?). She wants me to pick him up at the airport. Won't be able to get him back through your gates, of course, so we'll entertain each other. I'll have him back here tonight.
Duncan

Her frown deepened as she reread the message. Benjie had been scheduled to fly home with a paid baby-sitter on Sunday. Apparently Jason had seen a chance to save the escort's plane fare and fee by sending Benjie along with his girlfriend. But what would have happened if Duncan had not been here when the woman called? Eyes blazing, she started for the phone to give her ex-husband an earful, then swung back as the buzzer to the gate rang in the living room. She smacked the intercom button. "Yes?"

Duncan's voice came faintly, chanting, "Okay—one...two...three!" then, "We're he-ere!" yelled two gleeful male voices.

"Thank God!" She laughed and hit the button to open the gate. She tore out onto the porch and waited, hugging herself from the cold until Duncan's Jag pulled up before the house. The rider's door slammed open and a small, dark-haired boy tumbled out as she reached the car. "Benjie!" She swept him up and hugged him, laughing and kissing his face.

"Mommy!" He smelled like popcorn, and a stain of mustard streaked the sweatshirt he wore. "We went to a hockey game. And a museum with dinosaurs! And—and Duncan got me this." He grabbed a handful of his sweatshirt, which had New York Rangers emblazoned across its front. "Oh, and he gave me a rabbit! Did you see Alis—Alistair? And we went on a boat, a ferry, out by the Statue of Lib'ty. Let's go see Alistair." The last was directed at Duncan, who had strolled around the front of the Jag with a casual grin. Benjie squirmed out of Joanna's arms.

Her son was beat—she recognized the last burst of energy that preceded tears and collapse. Didn't Duncan know anything about children? They'd tried to cram a year's worth of excursions into one day. "Thanks for picking him up," she said hurriedly as Benjie dragged at her hand.

"My pleasure," Duncan assured her. "I'll get your bags," he told Benjie.

By the time Joanna had admired Al all over again for her son's benefit, Duncan had brought the luggage to the foot of the staircase. He strolled over to the rabbit cage to stand by Joanna and listen to Benjie's extolling Al's finer points. His hand smoothed up her back, slid under her hair and took the nape of her neck in a warm, possessive clasp.

Joanna stole a wondering look at him. He looked almost as exhausted as Benjie—like a boxer in the tenth round, especially with that eye, but a winning boxer. His solitary dimple deepened as he met her eyes. "Yep, he's some rabbit," he agreed, as Benjie invited compliments. "And now I guess you guys would like some time alone." He leaned to kiss the corner of her mouth. He kissed her again when she turned to look up at him.

Could her instincts be right, that he cared for her? The question was in her eyes, but she couldn't ask it, not here in front of Benjie. Smiling, Duncan kissed the tip of her nose, then he looked down at her son.

Benjie was standing, his dark eyes round with interest.

"Night, Benjie." Duncan ruffled her son's hair, then stroked the rabbit nestled in Benjie's arms. "Night, Al." He tugged a lock of Joanna's hair as he moved past her. "I'll call you," he said with a smile that warmed her down to her toes. He'd let himself out the front door before mother or son thought to move.

As the door shut behind Duncan, Benjie went straight to the point. "Are you gonna marry him?" he demanded.

Joanna's lingering smile slowly faded. *Oh, no.* It was one thing for her to cherish hopes that might never come to pass, but for Benjie to hope and then be disappointed... Hope could be the cruelest emotion of all.

"You ought to marry him," Benjie insisted. "He'd make a great dad. And anyway, I already asked him."

Joanna knelt—or rather, her knees buckled—and she caught her son's arms, pulling him nose to nose with her. "Oh, Benjie, you didn't!"

"He said he'd be proud to—to have a son like me," Benjie reported, frowning with the effort to remember the words. And it sounded as if he'd memorized them, for even the intonation sounded like Duncan's.

But what Joanna didn't tell her son, as she gave him a passionate hug, was that those words could be construed another way. To her they sounded like a gentle sidestep, not an acceptance of her son's proposal.

"READ IT TO ME AGAIN," Joanna said faintly, as a spasm of nausea swirled through her. Oh, why had Liza called today? Benjie looked up from the Sunday comics he was reading before the fire, then looked down again.

"Tip number ninety-four," Liza said. "'The surest way to a woman's heart is through her kids. If your target has kids, charm their little socks off. Take them to hockey games, bowling, whatever. Remember that when a woman looks for a lover, she's also seeking a father for her children. Play up to her rug rats, and you'll bowl her right over.'"

Joanna stretched the phone's long cord into the kitchen, out of Benjie's hearing. "So he used Benjie to get to me." That was unforgivable.

"Sure looks like it," Liza agreed. "The rat!"

Rat indeed. It was one thing for Duncan to play with her heart before seven million people. She was a big girl, after all, and if she'd let his counterfeit courtship turn her head, she had nobody but herself to blame. But to use Benjie, to turn her son's desperate wish for an at-home father to his own advantage, to disappoint a little boy who'd known too much disappointment already just for the sake of boosting his book up the bestseller list, that was despicable! Hardly hearing Liza's worried questions, she said good-bye and hung up the phone.

It rang again almost immediately, and she spun back to stare at it.

"I bet it's Duncan!" Benjie cried, appearing at her elbow.

So he was anticipating Duncan's call as much as she had been. She put her hand over the receiver as Benjie tried to lift it. "I don't think so, big boy. It's probably Susan, or someone else from the show."

"Oh." Benjie screwed up his face. "Then don't answer it!" He fiercely resented her career's encroachments on their time together. It was just another subtle symptom of how the divorce had hurt him. He didn't like to share his mother with the outside world.

"Good idea." The phone stopped ringing abruptly as the answering machine took over up in her bedroom.

But that wasn't good enough, she realized, as she prowled back and forth across the living room. If she stayed here, she would have to listen to Duncan's message. And right now, the sound of his laughing voice would turn her stomach inside out. The tears would come later, much later, after she'd forgiven herself for being such a fool. She swallowed painfully. "Why don't we go for a ride, Benjims? Want to drive up to Mystic and see the aquarium?" And after that, they would eat supper out. She was taking no chances that her son would encounter Duncan Flowers again. While she...she'd have to face him one last time. For tomorrow was Valentine's Day.

Chapter Eight

Susan Hadley looked worried. "I thought you'd want them on stage—"

"Well, you thought wrong!" Joanna snapped. She grimaced and put a hand on the senior producer's arm. "I'm sorry, it's not your fault. I'm just on edge." And it didn't help her wire-taut nerves to be told that a dozen red roses had arrived from Duncan. Nor that Susan had put them in a vase on her stage desk for all the world to see. Now there was no way to remove them without setting the studio audience to buzzing.

"Two minutes to air," the assistant director intoned.

Joanna drifted toward the curtain. Stopping before she stepped into view, she looked down at the note that had come with Duncan's flowers:

Sorry I missed you yesterday. Save the last five minutes of the show for me?
Yours,
Duncan

No, not hers. She wouldn't have him if he were a freebie thrown in with all the tea in China. When she'd dropped Benjie off at his private school this morning, he'd asked her, hope shining in his dark eyes, if she'd be seeing Duncan today. Crumpling the note, she tossed it behind her and stepped out on stage. The audience's applause engulfed her, a surge of adrenaline washed through her, and she lifted her chin. She would survive this. For Benjie, if not for herself, she would

keep on smiling. She smiled at her four guests and
took a seat behind her desk. Staring blankly at the vase
of crimson roses before her as her intro music played,
she drew in a shaky breath and inhaled the very scent
of love. Her eyes stung, and she blinked them furiously. Was Duncan sitting out there in the audience? She didn't have the time or the courage to search
for his face. It was—

Airtime. "Good morning," she said as she rose to
face her audience. "Happy Valentine's Day! And to
ensure that it's a happy day for you, we've invited
some very special people to be our guests. They bring
us a message of hope, that love *can* stand the test of
time." She nodded to the Sapersteins, who were holding hands like a couple of schoolkids on one couch,
and to Mr. and Mrs. Watkins on the other. "So today
we'll be asking them what they do to make their love
and their marriages last. We have 107 years of married experience on the stage here today...." She paused
as the audience broke into a round of applause, then
went on, "Maybe they'll have some helpful advice on
how to cherish the love of *your* life." She smiled at the
Sapersteins. "Elliot and Rebecca, could you start out?
Would you tell us how you happened to meet?"

The show went smoothly, but every word of it
clawed at Joanna's heart. If Duncan's courtship had
been a real one, they'd have had a story to tell someday to rival the funny one the Sapersteins told of the
way they'd met. Like Emma Watkins, Joanna, too,
would have hugged her love at least twice a day. She
would have respected Duncan's quirks and differ-
ences.... Her eyes misted again as she realized that she
didn't even *know* whether Duncan neatly rolled up his
tube of toothpaste as he used it, or if he was a fla-
grant squeeze-from-the-middle man like Elliot Saperstein. She suspected the latter, but she would have

put up with it gladly, would have bought him his own separate tube to abuse just as the finicky but charming Rebecca Saperstein had been doing for her husband for the past fifty years.

You're forgetting something, she reminded herself during the first commercial break. Her fingernails were biting into her crossed arms she was so frantic to create a distracting pain. But it was doing no good. *You're forgetting that he's not worth this sadness.* The man she thought she loved had never existed. That crazy and tender lover was nothing but moonshine and mirrors—a product of 101 trite tips for seducing a gullible female. *So you're breaking your heart over a smiling user. You ought to be smarter and tougher than that by now, Joanna. Snap out of it.*

To fight the pain that threatened to engulf her, she concentrated on her anger at Duncan while she showed the tape of the Bowmans' renewal of their wedding vows. Had it only been two days ago that they'd filmed this? Two days ago that she had fantasized about Duncan's slipping a ring on her finger someday? What an idiot she was! And what a jerk he was. It was so easy to con a woman, if you seemed to be offering the one thing she most wanted in life—love. Squaring her shoulders, she turned to the audience. "Would anyone like to ask our guests a question?"

But the first question was for Joanna. "What happened to your bet?" a young woman demanded while her husband seconded the query with a vigorous nod. "Where's Mr. Flowers?"

"Mr. Flowers will be joining us shortly," Joanna said briskly. "Now please, let's limit the questions to those for our guests."

But although she headed off further stray questions that way, the hour passed all too quickly. At the end of the fourth break, Joanna looked up as a ripple of noise spread throughout the audience. Duncan Flowers was striding down the center aisle toward her, his vivid blue eyes fixed on her face, his one dimple and the black eye lending him a roguish air.

"Where's your turkey suit?" someone in the audience called as he passed.

"I save that for formal occasions!" He laughed. Today he was dressed to the nines in a navy pinstripe, but somehow the suit's understated elegance only underlined the rugged power of the body beneath it. As he neared her, Joanna's knees were trembling so much that she had to sit on the front edge of her desk. Bracing her hands on either side of her, she hoped she looked cool and unshaken as she lifted her chin.

I'm not going to break, she vowed desperately. Not before seven million avid viewers. *I won't. I can't.* As Duncan mounted the steps to the stage with his tigerish stride, she could feel the blood thumping in her ears. Her voice would crack if she tried to speak now. Instead, she simply held out her mike.

He accepted it with two hands—one curling warmly around her wrist for a moment as he lifted the mike out of her fingers. Their eyes locked, hers green and brilliant with unshed tears, his sparkling with devilry. *And that's what he is,* she reminded herself desperately as he squeezed her wrist, let her go and turned halfway around toward the cameras. *He's an uncaring, exploitative, charming devil. Don't let him make you forget it.*

"I guess you know why I gathered you here today," Duncan announced with a note of laughing self-mockery that drew a rumble of affection from the audience. "In order to promote my book *101 Ways to Win the Woman of Your Dreams,* I made a bet with Joanna on this show two weeks ago. I bet that, using the tips in my book, I could win her heart by Valentine's Day.''

''And did you?'' a man yelled so loudly that the mike picked him up.

''I don't know.'' Duncan swung to give Joanna an unreadable glance, then faced the audience again. ''I guess we'll find out. What I do know is...'' He hesitated, and Joanna clenched her hands into fists. Even his pauses were artful—the man's crowd-swaying skills were fantastic. ''What I do know,'' he continued, his voice dropping to a huskier register, ''is that I chose the right woman to practice my wiles on. Joanna Hartz *is* the woman of my dreams.'' He turned to smile at her again, as the audience broke into a storm of sustained applause.

Hope swelled in her heart with the applause, as her eyes were trapped by his. She felt the tears welling up, and she blinked desperately, and when she could see him again, he'd turned back to his doting fans. She was dizzy with the drumbeat of her heart, thankful for the solid desk beneath her. As Duncan made a charming reference to the Sapersteins and the Watkins and the Bowmans—suggesting that his love might last just as long—her inner voice drowned out his words. *Of course, he'd call you the woman of his dreams, Joanna. This is the payoff. He's using your own hope, your own wishes against you. He knows that's what you want to believe, but don't you believe it!*

''But did you win her heart?'' the same man yelled again.

''Guess there's only one way to find out,'' Duncan said and chuckled. He dropped lightly to his knees at her feet and caught her nearest hand.

Oh, no. He wouldn't. Not even Duncan—

But he would. "Joanna," he said, his voice shimmering with laughter, "I never thought I'd do this on national TV, but here goes."

He *couldn't* mean it. But his blue eyes glowed with sincerity, and the hand holding her fingers seemed to be shaking. Or perhaps it was she who was shaking.

"Joanna," he said, while the audience collectively held its breath and leaned forward to listen. "Would you consider...uh...do you think...ah, heck. Marry me, would you?"

Her eyes glistening with tears, she swallowed painfully, but it didn't help. Her throat was a desert. All her words had withered and blown away.

"Would you?" he insisted, his hand crushing her fingers.

She couldn't speak, could barely see as the tears overflowed, but she still had her sense of touch. Her free hand groped, found the vase of red roses and lifted it. Slowly, deliberately, biting her lip with her concentration, Joanna Hartz poured one dozen long-stemmed roses and a quart of cold water over Duncan Flowers's upturned face and hopeful smile. Except for the gentle splash of water the silence in the room was complete. Then, as Duncan started to cough and sputter, the audience caught its collective breath and expelled it in a roar of protest.

"No! Boo! Boo-oo-oooh!"

As Duncan let her go to pick a rose off his head, the vase fell from her numb fingers. She could barely hear it smash above the noise of the crowd.

Joanna, you idiot! She didn't know if the words came from without or within—didn't care. Shoving herself off the desk, she felt glass crunch underfoot. Duncan was a tear-blurred shape before her. She dodged his outstretched hand, stepped on a rose and stumbled offstage with the boos of the crowd pursuing her.

She ran smack into Susan Hadley behind the curtain. "Joanna, you've got one minute left. You can't leave!"

"Oh, can't I?" she sobbed. "Tasha, where's my purse?" She didn't wait for an answer, though the purse held her car keys. But as she reached her private exit, a hand caught her shoulder.

"Let go of me!" she stormed, wrenching open the door.

"Joanna, honey, don't turn him down!" Tasha groaned, but she thrust the purse into her boss's hands.

"You take him, Tasha, if you think he's so hot!" She couldn't go fast enough in her high heels. She had to get to her car before she broke down entirely, because when this sorrow hit, she'd cry for a week. A year. The rest of her life. She kicked off her shoes and ran.

Hallways. Startled faces jerking up to stare as she fled, panting, past them. At last the elevator. She half fell against its call button, then spun around at the sound of pounding footsteps.

Running head down, as if he held a football and faced a seven-foot wall of teeth-bared tackles, Duncan Flowers sprinted after her, a forgotten rose clutched in one hand.

The elevator slid smoothly open, and Joanna stumbled inside. Whimpering, she scrabbled at the control panel but couldn't find the door-close button. She slapped her hand across the row of numbered floor buttons. The doors sighed and started to close.

"Joanna!" Duncan dived through the closing gap, thumped into the opposite wall, then spun around.

"Get *out* of here!" she stormed. Not that he could. The elevator descended with an almost inaudible hum.

"No," he panted and wiped the wet hair out of his eyes.

"Then I will!" The elevator was slowing its rush as they approached one of her chosen floors.

"Not...until you hear me out." Duncan pushed the emergency stop button, and the car jerked to a halt. Somewhere far off, a bell began to clang.

"Get out," Joanna sobbed hopelessly and pushed herself into the farthest corner of the cubicle.

"Jo...anna..." Still panting, Duncan braced a hand on the railing to either side of her, trapping her. "I'm sorry, Joanna." His face was so close to hers that water dripped off his hair and onto her cheeks.

"No, you're not! You don't give a damn. You did exactly what you set out to do. You'll be number one on your rotten bestseller list after this."

"I give a damn, Joanna!" He brushed his lips across her wet cheek. "The list doesn't matter. What matters is I'm sorry."

She twisted away, bumped his arm and recoiled. "Yeah, you're as sorry as they come."

He laughed, a breathless panting sound, and kissed her ear. "Guess I am. Sorry. But listen."

"I won't!" She shoved at his chest, but she might as well have shoved one of the walls, except that he was warmer and wetter. He'd discarded his jacket somewhere. She snatched her hands away from his soaking shirt.

"Joanna, look, what I said back there—I meant it." He smoothed the hair back behind her ear, and his face tensed as she flinched again. "You were right— that wasn't the time or the place to say it, but I meant every word. You *are* the woman of my dreams."

"The promotion of your dreams, you mean," she snapped. She couldn't believe him. Because to believe and then to be betrayed one more time...

Her eyes filled with tears at the thought, and he groaned and wrapped his arms around her. "Oh, Joanna, I stopped caring about that five minutes after I met you." He kissed the top of her head, then rested his cheek against it. "I mean..." The familiar note of rueful laughter crept into his voice. "I mean I cared about it, but you came first." He kissed her ear again. "You *come* first," he whispered. "And I'd have asked you yesterday if you'd only stayed home to answer your phone."

"You... you would have?" Her voice came out in a strangled squeak.

"I swear. Here, I bought this Saturday. Benjie helped me pick it out." Without letting her go, he groped awkwardly in his pants pocket, then pulled out a small black box. He flicked its lid up with his thumb.

Her eyes were swimming again. The stone appeared to be an emerald, and it was flanked by two small diamonds. Not that it mattered—a pop-up top from a beer can would have shone as brightly if he'd offered it. "Benjie d-didn't say..." she choked. "He told me about the ferry ride and the dinosaurs, but this..."

"Well, a kid's got to keep his priorities straight," Duncan said sensibly. "And I didn't tell him it was for you." Then the laughter left his eyes, leaving them watchful and very, very anxious. "But it is. With me or without." A hint of his dimple reappeared. "So... where were we?"

Letting her go, he sank to his knees, then caught her hand and smiled up at her. "Now you can say yes, or you can say no, Joanna, but keep in mind, if it's no, that I only used eight of my tips on you. I've got ninety-three more, and by God I'll use every last one of 'em—and if that's not enough, I'll start over from the beginning and use 'em all again. You know this is right as well as I do. So—'' he cleared his throat nervously ''—Joanna, will you m-marry me?''

Her legs couldn't hold her any longer. Slowly she slipped to the floor, and his hands caught and supported her until she was face-to-face with him. ''Yes,'' she whispered, then gasped as he pulled her into a rapturous bear hug.

''Whew!'' He laughed, his face buried in the curve of her neck. ''Whew!'' Then his breath tickled her skin as he laughed again soundlessly.

''What?'' she murmured, brushing her lips across his damp ear.

He lifted his head to prop it against hers, their brows and noses touching. ''I was just remembering the last tip in my book.'' His body vibrated against her as he laughed deep in his chest. ''Tip 101. Remember that, when you're in love, *every* day should be Valentine's Day,'' he quoted. ''Happy Valentine's Day, Joanna.''

''You crazy goof!'' She laughed, too, her eyes flooding with tears.

''Yeah,'' he agreed with a touch of smugness, ''but I'm *your* goof.'' As their lips met in a light kiss that quickly deepened, and their arms locked tight around each other, they failed to note the silence when the alarm bell ceased its ringing.

Gently the elevator began to rise.

HARLEQUIN
American Romance®

THE ROMANCE THAT STARTED IT ALL!

For Diane Bauer and Nick Granatelli, the walk down the aisle was a rocky road....

Don't miss the romantic prequel to WITH THIS RING—

I THEE WED
BY ANNE McALLISTER

Harlequin American Romance #387

Let Anne McAllister take you to Cambridge, Massachusetts, to the night when an innocent blind date brought a reluctant Diane Bauer and Nick Granatelli together. For Diane, a smoldering attraction like theirs had only one fate, one future—marriage. The hard part, she learned, was convincing her intended....

Watch for Anne McAllister's I THEE WED, available *now* from Harlequin American Romance.

ITW

History is now twice as exciting, twice as romantic!

Harlequin is proud to announce that, by popular demand, Harlequin Historicals will be increasing from two to four titles per month, starting in February 1991.

Even if you've never read a historical romance before, you will love the great stories you've come to expect from favorite authors like Patricia Potter, Lucy Elliot, Ruth Langan and Heather Graham Pozzessere.

Enter the world of Harlequin Historicals and share the adventures of cowboys and captains, pirates and princes.

Available wherever
Harlequin books are sold.

NHS